PENGUIN BOOKS

THE ONLY DAUGHTER

Jessica Anderson is the author of several novels and radio plays. She has twice won Australia's most prestigious literary prize, the Miles Franklin Literary Award—in 1978 for *Tirra Lirra by the River* (also available from Penguin), and in 1980 for this book. She lives in Sydney.

THE
ONLY DAUGHTER

Jessica Anderson

PENGUIN BOOKS

PENGUIN BOOKS

Viking Penguin Inc., 40 West 23rd Street, New York, New York 10010, U.S.A.
Penguin Books Ltd, Harmondsworth, Middlesex, England
Penguin Books Australia Ltd, Ringwood, Victoria, Australia
Penguin Books Canada Limited, 2801 John Street, Markham, Ontario, Canada L3R 1B4
Penguin Books (N.Z.) Ltd, 182–190 Wairau Road, Auckland 10, New Zealand

First published in Australia under the title *The Impersonators* by
The Macmillan Company of Australia Pty Ltd 1980
First published in the United States of America
as *The Only Daughter* by Viking Penguin Inc. 1985
Published in Penguin Books 1986

LIBRARY OF CONGRESS CATALOGING IN PUBLICATION DATA
Anderson, Jessica.
The only daughter.
Previously published as: The impersonators. 1980.
I. Title.
PR9619.3.A57I5   1985b   823   85-21786
ISBN 0 14 00.0333 1

Printed in the United States of America by
R. R. Donnelley & Sons Company, Harrisonburg, Virginia
Set in Baskerville

PART ONE

Some of the Characters

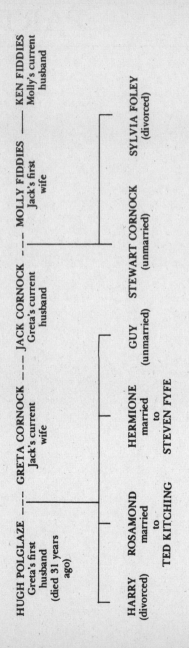

HUGH POLGLAZE --- GRETA CORNOCK --- JACK CORNOCK --- MOLLY FIDDIES --- KEN FIDDIES
Greta's first   Jack's current   Greta's current   Jack's first   Molly's current
husband   wife   husband   wife   husband
(died 31 years
ago)

HARRY   ROSAMOND   HERMIONE   GUY   STEWART CORNOCK   SYLVIA FOLEY
(divorced)   married   married   (unmarried)   (unmarried)   (divorced)
                  to   to
              TED KITCHING   STEVEN FYFE

The year is 1977

One

'Jack Cornock's daughter is coming back,' said Keith Burtenshaw.

Marjorie Burtenshaw sat at her dressing table, dabbing and fussing, making the best of her daytime face. 'I didn't know he had a daughter. What's her name?'

'Sylvia Foley.'

'Then she's married.'

'Divorced. She has picked her time.'

'How old?'

Keith Burtenshaw surmised as he selected a shirt. 'There was Bruce, killed in the war. Then Stewart. Then Sylvia, a long time after. In her late thirties? Yes.'

Marjorie Burtenshaw had not known Jack Cornock during the marriage that had produced this family. It was only after he divorced and remarried, and moved over to the north shore of the harbour, that she had met him and his second wife. She did not regard them as friends. 'Does Greta Cornock know she's coming?'

'I don't know. I'm not in daily contact with Greta.'

'Sometimes it sounds like it.'

'If I mention her a good deal lately, it's because she's in trouble.'

'I should have thought Jack was in trouble.'

'Yes, yes, both of them. I wish you would give Greta a ring.'

'I'm in trouble myself. I don't know what to do about this elbow. Who told you Sylvia what's-her-name is coming back?'

Keith Burtenshaw was knotting his tie at the mirror of which his wife occupied the lower half. He was sixty-five, thin, finely jointed, with a long jutting censorious chin, a sour taste in his mouth, and a calm, bleating voice. 'I am acting for a woman who is buying a property in the Eastern Suburbs. Stewart Cornock is the selling agent. During the course of the transaction I had occasion to ring him, and he mentioned that his sister is coming back to Sydney.'

'Stewart Cornock has done very well,' said Marjorie Burtenshaw, with weight in her voice. 'Very well indeed.'

Greta Cornock, after talking on the telephone with her son Harry, rang her elder daughter Rosamond. While waiting for an answer she drew cubes on the telephone pad. Rosamond's phone rang and rang. Greta broke the connection, dialled the number of her younger daughter Hermione, and went on drawing her cubes, very small and neat. Hermione and Steven Fyfe lived at Wollstonecraft, about fifteen kilometres down the North Shore line from Wahroonga, where Jack and Greta Cornock lived. Hermione was at home.

'Hermione,' said Greta, 'Harry just rang.' She raised her voice because at Wollstonecraft a train was passing. 'Yesterday he met Stewart in the street.'

'Stewart Street?' cried Hermione in distraction. 'Imogen,' she said to her youngest child, '*let go*!'

'Are you talking on the kitchen extension? That was a train.'

'Just a tick.'

Hermione put down the receiver, extricated the hem of her jeans from the powerful infantile grip of her daughter, then high-stepped over the child and shut the door between the kitchen and the balcony. She and Steven had sold their house a month ago, and while waiting to buy another were renting this second-story flat near the North Shore railway line. Greta, sitting in the hall at Wahroonga, had filled a page with her cubes; she turned it over and began another. The hall was big, square, rather dark. Red and green reflections, cast by the stained-glass panels beside the door, looked subacquous in the polished floor. At Wollstonecraft, Hermione gave a rusk to the baby, then picked up the phone again.

'Oh, you mean Stewart *Cornock*. Stewart was going to find us a house, but he hasn't. Imogen is trying to stand.'

'You were all very forward. Stewart told Harry that Sylvia is coming back.'

'Oh?' said Hermione, on a rise of interest. 'When?'

'Next Wednesday.'

'I wonder why.'

'Why shouldn't she?'

'Well, I always think of her as fixed, joined, wedged into Europe—oh, you mean because of Poppa?'

Greta was shading a cube. 'I don't know, of course.'

'Have you heard from her lately?'

'Not since it happened. I've been rather puzzled about that, when I've had time to be puzzled about anything.'

'What did Stewart say to Harry?'

'Only that she rang him, and gave him her flight number, and asked him to get her a flat.'

'Can she be coming back for good? Things are pretty bad in England now.'

'She rang from Rome.'

'They're worse there.'

'They're not very good here, in spite of Steven's wonderful government.'

The prickliness between Hermione and her mother, by both helplessly regretted, was by both inexorably increased. Hermione stood up straighter and said curtly, 'Excuse me, I must go.'

'Why?' asked Greta calmly. 'What is it?'

'The cat.'

'You should not have cats, dear, where there are very young children.'

'You did.'

'In my day we didn't know the dangers.'

'You get out of everything.'

Greta smiled and wrote lightly across the pad, NOT EVERYTHING. Hermione swooped to pick up the rusk the baby had dropped. There was no cat in sight. Her eyebrows were contracted into a single bar across her dark poetic face. When she rose again to the phone, she spoke with excessive politeness.

'How is Poppa, mother?'

Greta's two sons spoke of Jack Cornock as Jack, or sometimes Knocker, but Rosamond and Hermione continued to call him Poppa, as Greta had instructed them all to do from the start. Greta said, 'There is no change, Hermione.'

'Frightening, really. Well, I must go. This cat. Goodbye.'

'Goodbye, dear.'

Greta rang off and went, hitching the cardigan hanging from her shoulders, through the front door. The porch which darkened the hall overlooked the front garden and the road. On Orlando Road or its wide grassy verges nobody went on foot but school children, domestic servants, and joggers. In the south-west corner of the garden, a man knelt planting the annuals Greta liked to pick for the house. Her voice dropped to its croon of fondness.

'Siddy?'

Siddy got to his feet and came to the porch, his eager tumbling walk seeming part of his general purpose to propitiate and console. Probably in his fifties, he was a native of the same north-west district as Jack Cornock, who had picked him up to do odd jobs round his pub more than thirty years ago. He had bottle shoulders, an unusually narrow head, and rosy cheeks. He wore a striped business shirt and thick woollen trousers with braces, and carried with him the sour, unwashed smell that also permeated his two-roomed cottage at Brooklyn on the Hawksbury River. A hand-made cigarette, half smoked, rested on his lower lip.

'Siddy, just go round and check on him, will you?'

Siddy nodded and went, and Greta returned to the telephone and dialled Rosamond's number again.

Greta's elder son Harry, whose name was Hilary, but who had been overtaken at his first rough semi-rural school by the name he had used ever since, had once said that by the names Greta had given her children (Hilary, Rosamond, Hermione, Guy), she had exposed her ambition for them. Rosamond and Ted Kitching were the richest of the family, and lived on the southern shores of the harbour, at Point Piper. Rosamond was the only one resembling her mother, with far-sighted blue eyes and fair hair. As they talked she was watching a Japanese container ship come to a stop in the harbour, which at first made her sound rather absent-minded.

'Sylvia? Oh, how lovely. Did she write?'

'No. Harry saw Stewart in the street.'

'So do I, quite often. He looks terribly lean and hungry, and lately he's always with a hungry looking woman. But maybe he's only trying to sell her a house. Once I saw him with Min in his car.'

Min, or Minnie, was what Rosamond called Hermione. Rosamond stood with one knee on the arm of an upholstered chair, and twirled the telephone cord. 'How long since Sylvia went away. Wait—she was nineteen, and I'm thirty-seven, and she's two years older than me. Help! She's been away twenty years.'

'Stewart must have written to her about Jack.'

'Twenty *years*! Yes, I expect so. Oh—you mean that's why she's coming back?'

'I don't know, of course.'

'But she never even wrote to him.'

'She wrote to me. You know what he's like about letters. I gave them news of each other.'

'But you didn't write and tell her about the stroke, because you just said Stewart must have.'

'I left it to Stewart. I had enough to do without that.'

'Oh, you *did*! But listen,' said Rosamond, raising her chin, 'I wonder where she got the money to come. Last time Ted and I were in London, she was living in a bed-sitting room with a lav down the hall.'

'You know as much as I do.'

'Is Poppa pleased?'

'I'll tell him presently.'

'How is he, mother?'

'Just the same, Rosie. But I've asked Siddy to sleep in the room over the garage.'

'But Guy's there to help. And anyway, the smell.'

'Guy's gone off again.'

'When?'

'Yesterday.'

Two chesty little black tugs were racing up to the container ship. Rosamond took her knee from the arm of the chair and sat down. 'Mother, I want to ask you something.'

Greta's voice sounded a warning note in advance. 'Yes?'

'About Poppa's will.'

Greta's intake of breath was audible, and was let out bit by bit into her words. 'This is about—the—eighth—time—'

'Don't be like that.' Rosamond was still watching the tugs, but her mouth was faintly smiling. 'I'm only thinking of you.'

'—about the *eighth time* I have told you that if Poppa dies first—'

'Mother, he's seventy-six.'

'—if Poppa dies first, the house is mine. How are the boys, Rosamond?'

'I know the house is yours, but what about the money to keep it up? And not only after Poppa dies, either, but now, right now. Please don't deny that he has stopped giving you any.'

'It must be understood that these moods are symptoms.'

'Keith Burtenshaw was with him twice this week.'

'I shall be more careful what I tell Harry in future, if it leads to this victimization.'

'Harry didn't tell me that. Guy did.'

'Victimization. Jack is quite entitled to see his lawyer.'

'Ted says you ought to have power of attorney.'

'Rosie, if I decide a man's advice is indispensible, I have two sons of my own.'

'Oh, now, come *on*. You can't call Harry or Guy practical. And Ted is. He's a pig, I know, and a barbarian, but he is practical.'

Greta descended to weariness. 'Yes, my dear, I know. He has proved it. But I must do things my own way.'

'Which means doing nothing.'

'Oh, Rosie,' said Greta, pleading, 'I rang to tell you about Sylvia, not to talk about money.'

'But that's what made me talk about money. Sylvia's his only daughter, after all. Stewart and Sylvia are his only real children.'

'Rosamond—'

'Not that I think he would leave Stewart anything. They had that running battle, didn't they? But Sylvia's been far enough away to be idealized.'

'Rosamond, I am an old woman.'

'I wondered when that was coming.'

'I am an old woman,' said Greta with resolution, 'and if it turns out that I have only the house, I'll still have enough for my needs. And all you children are all right.'

'Were,' said Rosamond.

'What does that mean?'

'You must have seen this morning's paper.'

'I did. But Ted's been saying for years—'

'This time it's true. This wolf is real.'

'He's really losing—?'

'Hand over fist. Wow.'

'In that case he can sell the boat.'

'He has.'

'What did he get for it?'

'Nothing yet. But he's sure he has a buyer.'

'Oh,' said Greta, 'I see. Well, I think you'll find that Ted's all right. Ted's the kind of man who's always all right. I wish I felt as happy about Steven and Hermione. They'll never get out of that flat. How can they borrow money in times like these? Enough money for what Hermione wants? When they sold the Baulkham Hills house Steven made a very bad deal.'

'It's no use blaming Steve, mother, when it's always Min who craves so much to move. And you can't blame her, either, because she can't help it.'

'I don't believe in people not being able to help things.'

'No, but if God made Minnie looking like a goddess, he ought to have made a marble hall to put her in.'

'Goddesses! Marble Halls! They had a perfectly good house. Anyone could see hard times coming. And then to go and have another child, even if it is Imogen.' But Greta's voice had lost its sharpness, and was taking on its croon. 'Oh, Rosie, what a lovely child she is. Those eyes!'

'I would like to keep Imogen's eyes exactly as they are,' said Rosamond, smiling, watching the ship. 'It's not fair that they must change.'

But Greta's response, her sudden expelled breath, almost a hiss, made Rosamond sit straight in her chair, and move her eyes quickly to right and left. 'Mother?' she said with caution.

There was no reply. Rosamond darted glances of alarm all over the big plate glass window, at one point or another of the sky, the harbour, and the northern shores. 'Mother, what's the matter?'

Greta spoke in a flat, drained voice. 'Nothing I can explain.'

'It's my fault,' said Rosamond. 'I shouldn't have started talking about hard times, and Min and Steve. But Min and Steve are like Ted and me, mother. One way or another, they'll be all right. I wouldn't have mentioned what's happening to Ted, either, only I knew you would have read it in the paper. And Harry's fine, now that he's stopped pining for Margaret. And Guy, well, worrying doesn't help, does it? Yesterday, did you say he went?'

'Yes, yesterday. He won some money on some sort of gambling.'

'He'll be back in a week. You'll see. Next week you'll be keeping his meals hot again, on that gadget.'

'I don't want him to come back. I have to shed things. I have to be light.'

But Rosamond, though she looked startled, would not relinquish the safety of her mock bullying. 'That gadget you bought especially to keep Guy's meals hot. I throw Ted's out, but not Dominic's and Matthew's, because they're growing boys, and if I did, they might stop.'

Greta's voice was regaining resonance. 'How *are* the boys, Rosamond?'

'They've just come in. Hullo, darlings.'

Rosamond turned in her chair to look at the two schoolboys who had dawdled in from the hall, and stood banging their straw hats against their legs. 'How are they?' asked Greta's voice again.

Rosamond surveyed her two sons from head to foot. Fifteen and sixteen, they were of similar appearance, both dark, with not an angle of face or figure lacking in harmony. She turned again to the phone.

'They have changed into their summer hats.'

'Give them my love,' said Greta in her croon.

'Nan sends her love,' shouted Rosamond at her sons' departing backs. 'They send theirs,' she said into the phone. 'They've gone to feed their faces, the pigs, and then they'll go and smoke a joint, or whatever it's called these days.'

Greta spoke in a hushed voice. 'They don't really smoke marijuana?'

Jessica Anderson

'I only know what I read in the papers.'

Greta said indignantly, but with slight uncertainty, 'Just as well I know you are joking.'

Greta put the receiver in its cradle and stood up. She was in her sixtieth year, and her daughters often spoke, with sighs of pretended envy, about her perfect health and the durability of her good looks. What had once been a helmet of flaxen hair was now grey, but her eyes, tilted upward at the corners, were still startlingly blue, and her body still moved pliantly beneath her clothes. As she crossed the hall she whispered to herself, looking indignant. And indeed, there often hovered about her mouth this look of indignation, or defiance. Her knees, too flexible, gave her walk the hint of a crouch. It was her habit to walk quickly, and never to look aside without purpose. She straightened a rug with one foot, and passed under the wide arch into the dining room. And here she did look aside, obliquely, at the long shining table as she passed it. The eight chairs set close to its sides, and the others against the walls, seemed only to attest to its disuse; it was a long time since this room had been transformed into the party bower of her children's childhood and early youth.

Never since she had come into this house had Greta allowed herself the informality of trousers, even when most fashionable, nor the comfort of bare legs, even in summer. Now, in spring, she was impregnably dressed in a cotton shirt-dress and low-heeled shoes with crepe soles. As she walked and whispered, she occasionally hitched a shoulder to keep in place the cardigan over her shoulders. The dining-room opened onto a large bright kitchen. The windows here faced west, but the exterior awnings were not yet in use, and the spring sunlight, when Greta put her face to the glass, revealed the crumpling of the thin bluish skin beneath her eyes, a few broken capillaries in the eyes themselves, and down her cheeks the faint raking of vertical lines. Below a long feline upper lip, the underlip was slightly compressed.

The back garden was planted with herbs near the kitchen door, and beyond that only with trees and the tall shrubs grown to hide the fences. Beneath a prunus tree, in full flower of a pink so pale as to be almost white, Jack Cornock sat where Greta and Siddy had settled him an hour ago in his extended wheel chair. His legs lay horizontal, slightly apart, with one toe pointing outward and the toecaps of his highly polished shoes catching dapples of sun. The double-breasted jacket of his pin-striped suit was buttoned, and the brim of his hard felt hat rakishly slanted over one eye.

Jack Cornock had never thrown away a garment, and because in his youth and middle age he had strenuously pursued an ideal of smartness forever fleeing, he now had cupboards full of suits and hats and shoes dating from the early twenties onward. When he had married Greta, she had objected to nearly all of his clothes, so that he had angrily lost confidence in them, and put them away and bought new ones. But after a brief and undiagnosed illness (two months before his stroke) he had taken to wearing only the clothes she had persuaded him to discard. Each morning, between that illness and his stroke, he had dressed with finicky care, eyeing himself threateningly in the mirror, in the 'sharp' clothes of the post-war boom, until, turned out at last in a suit with very broad shoulders, a wide silk tie, and a hard felt hat, he would come and place himself in Greta's line of vision. 'Is it some mad sense of economy?' Hermione had once asked her mother, but Greta had replied with grim composure that no, it wasn't that. After his stroke, on his return from the hospital, it was assumed that at last he would discard these garments, but he rejected, at first in furious garbled speech and then with his glare and his good hand, all offers of the more relaxed garments of his later years. 'How will he get through the January heat?' Hermione asked Rosamond; but Rosamond's silence and doubting mouth asked whether he would be here in the January heat.

Greta, with her hands behind her back, crossed the grass between the trees and stood beside his chair. Though he could not rise without help, his stick must always be propped near his good hand. His body was still big, but it had been massive, and the padded extended shoulders of cloth dropped away from the shoulders of flesh beneath. His wide pale lips, dry and chapped and puckered as they had always been, were now hardly distinguishable from his facial skin. Behind thick-rimmed spectacles, his eyes, of a reddish brown watered by grey at the perimeters of the pupils, followed his wife closely but without expectancy.

She asked him if he wanted anything. With a solicitous tilt of her head, she offered tea, water, fruit juice, soup, or the services of Siddy. Raising a thumb or nodding were his usual gestures of assent, but to Greta's offers, though he continued to watch her closely as she made them, he gave not the faintest response. She waited for a moment or two, then smiled at him, and came closer to pluck from the dark cloth of his suit a few of the bridal pink blossoms.

'Sylvia is coming back,' she said.

His face did not change.

'You heard me, Jack, all the same.'

She crossed to the other side of his chair. His alphabet card, red felt pen, dictionary, and the *Sydney Morning Herald*, folded in four, lay on the grass. They could not have fallen of their own accord. Doctors said he had been lucky; both legs were affected, one was totally inert, but with his good hand he had learned to sign his name and he could usually convey his meaning by pointing to letters on the alphabet card or to words in the dictionary. But his silence was complete; he could not, or would not, speak a word.

The article about Ted Kitching's companies, on the outer fold of the newspaper (where she could not help but see it), was ringed in shaky red. As Greta rose to her feet and returned the things to his tray, she would not look at his face.

'Sylvia arrives on Wednesday. I will get her here as soon as I can. And if you want to see Keith Burtenshaw again, please don't ask Siddy to ring him. *I* will ring him. I will get him whenever you like.'

But as she turned away she said softly, warningly, 'But about the other thing you want—I will resist, Jack. I will resist.'

She dropped her cardigan on a garden seat, and from the same seat took up the rake she had propped there when she had heard the telephone ringing in the house. Several piles of debris already lay on the lawn, and she now began to rake these into one. The adjoining gardens were also thickly planted, and the many bird cries made a ceiling of sound from which continually, above the rest, sprang the loud, cupped call of the currawong, a chorus rising so far from that lesser ceiling of sound, and echoing so far, that the quietness under the trees seemed by contrast torpid.

Presently, at this level, Greta's indignant and sibilant whisper could be heard, as if tricked by the false silence, and the lonely regular sound of her rake, into venturing out. Until, hearing it herself, Greta looked up sharply, saw Jack Cornock's eyes upon her, and received the subtle emanation of his triumph. She abruptly turned her back on him then, and worked in silence, often moving awkwardly to avoid directly facing him. She had finished raking the debris into a single pile near the children's swing, and now eased it in a straight line toward the compost bins. The circle of blossom under the prunus tree she left undisturbed, just as she would never allow to be raked, in summer, the jacaranda flowers that reflected so beautifully the mauve of the tree above.

The Japanese container ship, drawn by one tug and nosed along by the other, was moving down the harbour. Rosamond watched it as she talked on the phone to Hermione.

'She still has that moon face and all that frizzy hair. At least she did last time Ted and I were over. And she was still skinny, with a sort of hollow between the hipbones, like I wish I had.'

'Like Stewart has,' said Hermione. 'Stewart showed me some houses, but they all cost too much.'

'Clothes always look good on that sort of figure. I'm truly going on that diet. Not that Sylvia cares about clothes any more.'

'She used to be obsessed with them.'

'Weren't we all!'

'Nothing like her. I suppose Molly knows she's coming.'

Molly—now Molly Fiddies—was Jack Cornock's first wife, divorced for adultery when he had so badly wanted to marry Greta. Greta's children had never seen her, but she had become a legendary figure for them when Harry, browsing in the newspaper room of the public library while waiting for a girl, had come across an account of the divorce proceedings. The headlines had become a bold joke among them. 'MONEY STASHED AWAY IN SEATS OF CAR,' they would shout at each other; then, almost inaudibly, to indicate the reduction to small print, 'SAYS DIVORCED WIFE'. Rosamond watched the container ship and said, 'Stewart will have told his mother.'

'Mother seems to think she's coming back because of Poppa.'

'She may be right. It's naïve to think that people never think about wills.'

'Is it? Do you think about wills, Rosie?'

'Not on my own account. But I guess I would if I needed to.'

'Is it true about Ted?'

'Is what true about Ted?'

'What was in the paper. Not his name, but about two of his companies. It can't be true.'

'I don't know, Min. He won't be serious about it. Neither will I.'

'Yet,' said Hermione.

'That's right, not yet. Do you think about wills, Min?'

'If you mean about Poppa's, of course not. Everything will go to mother.'

'It would have before his stroke. Or maybe before that illness. Remember? When he wouldn't get the doctor? That's when he started to change.'

'Those moods are symptoms.'

'Keith Burtenshaw has been there twice lately.'

There was a silence. Then Hermione said, 'He couldn't leave her only the house. It wouldn't stand up in law.'

'Not even if he left the rest to his own children? Or one of them?'

There was another silence before Hermione said flatly, 'I don't know.'

'Ted says he will leave about three hundred thousand. Quite apart from the loot.'

'Oh,' said Hermione with discontent, 'you and your loot.'

'Money stashed away in seats of car.'

But Hermione was in no mood to laugh at the old joke. 'I hate money,' she said. 'I *hate* it. I suppose mother ought to have legal advice. I mean, from her own man. Not Keith Burtenshaw, who is Poppa's.'

'I didn't get around to suggesting it. It was bad enough as it was.'

'Hang on a tick,' said Hermione. 'Jason,' she shouted, 'turn that down. God,' she said into the telephone, 'this flat.'

'Matthew and Dom have theirs on too.'

'Yes, but with all your rooms.'

'Never mind, Min. You'll soon be out of it.'

Hermione was silent. Rosamond chose to be brazen. 'Poor darlings, how can they read the *Financial Review* with that noise going on? They are so worried about their trust accounts. It isn't only about Poppa's will that mother needs legal advice, Min.'

'I must go,' said Hermione curtly, 'and start the dinner.'

'It's about getting enough money to carry on.'

'What!' cried Hermione, diverted. 'Is he still not giving her any?'

'Ted thinks she should have power of attorney, but when I told her that she talked at me through her teeth.'

Hermione laughed. 'Did she say she was an old woman?'

'Yes, we had that. And the bit about doing things her own way. But then I said something about Imogen's eyes, and a new thing happened.'

'What did you say about Imogen's eyes?'

'Only that they'll change.'

'All eyes change.'

'That's what I said.'

'They're perfectly straight now. A baby's eyes are often a bit crossed.'

'Oh Lord, Min, will you shut up! I had forgotten they ever were. What I'm saying is this—mother is under a strain.'

'As we all know,' said Hermione.

'More than we make allowances for.'

The silence this time went on for so long that strangers might have believed themselves cut off. But at last Hermione said judiciously, 'You're right. We don't make enough allowance.'

'It's because she covers up all the time. Or did. So we forget.'

'We must try to remember.'

'Only, lately her cover has been slipping a bit. And do you know what she said today? She said she had to throw things off. She had to be light. *Light*! And did you know Guy's gone off again?'

'About time he went for good, isn't it? Thirty-one.'

'But that's the trouble, he doesn't.'

'No, and she's so besotted—'

'Oh, I don't think so,' said Rosamond. 'Not besotted.'

Again they might have been cut off. Then Hermione said slowly, 'I haven't been out there for three weeks. Longer. I must go.'

'So must I.'

'But why does she have to be so hateful? Why does she have to be so critical, and get at the men we married? And Margaret, when Harry and Margaret were married.'

'Born bossy. Only, lately, hasn't she just been rapping it out from memory?'

'I don't think so at all. If you had heard her on the phone today—'

'Be like me, Min. Laugh, or take no notice.'

'I haven't your lovely nature—'

'I didn't mean—'

'—as she makes quite clear. Excuse me, Rosie. There's the door.'

'Can't Em or Jazz go?'

'They've just gone out. Excuse me, Rosie. Goodbye.'

Hermione rang off and went to the living room door. 'Emma,' she said vehemently, 'put Imogen in her play-pen and come and do these vegetables. And Jason, I thought I said to turn that down. Now you can turn it off instead.'

'If I help with the dinner,' said Emma, 'Jazz should too.'

'Quite right. Come along, Jason. You can chop the meat.'

Emma and Jason came into the kitchen, and all three of them, dressed alike in blue jeans and cotton-knit tops, stood side by side at the bench and sink, peeling and chopping and slicing. Emma was twelve and Jason thirteen. Of the same darkness and grace as Matthew and Dominic Kitching, they were often mistaken, when with those cousins, for their brother and sister. Hermione, too, was of this rich darkness. Thirty-five, her face unlined but beginning to take shadow, she was tall and unfashionably big, her breasts high and full, her neck stately and outward curving. Down her back hung a thick plait of hair secured by a rubber band. No photograph survived of Greta's first husband, but Harry, the only one who remembered his father well, said that one had only to look at Hermione and the five grandchildren to appreciate Hugh Polglaze's great physical beauty.

Harry was also in the kitchen of his flat when Rosamond rang. He was grilling a steak, and turned it with his free hand as he talked.

'Stewart spoke to Jack about it,' he said, 'at my suggestion. And then I did. But Jack's in a position of strength. He has only to be silent. Double strength, because he's a very sick man. I've offered mother money to tide her over, and so have you. What else can we do?'

'I'm trying to think of something,' said Rosamond.

That Rosamond also remembered their father, remembered his death, and how they had all lived afterwards, gave her relations with Harry a different tone from that used with the others. With him she was quieter, more sober, repressing her levity, as if those times when she and he had helped and guarded the two younger ones had struck a cast too firm to be moderated by time.

'Perhaps Sylvia would try,' she said at last.

'Would mother like that?'

'Did she object when you tried?'

'I didn't tell her I had. I felt I had made a mistake, got into something I didn't understand. Gone into *her* territory. His and hers.'

'Somebody ought to go in.'

'Not me again. Not unless she asks me. I'm around. I go out there at least a couple of times a week. Is Sylvia coming alone, have you heard?'

'I suppose so,' said Rosamond with surprise.

'She doesn't always travel alone. When Margaret and I were in London she was going off to Spain with a man. Eight years younger. My steak's cooked.'

'Why are you eating so early?'

'I have a meeting, and I want to check the minutes of the last one.'

'I'll let you go, then.'

Rosamond rang off, curled her legs up into her chair, and

rested her head against its back. The inward Manly ferry was off Vaucluse Point, the Lady Cutler was entering Sirius Cove, and the little Kaloon, newer and of a brighter blue, was moving away from the wharf at Cremorne. Rosamond could identify all the ferries, and remembered those that ran no longer. She knew all the tankers and container ships, and, when a new one came through The Heads would examine it through binoculars. With pleasure in her blue eyes, she greeted the passenger ships that continued to come, and she had an especially fond look, almost maternal, for the busy little tugs, the pilot boats, and the black police launches. Pleasure boats she liked less, even when under sail, and she positively disliked hydrofoils, which she said exploded out of the frame.

She was still there, watching the water darken, when her husband came into the room. She did not turn round. He leaned over the back of the chair and kissed her on the mouth. She got up and held out her arms. She was indifferent to clothes nowadays, and wore the same long cotton dress and old shawl in which she had said goodbye to him that morning. They embraced, exchanging a number of quick hard kisses.

Ted and Rosamond were cited as one of the few couples anyone knew who had remained in love, and in this state they were supported by the legend itself. Apart from one accident early in their marriage, Rosamond was faithful to Ted, and Ted had sexual relations with no other woman in Sydney, and when he was away, only with first-class professionals. He was a bull-necked man whose fashionable proportions were maintained always on the verge of erupting into fat. He released her and said, 'I'll get out of this bloody gear and we'll have a drink.'

He spoke in a very fast staccato way, as always until he had unwound. He was a director in a number of companies, some of them registered in obscure and faraway places. He was wearing a suit as rigidly structured, in its modern way, as Jack Cornock's. Between his style and Rosamond's there seemed a century of difference. After working before marriage in an office full (she said) of thundering typewriters, Rosamond had retreated with relief into one of the past traditions of her sex. She now detained him by unknotting his tie.

'Before we have a drink, Ted, shouldn't you jog?'
'I went round the Gardens at lunch time.'
'Mother rang. I've been running you down to mother.'
'That's the way. Your shawl's fallen off.'
'I said you were a pig.'

'Quite right.'

'And a barbarian. Yum. And that you're losing money.'

'Let me go, love. I need that drink.'

'Hand over fist, I said.'

'I couldn't have put it better.'

'So the boys will have to leave their school, and we must move. Well, as long as I don't have to go to work.'

He picked up her shawl and put it over her shoulders. 'No chance of that.'

'Is that a cryptic remark?'

'Hardly.'

'I wouldn't mind doing my own housework. I could always leave the place dirty.'

'You would, too. Come and talk to me while I get out of this gear.'

Rosamond followed him up the stairs to their bedroom. 'All the same, Ted, we'll have to start being serious about it sooner or later.'

'Right! Later. How's old Knocker, did Greta say?'

'Just the same. It's true Keith Burtenshaw has been there twice.'

'The old bastard's up to something,' said Ted with appreciation.

'And Sylvia's coming back.'

'Who's Sylvia?'

'You met her in London.'

'Yes yes yes.' Ted flung his coat on the bed, his tie after it. 'Thin. Fuzzy hair and little pointed tits. Smiles a lot. I remember.'

'I wish I could be more like Rosie,' Hermione was saying. 'She lives such an external life. It must be much easier.'

'I love you more because of your problems,' said Steven.

Hermione's dark brows drew together. 'Problems?'

Steven was holding Imogen in his arms; he turned and kissed her cheek. 'Because of the light and shade in your character,' he told Hermione. Steven had just come home from work. Like Ted Kitching, he dressed to harmonize with his clients, but was luckier than Ted, because his natural taste was closer to theirs. He was a youth counsellor in government employment; he wore blue jeans and a cotton-knit top, and had just removed a denim jacket. He had a look of cleanliness and health; his manner was gentle, his diffidence perhaps cultivated. He and Hermione had met during a demonstration against the bomb, and in the sixties had joined the protest against the presence of Australian troops in Vietnam.

But since the dismissal of the Labor government by the Governor-General (nearly two years ago), Hermione had declared all political action hopeless while, even before that event, Steven's mild radicalism had given way to a conservatism weakened by periods of confusion. He had recently shaved off his beard, an act regretted by Harry Polglaze, who said that in Steven's beard he had been able to trace his politics, having seen the prophet's beard of his Vietnam days trimmed until it had resembled that of George V of England. Steven came from New Zealand, where his father was an Anglican clergyman. He now turned his clean-shaven cheek to the tender cheek of his infant daughter, kissed her again, and set her on the floor. 'Look in my back left-hand pocket,' he said to Hermione.

She drew from the pocket of his jeans a ribbon of dusty pink. 'I thought of your hair as soon as I saw the colour,' he said. 'Turn round.'

She turned to let him loosen her hair and weave the ribbon into her plait. 'Sylvia is coming back,' she said contentedly.

'Poppa's daughter?'

'Yes. The one we kept missing during our year in Europe.'

'That's nice.'

It was peak hour. Two trains passed each other, shrieking on the points. Steven clenched his jaw, then opened his mouth wide to relax it before he spoke again.

'I saw Ted today, while I was going round the Gardens. I didn't stop. Maybe I should have. If there's one man I don't envy, it's poor bloody Ted.'

A look of irony appeared on Hermione's face, and Steven, as if it were visible to him, said curtly, 'He won't get out of this one.'

Hermione said lazily, 'He thinks mother should have power of attorney.'

'What Ted thinks doesn't seem quite so clever as it did.'

'But don't you think she ought to?'

'Not necessarily, darling. In a stroke situation, it can't be taken for granted that a man isn't capable of exercising his judgment. The results of a stroke are infinite, infinite, and nobody can be quite certain—'

'Yes, but listen, he's keeping on with this business of not giving mother any money.'

Steven was making symmetrical the loops of the pink bow. 'I see the problem, but it must be remembered that, basically, these moods are physical symptoms. Do you think we could get Jason to turn that fucking thing down?'

Two

Stewart Cornock, carrying Sylvia's suitcase, unlocked the door of the flat and pushed it open to let her pass. Sylvia's eyes, golden-brown and slightly protruberant, were dull and strained, though her mouth still absently smiled. There were people who said Sylvia smiled too much, and others who said it was a defensive habit picked up when she had worked on the tourist coaches. But it was a long time since she had worked on the tourist coaches. She went to the divan bed, eased the bag from her shoulder, and flopped into a sitting position, but then, straight away, crying out in protest that she had been sitting for more than twenty hours, she jumped to her feet, clasped her hands at the back of her head, and rapidly twisted her body to right and left from the waist.

Stewart was raising the blinds. 'Mary doesn't let this place to anyone as a rule, just shuts it up and goes off. She's like you, a nomad.'

Through the windows, beyond the plane trees, Sylvia saw the evergreens of a park, and beyond the park a round white tower block thrusting into a sky of which she had already remarked, at the airport, that it was a true tourist blue. She lowered her arms. 'It's inaccurate to call me a nomad. This is exactly the kind of place I had in mind.'

'Flukes fall to the capable.'

'You don't mean me?'

This supposition being too absurd, Stewart didn't bother to answer. The telephone was on a table beside the bed. He picked up the pad and pen, and wrote a number in large numerals.

'Mum's number, Syl, in case you don't have it handy.'

She grasped her bag, eager to prove it. 'I have it here.'

'Well, I'm going out to get you some tucker, so now would be a good time to ring her.'

Stewart had a good-humoured way of taking for granted that people would do as he said; Sylvia, too tired to think for herself, sat on the edge of the bed and dialled the number as soon as he left.

Since she was about twelve years old, she had not spoken or written to her mother without painful constraint. When the telephone rang unanswered, she was filled with relief, and began to rehearse her excuse for Stewart— 'Later . . . after lunch . . . coffee . . . a shower . . .' —so that when it was suddenly answered, she was startled into her first mistake.

'Is that Mrs Cornock?'

'No it is not,' said the voice in offence. 'It is Mrs Fiddies.'

'Oh, mum, I'm sorry. It's me, Sylvia.'

'Oh, it's you, Syl.'

It had never helped to know that the same constraint afflicted her mother. Molly had always declared with aplomb that she 'never wrote letters', but by that very neglect, and the absence of even a message in her greeting cards, and the triteness of the messages sent by Stewart, Sylvia had long ago accepted the widening of the rift between them. She said, 'I've just arrived.'

'At the airport, have you?'

'No, at the flat. Stewart got me a flat.'

'Ah yes, he did say.'

'One big room and a kitchen and bath.'

'You wouldn't want the work of anything more,' Molly told her.

There was a silence. 'Anyway, mum—' said Sylvia, while at the same time Molly said loudly, 'Anyway, Syl, it's nice you're back. How was the flight?'

'Too long. My first in a Jumbo jet.'

'Fancy that.'

But this was said in a voice suddenly so faint, so mechanical, that Sylvia was unnerved. She leaned forward and said anxiously, 'Well, you remember I went over by ship? And somehow or other I've done all the rest in smaller planes. Or in buses and trains and ships again.'

But now, though there was no reply at all, the anxiety left her face, and she relaxed her posture; she had recalled how her mother used to lift one slat of the Venetian blind to peer at someone in the street, while the phone in her hand rattled on. As a child, ringing from the hall in Wahroonga, she had wailed, 'Oh, mum, stop looking through that blind. I'm *talking* to you.' But the day had come when she had said, in Greta's voice, 'Oh, do stop that. It's so rude.'

She covered the mouthpiece, let out her sigh, and as she waited turned her head to look through her own windows. During her months in Rome the swathe of spring had travelled south and the breaking leaf-buds she had seen when she left London in April she now saw, with the dark winter seed pods, on these plane trees in Sydney. Through the receiver came the sound, also familiar from long ago, of Molly nervously clearing her throat. Those withdrawals of her attention had always left her apologetic.

'What was that again, Syl?'

'Nothing important. How are you, mum?'

She had not intended to sound stern, but her mother's reply was guiltily animated.

'Real good, all in all. All things considered. Real good. How about you, Syl?'

'I'm fine, mum.'

'That's good to hear. Real good. And what are your plans, Syl?'

Sylvia had expected this, and had her reply ready, but Molly was under too much pressure from her own vivacity to let her make it.

'Must feel funny being back. Haven't got that jet lag, I hope.'

'No. A bit tired, that's all.'

'Stewart never gets it neither. But I would, I know I would. You wouldn't get me to go, not if you was to pay me. Nor Ken. Ken wouldn't go.'

And now there was a silence neither seemed able to break. Sylvia was incredulous of her own incapacity. She had expected constraint, but not that she would revert to the painful unskilfulness of her childhood and early youth. She began dumbly to frame an enquiry after her mother's husband ('Is Ken well?'), when her mother said humbly, 'Stewart isn't still there by any chance, is he, Syl?'

'He just went out, mum, to get me some food.'

'Now isn't that just like his thoughtfulness?'

She was more at ease. 'Yes,' said Sylvia, 'he's very good.'

'Of course, you know about him?'

Sylvia was confused for only a second before recalling that 'him' or 'her', said with that shade of grimness, always meant Jack and Greta Cornock. Molly never spoke their names. She said, 'Yes. Stewart told me.'

'I'm glad you come back when you heard, Syl.'

'I didn't hear till today, mum. Evidently Stewart wrote to me about it. He told me so at the airport. But neither of his letters reached me. And when I rang him from Rome, and said I was coming back, he took it for granted that they had, so he didn't say anything about dad except that he would be pleased to see me.'

'Fancy that.'

This phrase of Molly's, though always used to gain time, had various intonations; it was now suspicious. 'I was unlucky about the letters,' Sylvia said patiently. 'The Roman post office surpassed itself. Stewart and I sorted all this out in the car, and that's the first time I knew dad was sick.'

Molly said tentatively, 'Must've given you a shock, then.'

'Well, I certainly wasn't expecting–'

'And no more you would! It shocked me, I can tell you. Fancy, Syl. A great big feller like that. Down like a tree!'

On how many occasions had the introduction of Jack Cornock in to the conversation broken the dam, released the flood of Molly's loquacity? Sylvia felt that she could relax on its tide, contributing only automatic replies.

'Down like a tree! It makes you think, doesn't it?'

'It does, mum.'

'No one of us knows whose turn it is next.'

'No.'

'His ladylove will have her work cut out now.'

'I suppose so.'

'Ah yes, it will be telling on his ladylove.'

'I expect so.'

'The human brain, Syl. Think of the human brain. I suppose Stewart told you that whilst he could not get a single word right, he could swear? Go on and on and never miss a beat? Did Stewart tell you that?'

'No.'

'Well, you ask him. I had a premonition. Did Stewart tell you about my premonition?'

'No.'

'You won't believe this, Syl. But the night before it happened, I had this dream he was falling. It was off a ladder, and there he was, falling, as clear as I can see you now. He was just going to crash when I wake up. And straight away, I knew. "He's gone," I said to myself. And next morning, when Stewart rung, I said, before he could get a word out, "Don't tell me, love. He's gone." You ask Stewart.'

'But he hasn't.'

Sylvia's automatism had betrayed her. She put a hand across her aching eyes. She could hear Molly fighting her way out of a thicket of sullen Ah's and Well's. After having been carried away by one of her own fictions, Molly had always had this difficulty in retracting. When she cleared the thicket at last, her voice was offended again.

'It is a well-known fact that dreams are not that exact.'

Sylvia, even as a child, had hurried at this stage to help her. 'Of course not.'

'He did not fall off a ladder, neither, come to that, but that does not alter the fact of what I dreamt.'

'It's really most curious.'

Molly was willing to be appeased. 'There's a lot in this life we don't know, Syl.'

'There is, mum.'

'What did you come back for, Syl—if it's not a rude question—if it wasn't for that?'

'Oh . . . most people do, mum, at one time or another.'

'It's natural,' said Molly with vigour.

But Sylvia had heard a key in the lock, and turned eagerly to the door. 'Oh, mum? Here's Stewart now.'

'Well, you just ask him if I didn't dream that.'

Stewart, carrying provisions in a cardboard carton, shut the door behind him. Sylvia spoke to her mother with the animation of relief.

'When shall I see you, mum?'

'Well . . . you say.'

'Tomorrow?'

Nodding approval, Stewart took the carton to the kitchen. 'Tomorrow will do me,' said Molly, with a stoical inflection.

'What time?'

'Any time will do me.'

'Two-thirty?'

'All right, okay, good. Have a chat before our cup of tea. I'll just have a word with Stewart, if that's okay.'

'Of course. Of course. Here he is now, holding out his hand.'

Smiling in advance, Stewart took the receiver. 'Hullo, old dear. Now what do you think of that? Your daughter home again, eh? Bet you wag your chins off tomorrow.'

As Sylvia went to the kitchen she heard through the phone the laugh she had called as a child her mother's 'man laugh', because it could be provoked only by men. Starting with a shriek before settling to laughter, it made her see again Molly in her early forties. Wearing one of her black dresses, and bedizened with art jewellery, this Molly stands with her weight on one high heel, and the opposite hip widely canted. One hand holds a glass of beer, and the other slaps her chest to prove how helpless is her laughter. As Sylvia put away the food she listened to Stewart, trying to detect in his voice the strain, the false note. She did not hear it. His loud affectionate raillery was not forced; he was himself enjoying it. She was depressed by the comparison with her own attitude towards her mother—so stiff, dumb, and unloving. Yet on the other side of the barrier, in the far, incredible distance, was the landscape of early childhood: of giggles, secrets, and walks to the shops hand-in-hand. She put the fruit on a dish and carried it to the living room.

'I know,' Stewart was saying. 'Sorry I can't drive her out, old dear. But you know the way it is—got to get out and get a buck.'

'Well,' he said, as he rang off, 'she's pleased as Punch.'

He was still smiling, as pleased as Punch himself. 'She thinks it's great you're back, Syl.'

Whatever her words, Sylvia's voice was always gentle and soft. 'Back to where I'm going to be called Syl?'

'How are you getting out to Burwood tomorrow?'

'Train. How would you like to be called Stew?'

'Sometimes I get Stewy. Get a taxi. My shout.'

'I want to go by train. I want to read the graffiti. What shall I do with those pizzas? They're warm. Are they for lunch?'

'Sure. You've got a guest. Me. Just shove them in the oven.'

But before she could move, he strode past her and shoved them in the oven himself. She leaned in the doorway, watching him put plates on to heat, open a bottle of wine, take cutlery from a drawer. He darted her several glances.

'You're not looking so hot now, Syl. How do you feel?'

She wanted to say, 'Unsynchronized. Mum and I bang away at opposing keys.' But where Molly was concerned, she and Stewart also played in opposing keys. He was eight years her senior; at the time of the divorce, when she was the child divided between two households, he was the young man staunch and wrathful in his mother's cause. Sylvia had continued to be inhibited by respect for such blind love and loyalty. She said, 'Something has crept up.'

Though his glance this time was acute, he rejected the invitation to honesty, as he always did, and always had done. 'Jet lag,' he said.

Sylvia always tried to give reason a chance. Never having experienced jet lag, she could not reasonably deny it. 'Possibly,' she said.

'It's not neat,' said Stewart. 'It's littered with exceptions. You wouldn't think he would be able to spell. But he can. Well, about as much as he ever could.'

Sylvia remembered 'sholder' for 'shoulder', but had to go a long way back to do so. Like Molly, Jack Cornock 'never wrote letters', but because the messages he sent by Greta had a personal or bantering cast, and because wives of Greta's generation so commonly write letters for both themselves and their husbands, his omission had not seemed so culpable as Molly's. 'Mum said he swore fluently,' she said.

'Not fluently. It was more a case of him getting those words right, and no others. Then one fine day he just shut up entirely. Don't blame him, either. Think of wanting to say 'door', and hearing 'fork' come out instead. Humiliating. I totally agree. Did I tell you they think this was the second stroke?'

The line of Stewart's eyebrows, raised in enquiry, was repeated in the three deep furrows across his forehead, and again in his low, peaked hairline. Sylvia shook her head.

'Well, they do. He got sick in April, and now they think that was a small stroke. He reckoned it was a wog. But *he* knew.'

Sylvia heard in his voice that grim satisfaction, almost an appreciation of his father, which she knew to be the condensation of that wild fruit, his youthful fury. 'How do you know?' she asked.

'Because that's when he started to get nasty and surly again. Oh, sweet as pie when everything was going his way. Oh, yes. For a while there he even seemed to forgive me for not being old enough to get killed in the war like poor old Brucie. But the moment there's any indication things are going to stop going his way—i.e. that first little stroke—and in goes the benevolent gent, and out comes the old brute. That's it, Syl, that's the fact. They say these things, these moods of his, are symptoms. But in that case I want to know what they were symptoms of when Brucie got killed, and he turned round and made an enemy of me.'

Sylvia hardly remembered the big fair noisy boy, the football hero, killed by the Japanese in New Guinea. 'Is dad allowed visitors?'

'Lord, yes. You'll go, of course.'

'Of course.'

'Don't worry, Syl. He'll be okay with you. Just before his stroke, the big one, he asked me when you were coming back. Took me aside, made a real point of it. I could tell he wanted it passed on, but he wouldn't ask, and I'm the kind of bastard that wouldn't do it unless he *did* ask. I relented after the stroke, though, big-hearted, and put it in the first letter, the one to London. I'll tell you what he said. "Time she came back," he said. "Bonzer little kid." '

Sylvia's eyes widened in startled reminiscence.

'Quite so,' said Stewart. 'Language of another era. He sort of reverted. In more ways than one. You'll see. Which reminds me.'

He got up from the table, took the pad and biro from beside the telephone, then sat on the edge of the bed and began to draw.

Sylvia turned her head and looked with unfocused eyes into the boughs of the trees. She was pursuing one particular memory of her father, seeing him from an angle too sharp to be accounted for only by her childish stature. He was walking towards her, and as she saw the dark shape of his shoulders and hat against the sky, she identified her watching post as the back verandah of the house at Burwood. On this verandah she stood level with the sunken paved area from which rose the retaining wall of the back garden. He was crossing the garden from the garage, and when he saw her he pretended not to, but began earnestly to scan the plants while she waited happily for the next stage of the game, for his astonished eyes to alight on her face, and for the playful and confidential tone of his greeting. He reached the top of the steps and, one foot slipping on something there, he teetered wildly for those few seconds that had filled her with such alarm. She had run out, crying, but by that time he was kicking at something on the top step, and swearing. 'Down like a tree,' her mother had said. She turned to Stewart. 'Was the stroke sudden?'

'Not the kind like a shot from a gun.' He tore off the page and brought it to the table. 'Look. You are *here*. Buses to Wynyard station go from there, and *there*. Trains to Burwood and Wahroonga still go from Wynyard. Branch of your bank *here*.'

'Thank you.' She folded the paper and put it in a pocket. 'You said in the car he was difficult about treatment.'

'He won't have any more tests made, but he takes a pill or two, and he lets the physio come and move his limbs.'

'What does that mean?'

'That he doesn't want them to stiffen.'

'Then he thinks he'll get better?'

'Or hopes he will. Don't ask me.'

'Stewart, these days, can't they retrain—'

'*Retrain?* Nobody could retrain Jack Cornock. He put himself into training once and for all sixty years ago.'

'An ignorant bush boy, pushed out into the world alone.'

'Sure. So his mental joints got welded. And he liked it. He loved it. He thinks it should be done to everyone. Have the rest of this wine.'

'I don't think it would help my jet lag, if that's what it is.'

He poured the wine into his own glass. 'Sorry I have to tell you all this, Syl. But I mightn't see you again before you go out there, and it's best you know how things stand. The fact is, he wants to go on being boss, and if he can't be boss one way, he'll try another, and no way's too low. His big stick these days isn't money. It's

27

doubt. He won't give Greta the money to carry on, or even tell her how much there is. He never has told anyone, except Keith Burtenshaw. But it's different now. It's her who has to manage, and he's letting her blunder along blindfold. I tried to intercede, and so did Harry. But no go. I guess someone will ask you.'

With one hand on her chest, and her eyes wide open, she silently mouthed, 'Me?' Stewart laughed. 'You wouldn't?'

'Most certainly not. Surely there's some law. Can't Greta apply—'

'She would have to prove him incapable. I reckon that's why he won't have more tests made, in case they give her that lever.'

She rose to her feet. 'I'll get the coffee,' she said absently. But halfway to the kitchen she turned. 'You make them sound like deadly enemies.'

'Well,' he said in doubt.

'And yet,' she said, 'there was always something in his attitude towards her, a sort of enmity.'

'I only know he was mad about her.'

'Oh yes,' she said, 'he was.'

But in the kitchen, pouring the coffee, Sylvia consulted her memory. She was eleven when she first met Greta. She saw again the blurred coloured lights in the floor of the hall, and she saw Greta, kneeling in attendance on her little son. Greta raises her eyes, smiling, but Sylvia, after swiftly taking her in, will look nowhere but at the parting of her thick flaxen hair. Greta rises to her feet, still smiling. Jack Cornock, beside or behind her, is indistinct. Sylvia releases her hand from Greta's and turns away, dazzled and hostile, and her father leaps into definition. Barely catching his look, as she turns away, she sees that it is questioning, challenging, angry, and is directed at his new wife. Sylvia took up the two full cups and carried them to the table. 'I saw more of them than you did. He was mad about her, yes, but hostile, too. Now that he has these moods, is Greta afraid of him?'

'Not her! She never was. Everyone else was. Mum. Me. You. Greta's children—'

'The Polglazes? They weren't! What about those jokes?'

'An outlet for fear. What people won't admit is that bullying, that small patient daily bullying, never letting up, really works. You can clear out, make war, give in, or go underground. Kids go underground.'

'Perhaps I was too close. Do the grandchildren like him?'

'I never see them together.'

'Small children,' said Sylvia, 'have such a marvellous capacity for uncritical love.'

But Stewart was suddenly glum and absorbed. 'They're all thumping great beauties, those grandchildren.'

'Harry told me they're all like their grandfather. Now why weren't there any jokes about *him*, if he was really a religious maniac?'

'They're all like Hermione,' said Stewart. 'Nobody knows what I go through, with that woman in my car.'

'What are you doing with Hermione in your car?'

'Showing her houses she can't afford. A woman like that, and all she ever thinks of is houses.'

Sylvia smiled across the table at him. 'Do you still deal only in the top bracket?'

'Where else? Always plenty of money at the top. And I don't know what I'm doing sitting here, either, when I ought to be out getting a bit of it.'

But he sat more easily than ever, an elbow on the table, an arm over the back of his chair. 'What are your plans, Syl?'

'I'll stay here two months, maybe three, then I'll settle in Rome. I'll teach Italian to English-speaking people, and English to Italians.'

'If you're going to settle at long last, why not here?'

Sylvia raised her coffee cup and turned a glance, deliberately vague, into the trees. She knew that many English, as well as Australian expatriates like herself, as soon as they set foot in Australia, felt compelled to make ill-tempered and contemptuous remarks about the country and its people. Whatever irritant accounted for this, Sylvia intended to have no part of it. Knowing about it, she was on guard. She would resist it. At all costs, she would be polite. She dipped her head to her coffee cup. 'Rome has been my goal for such a long time.'

'Can you work there legally?'

'It's done.'

'But you would have that insecurity, and here you wouldn't. Not on that account, anyway, and probably not on any other, seeing you're the one who might inherit from dad.'

But now her stare—all vagueness gone—made him falter. 'Is that surprise?'

'It is,' she said, with the same surprise in her voice. 'I've never thought about it.'

He was silent. She gave a brief laugh. 'Is *that* surprise?'

'Why wouldn't you have thought about it?' he asked reproachfully.

'Yes, why?' She drank coffee, staring downwards over the rim
of her cup, before she replied. 'I suppose, in the first place, I've
always taken it for granted that with dad, it was Greta, Greta, all
the way. Yes, hostility notwithstanding. And in the second place,
there's my providence, that I told you about, and that you found
so comical. I'm not sure that's not the main reason, in fact.'

'What about that legacy you got? Didn't that disturb your so-
called providence?'

'A bit, at first. But then I thought, well, it's really only enough to
pay for my visit to Australia, and to start me off in Rome. I'm
happy with my present arrangements. I like them. They suit me.
They're what I'm accustomed to. I've never calculated on anything from dad, and I would still prefer not to.'

'The house will be Greta's. That's something he can't change,
much as he might like to. It's the money that could go elsewhere.
But it mightn't, either, so maybe you're wise not to calculate. If
Greta gets none of it, it means she can't keep up the house. 'But,'
he said, raising then dropping the hand resting on the table,
'that's life.'

'I suppose so,' she said with a shrug.

'You never did like Greta, Syl, did you?'

His look, teasing, too reflective, challenged her into a smiling
impartiality. 'Oh, I don't know. Greta was good to me, in her own
way. After doing the one big, wrong thing, she was always careful
to do all the little, right things. You were too old for the birthday
parties. I've never forgotten them—how she transformed that
dining room, and the ingenuity of the games, and the marvellous
food. They were simply the best juvenile parties around. The
local matrons had to let their children come. She forced them by
child pressure. And you know how Harry and I had our birthdays
in the same week? On the invitations it was always Sylvia Cornock
and Harry Polglaze. My name always first. Little things like that.
No, Greta was very good.'

'And you still didn't like her.'

'Why do you always say that? Why must you bring it up? As if
what was true when I was a silly girl must be true for the rest of my
life. Don't you think that in all these years I haven't thought about
it? Understood how it happened? Well, understood most of it.'
She hesitated, shifting the spoon in her saucer. 'Stewart, those
jokes of the Polglazes, about the loot. Were they true?'

Stewart was looking at his watch. 'What loot?'

'Those headlines Harry found, about money stashed away in seats of cars—'

'By God, it's time poor old mum was allowed to live that down.'

'But there really was some loot?'

'If you like to call it that,' said Stewart with disparagement. 'But he would have converted it ages ago—leaked it into the house, into furnishings, cars, etcetera, and probably the residue was what he put into minerals. He was lucky, you know, to get out before the bust.'

'But he got his money as it said in that newspaper, on the wartime black market?'

'He made his living in legitimate trade, Syl. He was into a lot of small stuff. Dry cleaning shops, cinemas, taxis, food joints. He worked like a dog. Then he got a liquor licence, and the war came, and Sydney was full to the brim with Yanks, and he hopped in, feet first, and made a killing on the black market in grog, as many another did.'

'Mum didn't seem to know.'

'Now who could be easier to deceive than mum?'

Or less safe to trust, thought Sylvia.

'You've heard her go on about his marvellous winnings at the races,' said Stewart.

'Did Greta know?'

'Nobody knows what Greta does or doesn't know. Greta doesn't let much out. This seems to be on your mind.'

'A bit.'

'Then why didn't you ask me any of the times I was in London?'

'I wasn't close to them in London.'

And indeed, it had been Sylvia's long, half-dozing reverie on the plane, in the anticipation of visits shortly to be paid, that had made her try to fit into the general design these old discarded pieces. She had not succeeded; the design itself had become too obscure, the puzzles it provided given up too long ago. But her attempt had been overtaken by sleep, full of haunting dreams that had seemed a kind of answer. Stewart was looking again at his watch. She lifted the spoon and asked, 'How did you find out?'

'What? Me? I was a moral to find out.'

'How? Why?'

'Blokes used to tell me. They don't do it now—not now I've got it made—and anyway, half of them are dead—but they used to button-hole me in bars and say, "Hey, that old man of yours, he was a beauty," and then go on to relate some villany of his in '42, or whenever. No harm intended, mind. They admired him.'

'Did they?'

The dryness of this made him look at her sharply. 'You must have known he was crook, Syl.'

She looked at her own hand shifting the spoon. 'I suppose I guessed something. Mostly from the Polglaze's jokes. But I thought they *were* jokes. So did they.'

'What, guessed something, or thought they were jokes?'

'Both, I suppose,' she said with a shrug, 'since I've just proved it possible.'

His voice was soft, baffled, slightly resentful. 'Yet you've seen so much of the world.'

'Not that world.'

He rose to his feet. He went to the bed and picked up his coat. 'Syl, Sylvia, as far as that's concerned, it's all one world. You've only got to scratch a bit beneath the surface, and not very far either.'

She dropped the spoon into the saucer and got to her feet, smiling. 'I must have been looking for other things.'

'I guess you have quite a talent for looking for other things. Banks still shut at three, Syl.'

'I'll go there first, then ring Greta.'

'Do that.' He was settling his cuffs. He gave her a glance, up and down her figure, in which she detected a splinter of criticism. 'That legacy didn't exactly make you splurge on clothes.'

They had entered one of their areas of contention. She looked down at herself and said mildly, 'Old, but French.'

'All those pockets,' he said with dissatisfaction.

She looked bored. 'Where do I pay the rent?'

'I'll ring you about that tonight. Got to go.' He took hold of her by one shoulder and kissed her cheek. 'Be careful of muggers, joggers, murderers, and kids on skate boards.'

The flat was on the third floor. She stood at the window, looking down through the branches of the plane trees, watching Stewart dodge through the traffic to his car on the other side of the street. The car was a Ford Fairlane. He had once told her that if you sold real estate you had to have a good car, but not too bloody good, or people would say there was only one way you could have got a car like that.

He settled into the driver's seat with an air of relief, of satisfaction, like someone saying, 'Home at last!' She watched him manœuvre out of the cramped parking space and drive round the corner as the lights changed from green to amber.

She opened the window, and up rushed the seethe of traffic and the plashing of the fountain in the park. A man and a woman stepped out onto one of the balconies of the round white tower block. They wore heavy coats; they had just flown in from a cold climate. She thought of their baggage waiting in the room behind them, and then of her own, and drew the casement window shut, saying to herself, bank—shower—unpack—Greta. But Greta, the name, caught her as if by some hitch, and held her to the slow disclosure of the memory diverted from its course by Stewart's presence fifteen minutes ago. In the hall at Wahroonga she now saw, clearer than Greta, the child on the floor, or her father, herself. Greta rises from her attendance on the child on the floor, and extends her hand to the other child, the girl who has come in the front door, and who is refusing to meet Greta's eyes. The girl takes the hand and smiles, but to express yet hide her enmity, smiles only at the child on the floor. 'It is Guy, isn't it?' Her father looks into her face, then looks at Greta. Sylvia withdraws her hand from Greta's, and as she bends to the child, catches—light on a blade—the flash of hostility her father directs at his new wife. She kneels on the floor, and so that her joy shall sound like enthusiasm, she takes the child's hand.

'Oh, but he is like an angel. Hello, Guy. My name is Sylvia. Syl-vee-ah.'

The bank was round the corner at King's Cross. Sylvia had lived at the Cross before going away. The ground plan was familiar, and for the changes she had been prepared by friends. Over-prepared? She had almost expected the erotic and the porno-graphic to have ousted entirely the former population of residents and transients. She was pleased that they had not. She looked with a shade of affection at the people clustered round fruit barrows with bags and baskets, and at the formal aged, in hats and gloves and with walking sticks, still inching immune past the prostitutes, kinky books, adult films, and strip-teases. She had done her share of arguing for sexual frankness, and considered her distaste for its cruder manifestations a perverse quirk, which she would deal with one of these days, when she had time.

A secondary preoccupation of the Cross seemed to be with takeaway food, but about this too she had been told, and also that buyers did not take it far away before starting to eat it. She was made curious only by the number of Asians and Pacific Islanders, whom no one had happened to mention. She walked quickly, intent on a shower and a change of clothes. Her flat was in

Macleay Street, where there were more trees and no overt insistence on the sexual trade. Hesitating, doubtful of her doorway, she caught sight of a young man looking in the window of a cake shop. He resembled those Romans she liked least, and held her attention only because she believed him to be Guy Polglaze, and yet could not believe it. Many times she fancied she had seen in Renaissance paintings, as page boy or young flute player, the beautiful tender-skinned child with the dark curls, and she could not imagine by what freak of growth he had turned into this stocky, morose, blue-jowelled, over-dressed man. Though Rosamond, Harry and Stewart had spoken of his alteration, they had not given physical particulars, so that Rosamond's 'Oh, Guy, he's hopeless, he won't work', like Stewart's 'That Guy's a real no-hoper', and Harry's impatient sighs, had only made her imagine him as living, somehow or other, on his good looks. It had not occurred to her that he would have no good looks left to live on. Yet as she sped past him, pulling her keys from her bag, she was again certain that her first intuition had been right, and that embedded in those remarks about him there must have been some hint that Greta's Ariel had become her Caliban.

Sylvia's suitcase and shoulder bag held everything she owned apart from a tea chest full of papers and maps stored with friends, Richard and Janet Holyoak, in London. Taking a change of clothes from the suitcase, she saw again Guy's heavy head bent to the glass as he scrutinized the cakes, and remembered that even the slender child, the angel with the dark curls, had been greedy. They had laughed at him for it, and he, reaching all over the table for the best bits, had happily laughed back.

She had undressed, and was looking for her bathcap, when the phone rang. A firm crooning voice responded to hers.

'That is Sylvia.'

'Greta, isn't it?' Hearing the dismay in her voice, Sylvia again felt ineptitude, like a doom. And as if to confirm it, she said, 'I was just about to have a shower.'

'Then shall I ring later?'

'No, no, I didn't mean—no, it's all right.'

'I rang Stewart's office, and he gave me your number. Stewart has been so kind with Jack. Stewart is kind. We are all so pleased you are back, my dear. Rosie wants to see you, and so does Hermione. And of course, Harry.'

The warm crooning voice and the confiding manner (which confided so little) were having their old equivocal effect. So firmly, from the very start, had Greta been established in Sylvia's mind as malignant, the sole cause of her father's desertion and her mother's screams and tears, that Sylvia could never give in to her coercions without hating herself afterwards, or even while giving in. She said curtly, 'How is dad?'

'Why not come and see for yourself? I'll drive over and get you, shall I? and bring you back here to dinner.'

'Tonight?' She had not been like this, dumb and laboured, with Stewart. Only with her mother, with Greta—

'Why not tonight?' said Greta.

'I couldn't, Greta.'

'I told Jack I would bring you.'

Her mother, Greta, and her father? She said in open and uncaring panic, 'I simply couldn't.'

'Have you got jet lag?'

'Yes, yes.' Sylvia burst suddenly into laughter. 'I am a very bad case.'

'You sound pleased about it.'

'No. Only past caring.'

'I see. Yes, you had better go and have your shower. What about coming tomorrow?'

'I am going to see my mother.'

'Of course.' Greta had always been prompt, almost pious, in admitting Molly's prior claim. 'Friday, then?'

'Friday. Certainly.'

'Come about four. And I'll ask Harry to come, after work.'

'I look forward to seeing Harry and Margaret.'

'Oh, there's no Margaret any more. Didn't anyone tell you? She went and got herself one of those new little divorces two months ago.'

'Margaret did?'

'Or they got it together. I think that's the way with these little new divorces. Harry is looking forward so much to seeing you.'

Her tone of complicity embarrassed Sylvia. 'I think I saw Guy,' she said helplessly.

'Guy?' said Greta, in a changed voice, raised and anxious. 'And you knew him?'

'Yes, something about him—I don't know—he was looking at cakes.'

There was a silence. Sylvia turned over the contents of her suitcase with one bare foot. Greta said, as if musing, 'He has such a sweet tooth.'

'I wasn't absolutely sure—'

'Never mind, never mind. I have taken up too much of your time. Friday. Do go and have your shower.'

Sylvia rang off, laughed, and struck herself on the forehead. Amusement was a gain. She emptied her suitcase, but she had left her bath cap in Rome. Her hair, bulky and frizzed when let out of its knot, stood like a cape round her shoulders. She improvised a cap out of one of the plastic bags Stewart had brought with the provisions.

The tall cap increased her resemblance to the women painted by Hieronymus Bosch. Securing it with pins before the mirror, she saw her mouth irresistibly smile, and felt her mood sweeten with hope. It was Harry who had first pointed out her resemblance to the women of Bosch. She had been angry. They had high stomachs, she said, and she didn't.

In Harry's divorce she could foresee an end to their long story of obstructed love. It had begun when they were children, but when they were old enough consciously to seek each other out, they were inevitably thwarted. The little obstacles and coincidences by which this happened were so ludicrous that they added a despairing humour to the search, making it like a game with hidden rules. In its early stages this game was monitored by Greta, but Sylvia's attribution to her of all the blame had been disproved when, even after they were out of her reach, the bafflement continued. Then, with half a world between them, the game became impossible to play until four years ago, when Harry visited England with Margaret.

Harry's love for Margaret did not exclude the revival of his amorous friendship for Sylvia, nor did her current involvement exclude her similar feelings for him. Indeed, the seriousness of both of their involvements seemed only to foster the charms of this lighter one. But here were more obstacles, not only Margaret herself, but their scruples about hurting her, as well as their conflicting plans. Harry, an engineer working with earth-moving equipment, was in England on business that soon took him to the Midlands, while Sylvia was pledged to go with her lover to Spain.

Under the shower, Sylvia wondered why Greta now seemed willing to bring Harry and her together when she had once so resolutely shooed them apart. The answer that immediately occurred—the money Stewart thought she may inherit—she blocked off, not only because of its possible injustice to Greta, but to avoid bringing herself to an examination of alternatives which for so many years she had disciplined herself to ignore.

Sylvia had left Sydney in a Greek ship during the exodus of

young people from Australia in the fifties. After a few years of travelling in Europe carrying a pack, she married one of her travelling companions, Geoffrey Foley. By this time most of their friends had taken jobs in London, and Geoffrey was about to do the same. He was tired of the pressure of straps on his shoulders, tired of reading flapping maps on windy streets, exasperated by the intricate assembly of his pack and, above all, humiliated by the menial jobs they had to take in London to finance the next journey. Sylvia was neither tired, exasperated, nor humiliated, but she was in love with this young Englishman, and love made her tractable. Geoffrey went back to his copywriter's job, and Sylvia got a typist's job in the same agency. She had published a few travel articles, and it was assumed that she would soon be given a chance to write copy.

But Sylvia could not settle to a life of routine and constraint. She found casual work conducting tours of London, and in her free time read history and studied languages. Then one day she brought home a bundle of timetables and said she was going to Spain. She was alight and glowing, as when they were first in love. Geoffrey got leave and went with her, but though he tried to regain the insouciance of their former life, he was a sullen travelling companion and she, when they returned to London and she tried again to settle down, was a sullen wife. In the stream of their times, they were caught in conflicting currents. The more domestic Geoffrey became, the more Sylvia was attracted to the nomadic. When he browsed in a shop among kitchen ware, she would wait restlessly in the doorway; when he talked about having children, she would thoughtfully screw up her face; when he went to look at houses, and to talk of loans and leases, she stayed home. The tours she conducted took her further and further from London, and raging quarrels were alternated not with their former sensual reconciliations, but with silences and tired sporadic attempts at healing. Geoffrey, knowing her so malleable when in love, and finding her now so resistant, came to the obvious conclusion. It was not the only one he could have come to, but he thought it was.

'But it's not that at all,' she said. 'It's only that I think it's insane to spend most of your life getting things you can do without.'

'The usual dropout argument. Like Chris and John and Marion.'

'No. Not that I blame Chris and John and Marion. The getting and spending routine pushed them further out than they ever meant to go. I've learned from Chris and John and Marion. I don't want to drop out. I only want to drop down.'

But he was not listening. 'And shift around all the time, and be as poor as a rat.'

'No! I would loathe it. But there's a compromise. I've been thinking a lot about this. I know you can't have absolute freedom. But you can have some. It's only a matter of reconciling yourself to a low standard of living. I don't mean poverty, like in Calabria, but a low standard in our own society. Once you set a low but decent standard, and refuse to consider anything else, I'm sure it's quite easy. The trick is,' she said, 'to refuse to consider anything else. No dreams!'

'How do you set your decent standard?'

'You have to be practical. You have to draw a line.'

'Where do you draw yours?'

'At decayed teeth and inadequate contraception.'

Although serious, she tried to soften his mood by putting it with the air of a joke, but Geoffrey remained absolutely grim and silent. The blood rose to her face.

'Must I change my whole character?' she shouted.

'One of us must.'

Italy, the first European country she had ever seen, had remained for her the place to which she must always return. She was in Rome when Geoffrey Foley divorced her. She was surprised by how much it hurt her to lose that central figure, and that stable place, home. But she had not cast herself into this stream in order to resist it. The tourist industry was booming; for three years she moved about Italy, earning her living by conducting tours, which she came to dislike, and finding her way with delight through the intricacies of the language. But then the countries she had never seen began to lure and goad her. In another few years of travel and return, of trial and error, she let evolve the plan by which she had since lived. She spent the spring and summer in London, where she taught Italian, and by frugal living was able to save enough to take her, in October or November when the tourists began to leave Europe, on her own travels. It was not perfect, but it was the best she could do; it was her compromise. Sometimes she went with friends, sometimes with a lover, lately more often alone. As her thirties advanced, those of her friends who had settled and prospered, especially Richard and Janet Holyoak, began to worry about her. The productions of their own thirties were tangible: academic degrees, children, a house, furniture, a car. At first it was understood that Sylvia was collecting material for a book about the history of the British traveller in Europe, but as time went on, and she filled a tea chest with diaries, maps, and photographs, and wrote not a word of the book, Janet and Richard dropped the subject and urged her to concentrate on her teaching. She replied with surprise that it had always been her intention to settle one day, if possible in Rome, and to teach, and write the book. But more years went by, and still she went on in the old way, still getting most of her living by teaching, but filling an occasional gap by taking a tour. Twice she was engaged by American families, and one spring she drove two old Canadian ladies, sisters, all over Scotland and Eire in an attempt to trace their ancestry.

She never set out on a journey without an intense but peaceful elation, a deeply private triumph. But though this mood of departure never failed her, other changes took place. While the tourist boom had gone on, so had the boom in development and the motor industry, and the failure of restoration to keep pace with decay. Since settling to her plan she had become a lover rather than an explorer, returning to places she knew instead of seeking new ones, and now, to protect herself against rawness and incoherence, she limited her track even further, going only to places which had not been subject to great changes, or which had managed, like Rome, to absorb them. She noticed that a number of her old friends lived in the same way in London, sticking as much as possible to their 'villages', or to others of the same pleasantness, and making themselves blind to all that offended them while passing from one to the other. She saw that their fastidiousness reflected her own. The limitations and losses it forecast appalled her. She made attempts to reconcile herself to the changes, and now and then had successes. When at some small airport, instead of the windy tarmac she remembered, she found herself in the tepid unnatural air of a concrete and glass enclosure, she remembered that there must also have been sorrow when that first tarmac fractured a rural landscape. In street cafes she refrained from remarking on plastic tables and chairs, and when, instead of a building remembered with affection, she was confronted by a towering façade of glaring glass, she would try to assess it, as architect friends had instructed her, in its own terms. Sometimes she succeeded, and sometimes she pretended to.

In this way, her cycle of travel and work survived these changes, and was not interrupted until her thirty-eighth year when, in the harder financial times, the spring and summer yielded her only enough for three months of freedom. She returned to London, resigned to curtailment, and found awaiting her a letter from

Canada. One of the sisters she had conducted over Scotland and Eire had died, and had left her eight thousand Canadian dollars 'as a token of the happiest holiday of my life'. The other sister wrote a rather tart note saying, well, it was rather a lot of money to be called a token, but if that was the way Amy wanted it ...

At first Sylvia was strangely dismayed. It seemed almost a consolation that the rate of exchange was not in her favour; but by the time the money came through, the rate of exchange had altered, and so had her attitude. It no longer seemed a large sum of money; it was barely enough to make a journey to Australia and to help her to settle in Rome. In the lives of all her Australian friends, return was an imperative, either for a visit or for a period of work; she alone had never been back.

The Holyoaks told her that Rome was falling apart, and that she was out of her mind to think of settling there. Sylvia listened with her usual courteous attention, then said she would go to Rome for a few months to think about it, and would fly from there to Australia. The Holyoaks were mollified when at last she discarded her pack and bought a matching suitcase and shoulder bag. Yes, they said, they would be happy to mind her tea chest.

While she was in Rome the spring passed into summer. She watched the tourist coaches, from which she had once happily made a living, spill out their corrupting loads. She saw the untended grass in the parks grow long and bleached and dusty, and to defeat the *scippatori* she left her handbag at home and carried her money in her pockets. Twice she turned into streets and saw the drifting smoke from a recently exploded petrol bomb.

And yet, as she walked, and stood, and looked, and listened, she knew her devotion to this city to be still intense. Perhaps the amazement and delight with which she had first seen it, twenty years before, had constituted an unbreakable pact. When she was engaged by a shopkeeper to give English lessons to two of his sons, she thought it a good omen, for though the boys were emigrating to an uncle in Australia, it let her envisage similar work in the future, in which she would have the pleasure of imparting the structure of her own language. One disadvantage of the division of her year had been that most of her pupils wanted only a smattering. These two clever boys kept her in Rome until the second week in September. When she seemed likely to get the lease of a flat on the Janiculum, she decided to put off her visit to Australia, but the negotiations broke down, and she bought an airline ticket and rang Stewart on the same day.

Sleeping on the plane, she dreamed of her mother and father, seeing them as two shapes in confrontation, the one towering, massive, slow, the other thin, shrieking, volatile, with bits of moving glitter about her dress. When she woke she tried to oppose to this exaggeration of a childish vision the photographs sent to her by Stewart and Greta: the old woman standing on a garden path, shading her eyes with her hand; the old man getting out of a car, holding his hat. But the weakly accurate lines of the photographs could not hold down that other reality beneath, and when she went to sleep again, she saw the two long-tasselled, gilded ear-rings striking her mother's cheeks as she swung her head to and fro, and her painted red mouth shrieking in denial of some accusation, and she saw her father, huge, dark, and hovering, feeding with his silence his wife's hysteria.

She woke with a depression that did not lift until they had landed, and she came out of the baggage room and saw Stewart in the forefront of the waiting crowd. He did not see her; he was too engrossed in appreciation of the Greek woman who preceded her. Catching him in such a typical attitude had made her laugh, and lightened her mood.

She was careful never to count on pleasant accommodation, so the flat Stewart had found was a bonus. But she had counted on that Australian necessity, a shower. After turning the water from warm to cold, she let it run on the nape of her neck, and even after drying herself felt freshness like an aura round her body. The blunders of the day seemed less important. Equably, she told herself that arrivals were always confusing.

Stewart, in his flat, silhouetted by a low light against a wall of glass which framed a brilliant view, tugged off his tie while waiting for Sylvia to answer his call. As soon as he heard her voice he said vigorously, 'Syl, why I rang, I said I would, about the rent, I've paid it for two months, homecoming gift.'

'You shouldn't have. But don't let's talk of it now. I was almost asleep.'

'That's not an irreversible state. Get a taxi and come and have dinner with me.'

'I've had dinner.'

'Then come and have a drink.'

'You sound a bit drunk already.'

'Am I a bit drunk?' Stewart asked himself. 'Only a little bit,' he replied. He yawned, unbuttoning his shirt. 'Come on, come and see my flat. Not bad. Harbour view. City lights. The lot.'

'Another time.'

'Better hurry, then. I think I've got a buyer.'

'Is that why you move so often?'

'Yeah. I'm like you. A nomad. I'm an economic nomad. Pick up a good buy, sell at a decent profit, pick up another. Come on, Syl, how about that drink?'

'Did somebody stand you up?'

'*Shrewd*! Yeah, my girl. More than stood me up, finished it off. Mind, she did the right thing. The heart's gone out of it lately. I'm the type hangs on out of politeness.'

Her voice was now alert, curious. 'When you say girl—'

'Yeah, yeah, I meant woman. Thirty.'

'Thirty.'

'Yeah.'

'I rang Greta,' said Sylvia, 'and I'm going there on Friday. I saw Guy, too, in the street.'

'He's rubbish, that Guy. He's one of those bastards thinks he's got it made if he has Gucci shoes and one of those damn silly watches without numerals. He bludges on old women. He bullies them, and they cry. They seem to like that. Avoid him. Syl.'

'I'm not old enough to be at risk.'

'I didn't mean that. You know I didn't—'

'Stewart, I'll give you the rent for the flat. I would rather pay it myself. You don't mind? And now I'm going to sleep.'

'Right, but listen, Syl, why I rang, why I really rang—this is important—on the way to mum's tomorrow, pick up a bottle of Great Western, semi-dry, she likes that. A homecoming celebration, just you and her. Get it at the corner pub, not far to carry it. My shout, but no need to tell her that. Yeah, sure, go back to sleep. The view can wait.' He looked across one shoulder at it. 'Actually, living here, you get so you hardly notice it.'

Sylvia folded her hands behind her head and wondered why it had not occured to her before that Harry would be attached to a woman twenty years his junior—in fact, a girl. She was of an age when former admirers were apt to appear with girls; it demonstrated a biological truth she had done her best to accept, but which she still sometimes forgot to take into account.

Three

Sylvia slept late, and woke with a restlessness that snatched her attention from everything she tried to do. To give it play, she decided to walk to Wynyard station across Woolloomooloo, the Domain, and the Botanic Gardens, and at half past twelve she took a lift up to the roof to confirm her memory of the route.

On the roof a wind met her. During her adolescent mania for clothes, the winds of Sydney had harassed her, tugging at her many petticoats and penetrating her laboriously quelled hair. But though in her dress it was agony to be less than perfect, in her handbag was always evidence of concurrent passions: a blue Pelican or an orange Penguin, history or poetry. As she crossed the roof the memory of these past discords brought comfort for her present self. At this moment it was enough to be thirty-nine, self-possessed, comfortable and mobile. The wind did not dislodge a strand of her high-pinned hair, but stirred only a nimbus of frizz round her head. At the parapet she put a hand—an Australian gesture, recalling that snapshot of her mother—like a visor above her eyes.

She stood on the roof of a building itself on the high escarpment above Woolloomooloo, but the map of the city she had carried for two decades in her head, the attempted British gridiron of streets disrupted by the lay of the land and the intrusion of water, was visible only in Woolloomooloo and the green rise of parkland beyond. Woolloomooloo, low-lying, was slung between Pott's Point, where she stood, and the green rise of the Domain, which extended itself, like a long green finger from a green fist, into the harbour where its splayed tip was called, she thought, Mrs Macquarie's Point. Beyond this green fist and its finger rose the towers of the city, some bearing construction cranes. Distance impacted them, and their bases, around which lay the rest of her mental map, were hidden from her view.

But it was easy to confirm the first part of her route. There were the McElhone Stairs, just as she remembered them, leading from the escarpment of Pott's Point down into Woolloomooloo. During the pared-down and frugal period following her resolution to discard fashion and save to go abroad, they were part of her way to and from her drink waitress's job in a city night club. Watching her feet in thonged rubber sandals (five shillings at Woolworths), she used to count the steps as she went. Rosamond and a school friend had once mounted them with her, groaning at the hundredth step. Playing at wickedness, they had changed in her room into the kind of clothes forbidden by Greta, and had gone agog into the streets.

The McElhone Stairs led into Cowper Wharf Road, which still curved unchanged between dockside and pubs. She followed it with her eyes until she found the steps cut in the steep grassy bank she must ascend to reach the Domain. The gulch of an expressway was now carved out of that bank; the steps followed one of its edges. When she had climbed them she would stand between the Inner and Outer Domain and would have only to choose her path through the Gardens, in which she could trust herself entirely to memory.

Yet still she lingered on the roof, from another part of the parapet looking westward, where Burwood lay beyond a haze of smog, and from another, past the lustrous roofs of the Opera House and the meccano arch of the bridge, to the clean north, where her father lived with Greta. She found Neutral Bay, and wondered if Harry still lived there, and Point Piper, where Rosamond lived. She was defeated by Hermione's last-remembered address. Baulkham Hills? But she knew that many suburbs had pushed into land formerly rural.

But what kept her longest on the roof was her puzzlement that familiarity seemed a glaze which, while not obscuring the scene, made it inaccessible in all but its pictorial aspects. Memory itself seemed a glaze, without penetration to feeling. She stood at the eastern parapet, staring as if hypnotized at the glimpse of ocean between the headlands. From her angle of vision the two heads bit in, South Head overlapping North Head, and allowed to be seen only a triangle of a denser blue than the harbour. The Pacific. That denser blue had once filled her with determination. It had flashed through her mind as hands moved her tip to the edge of the tray. She remembered, as dispassionately as if it had happened to someone else, the masculine hands, the money on the wet tray, and that blue flash, expanding, promising distance.

Steven Fyfe entered the Inner Domain by Art Gallery Road and ran under the blackish-green figs. He wore white shorts, an old red T-shirt, and a blue headband woven by Hermione.

His gait was plain, rhythmical, and relaxed, a triumph of the biped state. As he crossed the bridge spanning the gulch of the expressway he saw down in Woolloomooloo Bay a merchant ship from mainland China, black and ochre, high out of the water. Five small men dressed in blue-grey were mounting the steps from Woolloomooloo to the Domain, and others in the same colour were radiating away from the wharf and dispersing through the streets of Woolloomooloo.

Sylvia passed a group of these Chinese on the McElhone Stairs, ascending as she descended. The sandstone steps were hollowed with wear. She counted them—a hundred and thirteen.

Steven entered the Outer Domain by the top path. On this hillocky finger of land between Woolloomooloo Bay and Farm Cove, paths and roads were traced at different levels and connected by long and short flights of steps, and on all the paths and roads and steps men and boys were jogging.

Steven, his back straight and his head erect, ran up the slope of the first hillock and advanced along its crest. At a short distance ahead he saw Ted Kitching, in black shorts and a purple T-shirt. Ted's back was not straight, his head was not erect, and his arms moved as if rocking, rather desperately, a large baby.

Ted reached the Henry Lawson statue and disappeared behind its pedestal. When Steven reached the statue, Ted was standing in half-profile, his hands on his hips, staring down at the Chinese ship.

'Hi!' shouted Steven.

Ted turned and shouted something in reply, but Steven, who always set himself to do the course non-stop, raised an arm in salutation and ran on. He crossed the path and ran up the second hillock. The rumours about Ted's companies were accruing, the comments in the financial pages growing longer. Hermione, handing Steven the *Herald* that morning, had said, 'He will have to start taking it seriously soon, whatever Rosie says.' For a few paces, Steven ran faster and bounded higher. In the grass, among the clover and little yellow daisies, lay a derelict man, no flesh visible in the crumpled cloth except for a sheeny ankle above a loose shoe. Near him, a pair of peewits strutted and explored. In cars parked between the hillock and the railings of the gardens, salesmen ate or dozed or stared or pondered.

Sylvia had crossed Woolloomooloo and was mounting the steps to the Domain. She looked up and saw, on the bridge crossing the expressway, the jogging men. At the top of the steps stood five Chinese seamen, conferring. Stopping to rest after thirty-five steps, she looked at the traffic below, and remembered the simple green hill the expressway had broken. But this was different from the spirit in which she had paused, a week or so ago, to note the crudely painted hardboard replacing a marble panel in a Roman villa, or to smile at an angel lolling in a tympanum with a sheaf of green leaves growing from the dirt in the crook of her arm. In that protective refusal to criticize, there had been no suggestion of a glaze, a transparent but obtrusive substance between her and what she saw.

Steven, on Mrs Macquarie's Point, changed his course to avoid disturbing a group of aboriginal boys making football passes with a red practice ball. A FAR WEST coach stood nearby. He ran down the broad steps to the path that followed at water level the loop of Farm Cove. On the harbour wall sat five aboriginal children, all girls, dangling their legs. One of them jumped down as he passed and ran in his rear, in a parody of his gait, making the others laugh so much that they had to get down from the wall. Steven smiled when he heard them, but then became graver than before. That morning a girl, a heroin addict of seventeen, had said to him, idly, 'Yes, but you're just a middle-class fuckwit, aren't you?' When Steven and Ted met, Ted would ask, 'How's the bleeding-heart business?' Ted believed in the survival of the fittest, in sinking or swimming. 'Christ!' he would say, 'Who would be nanny to a lot of hairy-arsed louts and incipient tarts?'

Sylvia stood at the top of the steps from Woolloomooloo. She looked at her watch and estimated that there was not enough time to walk round Mrs Macquarie's Point and enter the Gardens by the gate at water level. This was the gate through which Steven passed at that moment into the Gardens. Sylvia crossed the road and entered by the east gate. Ahead of her, the five Chinese seamen had clustered to look at a fountain.

Ted Kitching, with downcast eyes and pondering brows, left the Henry Lawson statue and departed at a dogged pace for Mrs Macquarie's Point. He reached the aboriginal boys and ran through their game. As they made way for him, they laughed at the legend on his purple T-shirt. Ted took no notice. He ran down the broad steps to water level, and passed the aboriginal girls on the wall. The same skinny little girl jumped down and ran in his rear. Laughter rose high behind him, but Ted's thoughtful expression did not change.

Steven ran on the semi-circular path between the harbour wall and garden beds cut to conform to the loop of the cove. In these beds, shrubberies full of birds were bordered by marigolds and candytuft, or scented stock and primula. 'Of course,' Hermione had said, taking back the newspaper, 'Ted's so ingenious, he may get out of it yet.' Crescents of sweat were creeping from beneath Steven's armpits.

Sylvia walked through banks of flowers, wisteria on one side, on the other tall azaleas. All were in full bloom, all exuded scent. When she had spent days here alone, in flight from her education (which, competitively managed from two households, had seemed to entail a double obligation), the Gardens had been cupped in the Domain, the cultivated area gripped by the natural, and broken only by the thread of a single road; but though that thread had expanded into the band and dipping gulch of the expressway, the Gardens still seemed to her (who had not been out of reach of traffic for many months) almost eerily quiet. She could hear the variation in the hum of the bees, her own light footsteps, and the light footsteps of the five Chinese ahead. They halted again to confer, and as Sylvia passed she saw how young they were, their skins as if lit from within, and on their black hair *en brosse* that shine that is almost a sparkle.

Steven completed the loop of Farm Cove, but prolonged his run by mounting the slope and following, at varying distances, the iron railings of the Governor's Residence. Drinking one fumy hot Sunday under the Cornocks' jacaranda tree, not long after the Governor-General had dismissed the Labor government, and Harry Polglaze had been talking of republicanism, Steven had said to Ted, 'I doubt the wisdom of discarding an institution that gives a sense of security to so many, simply because we don't happen to need that security ourselves.' But Ted had scratched a buttock and said that actually, he didn't give a stuff one way or the other. By glancing to his left Steven could recognize, among the other joggers, Ted's purple shirt and lumbering gait. Ted was taking a short cut across the grass, among the picnics, the flower beds, and the park benches, towards his usual egress by the main gate. Steven accordingly adjusted his pace.

Sylvia sat for a while in the palm grove where, once, in filtered light and deep silence, she had resolved to go away. The thought had first passed casually through her—I could go away—but had then returned and settled. And suddenly it was a fever. She got her job, got her room, and began to save. The five Chinese, walking faster, turned a corner and passed her seat. She followed them out of the palm grove. Her first obsession had been simply to get away. The seeds of addiction had not been sown until she had landed at Genoa. In Rome she was too impressed to speak. She could only shake her head. She almost cried. She had read about, yet had not expected, the impact of those visible layers of history, and she had not even read about the casual way the Romans lived with and used their treasures, the lovers in the shadow of ancient walls, the boys fishing their football out of a Bernini fountain.

She followed the Chinese onto a broad path parallel to the expressway on the other side of the railings. Ahead of the Chinese she saw a slowly ambling man in a purple T-shirt and black shorts. A tall man in a red T-shirt ran past her, past the Chinese, and slowed down beside the first man, clapping a hand on his shoulder. The taller man wore a blue headband, idly noticed by Sylvia across the barrier of the five Chinese. As he turned his head to speak to the shorter man, he revealed a delicate and regular profile.

Now that she was near the Main Gate, Sylvia turned suddenly about and surveyed the sloping stretches of grass, the big dense trees rising from their shadows, the agglomerated flowers, and the palm fronds streaming high out of shrubberies as if to return the signals of the flashing water. She had hoped to take herself by surprise, but either the glaze was as thick as ever, or the postcard brilliance of the scene made it impersonal. She knew that she had lain on that grass for hours, trapped in torpor and rebellion, but again the knowledge was dispassionate. Waking one day, lifting her face from her inside arm, wet with saliva, she had heard Harry saying, 'Sylvia? Sylvia?' She looked at her watch, and was startled into turning again on the broad path, walking quickly. The five Chinese were turning out of the gates.

'Gets the liver ticking over,' Ted was saying to Steven.

'It does,' Steven gravely agreed.

'I've been known to solve problems back there.'

Sylvia heard this as she hurried past, and heard the taller man say with sympathy, 'Then I sincerely hope you solved one today.'

But Ted, watching Sylvia walk away, was frowning. Steven had to repeat himself.

'I hope you solved one today, Ted.'

'I know that woman from somewhere.'

'A problem,' said Steven.

'Oh. Yes. That. Yes. I think I did.' Ted halted, put his hands on his hips, and winked at Steven. 'I just think I might have.'

Now that they were face to face, Steven saw the legend on Ted's T-shirt. I GOT TROUBLES. He stared, his lower lip becoming slack. Ted winked again, screwing up his face so that he looked idiotic.

'I think I did,' he said.

'Good for you,' said Steven.

They approached the main gate, Ted scratching himself. Rosamond often remonstrated with Ted because every time he and Steven met, Ted scratched himself to prove how coarse he was in comparison with Steven. Rosamond said she was sick of pulling Ted's hand off his arse, or even out of it, and that he needn't think Steven didn't notice, and wasn't insulted by Ted's presentation of himself as a comic-cut character.

Sylvia, outside the main gate, paused with her back to a fountain with perpendicular spouts, and looked across the expressway (here a flat band) to the low, heavy-columned public library, where she had spent so many days when driven from the Gardens by rain. There Harry had found the headlines about her parents' divorce, and there she had once read that the first requisite of happiness was to be born in a famous city. The five Chinese were mounting the steps to the library. She turned away, smiling, and walked towards the crossing at Macquarie Street.

Steven and Ted came through the main gate. Ted ran up the surround of the fountain and dipped his head in a spout of water. 'That's asking for trouble,' said Steven curtly, when Ted rejoined him. As they walked towards Macquarie Street, Ted wiped his face with a forearm, sniffing. 'Why don't you blow your nose with your hand?' asked Steven lightly.

Ted sniffed. 'See that woman up at the lights? Skinny. With her hair up. Passed us before. That's Knocker's daughter.'

'Sylvia? Is it?'

'I knew I knew her. Rosie and I saw her last time we were over.'

'Hermione and I hope to go over again when the children—'

'D'you know what her husband said about her? She told us this herself. "No awkward protruberances," he said. "Designed for folding and packing." I don't like her much, but Rosie does.'

The WALK sign came on, and Sylvia stepped into the street.

'I suppose she's going to Wahroonga,' said Steven.

'No. Out to Burwood to see her mum. She told Greta so yesterday. Rosie rang Greta last night. Rosie's worried about Greta.'

'Hermione's worried about Greta.'

They stood at the lights, watching Sylvia walk quickly down the slope of Bent Street.

'She's in no hurry to see her father,' remarked Steven.

'Well, not to make it too obvious, you know.'

'You really think—'

'Why not? Everybody's got to look after themselves in this world.'

Once the train passed the uniform, blackened roofs of the railway workshops, the remembered chaos took over, a hotch-potch of small buildings that stretched as far as the eye could see, and was arrested only by the stately clustered silos of the flour mills. The pubs were still on their corners, the spires of the little churches still on a level with the television antennae, and except where a weedy embankment cut everything off, she could still see, wherever she looked, the painted words:

HOOKERS BUY AND SELL... SPECIAL FILTERS... FUNERAL PARLOUR...
COME BACK TO GAS... LIME AND CEMENT... COKE ADDS LIFE...
NEW TASTE SENSATION... WE LEND MONEY... GOD WANTS YOU...

She sat too alertly, her legs crossed, her head slightly tilted. The new blocks of flats were quite unlike those desolate blocks surrounding the big Italian cities. Simply three stories of red or yellowish brick built on concrete platforms, they were neat, prim, and mean. Sighs began to fill her chest. The glaze had dropped away. As the train drew into Burwood she looked quickly in her bag to make sure she had brought enough money for the champagne suggested by Stewart.

Keith Burtenshaw, who had a younger partner, David Sole, did some of his work at home, and was speaking from his study overlooking a garden not half a mile from the Cornocks' house. 'It's been on my mind, Greta,' he said. 'And I want to tell you, for a start, how sorry I am that I failed to argue him out of what happened.'

Greta shaded a cube. 'But as I don't know what did happen—'

'No, and nobody is more sorry than I that I can't breach his confidence, but you must have gathered that you weren't left out entirely. I managed that much. And nor is the amount derisory. I only wish I could have talked him out of changing it at all. And I most certainly wish that he hadn't said, indicated, that it would do in the meantime. That's what's on my mind. I want to urge you once again, Greta, to apply yourself to getting round him. You could do it.'

'I can't.'

'Nonsense. Think of yourself.'

'I am thinking of myself. Putting my energies into myself.'

Keith Burtenshaw swivelled his chair, and flung some papers about on his desk, but his voice was as calm as ever. 'What you said the other day, Greta—that's superstitious nonsense. Turn your mind away from that.'

'You don't know what it is, Keith. You wouldn't listen.'

'No, and nor shall I. That isn't my field. I want to do my best for Jack, and for you, and I want those endeavours to be compatible. But I won't listen to superstitious nonsense, Greta, or to ancient tales.'

She put down her pen, and laid her clenched fist on the pad. 'I only thought, that someone of my own generation, who knows so much already—'

'Marjorie is always on the phone to this one and that one, some of them she went to school with. Her girl friends, she calls them. Has Jack's daughter arrived, Greta?'

Greta picked up her pen again. 'Yesterday. She's coming here tomorrow.'

'She certainly timed her arrival nicely.'

'Why should we expect her to be immune from the money hunger that afflicts everyone else?'

'I wish it afflicted you.'

'It did, in my day, as you remember.'

'No, I don't, Greta. Who was that fellow we used as a witness?'

'He was here to give a valuation on the rugs.'

'It hasn't come to that, has it?'

'There's nothing final about a valuation. How is Marjorie, Keith?'

Keith Burtenshaw made his sourest mouth. 'She's all right, I suppose . . .'

When Greta left the phone she returned to her seat in the back garden and picked up her sewing again. She was unpicking a wool skirt. After a while, when the silence had settled beneath the bird cries, she whispered something about Rome, then raised her voice to a normal conversation level and said, 'Every time I think of Europe, I think of blood.'

Again the silence settled, then again her whisper came out. She said that Harry was right in one thing—that house hunger in those days *was* like an infection. 'But Hermione was only a very little girl. It's absurd to think she could have caught it.'

She gave a sociable little laugh at the absurdity of it but, the laugh dying emptily away, she raised her head, startled, and looked about her in a dazed way before settling to her work again.

But in a few minutes, she was whispering that the girls had been only in their twenties when short skirts were in fashion. She let the skirt drop suddenly to her lap, stared ahead of her, and said aloud, 'On and on. Pointlessly, pointlessly. On and on.'

Siddy, coming round a corner of the house, showed no surprise at hearing her voice, nor did she show confusion at being overheard. Calmly, she watched him cross the grass. His unlit cigarette bobbed as he spoke.

'He says he hasn't got all the *Herald*.'

'The financial part is on the kitchen table,' she said with resignation.

As he turned to go, she called him back, but when he came back, she did not seem to recall why she wanted him. She looked about her, and at last said, as if at random, 'Oh, Siddy, that swing . . .'

'What about it?'

She put her sewing aside, and they went together to the childrens' swing suspended from the native fig free. She lifted one side of the seat to expose the rope. 'Isn't it rather frayed?'

'Good for years yet.'

'No. Either it will have to come down, or be made perfectly safe.'

'Well,' he said patiently, 'which?'

'The children come so seldom. We'll have it down.'

'Right-oh.'

'Still, Emma used it last time they came.'

Siddy made his dainty gesture of plucking the butt from his lower lip. He looked at it, and put it back.

'And there's Imogen coming on, though she would still have to be held . . .'

'No trouble to put in a new rope.'

'Well, and there it would be, wouldn't it? Good for the future.'

When she returned to the seat, and picked up the skirt again, she looked more contented. With her tiny scissors she bit at the cloth, again and again, patiently opening the seam. Scraps of threads fell around her. It was five minutes before her whisper came out again.

'We used to call that Guy's tree . . . Guy's branch . . .'

'He was dead set on Brenda,' said Molly. 'But I stuck out for Sylvia. I thought it softened the Cornock. Have a drop more, Syl.'

'You have it, mum.'

'No, you.'

'Just a bit, then. Here, let me pour it.'

The champagne had helped. Molly held out her glass like a

child, and Sylvia, standing to pour, felt slightly filial. Molly had not entered the nunnery of old age. She was dressed in floral nylon, too tight, too short, and cut to expose a rucked neck and a chest cleft into sections like a burnt-out claypan. Diamanté ear-rings hung from her softened, elongated ear lobes, and on one shoulder was pinned a matching brooch. Her lipstick, pink instead of the red Sylvia remembered, clung only to the edges of her big drooping mouth. With the rest she had imprinted crescents on the rim of the full glass she now raised to the light. The house was one of those often described by Stewart as 'the double-fronted brick bung, the curse of Sydney,' by which he meant a brick box with one of its two front rooms projecting beyond the other, and a small tiled verandah occupying the space thus provided. On the back a wide comfortable verandah had been added in Jack Cornock's time, and here Molly and Sylvia sat on chairs of plastic webbing, facing the raised lawn and the concrete steps on which Sylvia had once seen her father nearly lose his footing.

'Cheers, Syl.'

'Cheers.'

There was respect and satisfaction in the approach of Molly's big puckered lips to the glass. She drank a little, said it was nice, and leaned back.

'Did you notice how our shops have sprung ahead? These days you never need go to town at all if you don't want.'

'I can't imagine you never going to town.'

'Ah, great old shopper, wasn't I?' She lapsed into a moment's thought. 'Ah well, never mind. Sorry I never answered your lovely letters, Syl.'

'Don't be sorry. I know how you hate writing letters.'

'When Stewart come out I always save them for him to read. Did he write?'

'Stewart? Oh,' said Sylvia then, realizing who she meant. 'No, he didn't.'

'Did she?'

'Yes, for them both.'

'It's not the same as if he wrote hisself. Well, I should talk. But he can write.'

Sylvia was resourceful enough, in the shocked pause, to repress her exclamation. Molly gave a shriek.

'The things I come out with! Sounds like I can't write. But I wouldn't have got through life without I could write. Now would I?'

Sylvia gave her smile. 'Hardly.'

But it was from her mother she had inherited her blushing skin, and both were proving it now.

'It's this right hand that's the trouble.' Molly changed her glass from her right to her left hand, and extended the right to Sylvia's view, flexing and unflexing the fingers. A moment ago they had easily held the stem of the thin glass; now they looked crabbed. 'See that?' said Molly keenly. 'See that?'

Sylvia made a sound of condolence. The suspicion that Molly could not read or write must have lain dormant in her mind for a long time. Conviction could not otherwise have been so sudden. And how fast and lucidly her memory was providing confirmation, showing her Molly saying, 'Here, love, read out these ingredients. Save me putting on specs.' Or 'I've got no time to write to your teacher. Get your father to.' Or, if Jack Cornock were not at home, 'Get Stewart to, and I'll sign it.' And what a business that signature was, how laborious, and always Molly had to wipe her hands first, and sit down, and get the paper at a certain angle. And did illiteracy also explain the solicitor's letters Molly had so often threatened, and sometimes sent? Jack Cornock, at the phone at Wahroonga, had shouted at his former wife, 'You and your bloody solicitor's letters! If you've got something to say, write it yourself.' But Sylvia, though assaulted by a rush of questions, of incredible possibilities, was still looking with polite concern at Molly's hand, clenching and unclenching, and could feel Molly's anxious gaze resting on her face.

'Is it arthritis, mum?'

Molly also looked at her hand. 'They don't know. Not even the best Macquarie Street specialists. It's been like that ages, and not likely to get better at age seventy-three.'

But she remained silent and thoughtful, as if dissatisfied with her own deception; and Sylvia was also silent, sitting in rather a crouched posture over the empty wine glass held in her lap, and gazing, like her mother, out over the garden. Ken Fiddies had evidently seen no need to change the style of gardening set by Jack Cornock: the buffalo grass was as severely clipped as ever, and the citrus trees still stood in beds so exactly circular that they might have been sunk into the earth in barrels. Molly had finished her wine. She folded her arms, clutching the elbows.

'Are you chilly, Syl?'

'No, mum.'

'Say if you get chilly.'

'Are you?'

'A bit.'

'Let's go in, then.'

'Okay, good. That's the bottle gone, anyway. Bring it in, will you?' And Molly added, with one of her touches of hauteur, 'If you would be so good.'

Sylvia picked up the glasses and bottle and followed her. Jack Cornock had much commended himself for giving Molly the house when, having divorced her for adultery, he was under no legal compulsion to give her anything. Molly had defended herself in court by the disclosure that they had an understanding by which each was allowed to be unfaithful to the other, but that he had betrayed it because he had lost his head over 'a nasty blonde piece years younger'. Stewart always claimed that the court had believed her. Sylvia had certainly believed her, knowing her to be so shy with what she called 'perfessional people' that only true indignation would have given her the courage to clamour and shout before so many of that class. But whether the court had believed her or not, Jack Cornock had hired detectives, who had proved Molly's adultery by climbing in a window and finding her in bed, with a man, while Molly could prove nothing, and so was proclaimed the guilty party, and punished accordingly. Barbarous times, thought Sylvia, following her mother into the dining room. After the divorce Molly had taken in boarders, and into one of her rooms, when she was in her fifties, had come Ken Fiddies, a widower with adult children. Molly, though still thin and light, now walked with a stumping gait, her veined legs apart. A television set stood across one corner of the dining room. As she passed she turned on the picture without the sound.

'Take those into the kitchen, Syl. And switch on the kettle, will you? I filled it already, but better check.'

When Sylvia came out of the kitchen a silent advertisement for cat food filled the screen. The table was veiled with a cloth. Molly took it by two corners and whisked it off.

'Like old times, Syl.'

Sylvia's usual soft little smile, the abruptly curved double lines appearing on either side of her plump mouth, hid her dismay. Such food as this—a raisin tart, cup cakes filled with stiff cream, an iced chocolate cake on a pedestal—had invariably greeted her for the first few years of her division between the two households. And while she ate, Molly would question her in a casual tone disproved by her persistence. Did he still always wear a hat? Did she? What kind? What colour? Did he take her to the pictures? the theatre? out driving on Sundays? What make was their fridge?

their vacuum cleaner? their toaster? No question was too trivial; no answer could be too particular: all were welcome irritants to Molly's wound. Sylvia, intimidated by pity for her mother, had kept up the replies in an agony of evasion, but one day had gagged, broken into a sweat, and rushed from the table. Molly did not connect her sickness with either the food or the questions. It was something she ate at the other house. Or it was all that dancing. What right had they to send her to ballet when Molly had just enrolled her in Folk. She had access, which she hoped gave her *some* rights. She would write a solicitor's letter.

Sylvia had never quite understood why, after about three years, the interrogation had lost its compulsive force and become feeble and sporadic. She supposed it was sheer tiredness. The table was no longer set for her arrival, and Molly, untidy and disgruntled, would only say, 'Oh, it's you. Get yourself something if you're hungry.'

Only the battle over her education had continued. Molly wanted her to have only the best, by which she meant the most expensive, and since Jack Cornock had money to burn, she didn't see why she shouldn't have it. A local solicitor, with rooms in the shopping centre, wrote the letters. There were counter-attacks by Jack Cornock, and hidden attempts at accommodation by Greta. Knowing herself to be not really the issue in this battle, Sylvia had tried to curl up under the rain of missiles, hoping not to be noticed. But she was always being pulled upright by an arm, usually by Molly, and displayed, and ranted over, until at last she was old enough to shed her disabling pity, and to remove herself from between them, leaving nobody with an excuse for combat.

'I must confess they aren't home-made these days,' said Molly. 'The hours I used to spend! My word, you used to look forward to my spreads when you come home from there. Ken's due any time, but he doesn't like tea this late, so whatsay we start? There's the kettle boiling now.'

'Let me make it.'

'Right-oh. I'll just get the milk.'

At the refrigerator, Molly said, 'Funny you bringing champagne, Syl. Great minds. I got some in myself.' She took a bottle of champagne from the refrigerator, and as she put it at the back of a cupboard, darted a quick upward glance at Sylvia.

'Don't let on to Ken I got this, Syl.'

After one of Molly's shopping sprees in town, she would stand in her bedroom trying on a new dress, or a new hat, and turning her head this way and that, her eyes always on her own in the mirror, she would murmur to her small admiring daughter, 'Don't let on to your father I got this, love. I'll tell him later.'

At the table, as they finished their tea, the last effects of the champagne wore off, and between them swelled the afflatus of their estrangement. Sylvia had once thought of these silences as vacuums, but this was not so; they were haunted by the infantile and maternal love they had displaced. Unbearable she had always found them, and still truly found them. She felt compelled to embark on talk of the other house.

'I haven't been out to Wahroonga yet.'

Molly was dull but prompt. 'I thought last night, maybe.'

'No, early to bed. Tonight too. I'll go tomorrow.'

'Stewart says she's not looking all that chirpy. But he looks all right, according to Stewart. Dresses as well as ever, too. Ah, but he was always dressy. Yes, everything had to be just right. And I was the same. Oh, I was! Though you mightn't remember.'

'But I do,' said Sylvia.

'I'll never forget the big race meetings, and him and me, the looks we used to get. Standing at the enclosure, watching all the dirty little jocks come out. And he used to win. Win! He had that real lucky streak. More tea?'

'No, thank you, mum.'

'Plenty more in the pot.'

'No, really.'

'Yes, he couldn't put a finger wrong. Ken reckons it's a waste of good money, and they're not getting any of his. Nor the pokies neither. Ah well, quite right. The races aren't what they was, anyway. You see them in jeans, and somebody said, bare feet. Here are these two again.'

Sylvia had forgotten the television. She turned her head and saw a girl lying in bed, propped on pillows, her long shining hair disposed on each shoulder. Her face was very sad. A young man was crossing the room, looking equally sad.

'I knew he was going to do that,' said Molly, 'grab her hands. You can always tell.'

She reached over and turned up the sound. Tears ran down the girl's cheeks. The man bowed his head over her hands. 'I would give anything—' he said.

Molly, her head sunk into her shoulders, snorted. 'A fat lot you would give, sonny boy!'

Sylvia found her own sense of grievance, of neglect, absurd yet irrepressible. Just inside the doorway to the living room stood a telephone on a small round table. Sylvia had noticed it before, but only now understood its significance; when Molly had absented herself from yesterday's conversation, she had not been looking through the blind. The young man said, 'From now on, I promise—' and Molly retorted, loud and bitter, 'Ah yes, we know all about you and your promises.'

Sylvia, as quietly as she could, packed the tea tray and took it into the kitchen. 'Leave all that, Syl,' said Molly, without turning round.

Sylvia washed up the tea things, and was putting the last of them away when Molly came into the kitchen. 'She lost the baby,' she said tranquilly, 'and whilst that was happening, where was he? Out on the razzle-dazzle. I told you not to bother with those, Syl.'

'Do you still empty the teapot on the garden?'

Molly gave a quick nervous look at her face, then fell into her artificial vivacity.

'That's one of the ones I follow. It wasn't much today, but as a rule it's real realistic. Here, no need for you to do that. You give that to me.'

Sylvia, who had believed not only that her irrational resentment did not show, but even that she no longer felt it, was amazed to find herself engaging with her mother in a small sulky struggle for the teapot. Molly gave in.

'Oh, all right, then. On the garden, but only on the ferns.'

Taking the teapot away, Sylvia again felt betrayed by herself, belittled, all the gains of her maturity gone for nothing. As she crossed the verandah an old man appeared at the top of the flight of concrete steps. He was gnarled but agile. He wore shorts and a tight pink T-shirt outlining a small hard belly like half of a rugby football. His socks were crumpled above canvas sneakers. He ran down the steps, extending a hand.

'Sylvia? Ken here. Pleased to meet you, Sylvia.' He looked at the teapot. 'What are you doing with that, Sylvia?'

'Emptying it on the ferns.'

'Who said to do that?'

Memory instructed her. 'Nobody.'

'Give that to me.'

He took it from her as he spoke. She followed him into the house. Ken Fiddies was a carpenter, still working at seventy-two. 'Hoy!' he shouted. 'Hoy!'

Molly was standing in the dining room. 'Here,' he said. But in the act of giving her the teapot, he drew it back, and looked her over with exaggerated astonishment.

'What have you got yourself up like that for?'

She flapped her hands at her dress, frightened yet flirtatious. 'Oh, *Ken*, I've had this ages.'

'Race day, hey? The grand old days back again, hey? Jew-els and all.' But now his voice changed to horror; he advanced to examine her. 'Hey, take a dekker at those ear-rings! They're bloody filthy!'

Sylvia, who knew that he was not addressing her, but some invisible and probably habitual audience, stayed silently in the doorway. Molly grasped one ear lobe. 'They are not.'

'They are so. Every one of those bits of glass has a rim of muck around it. Well, it's nothing to do with me if you want to show your daughter your filthy habits. I've been working hard all day, and I got to go and have a shower. Here, take this and empty it in the right place.'

'Which is the ferns,' said Molly. 'And you let my ear-rings alone.'

'I wouldn't touch them with a forty foot pole. Shit and muck all over them. And the ferns have had enough of the tea treatment.'

Molly was doing her best to be haughty. 'It so happens they are my ferns.'

'Look, I'm not here to argue the toss. Just take this pot and cut the cackle. I've been working hard all day, and Barry and them are coming over to tea.'

'The cheek.' Taking the pot he thrust at her as he went, she dropped the ear-ring she had removed. 'Like his nerve.'

Sylvia picked up the ear-ring, gave it to Molly, and took the tea pot. As she emptied it into the kitchen strainer she told herself that it was not really surprising to find her mother married to another lion tamer. Given her upbringing, and the conditioning of her first marriage . . .

But Sylvia could not maintain this cool deductive attitude. She gripped the edge of the sink, stared at the shrouded windows, only a few feet away, of the house next door, and on a rise of grief or fury told herself that she was glad, glad, that her mother's first tamer had exchanged her for a beast more difficult to subdue. The whip-crackings and shoves she had just witnessed would not have worked with his second beast.

Molly came grumbling into the kitchen. 'They're not all that dirty. Just let me in there, Syl.'

Sylvia moved aside, and Molly took a pot brush from its hook, wet it, and wiped it on a cake of soap. 'Bit of powder,' she muttered as she scrubbed the ear-ring. 'Bit of moisturizer. Calling it what he did.' She gave Sylvia one of her sidelong looks, quick as a blink. 'I am seriously annoyed,' she added primly.

'Who is Barry, mum?'

'Ted's oldest. A good chap, Barry, and a real hard worker. Whatever objective Barry sets hisself he attains. And Joy his wife is one of them real outgoing persons. And four nice kids too. Ken's got nine grandchildren in all, and I'm nan or grannie to the lot. It's only the eternal cooking and the baby-sitting. I could sure do with less of that. There, that's all it was. Bit of powder and moisturizer.'

She took off the other ear-ring. 'That's Joy their mother Barry's wife I was telling you about had the kidney complaint. Or was it someone else I was telling?'

'I'll go and get my jacket, mum.'

'I told you it was chilly.'

'No. I'm going home.'

'That jet lag.'

'I'm afraid so.'

'Well, all right, okay. I never knew Barry and them was coming to tea.'

Molly still kept the old custom of laying the coats of guests across her own bed. From the dressing table Sylvia picked up the framed photograph of a girl standing on the edge of a narrow timber verandah. She wore a low-waisted dress, shoes strapped across the instep, and a cloche hat. She stood in a Hollywood pose, her head tilted away, and her eyes looking back at the camera in challenge and foolish pride. Her surroundings were masked, so that she seemed to be standing in a clearing of white mist except for those few boards that gave her a footing, and which Sylvia would not have recognized as a verandah had she not been able to recall the original photograph, which had shown the whole of that gimcrack structure, its disrepair and peeling paint, and the bottles and empty jam tins littering the ground at its base. Somebody, probably the local photographer who had obliterated those surroundings, and who Molly always used to say was 'a bit her way', had written in black ink, obliquely across a corner of the white mist—

"Cheeky."

Twenty-five years ago, Sylvia had been frightened by her resemblance to that girl, and even now, there was something gingerly in the way she set the photograph down. A small photograph of Bruce in uniform was eroded at the edges, and a large one of Stewart so retouched that the face looked moulded of soap.

There was none of herself. Armed now against absurd grievances, she would not let its absence touch her. She found her mother still in the kitchen, scrubbing the matching brooch.

'Hang on a bit, Syl, I'll come to the door.'

On the little tiled verandah they gripped hands. For the sake of her composure, Sylvia blocked off sensation before they kissed, so that the substance her lips touched might have been other than human.

'Well, Syl, it was lovely.'

'Nice. Thank you, mum.'

Molly's farewells were always protracted. She folded her arms and went with Sylvia to the gate. 'No need to say come again.'

'I'll ring first. Goodbye, mum.'

'Wait on.' Molly looked cautiously behind her, then lowered her voice. 'You done the right thing, coming back. His own flesh and blood. Why should she get the lot?'

'Mum,' said Sylvia, with tense patience, 'I told you. I didn't know he was sick.'

'Well, you know now, don't you?' said Molly sharply.

Sylvia smiled, shut the little wrought iron gate, and walked quickly away, waving a hand. Custom had always demanded that at the corner she must turn and wave again, but when she did so, she was disconcerted to see that though Molly still stood at the gate with her arms folded, she was now engrossed in talking to a woman on the footpath, who also stood with folded arms.

As soon as Sylvia turned the corner, and was walking under the tristania trees in front of the church, she put a hand on her chest, dragged in a breath, and let it out with a theatrical 'Phew!' It was the only response she dared to make, such melancholy waited beyond it. With this surface drama, she would stave off melancholy until she was less exhausted. She knew that her present exhaustion could not be explained by jet lag; it was too familiar from past visits to her mother. Yet there were similarites, and she thought it too bad that one state should be compounded by the other. It seemed that in both persistance against a barrier must be paid for by the loss of one's natural rhythm, by anxiety, and an urgent need to reassemble, or even to rediscover, one's self. Her walk to the station was almost headlong. She plunged into the grimy tunnel and ran up the enclosed stairway towards the gentle pepperina leaves that still hung swinging in the entrance, and which had so often seemed to say to her, 'Hush.'

Ken came out with his sparse hair slicked down with water, and wearing shorts with stitched creases and a short-sleeved shirt with the collar pressed open. These clothes, and his brown strapped sandals of a style commonly worn by children, gave him rather the air of an inmate of an institution where points are given for neatness and cleanliness.

He paused in the kitchen door and opened as far as possible his small grey eyes. 'She gone?'

'What did you expect?' asked Molly in her grumble.

'Oh yes, it would have to be something *I* did,' he said with genial sarcasm. 'Trust old Ken to piss in the pickles. But it so happens I thought she looked a real nice quiet girl. I was expecting a greasy old dropout. What are we giving the mob tonight?'

'I am putting in this joint, as you can see for yourself.'

'Well, glad to see you not trussed up like a sore toe any more. Want a beer?'

'I was chilly, was the reason I changed. And I have had champagne, as it happens.'

'Oooo,' said Ken, mimicking reverence. He took a can of beer from the refrigerator. 'Right!' he said conclusively. 'No beer for you.'

When he had taken his drink to the dining room, she took a can of beer from the refrigerator, and a glass from the shelf, and followed him. He sat on a dining chair in front of the television. One hand gripped a spread knee; the other made a tankard handle for the can of beer. The words on the screen gave way to the face of the announcer.

'There's Ian,' said Ken. 'Hullo, Ian.'

Molly sat down beside him. 'If you knew how depressed I am,' she said.

'Get that into you, love. You'll feel better. Hey, get a load of Ian's tie tonight.'

'When she was a kid, and come here from their house, after she went, I just laid across the bed and howled, every time.'

'Well, don't start again now.'

Molly drank a little beer, then sat up and pressed back her shoulders. 'All my tears are shed.'

'Let's listen to Ian, hey?'

'I stopped caring by sheer will-power. It was either that or crack up. I could see her drift further and further away, week by week, and nothing I done, all the nice things, never made a scrap of difference. It was like a tide taking her away, and me helpless on the bank, and no use of even singing out.'

'Just drink that up, love.'

'It was her done it.'

'How about giving Ian a go?'

'It wasn't Syl's fault.'

'You just said it was.'

'I said it was *her*.'

'Oh,' said Ken in comprehension. 'Well, now let's listen to Ian, hey? The mob'll be here soon.'

Molly drank some more beer, looking at the screen. Then she said in an aggrieved voice, 'What's wrong with Ian's tie? I like that tie. It's bright and modern.'

'She's not a dropout,' said Stewart. 'What gave you that impression?'

'I didn't use the word disparagingly,' said Hermione. 'Rather the opposite. This is the street, isn't it?'

'This is it. What do you think of it?'

'Not much.'

'I'm sorry about that. What Syl really is, is a teacher of languages who works half-time so she can travel for the rest. Nothing very freaky about that.'

'I didn't know you were so interested in semantics. I always liked Sylvia. Of course I was only a schoolgirl when she went away. Rosie's asking her to lunch, and I'm going too. How does she like you calling her Syl?'

'Not much.'

'It's a losing battle. Mother fought it for us, and ended up with Harry, Rosie, and Min—'

'*I* don't call you—'

'Only Guy escaped. And I fought it, and ended up with Em and Jazz and no doubt Immy. Although Rosie, I must say—and I don't know how she did it—does have her Matthew, though Dom's had it.'

'I never think of you as anything but Hermione. I never have. Syl, Sylvia's gone to see mum today. Mum's thrilled to bits, of course. Syl didn't know about dad until she got here.'

'Oh?'

'In some ways she's out of this world.'

'That's not uncommon. People do attribute the most mercenary motives, and are so often wrong. Is this the house?'

'No, the one over the road with the striped awnings. Only I don't want to leave the car in the sun.'

'No water views from that side of the street.'

Stewart turned sideways in the driver's seat, leaving a hand on the wheel. 'You want water views?'

'Built in the twenties, then added to.'

'That worries you?'

'The very worst period. Not that there are any good ones. But I suppose it could be painted white.'

'Why? You've got a good brick there, not too red. So if it's not a silly question, why add paint to the cost of maintenance?'

Hermione, who had been looking beyond him at the house, changed her focus and looked fully into his face. 'As the whole exercise is purely academic, I might as well have it painted white.'

'Well,' he said, 'now that you've brought that up.'

'Or perhaps one of those very washy pinks,' she said, looking at the house again, and judiciously tilting her head.

'Look, an academic exercise. You just said it.'

'Yes,' she said, looking swiftly into his eyes and speaking with controlled fury, 'because I can tell that's what *you think*.'

'And I'm wrong? You do have the money for this kind of property?'

'Oh, how I love the way they call any silly little house a property. There must be some way we can borrow enough.'

'Agents get a lot of women who fantasize. You learn to pick them.'

'Oh yes? And then what?'

'I'm polite.'

Her agression was unhesitating. 'But you don't show them houses.'

'Not as a rule.'

'Then why am I the exception?'

He was silent.

'Come on. Why?'

'Right,' he said. 'Because you turn me on. And have ever since that night at the Ericsons.'

'What night?' Her eyes wandered. 'I haven't seen Katie Ericson for ages.'

'So, since you started on this house bit, I've been fantasizing, too. But I thought it out, and saw it for what it was. Sheer fantasy. Nothing in it for me. No commission. Nothing. So I stopped fantasizing. So, right, now *you* tell the truth. Do you or do you not have the money to justify looking at the houses I deal in?'

She was bold and direct again. '*I* think we have.'

'Which means Steven doesn't. What did you get for the Baulkham Hills house?'

She said angrily, 'Fifty-two thousand.'

'How much clear?'

'Thirty.'

He dangled a hand over the top of the wheel. 'And Steven is how old?'

She smiled at him. 'How old are you, Stewart?'

'Forty-seven. And I'm not trying to borrow money. And as for anything else, I said I stopped fantasizing, and I meant it.'

'Good. Steven is thirty-seven, and I'm thirty-five.'

'And Steven earns—no, don't tell me, I've got a rough idea. No, you couldn't do it. Not these days. Money's too tight. You're established borrowers, right enough. But even so.'

'Established borrowers,' she repeated with distaste.

'If you were a two-income family, maybe—'

'When Imogen is a bit older—'

'Yeah, sure, fine, but as far as I remember about you, you got yourself an arts degree and then got married. I'm not saying you couldn't get a job, but a woman's job has to be pretty bloody heavy to be taken into account. So unless there are circumstances I don't know about, unless you or Steven have real solid expectations you can borrow on, I honestly, Hermione, I honestly don't see the point of me driving you round like I do. You'd be better off looking at something in your range.'

'I have. It's hopeless.'

'Not a bit. I know that range. It's a matter of adapting your taste. The northern beaches, that's where you ought to be looking.'

'Well, listen, and I'll tell you what I thought. It was Penny Newman's turn to look after the children—we take turns—so when I saw your advertisement for this I thought, well, if the layout is right, we could let part of it to help with the repayments.'

'Not here in Vaucluse you can't. Council doesn't allow it.'

'It's done.'

'Couldn't be used as collateral.'

'Well, I suppose you're right. I suppose there's really no point in disturbing the people.'

'They're not there. I told you. They're in Bali.'

'Have you been to Bali, Stewart?'

'Yeah. Not bad, Bali.'

'I didn't dream you were forty-seven.'

'Then you can't have bothered to enquire.'

'But listen, when I was at high school—'

'I remember you at high school.'

'—you seemed only a few years older than Sylvia.'

'Eight,' he said mechanically. He was looking across the street at the house again.

'Of course you're right about adapting my taste. What about Dover Heights?'

'I suppose,' he said, as if he had not heard her, 'now that we're here.'

'Yes,' she said, 'who is to say there is no point?' She unfastened her seat belt. 'Even if there's no direct point, the more places I look at, the more I get to know the market. And as you say, now that we're here.'

As they crossed the empty street he took her arm while looking hawkishly both ways for traffic. He stood in the porch and rang the doorbell, saying that you never knew, while she inspected the garden.

'I would do away with all this horticultural clutter, and have just one beautiful tree. I think a maple, like mother's.'

'Maples don't do well here.'

'They can't have been properly tried.'

'That kind of arrogance always delays the making of a garden. I've seen it so many times.'

Hermione's dark brows drew together. 'Arrogance?'

But he had opened the front door. 'Come on, Hermione, if you're coming.'

She went past him into the hall and stood turning her head to inspect walls and ceilings. He came behind her and put both hands on her shoulders. She walked away from under them, remarking that the hall was a good size. 'But rather dark.'

'A different paper would fix that.'

'They certainly were carried away by poor old William Morris.'

'Here,' he said, opening a door, 'is the dining room, and through those double doors, the living room. They call it the drawing room, but the people before them called it the lounge. You can see that without a harbour view they've done their best—made the garden a real extension of the house.'

'I see that.' Hermione sounded rather excited. She marched about and said, 'Yes, this part is *very* good.'

Stewart, with irony, bowed his head. She did not notice.

'Yes, the proportions, the light, the colours, everything but the furniture is good.'

'The furniture's not good?'

'I can see it's expensive, but no, it's not good. But of course they would be removing it.'

'Yes, Hermione, they would be removing it. And through here is the kitchen.'

In the kitchen he explained, 'This used to be a bedroom before the second story was added. Plenty of room for breakfast, as you see. Dishwasher, fridge, garbage compactor, all included.'

'Our fridge is new.'

'A second one in the garage for the beer.'

'We don't—'

'Of course not. Then for the Christmas overflow.'

'And the garbage compactor is all but useless. We would compost everything we could.'

'Watch it, Hermione. You'll convince yourself.'

She walked away from him. 'Show me the rest.'

They crossed the hall again. 'This is whatever you like—study, spare room, etcetera. Housekeeper's room at present. Bathroom and toilet through that door.'

'Then here's our room to let. Is that the only extra loo?'

'Another off the laundry. Do you want to see upstairs?'

But she was already in the hall, making for the stairs. As he mounted behind her he put both hands low on her hips.

'These stairs are quite a convincing addition,' she said coldly. 'I like to feel that rotary movement.'

'So often they aren't. William Morris *again*!'

'Through that door is the toilet and handbasin. And here'—he opened the door—'is the bathroom. Remodelled last year. Full bath, shower, vanity, bidet, indoor garden, the lot. This is the kind of thing that justifies the price.'

'Whoever designed this black and white wallpaper must have made a fortune. It's everywhere.'

'It's in my flat.'

'So *many* naked ladies!'

'See this one here, Hermione. She always reminds me of you.'

'Are these people middle-aged?'

'About my age.'

'I thought so. Is the main bedroom next door?'

He led the way out of the bathroom and opened another door, but did not go into the room with her.

'Oh, *very* good,' said Hermione, 'with the fluffiness removed.'

Stewart looked at his watch. 'Shall we go?'

'What about the other bedrooms?'

'They're just bedrooms.'

'Is something wrong with them?'

'Why should that stop me? They're the same standard as this.

Jessica Anderson

Just fluffy middle-aged bedrooms.'

'I've made you cross.'

'I'm not cross.'

She sat on the edge of a bed, smiling. 'You are.'

'This sounds to me like a futile conversation.'

'When you said you remembered me at high school, what did you mean?'

'Just that I used to see you at bus stops, etcetera. Let's go.'

'Watching me from cars?'

'If I happened to be passing, why not? I first knew you when you were only a little kid. I picked you for a real sweetie then, one of those dark gentle little kids like you see in Italian families.'

'It has always been my trouble,' she said gravely.

'What! Oh, hey, now, wait a *bit*. Then you hit the teens, and I used to see you at bus stops—and elsewhere, like at the Ericsons—and I used to think, There goes the makings of a very tough lady who will get what she wants.'

She raised her eyebrows, and said with complete and gentle perplexity, 'Tough?'

'Wait a bit—'

'*Me* tough? When for so many years—'

'Wait. So I was surprised when you went in for the anti-bomb and anti-Vietnam bit, and the pro-abo and pro-underprivileged bit. And then Steven and more of the same, plus conservation and organic gardening at Baulkham Hills. I thought, well, good, she's reverted to the gentle little kid.'

Hermione got up, opened a drawer, and banged it shut. 'Which was *true*,' she said.

'Which *was* true, maybe. But lately—oh, don't think I don't see your longings, Hermione—lately you've come to the conclusion that the children of the world are wiser in their generation than the children of light. I read that,' he said, smiling at her look of startled enquiry, 'in a book I found in a Koala motel at Kempsey. After giving a lift that day to one of those alternative lifestyle couples. And when I read it I thought, Damn right. They haven't a hope.'

'The bible's only impressive,' complained Hermione, 'because it's so cryptic.'

'I would have been very impressed to read it in the evening paper.'

'And when it's not cryptic, it's contradicted by something in some other part. All it means, I suppose, is that the children of light are before their time.'

68

'And unwise in their generation. Which is now. Which is the only stretch I'm interested in, that being all I've got. Oh, I know you have three kids, Hermione, and they're great kids, too. And if you had kept on being one of the children of light I wouldn't have said a word. But you've changed with no prompting from me. I've watched it happen. You're coming over to our side.'

'I also have a husband.'

'Husbands can look after themselves. I don't believe you've forgotten that night at the Ericsons, any more than I have.'

'I recall one night in their kitchen, with Rosie and Sylvia and Kate, and you came in with Peter Ericson and his brother. Drunk.'

'You three ended up not too sober, either.'

She wandered off and opened a cupboard. 'Foolish children that we were.'

'Rosie and Sylvia weren't children. And you were fifteen.'

'To hear you, you would think there had been an orgy. This is a well-fitted cupboard. What about the other bedrooms?'

'Okay. Come on.'

'That's the trouble,' she said in the third bedroom. 'They always skimp on these.'

He sat on one of the single beds and addressed her back. She was looking in a clothes cupboard, which was empty. The upward angle of his vision made the three furrows across his forehead, between the line of his eyebrows and the peaked line of his hair, very distinct.

'That night at the Ericsons, you were sitting on the edge of the kitchen counter. Mini-skirts hadn't come in then—'

'And how glad I was when they went out again. I was too big to look good in them.'

'Your size wasn't the trouble. They didn't go with your dignified face.'

'Dignified? Look at these handles. Funny how in this country we spoil everything with shoddy details. Dignified?' She turned from the cupboard, smiling. 'I don't know how I feel about that.'

'You've no need to feel bad about having a dignified face, Hermione. That night, that night, there was a bit of horseplay with me and Peter's brother, and he pushed me out of the chair—as I can see you well remember—and sent me reeling across the kitchen, and I finished up where you were sitting, and my head went under your skirt, and butted your legs apart, and everyone was dead silent.'

'I don't—'

'Including you.'

'I don't remember the silence,' she said languidly. 'But if I was silent, it must have been from shock. I was only fifteen.'

'Don't think because I was twenty-seven it wasn't a shock to me. I couldn't move. Then Peter called out something like, "Get out of there, you dirty so-and-so!" I never forgave that bastard. I never had dealings with that bastard again.'

'Really?'

'God's honour! I picked on him for something else.'

'I do remember you went straight home.'

'When I finally got my head out, yes.'

'And that Sylvia and Rosie were embarrassed. But really, the incident was so trivial.'

'Trivial. I totally agree. So why have I never forgotten it? I've had a hundred dreams about it, Hermione. And all this driving around has revived it worse than ever. Do you know one of the things I want, Hermione? I keep thinking about this. I want to go to sleep with my head between your legs.'

'You ought not to say that,' she said. 'That is too intimate.'

He gave her a look of caution.

'It's true,' she said. 'It's the way you made it sound.'

The same caution, as well as a little cunning, was in his voice. 'I could go on. Do you want me to go on?'

'No. I think you must be an innocent sort of a man, in a way. I don't believe you know *how* intimate—'

'And I don't believe that in the course of all the passes you must have had made at you—'

She was shaking her head. 'You're wrong. Most men are afraid of me. It's always been like that. Rosie got all the boys. They would start with me, but Rosie could wiggle her bottom and wink.'

He laughed, as if he would have liked that himself. 'There you are!' she said. 'And since I've married and had children, I've been treated like a monument celebrating maternity. I don't mean by Steven, of course, but by other men. Not that I've looked for anything else, but it has made me unused to reacting—'

'You're nervous.'

'I am. That's what I'm saying. I actually feel shy.'

'Quite normal. Pre-fucking nerves. If we fucked, you wouldn't be shy any more.'

She turned, her face expressionless, and made for the door. He sprang to his feet and grasped her arm.

'Wait, Hermione, listen. I don't get this. I remember when you and Rosie used to shock *me*. I had never heard girls like you use the bar-room words before. It was fuck this and shit that all day long. Yes, and Steven too.'

'You don't understand.'

'What don't I understand?'

'Please let my arm go.'

He released her; she rubbed her arm. 'We were reformers,' she said, with a sidelong smile. 'Or so we thought. We were cleansing the language of cant. It was a movement, all over the world. And I do think it partly succeeded, you know. There's definitely less verbal prurience now than there was.'

'Sure. I agree. So why object to me using the word fuck?'

'You make it sound so personal.'

'It's a pretty personal business.'

'Oh, stop it,' she said, laughing and going to the door. 'I still haven't seen the laundry.'

'Yes,' he said, following her, 'if you want an impersonal fuck, you've got the wrong man.'

She walked faster. They reached the head of the stairs. 'Although I should be grateful,' he said, as he descended behind her, 'that you're not having any. All my instincts but one are against it. You're too married. You've got too many kids. And you're too irritable.'

They were in the downstairs hall. She wheeled to face him. 'Irritable?'

'Yes,' he said, seriously and without heat, 'you are an irritable, dogmatic woman. Don't you want to see the laundry?'

'No!'

He reached the door before her, and barred her way with an arm. His voice was cold and curt. 'Now, Hermione, don't go storming out there with that face on you. There are neighbours. I've got a good reputation in this business, and I mean to keep it.'

She was as curt as he. 'You needn't worry.'

'I was serious in what I said, though I never meant to say it. Whether I've ever been in love with anyone is doubtful, but if I have, it's with you.'

She looked at the door, waiting for him to open it.

'And there's one more thing I'll toss in the ring, for what it's worth. I'm richer than people think. I got into a few good sub-divisions in the fifties. One of them with Peter Ericson's brother, in fact, which is what I was doing there that night. It was those sub-divisions gave me my kick-off, and I got out before the wipeout. My money doesn't show much. It's a queer position. I can't *make* it show much. What do I need apart from what I've got?

A boat? When would I get the time to sail it, let alone mess about with it like they do? I work a bit of cash to mum, but not much, or it makes trouble with her and Ken. If dad doesn't leave anything to Syl, which I think he will, I had in mind setting her up in some way, but she's got her own queer arrangement. To me it looks a bit like over-planning, too much on the tight side, but it seems to suit her, and she mightn't want it broken. There's been speculation about dad's money, as is only natural, but I'm richer than him. If dad knew how much money I have, he would either respect me at long last, or want to kill me. I reckon I'm about as rich as Ted, or as Ted was before he got into strife.'

She raised her eyebrows and addressed the door. 'What am I supposed to do with this information?'

'I just thought you might like to kick it around, that's all. If you want to do anything about it, tell me. I won't say anything more. And in the meantime—bearing in mind your three kids, Hermione—you and Steven try the northern beaches.'

On Wynyard ramp, making her way up the incline against the pressure of the crowds going home to the suburbs, Sylvia felt a strong upsurge of hostility against her surroundings.

This hideous ramp. I hate it. I've always hated it. It's like the black inside of someone's mouth.

She was startled by her own vehemence, which, she thought, as she looked around her, paid too much of a compliment to a commonplace commercial muddle no worse than she had seen hundreds of times before. Yet it made her notice for the first time in her life the part played by bitumen in the Sydney scene. She had always sensed that, in her visual memory of Sydney as a city predominantly blue and green and terra-cotta, there had been an element missing. And here it was, this ashen skin covering not only the roads, but the footpaths as well. Her interest in the discovery eased her melancholy. On her way to the bus she noticed how the trampling of feet had overcast it with a dirty yellow, and how in many places it was cracked and patched, and in others slackened into hollows. From the bus window she saw how it lapped up to the stairs and walls of buildings, but was interrupted where a new tower block sent forth a band of paving, like the butt of its own shadow, across the footpath. And in that way, she supposed, the city would one day be paved, in multifarious stripes.

As she opened the windows of her flat she saw, in the little park opposite, the five Chinese seamen she had seen in the gardens. They were walking about, listless but still decorous, and clustering to examine beds of spring flowers.

At six o'clock she rang Stewart.

'Oh, hi, Syl. How did it go with mum?'

'She seems in good health.'

'Doesn't she! Look, can I ring you back?'

'No, Stewart. This won't take a minute. I want to know if mum can read and write.'

He said quietly, 'Hang on. Won't be long.'

When he came on the line again, he said, 'I'm on the extension now. I couldn't talk before because I've got a guy in there interested in the flat. No, mum can't read or write, Syl. She does her signature by sort of making a drawing of it.'

'How did you find out?'

'I noticed.'

'When?'

'Too far back to say. I was only a kid. I used to help her hide it. Listen, whatever you do, don't let her know you've tumbled. She's sensitive about that like about nothing else.'

'But what I can't understand is dad. He must have known. Yet I remember him on the phone at Wahroonga—'

'He didn't know.'

'He lived with her for more than twenty years, and didn't even notice—'

Stewart became impatient. 'That's right. He didn't notice. I've got to go now, Syl.'

'Sorry. I didn't know you worked at night.'

'I work any time. And today I wasted most of my afternoon.'

Stewart rang off and returned to his living room. His visitor was no longer there. He found him in the bathroom, his replenished glass of whisky in his hand.

'Not a bad set-up, is it?' asked Stewart.

'Marvellous,' said the man, 'what they can squeeze into a little tiny bit of space.'

'Nothing tiny about that bath. Bath for a six-footer. Rare thing these days.'

'I'm strictly a shower man.'

'Well, here's the shower.'

'Yeah, but I mean, the bath's wasted on me.'

'You're not into these herbal baths?'

'Never heard of them.'

Stewart opened a cupboard. 'Here, try it next time someone lends you a bath.'

'You got shares in the stuff?'

'If you look at the label,' said Stewart, 'you'll see it's German. What do you think of the wall paper?'

'I'm never averse to nudey ladies, but you wouldn't exactly want to cuddle up to any of those, would you?'

'Wouldn't you?'

'I wouldn't.'

'Well, they're classical, see? Greek.'

'Is that what they are? Get a load of the face on that one.'

'Don't you like that one?'

'No, I do not like that one.'

'Why not?'

'She looks scornful. She looks as if she doesn't even *know* she's naked.'

Steven and Hermione were in the kitchen, leaning against opposite benches, and drinking vermouth while the casserole was cooking.

'What does this mean?' said Hermione. ' "The children of the world are wiser in their generation than the children of light." '

'Wrong,' said Steven. ' "The children of *this* world are *in their generation wiser*—" '

'Yes, but what does it mean?'

'I doubt if it yields to analysis.'

'Didn't you ever ask your father?'

'I did once. I forget what he said. I wasn't satisfied.'

'It can't mean what it says.'

'The bible is ambiguous. Like Hamlet. Which is probably why it's lasted even as well as it has. Where did you come across it?'

'Stewart Cornock quoted it at me today.'

'*He* did? It must have lasted better than I thought.'

'He's not illiterate.'

'Let's say semi.'

Hermione said musingly, 'He certainly hasn't read Freud.'

'How did Sigmund come into it?'

'Oh, just one of those naïve remarks people make if they haven't read Freud. It's only then you realize how basic he is. How basic Freud is,' she added.

'People like Stewart tend to dip in and take things out of

context. Were you looking at a house?'

'Yes.'

'Where?'

A train passed another going in the opposite direction. Hermione shut her eyes, and laid the fingers of one hand across her forehead until it was quiet again. Then she said in a weak voice, 'Dover Heights.'

'Dover Heights! That's almost as silly as if you looked in Vaucluse or Point Piper. What the hell's wrong with you, Min?'

'What's wrong with *you*? You've been in a shitty mood ever since you came in.'

Steven nodded warningly towards the living room, where Emma and Jason were doing their homework. He asked evenly, 'Was the house any good?'

'Of course the bloody house was no good.'

'You know where I think we should look.'

'The northern beaches. Tell me again. The northern beaches. All right, I'm being hit over the head with the northern beaches, so we'll *look* at the northern bloody beaches.'

'Now that's constructive. We'll go together. This Saturday's the Collisons' party. Make it Saturday week.'

'Right. Saturday week.'

'Ted was in the Gardens today. He got winded and had to rest, pretending to look at a Chinese ship.'

'I saw that Chinese ship on my way to the eastern suburbs. And Chinese all over the place.'

'I've never seen so many get shore leave. Perhaps the masters of China have decided that they won't be traumatized, after all, by subjection for one day to conflicting influences.'

'Well, that's just where the masters of China could be wrong. Sometimes it's enough to be subjected to ten seconds of a conflicting influence.'

'In a highly charged emotional situation, yes. I was talking to Ted at the gates.'

'Did he say anything about—'

'Not directly. But he can be a very amusing fellow, Ted.' Steven was interrupted by his own laughter. 'He's a man I have absolutely no respect for, but today I couldn't help laughing. He had on a purple T-shirt . . .'

Four

When Sylvia woke next morning she accepted without hesitation
the view through the windows of treetops, sky, and the round,
white tower block. Today she must visit her father; today she
would talk to Greta; today she may see Harry. Leaving at respite
in her mind her dread of the first encounter, her need for care in
the second, and her reduced hopes of the third, she lay staring at
the sky, combing her hair backwards with her fingers, and began
to think about money. The owner of the flat, Mary Yates, had
gone to India for three months, and since she did not usually let
the flat at all, but had done so only as a favour to Stewart, Sylvia
was not committed for that time, but could return to Rome, if she
pleased, in two months. By cutting that month off her stay, she
would have more money on which to start life in Rome. She
roughly estimated her costs for eight weeks, and subtracted it
from the whole. Her thoughts lingered on the remainder with
unusual persistence, and when she got out of bed she scribbled it
on an envelope and put a ring around it.

Later in the morning she settled down to write air letters. All
but one were to be brief, hardly more than notices of her address,
but for Richard and Janet Holyoak she intended a longer letter.
Richard was an Australian (he had left Sydney in the same ship as
Sylvia), which made her feel a sort of obligation to remark upon
the place. This she found she could not do; the long letter of her
intention was not only brief, but distressingly vapid, and had to be
redeemed by a promise of a better one very soon. After she had
taken her letters to the post office, she bought a newspaper and
walked down to Rushcutter's Bay park. She sat on a seat at the
harbour wall and scanned the newspaper with facile attention,
but presently put it aside and looked in much the same manner
over the pinch-necked little bay. She raised her eyes to the sky.
The clarity of the light, of course, was marvellous; she did not
know why she sighed. She raised her feet and set them on the low
stone wall, and recalled Harry's feet on this wall beside hers, his
legs bent at the knees while hers were almost straight. When she
had worked at the night club, this park was her nearest access to
fresh air and sun. Sometimes she had brought a rug and, to the
whispering sound of these little waves, had lain on the grass
sleeping, reading, or making her calculations on time and money.
Once, when Harry had joined her there, they had exchanged

kisses of increasing urgency, and had then gone back to her room. The obstacle on that occasion had been notably ludicrous. A plumber was lying on the floor under the sink, and while fixing the trouble had discussed with the landlord, who stood in her doorway, the merits of the Holden motor car. By the time they both went, Sylvia had to leave for work. She would not forgo a Saturday night's pay, and Harry had told her she was setting a pattern of meanness that would last all her life. Her ship had sailed a week later.

When Sylvia opened the door of the flat, the telephone was ringing.

'Sylvia? Rosie.'

'Rosie.' Sylvia sat on the edge of the bed, smiling. She had always liked Rosamond.

'Ted saw you yesterday,' said Rosamond.

'Did he? Where?'

'In the gardens. He was jogging. He had on a purple T-shirt, and you walked right past him.'

'Was that Ted? I only saw him from the back.'

But Rosamond was pretending to be hurt. 'You snubbed him. And that was Steven he was with. Min's Steven. You snubbed our husbands.'

'How is Hermione?'

'Beautiful. Touchy. Restless as hell. What are your plans?'

'You mean today, or long-term?'

'I know them today. Mother told me. I meant long-term.'

'I'm staying here for two months, then settling in Rome.'

'For good?'

As if infected by Rosamond's surprise, Sylvia hesitated. 'Yes.'

'Of course I adore Rome,' said Rosamond politely. 'It's only that those old buildings make the air so dusty. Would you like to come here on Saturday week, Sylvia? For lunch? I'll ask Min and we'll talk about false eyelashes and pancake make-up. No, we won't, because Steven will be here. He and Min don't go out much apart like Ted and I do. I'll ask Harry, too. Not that he'll come. And as for Ted, he's selling his boat, so will probably be out on the harbour. Will you come?'

'Thank you, I would like to.' Sylvia felt relieved, lightened, by this talk unburdened by past tensions, for the rancours and rivalries of their elders had been steadily, even perversely, rejected by the older children. 'Why won't Harry come?' she asked.

'He'll say he has too much work to do, but his real reason is that he doesn't care to meet Ted. I don't mean they fight, like Ted and

Steven could do if they tried. No, Harry just draws off and avoids him. It happened when the Governor-General sacked the Whitlam government and put Fraser in as P.M. What's called the Fraser coup. You heard about it?'

'Only after it happened. When it happened I was in Spain.'

'Lucky you. The fights! the passion! the headlines! the indigestion! I admire Gough Whitlam myself, he's such a brave guy. But Ted said he was bad for business. How clever you are to say nothing, Sylvia. When Ted said that to Harry, Harry didn't say anything, either, but ever since then it's as if he can't bear to look at Ted's *face*. They're all like that about Malcolm Fraser's face, too, you know, all the Labor people are. And his voice. If he happens to come on the telly, they just get that closed, hurt expression, and look slightly to one side until he goes away. Oh, it wounded them, it really did. It's not exactly hate they feel for him . . . I don't know how to describe it. And when it was over Harry joined the Labor party, and a lot of other things, but Margaret, who was as hot as he was during the crisis, decided that nothing succeeds like success, and swung around.'

'No need to ask what dad thought. What about Greta?'

'Mother treated the whole thing like a rather irritating farce. But she was like me, and banned all talk of it in the house. Well, she had to, with Poppa crowing like he was, or the roof would have blown off. When you go there today, Sylvia, you'll see Harry, and Guy, too. Mother says you saw Guy in the street, but I don't know how you knew him. He was such an angelic child, then all of a sudden he got those lowering brows, and that great blue chin, and all that hair all over him.'

'Adolescence. That's when the bad fairies show their hand.'

'Isn't it! Though he's been rather clever, in a horrible sort of way, in developing a character to fit. Only it doesn't *quite* fit. Thank God Matthew and Dom don't look like going the same way.'

'How are they?'

'So self-absorbed they seem stupid. Perhaps they are. Do you have a harbour view?'

'No.'

'There's a marvellous Stoldt container ship coming in. What colours! Sylvia, do you know, did Stewart happen to mention, what Poppa is doing to mother about money?'

'Yes, Rosie, he did.'

'It's a symptom, of course, but from mother's point of view I really think it's too bad, Sylvia, don't you?'

'I do, Rosie.'

'Harry would help her, and so would Ted and I. But I don't see her taking help from us. Not that Ted isn't in trouble himself, you've probably heard, but it doesn't seem the kind of trouble where he can't lay his hands on ready money. I must say I don't understand Ted's trouble myself.'

'But Greta isn't down to bedrock, surely?'

'At the moment I'm rather confused about what bedrock is. I'm sure I don't know what it is for Ted. But I think mother's pretty near cash bedrock. And you know what a horror she has of borrowing.'

'Yes, they both had. Yes, I see.'

'Harry and Stewart both had a go at him, but all they got was the look. Poppa gives us all the look now. When I go in to say hello, that's all I get, the look. I don't mind, because he's a very sick man, though it does rather leave me wondering what to do with my face. But you've been away for such a long time, Sylvia, he has idealized you. You may be able to do it.'

'Oh, if it depends on *me*—'

'Oh, you do sound *grim*. Who knows? The subject might just crop up.'

'I can't imagine how.'

'Well, it just might, if he's having one of his good days,' said Rosamond coaxingly, 'mightn't it?'

The newspaper lay on the bed. To make a digression, Sylvia picked it up. 'Let's see what my stars say.'

'You're not into that, are you?'

'This newspaper is.'

'I always read mine, but I didn't think you would.'

'Here we are. Acquarius. Beautify the home, and buy perfume and art objects. Wear pink or lilac on a special outing.'

'Well, I don't think much of that,' said Rosamond, 'unless you've got on your pink hat. What do mine say? Pisces. I'm a little fish.'

'Pisces. Day negative—'

'I'll say!' said Rosamond.

'—but in the evening grasp opportunity to talk over difficulties with loved ones.'

'Now isn't that absolutely extraordinary. I don't care what anyone says, there's something in the stars.'

Sylvia went to David Jones's corner by bus, then walked to Wynyard down Market and George Streets. Here she was again away from the polyglot population of the Cross and among people from all the suburbs. But she had learned long ago not to strain after an impression of a people. One must simply let it happen; and she now supposed, when nothing much happened, that the freshness had been taken from the human scene by her familiarity with Sydneyans abroad, whose mostly Hogarthian presences had run like a thread of varying thickness through her life, forming great unforgettable knots on the tourist coaches. So today only the bold new towers made their mark. Set back from the old building line to provide broad paved areas, they sometimes tolerated nearby little old buildings with toy turrets or balconies, which made her wonder if what the developers meant to destroy, they first painted in humorous colours.

Yesterday she had travelled from Platform 3. Today she waited on 4, which was the other side of the same platform. When she first went to London, and she had been asked about the Australian classless society, she had not known what to reply, but later she was able to say that though there were no divisions of the complexity and rigour of the English classes, difference of income, sustained through two or more generations, was often visible and audible in the people, and that, she supposed, could be called class. And as she had spoken, there had always hung in her memory the curved walls of this tunnel, from the floor of which rose this platform, like an elongated box, onto which people arrived together by climbing the broad steps from below, but on which they divided into two, and stood back to back—the westbound on 3, and the northbound on 4. And on each side there were those whose habit it had once been to stand facing the other way.

From the upper deck of the train as it crossed the bridge she saw, through the flashing girders, the main harbour and, in the stream, solid as a building, the Stoldt ship spoken of by Rosamond. For Sylvia, water was the only convincing element of division. On catching sight of the familiar little church steeple, dwarfed by the sweeping north approach of the bridge, she physically felt the crossing made, the North Shore reached.

Janet Holyoak, hearing Richard and Sylvia talk of the North Shore line, had visualized a train line winding around all the intricate bays and points of the north shore of the harbour. She even said she saw a little Puffing Billy of a train, with a whistle that went toot-toot, but that was only to dramatize her disappointment on learning that after crossing the bridge (though a few miles of meandering did give an occasional glimpse of water) the North Shore line settled to a course, varying from north to north-west, through dry and rising country. Janet was also interested to learn (she too having heard of the classless society) that if you spoke of the North Shore, and left train lines out of it, you meant only the eight inland suburbs from Roseville to Wahroonga, though Roseville was disputed nowadays as being too mixed.

Stewart would have called the North Shore definitely good stuff, grade B, for in financial terms the best stuff was still on the harbour shores and hills of the eastern peninsula. But in the post-war years the newly rich adventurers who felt no misgivings about buying in the east were often daunted by the North Shore, because when its residents called it good they also meant seemly; it was spoken of as 'a good place to bring up children'. After Sylvia had left both her homes and taken a room at the Cross, it occurred to her that its seemliness was helped by its inaccessiblity to the north-easterlies. The big damp southerlies blustered their way through, as did the galling winds from the western desert, but from the sensuous salty north-easterlies, which on summer nights could saturate the eastern peninsula, the North Shore was removed, so that the children of the residents were not tempted out at night to roam the beaches or to pile all together into a car and drive away anywhere. Perhaps this knowledge, even if hardly conscious, was implicit in the comment that it was a good place to bring up children; and if a few of the newly rich adventurers did penetrate, it was usually because their wives wanted their children to be different from themselves, and so moved to this 'good' district, knowing that though they would be unlikely to be accepted, their children were likely to be. That, Sylvia had always taken for granted, was Greta's reason.

For Janet's amusement, and their own, Richard and Sylvia had pronounced the word 'good' in all the ways of its residents: the innocently factual, the unctuous, the respectful, the finical, the sophisticated wry, not forgetting to add that there were those who never used the word at all. Janet (and Geoffrey Foley, who had come into it by this time) said it sounded a bit like the Home Counties; but Richard and Sylvia, extending the joke, shook their heads and said that the North Shore was incomparable. When Janet came out in the sixties and stayed with Richard's parents at Pymble, she was disappointed to find what she called only a few rather pretty middle-class suburbs; but Richard added a post-script to her letter to say that she had failed to appreciate the mystique of the North Shore which, besides, had changed, the wild arrogant moneyed kids of the sixties having been let loose everywhere.

From her high seat on the train Sylvia saw little change. As the line progressed she looked more and more often down on the crowns of trees, evergreen and in spring flower. At Roseville station there were still roses, and at Killara beds crammed with spring annuals. The line now ran on a ridge from which spurs thrust into the bush as headlands do into the sea. On these spurs and the more accessible slopes were the 'best' streets. Though not visible from the train, Sylvia saw them in memory, radiating away from the central ridges, getting quieter and quieter as they went, the trees taller, and the ancestral notes of spring and autumn— the tender greens, the reds and golds—making strange and melancholic the grey-greens and umbers of the bush valleys below. Sylvia's memory of this was so positive that she had to struggle to reach the later information (from Greta and the Holyoaks) that new roads now plunged down to the floors of the valleys, and that housing estates, hardly accessible by foot, were laid out on their slopes. Joining and leaving the train were girls and boys of an adolescent bloom enhanced by the severity of their school uniforms, and whose released voices thronged the air. Travelling one afternoon from her room at the Cross, Sylvia had seen Hermione in a group like one of these, and had noticed for the first time her lack of modernity, the biblical quality of her beauty.

A number of these boys and girls got out of the train at Wahroonga and preceded her as she set out for Orlando Road. New fences bisected many of the gardens of the big houses, and new houses stood in the rectangles of land thus detached. The rectangle was less insistent than at bare Burwood but, in spite of trees and the hilly terrain, it did prevail. Hot from walking, Sylvia took off her jacket and hooked it by one finger over a shoulder. The boys and girls were slipping into gates. A car passed; a David Jones delivery van stood at the kerb; a man walked behind a motor mower on the footpath. If the wild moneyed arrogant kids of the sixties had ruffled the feathers here, they had left no evidence to the casual view, and had left unchanged that prime characteristic—that so little *was* evident to the casual view.

When the last of the boys entered his gate, Sylvia, in these streets usually reached only by car, walked alone. When a car passed her, then two and three more, she had a sudden vision of herself as almost emblematic, for if at any time in the last twenty years she had shut her eyes and spoken the name of this place, it was likely that she would have seen a child or a girl, walking alone in these quiet streets, approached and overtaken by the swish and whoosh of cars.

Once, aged twelve, coming from Burwood, she had walked in stormy rain that had blown in under her umbrella. She had made slow progress, head down, stumbling in flooded ditches, splashed by cars, and had arrived muddy and soaked. 'You met Hermione's train,' her father had said angrily to Greta. 'Why didn't you meet Sylvia's?' Greta had mildly replied that Sylvia had not told her which train to meet. Sylvia, taking off her wet shoes and miserably snuffling, had avoided confirming this, though it had been raining hard when she left Molly's. She had played the Iago game for years; she could blush for it now; only her provocation gave an excuse.

Orlando Road, old and 'good', though not 'the best', was in a slight dip. Sylvia walked soundlessly on the wide grassy verges. A woman with waved grey hair, rising from her weeding as Sylvia passed within touching distance, refrained from glancing at her. When Sylvia had first come here she had been unaccustomed to such decorum, for, though Molly had sometimes murmured to her not to stare, she was usually too busy staring herself to insist. So at first Sylvia was often abashed and shy and uncertain of herself. Then custom gave her ease, and then, in the few years before she went away, she swung round to criticism and attack. She had had intimations by this time that there were places in the world of a deep, rich, harmonious character. She did not know how they had acquired it. Someone had told her that Venice had no good and bad quarters, which she thought may have had something to do with it, but in any case she was certain that it was not acquired by putting together such people and such houses as these. She could see that they attempted some ideal, but suspected that their goals were timid and second-rate. There they sat, she said, each penned in its rectangle, like a well-trained dog at a dog show. She was oppressed by their petty privacy, the trivial discretion of their façades.

But the intensity with which she had condemned them now seemed exaggerated and silly. It was a fashionable chorus she had joined. No longer threatened, she could look about her and find the place pleasant, though rather comatose. Triumph rose in her, the gaiety of her freedom. Number fifty-two was in sight. The door opened, and Greta stepped into the porch with a man. She saw Sylvia and waved, fluttering her fingers. Sylvia returned the wave by describing an arc in the air with an arm. The man came out through the gate and, as he approached Sylvia on the grassy footpath, deftly removed the cigarette from his lower lip before he smiled. As they passed she smelled his smoky sourness.

'That's Siddy,' said Greta. 'He was worried about his own garden, and as there will be so many of us here . . .' She took Sylvia's hand; she patted and pressed it. 'How little you have changed.'

The hair springing from that centre parting was now iron grey, and the tilted blue eyes were tired and strained. Barely beneath Greta's smile waited the contortion of the other commedia dell'arte mask. Sylvia reminded herself to let nothing persuade her to the intercession suggested by Rosamond. 'I did enjoy walking from the train,' she said. 'The gardens are so lovely.'

This benign and easy falsity seemed part of her triumph. Greta was looking pleased. 'You used to go on about the fences,' she said. 'But come in, come in. Do the fences still seem so terrible?'

'There are so many of them.'

They were in the hall. Greta halted to say with concern, 'But other places must have them.'

'Somehow they're not so visible.'

'One of these days I shall travel.'

'Don't. It's a great distinction, not having travelled.'

Sylvia felt she was doing well, redeeming the blunders of the last two days. 'The hall looks bigger,' she said. 'Rooms are said to look smaller when you go back. But weren't there rugs?'

'At the cleaners,' said Greta. 'Jack is asleep. So perhaps you would like a cup of tea first.'

'I would like something first.'

'Come into the kitchen. You won't mind having it there. Jack is looking forward so much to seeing you.'

Following Greta through the dining room, watching the reflection of their two heads pass along the shining table, Sylvia felt her apprehension rising. 'Has he said so? I mean, indicated—'

'Not to me, but he did to Siddy. You had better know straight away, so that you won't be embarrassed, that he doesn't, to me.'

'Speak? Indicate?'

'Not unless he is forced to by some physical need, and there's no one else available, which he hates doing so much that I asked Siddy to sleep in the house.'

They were in the kitchen, from which Greta had fuelled all those birthday parties. Greta went to fill the kettle. 'He ignores Rosie, too,' said Sylvia. 'Rosie told me. So there is nothing personal—'

'Oh, I hope it is personal,' said Greta, softly and drily. 'I hope at least it is that.'

Again Sylvia was touched by apprehension. Her composure, as with her mother the previous day, depended upon a certain distance maintained. She said brightly, 'I was thinking just now of the birthday parties.'

'Those were the good days, Sylvia.'

For Sylvia they had been such bad days that she was embarrassed. She was aware of ambushes; she was not to be allowed to keep her triumph, but could fall back on her composure. She turned to the window. 'And the garden looks smaller!'

'Because the trees are bigger.'

'It looks beautiful,' said Sylvia, overtaken by sincerity.

Greta joined her at the window. 'My pink tree is a week past perfection.' She spoke with the care and justness of a connoisseur. 'The flowers have lost their first crispness, but it gains in softness. The Port Jackson fig is too big and greedy, and must come out.'

Sylvia remembered the child lying on the broadest branch, concealed from anyone standing beneath. 'Guy's tree.'

'Yes. I delay taking it out because of the swing. Yes, the garden is the reason I will stay here. If it is possible.'

This made Sylvia suspect that when they were sitting down with their cups of tea Greta would ask her to intercede with her father. But when they sat facing each other across the table, Greta, holding her full teacup raised, looked aside and said musingly, 'Yes, I have thought of travelling, of going to Europe, since everybody does. But every time I think of Europe, I think of blood.'

'Really?' said Sylvia, and instantly thought how foolish, how trite, the bright vocable sounded. But Greta took no notice. Her cup still raised, her head turned to the garden, she went on speaking in the same hesitant way.

'My father was killed in the war in France, the year I was born. In that old war, of mud and blood. And one of the first things I remember is someone saying, a man saying, "He gave his blood for his country." '

Sylvia said, 'Wouldn't it have been, "He gave his life"? '

'No. blood. Always blood. That old war, it clung and clung. There was an Anzac Day service, at dawn, in a big park, and a man saying, shouting, "These shed their blood." My aunt took me, the first aunt, the married one, Aunt Maud, so it was after my mother died. She died in the influenza epidemic, after that war . . .'

Sylvia had only occasionally heard of Aunt Maud, though a

spinster aunt, Aunt Edith, had often been mentioned. As Greta irresolutely went on with her references to blood, Sylvia drank her tea, and tried not to show her discomfort. She had set herself—she supposed, steeled herself—to meet a Greta firm and clear-spoken, persuasive and bossy by turns, a Greta who stood tough and alone in her privacy, behind the shield of her skilled volubility. She was, besides, made uneasy by the tilt of Greta's raised cup, from which the tea seemed about to tip; she tried not to look at it.

'... and the poems in our school books. Blood red was the wreck of the square that broke. Blood red were the something something fields. How that red rain hath made the harvest grow. And the ones about blood on snow.'

'The irresistible colour contrast,' said Sylvia briskly.

Greta turned her gaze to Sylvia's face, and after a moment, gave her broad, strained smile. 'But of course we had poems about daffodils and spring, too.'

Sylvia saw with relief that she had re-entered her usual impersonation. She was drinking tea.

'But we had daffodils and spring here, too, so they didn't make so much of an impression. When you girls were at school, your poems were all about Australian flora and fauna.'

Sylvia laughed. 'I can see where Rosie gets her habit of simplification.'

'Rosie tells me you are going to lunch with her, and so is Hermione. You must have passed Hermione's flat today, in the train.'

'Doesn't she live at Baulkham Hills?'

'No, they sold their house there, very foolish, and moved to a flat while they look for something else to buy. Something bigger and better, of course. Status is Hermione's first concern, and always has been, though she has called it all sorts of other things, as she has swung this way and that with the trends. Well, I don't know what else I was entitled to expect.'

Her impersonation was wavering again, but instead of musing as before, she now spoke recklessly, while looking at Sylvia in uncertain appeal.

'Guy is coming today. I don't see how he can actually be stopped from coming. But I can't afford Guy any more. I don't mean financially, though money does get muddled up with everything, doesn't it? No, I mean, like ballast.'

It was as if from her disciplined body another woman longed so much to get out that she could not help but give these hints and nudges and forebodings. But Sylvia, torn yesterday by her own mother, could not help shrinking from this importunate other woman. She said unwillingly, 'Like ballast from a boat?'

'Yes. Yes. The difficulty is, Guy is still recognizably my child. The other three, those three middle-aged people, often seem more strange than actual strangers.'

Sylvia did not know the adult Hermione, but was slightly offended on behalf of Harry, and perhaps of Rosamond. She looked discreetly into her teacup.

But now the importunate other woman was again pulled back, closed up.

'Life is not easy for anyone in this house, Sylvia. Except for Siddy, who knows nothing but obedience. How is your mother?'

'Very well,' said Sylvia with reserve.

Greta finished her tea, set down her cup, and smiled across the table, directly into Sylvia's face. 'Why should you want to know about me? I am like you. I am reasonable. I can understand why you don't. When Rosie and Hermione used to ask their questions—those questions girls always ask, so persistent, so inquisitive—wasn't it me who always said I wanted no invitations to introspection. I can hear myself now. "Introspection is unhealthy." "Always look forward! Never look back!" '

Sylvia's smile was as direct as Greta's. 'You mean you are trapped by your own good example?'

'I do seem to be. But you call it good. Do you really think it was good?'

'I think so. Yes. In fact, I've always tried to take it.'

'Well, perhaps it was. In any case, it would be ridiculous if at my age, after all this time . . .'

But she seemed to lose the thread of that thought, and after looking for a few moments into the garden, she spoke in her coaxing voice. 'The boys are to take the swing down for me today. And next week Siddy will put up a new one.'

'How are your grandchildren?'

'Just wait till you see them. Hermione's Imogen has started to stand already. Of course,' she said, fully in her old style, 'they are all very advanced. So were mine.'

'I will see them at Rosie's.'

'Yes.' Greta was now quite composed. 'Sylvia, your father is often difficult. The best thing is to be steadily gentle with him. He needs it, but he can't take it from me.'

'I should have thought it could be taken for granted—' Sylvia heard with distaste the umbrage in her voice, the haughtiness reminiscent of Molly; yet she went on '—I should have thought it could be taken for granted that I would be gentle with him.'

Greta was polite. 'Of course.'

'I should have thought—'

'Just listen. I wish he could take it from me. But he can't. He would see it as a defeat. Yet it is the only thing that may bring him round.'

'Round to what?'

'Acceptance. It's a dreadful thing, the way he fights.'

'Acceptance of illness. But shouldn't he fight?'

'I said the *way* he fights. And I mean acceptance of his death.'

'But will that be soon?'

'Soon? It can't be years. Months, perhaps. Weeks. Days.'

'How can you know that?'

'He knows it himself.'

'But Stewart said—Stewart said—'

Into Sylvia's pause, Greta said flatly, 'What did Stewart say?'

'That he lets the physiotherapist move his limbs, Which means he must hope—'

'There are remissions in that kind of knowledge.'

'I don't see how you can be so positive.'

Greta rose abruptly from her chair. She spoke impatiently, as if, in giving up the subject, she also gave up her hopes of Sylvia. 'Well, I'll go and see if he's still asleep.'

It was like an echo of those past scenes with Greta, always undramatic, which had invariably ended by Sylvia feeling in the wrong. Rising now was the slow tide of her sullenness. She jumped to her feet, with an impulse to combat it by movement. But there was nowhere to go. She stood at the window and, suddenly pressing her forehead to the glass, fervently hoped that she was not fated to repeat all her past mistakes before she could break away once more into her own world. Nor had her own world ever appeared so simple and clear and gay and desirable.

Greta returned in only a few minutes. 'He's still asleep. But go in, Sylvia, go in. He'll see you as soon as he wakes. That's sure to please him. And if he asks for Siddy, tell him he won't be back till after dinner, but that Harry will soon be here.'

Sylvia's first impression was that her father, in spite of obvious physical changes, had become in some indefinable way more fully himself. The impression passed even before she shut the door behind her, and as she crossed the room she saw him more simply as a sick but well-tended old man lying in dignified sleep in an extended wheel chair. The back of the chair was lowered so that he half-reclined, his head on a pillow. Beside him was a wheeled tray holding newspapers, a telephone, toilet articles, and the alphabet card and dictionary Stewart had spoken of. As she approached he stirred; the pillow slipped sideways, and he abruptly slumped, making the collar and padded shoulders of his coat rise like a dislodged cuirass to his ears. She waited to see if he would wake, and when he did not, sat on a chair between his bed and the window. His formal clothes surprised her, but recalling Stewart's remark that he had reverted in more ways than one, she supposed that he had dressed like this for her sake, for in his youth and middle age it had been common to dress in your formal best, however uncomfortable, for visitors.

The pillow slipped again as she watched, and his open mouth dropped suddenly awry. She wished she could adjust the pillow, pull down and settle his coat, comb his hair, and restore his former dignity, but even if she had not been afraid to wake him, she would have felt stiff and timorous in such services. When someone among the tourists she conducted had collapsed, it had always been some other woman, or sometimes a man, who knelt by the patient and did what was necessary for, though she had the theory of relief, and could advise, Sylvia was backward in its application; it seemed that she was capable of giving relief only in the embraces of sex or the light caresses of friendship. She had watched Italian women in villages where she had lived, and seen how natural and adept they were in birth, death, and illnesses, but had noticed too that there were some among them less willing and adept, and who in a society offering more choices would have remained as aloof as herself. Yet she had sometimes envied those different ones for having been forced by convention into that narrow track where sooner or later they must be confronted with the exigencies of others.

When the pillow slipped again she moved her chair forward and held it in place with one hand so that the loss of it would not give him a startled awakening. The coarse waves of his hair, still thick, had been ruffled by the dislodgement of the pillow. Stewart, running his hand over his own hair, had once said, 'My one inheritance of value.' Stewart's hair was brown; the former red of Jack Cornock's could be deduced only by a few rusty bristles in his eyebrows, and by the defensive weathering, scaling, and pocking of a skin evolved in another hemisphere. He had been born on his father's farm in the hot dry west, and had walked off it at sixteen, carrying his few possessions in a sugar bag.

'Blackfeller's country', he used to call it later. He was the youngest of five brothers. Two were killed at Gallipoli, and two came back. It was a year of drought and trouble and loss; soon there was a blazing row. Punching and yelling, he had claimed his entitlement by reason of four years of 'working like a bullock'. Punching and roaring, they had claimed theirs by reason of seniority. That land would not yield enough for three. The most bitter thing was that his father, who had called him his little mate during those years of work, had stayed out of it. His mother, who in bush terms was educated, had died when he was seven. When he walked out of the door of what he always called afterwards, contemptuously, 'that bush humpy', he had a fractured collar bone, a broken thumb, and was raw and swollen with lacerations and bruises. He never saw any of his family again, never wrote to them, and referred to them only briefly and with unrelenting venom, saying that no doubt they still lived out there like the low animals they were, in that bush humpy with cracks in the wall and an earthern floor. Sylvia saw the incident as having taken place in a landscape resembling the paintings of Russell Drysdale: the iron-grey humpy, the red earth stretching featureless as far as the eye could see, the arch of cloudless sky yellowing at the base, and the small figure of the youth, in dark silhouette, holding stiffly in one hand the gathered mouth of the sack.

The sack, cited too often as an example of bare beginnings, of the importance of hard yakker, and of noses kept to grindstones, had entered the Polglazes' jokes. But in spite of those jokes (which Sylvia had at first overheard, and then joined in), that imagined landscape had never altered, nor had the story of the embattled boy, the cowardly father, and the warrior brothers, lost its simple intensity.

Footsteps and voices in the hall made her look quickly at the closed door. Harry had arrived. She felt pleasure relax her face. She turned back to her father, and saw that he had opened his eyes.

Filmed and dull, they looked at her without recognition. 'It's Sylvia,' she said. He seized his spectacles from the tray and put them on.

When he had come home in her childhood, he used to greet her with this same look of tender amazement. It was part of their game. 'Now what is this? Is it a chicken that's strayed in? No, it's a little brown bird from the bush . . .' She rose from her chair and set a cheek against his. She felt a hand, clumsy as a padded ball on the end of a stick, patting her back; and still with her cheek against his, tears flowing down her face, she wondered in panic how she could speak to him, for his lack of speech had momentarily made her forget that he could hear. Remembering this with relief, she sat back in her chair and laughed as she wiped the tears from her face.

'I'm not crying because you look sick. The first thing I thought is how little you've changed. I suppose I howled because you're so pleased to see me.'

And indeed he did look deeply gratified. But then she saw that the little nods he was giving, over and over, were not only of gratification in her presence. She remembered those nods. They were conclusive. They approved a decision arrived at; they often approved his own stratagems.

Her tenderness sank away, and apprehension took its place. The droop on the left side of his mouth gave it the lopsided, vindictive line seen in her nightmare image of him on the aeroplane, as if that image had been a forecast with which she had now caught up. He had seemed more fully himself at first glance because in twenty years her strongest perception of him, fortified or even formed in dreams, was of a huge, dark presence looming over a screaming woman. This was like the face that had looked out from that presence, and this was like the silence with which he had fed that woman's hysteria.

Sylvia's quick, alert little smile appeared. Sociably, she inclined her head. 'Siddy had to go home for a while. But Harry is here. Greta asked me to tell you.'

She saw his face take on a grim amusement, as if he would say, 'Oh, she did, did she?' Her apprehension hardened into a determination that she would not be used in his contest with Greta. Believing now that it *was* a contest, she also had a conception, too swift to catch and hold, of what Greta had meant when she said that the way he fought was dreadful. He was awkwardly turning, moving his entire trunk. Eagerly, she leaned forward.

'Do you want the dictionary? Your card?'

But he had himself reached to swing the tray across his knees, and as he did so she saw his satisfaction give way to fury. The blood mottled his skin, the ragged brows contracted. She saw that his eyes, behind the glass of his spectacles, were looking with rage into his own, reflected in the long dressing mirror on the wall, and knew that his fury was caused by his own dishevelment. She got to her feet, as nervous, as anxious to appease him, as her mother had once been.

'May I help—? Do you want—?'

He struggled to raise himself, failed, and seized the bell. But before he could ring it the door opened, and Harry came in. Harry's eyes immediately met hers; he was smiling, and she knew that he had come to greet her, but she could only say, in a voice high with anxiety, 'Oh, Harry, could you help me with—Could you please help me make my father tidy?'

Harry, immediately at his most practical, came forward demonstrating how they should join arms beneath Jack's knees and behind his back. In the few years since she had seen him, his hair showed more grey, and his body a forecast, a first shade, of settling and gnarling. They bent to their task, and as their hands gripped each other's forearms, the very quick glance they exchanged recognized that the inert body between them was in startling accord with their old pattern.

Jack, as they raised him, looked straight ahead and ignored Harry's presence. This would have seemed grim to Sylvia a few minutes ago, but now, because Harry was here to share it, it gave an effect of childish huffiness, and she avoided Harry's eyes lest they be tempted to exchange a smile. As soon as Jack was upright, and the back of the chair brought to a right angle with the seat, he pushed Harry away, not violently, but with flips of his good hand, as if to disperse rubbish. Harry's submission was poker-faced; he and Rosamond had always been, externally, strictly affable towards Jack. He said to Sylvia, 'I'll see you later, then.' And to Jack, 'Well, I'll be here till Siddy gets back, if you need me.'

'We didn't even say hello,' she remarked with a laugh, as the door shut behind him.

Her father ignored her. Using the wall mirror and the swivelled shaving mirror on the tray, he began to tidy himself. When he also ignored her offer to help him, she guessed that she was included in his anger because she had seen him in his dishevelment, and could easily imagine his anger extended to Greta for allowing him to be thus seen. He had dragged loose the knot of his tie, and now, patiently, righteously, he used his effective hand, and at one stage, his teeth, to knot it to his liking. When Molly and he, dressed in their best (and always much too early), used to wait for visitors in the living room of the house at Burwood, he would advance again and again on the mirror above the mantel shelf, first to look keenly into his own eyes, then to stroke a lapel, run a hand with infinite gentleness over the greased corrugations of his hair, and press for a moment in the pincer of forefinger and thumb the knot of his tie. While Molly, cautiously dabbing at her sweat and powder, would not be able to refrain from crying out that he was a vain thing, and that he got on her nerves.

'Fancy! A great big man like you! Bad as a woman any day!'

But Sylvia, when she was older and saw that these occasions persisted into his life with Greta, suspected that in touching his expensive suit, his imported silk tie, and his expertly barbered hair, he was ceremoniously invoking, one by one, the symbols of his victory over the brothers 'still living out there in that bush humpy like the low animals they were'.

Molly's comments on this ritual never made him hurry it, or vary it, or alter it in any way at all. Jack Cornock's nerves were good, whereas poor Molly's were unstable, fit only for the short dash. He had ignored her as completely as he was ignoring Sylvia now. Shutting himself off had always been one of his techniques of punishment. He had called it 'letting them sweat for a bit'. And as she watched him from her excluded position, Sylvia could not help reflecting with asperity that this man, who was capable of giving himself such loving and detailed attention, had failed to observe in more than twenty years of marriage that his wife could not read or write. But now he was neat again, the collar and shoulders of his coat settled, his hair combed, his tie knotted. So he gave her a single nod, as he used to do when re-admitting Molly, and drew towards him the alphabet card and pen. The pen was used only as a pointer. His message was: HOW ARE YOU HOLDING?

'Holding what?' she asked.

He gave her a glance of suspicion. 'No, honestly,' she protested, 'I don't know what it means.'

He held her glance for a while longer, then evidently deciding to believe her, pointed with his pen to the letter M. And instantly she recalled the verbal usage, and was surprised that she had ever forgotten it. 'Oh,' she said, as he was still spelling the word out, 'how am I holding for money? I'm quite all right. I have all I need. So if you are offering me money, thank you, but I don't need any.'

As she spoke she lifted her handbag from the floor and pointlessly rummaged in it, dismayed to find herself so flustered. She did not look up until he gave two sharp raps on his tray. He was smiling, however, and looked rather ingratiating.

I HAV PLENTY

'Have you?' she said. 'That's good.' She held in her hand a few of the papers from her bag, and now looked down at them and saw that among them was her airline ticket. She intended to show it, to smile and tell him that some people kept them as souvenirs.

But she had a revulsion against all this pretence—all his, and all her own. She saw suddenly that she was in this difficulty with both her parents because her estrangement from them had never been acknowledged. Out of fear, or a queer politeness, or a denial of anything dramatic, or perhaps simply out of shyness, everyone, including herself, had pretended that it had never happened, and so now they were stuck with this old false act and couldn't get into any other. A mist passed quickly over her eyes, as it used to do when she was angry. Yet she thought she was not angry, only virtuously determined to demolish this old false act, to force her way through the pretence with truth. Nor did she deliberately choose the point at which she attacked it; the words seemed to come of their own accord.

'Dad, did you know that mum can't read or write? And never could?'

After his first stupefaction, all expression left his face. His eyes moved away from hers, towards the window.

'Well, neither did I. Stewart knew. He noticed when he was a child.'

He was eyeing her again. He still held the pen in his hand. With uncertainty, and several false starts, he pointed out a message.

I KNEW

But she had seen his stupefaction, and believed this to be a lie. They were still in the old act. She began to shove the papers back into her bag, but then changed her mind and proffered the ticket.

'Some people keep these as souvenirs.'

Now that there was no question of anything but falsity, she dropped easily into chatter, telling him of obscure small airports, of journeys delayed, of forced landings, of campings in airports. But though he watched her closely as she spoke, she knew that he was inattentive; he now seemed really deaf. After a while she said, 'I think you are tired. Do you want me to go?'

She had to repeat it before he nodded. On her way out of the room she remembered the tray, and went back to wheel it out of his way. He was looking out of the window again, and did not acknowledge her return. She wondered if periods of inattention were also symptoms of his condition. As she crossed the room again, she felt that he had turned and was watching her but when she reached the door she saw that this was not so. He was still looking out of the window. When she shut the door behind her, tears came into her eyes, and she set her lips and carefully stroked them away with a forefinger. She could hear Harry and Greta talking in the hall. She went to the bathroom and looked cautiously into the mirror.

On Stewart's face appeared, in a weaker form, the stigma of hardship and ignorance so apparent on her father's and mother's faces. She tried to remove the veil of custom, to look at herself with impartiality, and find it on her own. But she, the youngest, the only daughter, born into easier times, and loved and cosseted until the age of ten, had escaped it. She stared into the mirror, and a remarkably blank face stared back.

Harry and Greta were still in the hall. Under the arch of the dining room stood the man she had seen in Macleay Street. She smiled. 'Guy,' she said.

'Mother said you knew me.'

His voice had a slight break, almost a crackle, not unattractive. 'I wasn't sure,' she said. 'Did you buy a cake?'

'I was hanging around,' he said. 'I hang around looking at things. Cakes, clothes, jewellery. You must have heard how hopeless I am. I look in windows, with my mouth hanging open, wasting time.'

Smiling still, she turned to Harry. 'We didn't even say hello.'

'No.' His amusement, his nod towards Guy and Greta, remarked that the pattern was persisting.

'How did you find Jack?' asked Greta.

'I was amazed at the things he can do. And he still looks very—' She lifted a hand—'very—'

'Very what?' asked Greta.

'Strong.'

'Oh, he's strong,' said Harry wryly.

'Did he manage to give messages?' asked Greta.

'Oh, yes.' Sylvia heard herself sigh. 'Easily. Easily.'

'Sometimes he gets the letters all buggered up,' said Guy. 'Mother said you have jet lag, Sylvia. Have you got over your jet lag, Sylvia?'

Her grimace was of self-deprecation. 'I think I'll keep it for a day or two yet, in case I need an excuse for something.'

'We were having a row when you came in,' said Guy.

'Nothing of the sort,' said Greta.

'Mother has sold the rugs from this floor.'

'They are at the cleaners.'

'I didn't even notice they were gone,' said Harry.

'You wouldn't,' said Guy. 'But I'll tell you who would,' he said to Sylvia. 'Your father. And I bet that made his day.'

'This isn't for me,' said Sylvia.

Guy's laugh confirmed the odd attraction of his voice. As she turned back into the corridor she heard Harry say, 'Did you sell them, mother?'

The corridor led to a porch opening onto the back garden. Sighing deeply, she strode across the shadowed grass and flung down her bag, and herself beside it, under the flowering prunus. She stretched out on her back and folded her hands under her head. Only then did it occur to her that in disclosing Molly's illiteracy to her father, she had betrayed a secret her mother must have kept with enormous difficulty and a thousand ruses. She gave a cry, a whimper of helplessness and regret.

But the beauty of the tree was having its effect. The soft massed flowers, irradiated on one side by the setting sun, were neither pink nor white, and the new leaves unfurling among them neither bronze nor green. It was easy to believe that the purpose of such beauty was to bless and soothe, and Sylvia gave herself up to it with gratitude. She had left the house in the hope that Harry would follow her, but the footsteps that presently crossed the grass were Guy's. He stood looking down at her, his dark head and shoulders startling against the cloud of tender flowers, almost as if she were seeing the thick human substance for the first time. 'You'll get something or other lying on that grass,' he said. He was childish, petulant. 'Lumbago, I think it is. Mother did sell those rugs, I don't care what she says.'

Unnecessarily, under that filter of flowers, she raised a forearm to shield her eyes. 'I shan't stay here for long enough to get lumbago.'

He sat on the grass at her side, raising his face to look into the tree. 'Little cherubs should be sticking their faces out through those flowers.'

The remark gave her some notion of the kind of woman he might please. 'It's quite good enough without them,' she said.

'What a pity mother will lose it.'

'Who says she will?'

'She will if this goes on. The rugs are the start. It will end by her eating off the floor, while he lolls in his chair, king of the ruins. And if you tell me not to talk like that because he's your father, I'll say I will talk like that, because she's my mother.'

'I didn't tell you not to.'

'You looked as if you were going to.'

'I was about to say that extreme situation won't arise.'

'Who will stop it? You?'

There was sexuality in his pretended antagonism; she was

careful not to make the response it called for. She said idly, 'It's not my business.'

'Or do you mean he will die before it can happen?' He leaned closely over her. 'I love it when you blush. I used to watch you across the table. It was the first time I had ever seen a blush like that. *Do* you mean he will die soon?'

'This isn't my business.'

'If he dies soon? Oh, but I bet you know it is.'

'I mean—' she managed to maintain her dry and idle tone— 'that it isn't my business to intercede.'

'Of course it is. You're his daughter. It's up to you. You could try, at least. But I bet you won't even do that.'

Feeling the disadvantage of her supine position, she sat up, raising her arms to check the firmness of her knot of hair.

'Rosie and Harry say how fair-minded you are,' he said, 'how intelligent, and terribly unmaterialistic, and so on. But I think you're just evasive.'

She looked at him with interest. His heavy brow and pulpy lips had made her think him unintelligent. For a moment she was tempted to ask if it were true that he would think himself made if he had Gucci shoes and a watch without numerals. She took a hairpin out of her knot of hair, then put it back.

He said, 'And maybe you're cold-blooded, too.'

His smiling face was too close to hers. She said into it swiftly, shrewdly, and without intention, 'So are you, Guy.'

'Great. Now we're talking about money.'

She had not expected him to be so bold, and as if he sensed her retreat, he became bolder still. 'Future money. Yours.'

She was angry and silent. He pulled grass, smiling into her face, and she wondered if he would dare to class her with his wistful old women, and expose his simple mercenary purpose. In the past few months she had had several such duels with young Romans, they asking, 'Would you buy it?' and she as silently replying, 'No.' She threatened him with her eyes, and was pleased to see him falter. As she got to her feet, and picked up her bag, Harry opened the kitchen door and began to cross the grass. Harry walked fast, but with a new deliberation. He looked at the ground as he came, and clicked the finger and thumb of one hand. Guy groaned, flopped onto his back, and propped both feet against the trunk of the tree. Harry came to a stop near his head. 'Did he tell you?' he asked Sylvia.

'Tell me what?'

'Your father wants you. Mother asked him to tell you.'

'I forgot,' said Guy. 'I was too busy trying to make her.'

As Harry and she started back across the grass, he laid an arm across her shoulders. 'Was he?'

Her laugh was one of pure delight, surprising to herself. 'He is looking for irons for his fire.'

With the pressure of a hip Harry manoeuvred her towards the porch instead of the kitchen, and as soon as he shut the door behind them he put his arms round her and kissed her. She laughed, then gave a deep sigh of relief. They kissed again and again. When they drew apart she left one hand on his shoulder and looked into his face, smiling.

'This time we have both changed.'

'What happened to your Afro?'

She was thinking that in the prime of his middle age he would be a dark-skinned, thickset man with yellowish-brown eyes quick to burn with an anger on which he would be slow to act. 'I got sick of it,' she said, 'and let it grow.'

'When I heard you were coming back, I couldn't believe my luck. Exactly when I needed you.'

She let her hand slip from his shoulder. 'Oh, if you need me, I'll let you down.'

'You won't.'

'I will.' She came very close again, but touched him only with the palms of her hands. 'I shouldn't have come back.' She was almost whispering. 'I do nothing right. I say things I don't intend to say. I blunder.'

'Remember your journey.'

'No, it's true what I said. Jet lag is only an excuse. This place is bad for me. It curses me.'

'Hush,' he said, laughing at her intensity.

'I had better go in. My father—'

'One minute.'

This time she emerged smiling from their kiss. 'I thought you would have a young girl.'

'I thought you would have a young guy. Like that one in London. Eight years younger.'

'I thought your girl would be twenty years younger.'

'You have always been the only other important one.'

'Other than Margaret?'

'Yes. You don't mind that, do you?'

'No. I always liked it—the way you loved Margaret so much.'

'Will you come to my place tonight?'

'Yes. But I've told you, so be warned. I'll let you down. I'll blunder.'

All the same, she was smiling with joy as she opened the door of her father's room. Her feeling of absolute freshness, renewal, was hardly touched by the thought, as she caught sight of her own glowing face in the mirror, that she had been refreshed, renewed, so many times before. And when her father returned her smile, she felt that her former impressions were exaggerated, too much influenced by her nightmare on the plane. She tilted her head and smiled at him in enquiry.

He had before him an open address book. He pointed to a name, a telephone number, and then to the phone. She nodded. On his card he pointed out a message. She nodded again. She was to get Keith Burtenshaw on the line and ask him to come here without fail on Monday. The message was misspelt, but she understood.

A woman's voice answered. She sounded cross. 'Keith has just this minute come in the door. Who is it?'

'I'm speaking for Jack Cornock. I'm Sylvia Foley.'

'Oh, the daughter. I'll see if Keith can speak to you.'

Her father was repeating the message. NOTHING FALE. MONDAY. She nodded again, reassuringly. In the telephone a slow high voice said, 'Yes? I'm Keith Burtenshaw.'

'Mr Burtenshaw, my father would like you to come here on Monday.'

'Why, Mrs Foley?'

'I don't know, Mr Burtenshaw.' She was wondering, as she spoke, how early Harry and she would be able to leave. 'I'm only giving his message.'

The voice spoke with a sardonic undertone. 'You're only giving his message.'

'Yes.'

'Well, you tell him—let me see—yes, tell him I may manage Tuesday.'

She covered the mouthpiece. 'He says Tuesday.'

The lively side of Jack Cornock's mouth joined the deadened side to tightly clamp the chin. He picked up his pen. When he had pointed out MON she nodded and uncovered the mouthpiece. Harry and she could not leave, she had just recalled, until Siddy returned. 'He still says Monday, Mr Burtenshaw.'

'And you really don't know what this is all about?'

'I haven't the least idea,' she said, with a laugh of surprise.

'You had better let me speak to him.'

'He wants to speak to you,' she said to her father. And when he pushed away the receiver, she shook her head. 'He and I could argue back and forth all night. Please listen to him.'

When her father took the phone she went over to the window, forgetting that there was no need to place herself out of earshot of this silent man. Jack Cornock sat placidly enough with the receiver at his ear, and glanced inattentively around him as he listened. And in that attitude, in the fading daylight, he looked so much like the man of twenty or even thirty years ago that she almost expected to hear the voice, jocose, relaxed, yet with a hard edge of challenge to its banter, in which she had so often heard him talk on the telephone to colleagues. He was a man with no close friends; it was only business she had heard him discuss, though he might lead into it or break it with mention of sport or motor cars, or with enquiries about the other's health, or sometimes with reminiscences of old so-and-so, who had just died. She saw very few of the men with whom he spoke, but from those few, and from the hundreds of snatches of conversation overheard, she had evolved an idea of the type, and believed she could recognize it. Seeing one of them, she would think, 'That's the kind of man my father rings up'. She had seen this man avid at the wheel as he took a corner in his car. In the nightclub where she served drinks, he had called her with a raised finger. As he trotted nimbly down the stairs of an office building, he had done up one button of his coat. In the smaller Sydney of those days, these men had rather presented themselves to the public, conscious of being well known. Among the shabbier and less successful of them, she supposed, were those who had button-holed Stewart in bars to tell him of the exploits of his father. The man to whom her father was now listening seemed a new sort, atypical.

Jack Cornock was no longer looking about him. He had sunk his head to his chest, and had drawn his mouth down. She guessed that the man with the high voice had held firm in his refusal to come on Monday. She expected to be asked to convey her father's disagreement to this, but when he replaced the receiver, the dull tone told her that the other man had already hung up. She recalled the way her father had risen from those other conversations, so quietly, heavily, satisfied, giving his conclusive nods, and she could not help but be sorry, whatever his past chicanery, that he could now be treated as summarily as this. She went forward.

'Let me put on the light.'

His good hand still rested on the telephone. He looked at her with dullness; it seemed that his anger would return. But then, as

when he had awakened, recognition sprang to his eyes. He pushed away the phone, beckoned her, and drew from his pocket a flat rectangular box. She opened it and lifted out a short string of ungraded pearls. In her spontaneous 'Oh', resentment was oddly mingled with her surprise. He seized his pen and spelled out with childish triumph the word REAL. He pointed to her neck; she was to put the pearls on.

Greta, as she came in, turning on the overhead light, did not see the pearls at once. 'Jack,' she said, 'you will come out to dinner tonight, I am sure.'

Sylvia knew that only the utmost plainness would meet this occasion. She turned, spreading the points of her collar, and lifted her chin. 'Look what dad gave me.'

'Oh, the pearls,' said Greta. But when she turned to her husband, her voice was flat with despair. 'Who did you ask to get them from the bank? Siddy? But *I* would have done that. You had only to ask.'

His derogatory tilt of the head, lift of a brow, told his clear story; he took pleasure in publicly announcing his mistrust of her; Sylvia felt her blush rising from her body, under her pearls, upward to her neck and face.

Harry, looking in at the open door, brought a distraction. 'I've just taken the swing down.' He was holding his hands, covered with dirt, away from his body. 'I'll just go and wash these, then I'll get us all a drink.'

At dinner Jack Cornock sat sideways to the table, set apart by the bulk of his wheel chair. Sylvia saw Greta's attention gradually withdraw from him. Talkative with wine, pleased with the success of her meal, Greta put her hands on the table beside her plate and said with firmness and gaiety. 'Well, Rosie has taken the Saturday I wanted, but I will have the one after. Or would Sunday be better? Yes, Sunday is better for Stewart. Everyone must come. Children, husbands, grandchildren. Jack?'

At least he did not disagree. The childish manner in which he pretended not to hear made Sylvia want to laugh. It seemed a common situation, after all—a sullen family member resisting efforts to coax him back into the fold.

'We will have it in the garden,' said Greta. 'By then Siddy will have put up the new swing.'

'You said you wouldn't have another swing on that tree,' Harry reminded her.

'This is its last swing. In three or four years I'll have it out.'

Sylvia, who was about to address her father, to draw him into the conversation, was shocked at what she saw: his attitude, his face, so still, yet hatred blazing towards his wife like air channelled from a furnace. Guy was also watching Jack Cornock. He flicked a pleased glance from him to Sylvia, then picked up his glass.

'Well, happy parties, all,' he said in his petulant voice.

Harry refused to drive Guy to Elizabeth Bay, but agreed to drop him at Roseville station, from where he could catch a train to Wynyard. Harry and Sylvia sat belted into the front seats, which rose to a peak behind their heads, while Guy, unbelted in the back, leaned forward and spoke into the space between them.

'I'm the only one not asked to Rosie's.'

'I'm not going, either,' said Harry.

'You were asked, though.'

'I have too much paper work to catch up on,' Harry explained to Sylvia.

'I haven't,' said Guy. 'So I could go instead of you. I want to go. I want to see how Ted's taking it.'

'Taking what?' asked Sylvia

'Ted's going bust,' replied Guy.

'So that's what Rosie meant,' said Sylvia; and Harry said, 'It does really begin to look like it.'

'I'll tell you why Rosie doesn't ask me, Sylvia. I pinched her candelabrum and popped it, and she had to go and get it back. She was thrilled. She had never been in a pop shop before. But she said once was enough. Did they tell you I pinch things?'

'Do you?' said Sylvia politely.

'Margaret is working in commercial TV now,' said Harry to Sylvia.

'I used to pinch things from mother,' said Guy, 'because I knew it was safe. I knew she wouldn't tell Knocker. She wouldn't let him get that on her. But then Harry hit me, so I stopped.'

'She used to say she wouldn't touch commercial TV,' said Sylvia.

'He hit me in cold blood,' said Guy.

'I hit you in hot blood,' said Harry. 'I did my block. And if you touch one more of her things, I'll do it again.'

'Does Margaret like commercial TV?'

'I had sticking plaster over one eye,' said Guy, relaxing into the back seat, 'and everyone was sorry for me.'

'I don't know whether she likes it or not,' said Harry. 'We don't see each other. We thought we would. Neither of us dreamed we

wouldn't. Yet that's the way it turned out.'

'It so often does,' said Sylvia.

'Problems,' said Guy. 'Dear Diana Crap, can you help me? My divorced wife and I don't want to see each other, and as we love each other very much, and are both very lovely persons, this hurts us both very much.'

Sylvia and Harry laughed. Guy's voice rose and quickened. 'I bet Harry's taking you to Neutral Bay, Sylvia. Watch it. He'll hit you. And to think you could have had me. I never hit people, in case they hit me back. Of course, you would have had to lock up those pearls. I bet they were hot once, those pearls.'

Sylvia raised her hand and fingered the pearls.

'That's what Harry's after, your pearls. To say nothing of the money he hopes you'll inherit. He's known as a bludger from one end of Sydney to the other.'

Harry swung the car over and drew into the kerb. 'Here you are, Guy.'

'This isn't Roseville.'

'Out!'

'Shit,' murmured Guy, as he got out. He kept a hand on the door, preventing Harry from going on. He leaned into the car and put his lips to Sylvia's ear. 'You saw your father's face. He wants to take her with him.'

He drew away from the car and leapt through its headlights to hail a passing taxi. Sylvia watched him get in beside the driver. Harry was rejoining the traffic. 'Guy's poison,' he said tensely.

The taxi was speeding ahead of them. Guy's arm appeared, waving. 'When I first saw him,' said Sylvia, 'I wondered what attraction he had left. Now I know. He's so brazen he disarms you.'

'Not me. Not any more.'

'I mean me.'

'What did he say to you just then?'

'You would call it poison. I call it mischief.'

'What was it?'

'Mischief. Let's forget it.'

'What was it?'

'I don't want to tell you. It wasn't about you or me.'

'What could he have to say that I'm not allowed to hear?'

'Oh, I see. So Guy's going to be our obstacle. We always have had one.'

'Not this time.'

'I knew one would turn up.'

'To hell with Guy. Leave your pearls on instead.'

'All right. I hate these seats, don't you? Remember the seats in your first car? And how I used to put my arm along the back, and touch your shoulder?'

He was smiling. Drawing up for a red light, he put a hand on the top of the wheel, as if he would spin it. As they drove on again, she said soberly, 'Out there on the grass, Guy said I ought to intercede with dad on your mother's behalf. Do you think I ought to?'

'Did she ask you to?'

'Not a word. Not a hint.'

'Then why should you?'

'Her position . . .'

'Are you sure she wants anyone to change it?'

'She wants him to change it. Only him!'

'But anyone else? I'm not. Just be nice to him.'

After a while, she said hesitantly, 'I'm just that little bit wary of being nice to him, because of that money Guy just mentioned.'

'It's only a possibility. What about your ability to ignore possibilities?'

'It helps not to be reminded of them all the time.'

'I won't remind—'

'Oh *you* won't, I know.'

The Kitchings were eating in the kitchen, as they usually did. They employed a cleaner, who lived out, but Rosamond did her own cooking, and on the sink was the pile of dishes and basins and plates, and saucepans with their handles sticking up, with which the cleaner would start her day tomorrow. It was nine o'clock. Rosamond cut a slice of cheese and said to her sons, 'No, I've given you fair warning. I want you to stay home.'

'Just for this Sylvia someone,' said Dominic.

'She's not even a real relation,' said Matthew.

'You'll stay home anyway. I want to show you off.'

'Dad's not staying home.'

'She doesn't think I'm worth showing off,' said Ted.

'Daddy will stay home if he can, but he may have to take the boat out. And don't you boys ask to go, because daddy is taking out a buyer.'

'You selling the boat?' asked Matthew with aggression.

Ted ate a piece of cheese. 'Nothing settled yet.'

'Em and Jazz will be coming,' said Rosamond to the boys.

'If we stay long enough to be shown off,' said Dominic, 'then can we take Em and Jazz over to Derek's?'

'Derek is very fascinated with Em,' said Matthew.

'Derek is allowed to drink with meals,' remarked Dominic, watching his father fill his glass.

'Well, you're not,' said Ted.

'You have your pot,' said Rosamond consolingly.

'You had better watch those jokes, mum,' said Matthew.

'Oh, if I had to watch everything you two tell me to watch . . . Ted, I thought I would ask Stewart Cornock on Saturday, too.'

'Now why in heaven's name?' asked Ted.

'Stewart Cornock the greyhound man,' said Dominic.

'Well, he's Sylvia's brother,' said Rosamond. 'Why do you call him that, Dom? He doesn't keep greyhounds.'

'He looks like one,' said Dominic.

'Right,' said Ted. 'He does. Trained to within an inch of his life, but way past it. He might just win one more for his owners at a country race meeting.'

'I don't want to go into business,' said Matthew. 'I want to be a fisherman.'

'Oh?' said Ted. 'So what's happened all of a sudden to marine biology?'

'I would rather be a marine biologist than a fisherman, but I would rather be a fisherman than go into business.'

'Remember when we were going to be fishermen?' Rosamond asked Ted. 'When we were first married, and we were going to buy that land and that boat down the south coast.'

'Hey, that would have been great,' said Dominic.

'Yeah,' said Ted. 'Great. When all the housewives line up to buy frozen fish fingers from Japan.'

'People do fish down there,' said Matthew. 'They must make a living.'

'If you call that a living. Rosie, I don't see what being Sylvia's brother has to do with asking Stewart Cornock here. On that basis you might as well ask her mother as well.'

'Darling, I don't know her mother.'

'You hardly know Stewart.'

'Stewart has been so sweet about helping mother. And apart from that—You two boys may leave the table.'

The boys exchanged glances. Then Dominic said, 'We want to stay and listen.'

'Selling the boat?' said Matthew, aggressive again. 'Selling the house?'

'Derek's father says dad's going bust,' said Dominic.

'You heard your mother,' said Ted. 'Now piss off.'

'We want to stay and hear about your bankruptcy,' said Matthew.

'Piss off!'

'Now just a moment, Ted,' said Rosamond. 'Haven't they a right to know?'

Ted half-rose from his chair. '*Piss off*!'

'Well,' said Rosamond, when the boys had gone, 'I know you're under a strain, but that was very crude.'

'Smart arses,' muttered Ted.

'Don't eat any more cheese when you feel like that. You'll get an ulcer. You know, Ted, if the boys at school have begun to talk about it—'

'Fuck Derek's father.'

'*Especially* Stilton. Derek's father's a judge.'

'So he fucking well is,' said Ted with amusement. 'Well, I'll tell you what—he's the one who had better go and catch fish for a living.'

'I just wish you would be frank about it.'

'I've been as frank as I can be. We went into all this last night.'

'Last night the stars weren't right. You see, about Stewart, I thought it would give him a chance to value the house.'

'Who says we're selling?'

'Ted, we can't possibly sit on hundreds of thousands of dollars worth of real estate. Not in our position. And who would be a better man to handle the sale than Stewart?'

'Rosie. Love. Look. I told you last night. There may be a way out.'

'Ted, I read the papers, too.'

'They don't put everything in the papers. Merrymen and I are working on something.'

'I hate Merrymen.'

'I know you do.'

'He nearly went to jail.'

'Bull! They didn't even get him past the committal proceedings.'

'Tell me what you're working on.'

'Love, you wouldn't understand.'

'Simplify it.'

'Its merit is its extreme complexity. Just trust me.'

'Trust you to do what? Ted, I'm going to start crying again.'

'Keep us in this house, for one thing. Look, love, ask Stewart

Cornock if you like. Let him give you a valuation. It won't hurt to have a valuation. But don't be surprised if he can't come. Those guys sell on Saturdays.'

'Well, he can bring Sylvia, and if he can't stay for lunch, at least he can stay for a drink. And I'll say, "Oh, by the way, Stewart, while you're here . . ."'

'That's the shot. And if it wastes his time, well, that's part of his game. Will you have some more of this?'

'Half a glass, out of nobility, so that you won't drink too much. You mustn't think I would mind being poor, Ted.'

'You don't know what it's like.'

'*I* don't know?'

'Oh, that. That was so long ago.'

'All the same, I've never forgotten it. Those two crummy little rooms, and sharing a kitchen and bathroom. And while mother was at work, some woman or other, usually the one who owned the house, was supposed to look after us. One of them, when Guy shit his napkin, she used to beat him. She used to whack all of us. Then one day Harry got one of those carpet sweepers—you're not listening.'

'You only talk about it when you're worried.'

'The whacking that went on in that place was terrific. When mother came home she was beside herself. That's a good saying, isn't it? Beside yourself. As if you can divide into two people, one beside the other, and each doing different things. You can, too. I mean, without being schizo. Anyway, Harry got one of those carpet sweepers and butted her in the stomach, and she went round doubled up, pretending to be injured, and we had to move. We were always moving.'

'Well, then Greta married Knocker, and everything was okay. So stop talking about it.'

'No, then she got that job demonstrating cosmetics, and *then* everything was okay.'

'I thought—'

'No, I was five when she got that job. I remember it perfectly. She was so good at it, they paid her a lot of money, and we had that nice Spanish girl to look after us.'

'Right,' said Ted. 'I was mistaken. So stop talking about it. Okay?'

Sylvia, wakened by the moon coming round to the west, got up to draw the blind. The windows overlooked the head of a narrow bay crossed by the sinuous, spooky shadows of tall buildings on the opposite shore. The hum of traffic across the bridge had stopped, the bay was emptied of boats, and she could hear the plash of water against the sandstone wall below. She drew the blind and returned to the narrow bed, where Harry lay asleep on his back. She lay on her back beside him, touching him with a shoulder, a hip, a leg. But as soon as she settled herself to sleep, he woke up.

'Did you get up?'

The quiet question filled her with contentment. 'I drew the blind.'

'What's the time?'

'I don't know.'

'Why are we talking so quietly?'

'Because we still can't believe it.'

He covered her pubic mount with a hand. 'It was only you who doubted it.'

PART TWO

Five

'It's cleared up nicely,' said Keith Burtenshaw.

'Yes,' said Greta.

'After all that rain.'

'Yes.'

'I expect on a day like this, Jack is in the garden.'

Greta was drawing a five-pointed star. 'Yes.'

'Is anyone else there? Siddy?'

'In the garden with Jack.'

'The daughter?'

'Sylvia is going to Rosie's today. The Kitchings are having a party.'

'Fiddling while Rome burns?'

'Is it actually on fire?'

'It will go up on Monday. I have it on good authority. So be prepared.'

'Oh, they will be all right.'

Her rough impatience made him pause. 'I thought it best to warn you.'

'Is that why you rang?'

'Well, not primarily, no. One of those awkward things has cropped up, Greta. We find we have to go up the north coast for a few days, perhaps even a week.'

'You will get some golf.'

'It will do Marjorie good to see the grandchildren. But you know how I said, when I came on Tuesday to take Jack's instructions, you know how I told you I would stall him as long as I could? He wanted it drawn up and signed the next day, if you please. Of course there was no question of that, and I told him so. But, well, you know, and I know, how long the firm has been doing Jack's work, my father before me, and now me, and to stall him until I get back doesn't seem quite the thing. And neither does handing it over to David Sole. David does seem to have the knack of making him angry, and, well, we both know that anger isn't good for him, and, well, the document is all drawn up and ready, so I thought I would pop in with it today, on our way north. Marjorie could witness it.'

Greta had stopped drawing stars and had moved her eyes sideways, as if listening to something in the house. Keith Burtenshaw said, 'Are you there?'

Slowly, she began another star. 'Go on. You were talking about witnesses. Siddy will be here.'

'We can't use him.'

'That at least is good news.'

'I'll tell you what I'll do, Greta. I'll bring Vera Vance, one of Marjorie's friends, one of the girl friends. She's staying in the house to look after the cats while we're away. I can drop her off afterwards. How's that, Greta?'

'Very kind.'

'What else can I do? Unless of course you change your mind about going for that power of attorney.'

'Do you think he's incapable, Keith?'

'It's a long time since I've seen him in such good form as on Tuesday.'

'On Wednesday night he beat Sylvia at drafts.'

'She's very attentive.'

'Next week she's hiring a car and going into the country.'

'Good thinking. He won't tire of her.'

'You don't know her, Keith.'

'You mean to tell me she neglects the possibility?'

'She tries to snub it. She's nice to him, but as if he were a tourist on a coach.'

'Well, something seems to have done him the world of good. And she has a long way to come without a car, if she's not keen.'

'She comes when Harry comes. Harry brings her.'

'I see.' There was a long pause; then Keith Burtenshaw said, 'Well, it's a funny old world, Greta.'

'Isn't it,' she agreed, without irony.

'Everything may turn out well in the long run. But it will be a long, long run.'

'Don't speak of it,' she said quickly. 'Don't speak of it.'

He said guardedly, after a pause, 'You did say Jack was in the garden?'

She had filled a page with stars, and now began quickly to enclose them in squares. 'Yes, yes. And so is Siddy. Is that all, Keith?'

'Marjorie is looking forward to seeing you, Greta.'

'Yes, yes. I'll expect you some time today. Suit yourself about the time.'

After he rang off, she kept the receiver at her ear for about ten seconds. Then she replaced it, and returned to putting squares round her stars. When Guy came under the arch from the dining room, she spoke without looking up.

'What good can it do you to overhear my conversations? You are like a, like a, scavenger. How long have you been here?'

'Five minutes. I came in the back way.'

'You and Harry—you both seem to be haunting the place.'

He sat down, stretching his legs before him. 'The rugs aren't back from the cleaners,' he said with challenge.

Her back bowed, she seemed completely engrossed in making her squares.

'I've brought the rope for the swing. I'll put it up for you if you like.'

The plaintive note did not stir her; she did not raise her head.

'Like a scavenger,' he said, with the beginning of sullenness in his voice. 'It was you who said it.'

Scrubbed and showered and freshly dressed in his neat juvenile clothes, Ken was oiling his hair and combing it back before the bathroom mirror. Molly was pottering about, picking up wet brushes and washcloths, getting in his way.

'She's going to a party today, at Point Piper. She brought herself one of them Indian dresses. Calf-length. It's a nice length, the calf, but in my opinion, them pearls need something swishier. I told her so, day she took me to lunch in town. I didn't hide my opinion. I reckon, and Stewart agrees, them pearls are only a hint of things to come. You're off now, are you?'

Ken sniffed up one nostril. 'Might as well.'

'Trying to kid he doesn't want to go,' remarked Molly.

'I've been working hard all week.'

'And of course I haven't.'

'With your lunches in town.'

'One lunch, I beg your pardon.'

'What you doing this arvo, love?'

'Nothing.'

'There's movies on Seven.'

' "The Belles of St Trinians" and a "Abbott and Costello". And I seen both one hundred times. Go on, why don't you? Don't hang around. You needn't think I want you.'

When Ken reached the pub his mates were talking about women. 'I only know one thing about women,' said Ken loudly, as he joined them. 'Schooner please, Jean.'

Ken was admired in his group for his aged jauntiness and

aggression. 'What do you know, Ken?' asked someone, grinning in advance.

'You can't give them an inch,' said Ken. 'Give them an inch and you're a goner, you've had it, you're history.'

'You're behind the times, Ken,' said one young man, in a kindly tone.

'Behind the times, am I? You're just married, spending too much time on the nest, that's your trouble. You just wait and see, just wait and see, just wait and see if I'm wrong. Thank you, Jean.'

The first engrossment of love, which ten years ago could have made Sylvia heedless of all other obligations, now admitted a duty to her mother, and a duty to her father more happily fulfilled because it included the company of Harry. She was able to set aside her uneasiness with both her parents and Greta and to fill the awful space with her bright useful professionalism. She thought of this as temporary; she knew that she could do better, and believed that one day soon, when she had more time, she would.

In that first week Stewart was more blithely set aside (Stewart wouldn't care), until late on Friday morning, when she answered Harry's telephone.

'Syl! I've been trying to get you at the flat. I rang early and I rang late. Then just now I thought you might have stopped over at Wahroonga, so I tried there, and got Guy, and he said to try Harry's.'

'I've been here for most of the week, in fact.'

'Oh.' A pause enclosed his careful lack of comment. 'Are you going to the Kitchings tomorrow?'

'Yes.'

'Rosie asked me, too. Now tell me this—why should I be asked to the Kitchings? Our cars pass. Ted nods if he's in the mood. Rosie waves. They must be selling, is all I can think of. You'll be going with Harry?'

'Harry's not going.'

'And Guy's not going. He just said he wasn't. So who is going?'

'Me. You, I hope. Hermione and her family.'

'Steven?'

'Yes. I'm pretty sure of that, because Rosie said Hermione and Steven don't go out much apart.'

'No, I don't suppose they do.' He sounded slightly fretful. 'Rosie must know it's a bad day for me to socialize. It was her idea

for me to bring you, and stop if I can. But if they're selling
. . . Well, that's what I'll do, stop if I can. Can you be at the flat at
twelve?'

'Yes. I'll show you the pearls dad gave me.'

'I heard all about them from mum. Do you want me to get a
valuation on them?'

She touched them, as though they were threatened. '*No!*'

'Okay, okay. Mum enjoyed that lunch with you, Syl.'

'Oh Lord, that reminds me. Stewart, I must tell you this. I told
dad that mum couldn't read or write.'

'Jesus! What made you do that?'

'I wanted to say something that wasn't trifling or false, and
that's what came out.'

'Jesus! The very person she tried hardest of all to keep it from.'

'I'm sorry.'

'You haven't told anyone else, have you?'

She knew he was thinking of Harry. 'No, it stays here, with me.'

'Well, it was probably wiped clean out of dad's mind ten minutes later. Twelve on Saturday then.'

Now, on Saturday, wearing her Indian dress and her pearls, she
sat at Harry's desk. He was talking on the telephone in the bedroom; she could hear his voice (argumentative, sometimes breaking into laughter) but not his words. She pushed aside the political
leaflets to make room for her blue air letter, but moved with more
care and respect the pages of engineering design and calculation,
as abstruse to her as any of the Asian scripts. The windows
displayed the little bay, sunlit and busy; small craft gave way to a
densely black submarine gliding to its base at the foot of the
opposite shore, and one of those cruisers which Harry called the
whoopee boats, and she called the drunks' boats, was making its
first noisy circuit of the day. As she began her letter she heard the
thud and the churning of water as a ferry reached the wharf
below the windows, then the clatter as the gangplank was thrown
over. She found it not much easier than before to write to the
Holyoaks. She wrote rapidly and carelessly across the page.

*I've decided to stay the full three months after all, not because of my
father, who is a very strong old man and could live for years yet. I feel
sorry for his wife. Tending people so closely, one is prone to hysterical
convictions. No, my reason is Harry Polglaze, whom you met in 1973.
I won't go into details in case it breaks the spell, which will tell you
everything anyway. One night this week we visited some people
you—Richard—know. Mervyn and Stephanie Gisbourne . . .*

Harry had taken her to meet the Gisbournes. There had been six other people present, and they were standing about in one of those glass-walled additions so common at the backs of Sydney houses, drinking before dinner, when one woman spoke with indignation about the French nuclear tests in the Pacific. Sylvia joined in the general agreement, but with a note so different from the rest that Harry clasped her by the back of the neck and said with amusement, 'But *you* don't have to apologize for the French.' There was laughter, including her own, into which he broke to say incredulously, 'She really feels she must, you know.' Outside the glass room, rain had been pouring on a sodden garden.

> *. . . a week of warmth and cold and wind and rain. I had forgotten the suddenness of the climatic changes. To tell you the truth, Sydney confuses and bewilders me. I suspect that I've begun to resist it again, as I did before going away, but that if I could make myself stop, I could get to like the bright violent climate and the unaffected people. For unaffected don't read simple. But I can't make myself stop. I've driven about in Harry's car while he is at work, so have seen quite a lot of the city and suburbs, some of it pleasant, some of it terrible, like everywhere else, but nine-tenths of it new, raw, unstable—no, I can't say what it is. It is easier to say what it is not. What it is, is elusive. The girls in flowery floppy dresses made me feel out of date, though I saw last year in Europe that the long reign of blue jeans was over. But anyway, I weakened, and went and bought an Indian dress, as a compromise. India! From here it is temptingly close. I find myself thinking about it, trying to work out a cheap way of spending a few weeks there on the way home . . .*

Harry came into the room. Without looking up, she said loudly, 'I am trying to work out some way of stopping in India on my way back.'

'Back?' He leaned over her chair and kissed her neck. 'Back to where?'

She smiled to herself, finishing the letter. 'Be irresponsible. Come to Rosie's with me.'

'We could do a deal.'

'The weights are uneven.'

'Then come on. Or I'll be late for my meeting.'

The Chinese ship was still at its berth in Woolloomooloo Bay. Harry and Sylvia saw it as they drove to her flat, and Steven Fyfe, driving his family the same way more than an hour later, pointed out to his children that she was taking on wheat. The Fyfes were late for Rosamond's lunch because they had been to the northern beaches to inspect two houses advertised in that morning's *Herald*. No inspection had taken place; Hermione had disliked both exteriors so much that she would not even go in.

'It's a good situation,' Steven said, at the second one. They had left their children on the beach, and were alone in the car.

'It's a beautiful situation.'

To the north, headland after headland advanced into the Pacific. Deep blue below the bluff on which their car stood, it stretched away, paler and paler, until the last visible headland stood in a shimmer of silver. Hermione turned again to the houses around them.

'But look what we've done to it.'

'Pressure of fashion. Advertising. We get conned into these things.'

'We let ourselves be conned. Information is available. We have only to look. Come on, let's go and pick up the children. The high schools round here are no good anyway. All the girls are on the pill or pregnant.'

'That classifies very nicely as a reckless statement.'

'I don't care. Come on. Let's go.'

'You don't want to look at any others?'

Hermione turned over the *Herald* in her lap. 'Not at our price.' She tossed the paper into the back seat. 'I know I'm impossible. Why don't we get a divorce?'

Steven started the car. 'Three children are three good reasons. And you know the others, Min.'

'But with somebody reasonable, you could be so much happier.'

'Darling, don't start that again.'

'But I will always be impossible. I will never give in. Never.'

'I don't ask you to.'

'But you secretly think I will.'

'Don't those ivy-leaved geraniums do well down here?'

'And I will, too. I'll be forced to.'

'Stewart Cornock developed some of this land.'

'Did he?'

'According to Ted.'

'At least he didn't build the houses.'

'More profit in sub-division.'

When they reached the children on the beach, Imogen had to be fed. Then Emma said she was hot, and unzipped her jacket, revealing a T-shirt printed with the legend LOVE ANIMALS. KISS A

117

PUSSY. For the last month, she had been given her own clothes allowance. When Steven and Hermione explained to her why she must take it off, she burst into tears of rage or embarrassment, and more time was lost in soothing her, and taking her to the shopping centre to buy a new T-shirt, this time printed with an orange tree, with which she was well content. But she was worried about the marks of tears on her face, and after they passed the Chinese ship, she leaned forward and asked for the third time, 'Mum, are you sure it doesn't show?'

'No, dear. Truly.'

'Dad?'

'No, Em. Not a trace.'

'Is Uncle Harry coming?' asked Jason.

'Hardly,' said Hermione.

'What does that mean?' asked Emma.

'That he doesn't like Uncle Ted,' said Jason.

'That's putting it too strongly, Jason,' said Steven.

They drove round the point and turned into Macleay Street, where the plane trees forecast in palest green their leafy tunnel of summer. At King's Cross young people were rushing home to their flats with flowers and dry-cleaning on wire hangers. Old bachelors carried heavy airline bags, and old women their small parcels of fruit and meat, their cake in a cardboard box. Imogen, her head hanging sideways, was asleep in her padded, suspended seat. When they passed The Pink Pussycat, Jason laughed, and Emma burst into tears again. They had reached Double Bay before she stopped crying, and then she demanded to be put out because she couldn't go anywhere looking like this. '*Shit!*' whispered Hermione to Steven. Steven made shushing noises, and turned down a side street, where, under the pepperina trees in a small park, Hermione treated Emma's eyes with witch hazel from the glove box, while Imogen soundly slept, and everyone else assured Emma once again that nobody could tell she had been crying.

'And we are always hearing how cool and sophisticated today's children are,' complained Hermione, as she got back into the car. Emma was bright and giggly when they went on, but Hermione leaned against the back of the seat and closed her eyes. The car turned into Wolseley Road. 'Mum,' said Emma in a panic, 'I bet my eyes do show.'

'No,' murmured Hermione. She opened her eyes and looked through the window.

'You didn't even look. Do they?' Emma asked Jason.

'Na-ow,' said Jason, opening his mouth wide in reassuring scorn.

'There's your house, mum,' said Emma.

Hermione said nothing; Steven gave her a reproachful glance.

'The one you like, mum,' insisted Emma.

'I saw it,' said Hermione languidly.

'When you didn't even look?'

'It's way back there now, anyway,' said Jason quickly.

Emma continued to look at the houses, some barely visible behind walls and trees, and some exposing façades to the street. 'They are all nice,' she said.

'They are all *big*,' amended Hermione.

Steven sighed.

As the car took the wide bend in the road, Imogen woke up, struggled against the harness, and opened her mouth to roar but, distracted by something, peacefully gazed instead, the pupils of her eyes enlarging.

The Kitchings' house, about fifty years old, was in the Spanish or perhaps the Mexican style. Hermione, while she conceded that it was suitable to the climate, usually added that it had the decency to hide itself behind a wall. Rosamond came out of a door in this white wall as their car drew up. She kissed each of them as they got out. 'Oh, let *me*,' she pleaded, as Hermione began to unstrap Imogen. And she leaned into the car, crooning and making coquettish eyes, and took the baby from her seat.

'Oh, I love you. I shan't give you back. I'll eat you. Sylvia and Stewart have arrived. Go on in, everybody.'

'Stewart?' said Hermione.

'Well, you *know* Stewart. He brought Sylvia. And Ted is home.'

'Ted is?' said Steven, intently.

'Actually not sailing. Think of that. But he won't be appearing. You won't be granted an audience. He's locked in his study with that little weasel Merrymen. What a misnomer. And I'm taking them in food and sustenance.'

'Locked?' said Steven.

'Well, not actually. But shut. What importance! You would think it was a cabinet meeting at least. Come on.'

As she led the way with Emma and Jason, Steven said quietly to Hermione, 'Stewart Cornock. They must be selling.'

'I feel fat today,' said Hermione morosely. 'I always feel fat in this skirt.'

Dominic and Matthew, though they had protested against staying

119

home to be shown off, gave no sign of wanting to leave the adult company assembled in the living room. Steven, who was helping Rosamond to dispense drinks, had filled a tray for the young people to take into the garden, but Emma and Jason had to wait in the doorway, Jason holding this tray, while Dominic spoke of the theory of drifting continents. As Dominic and Matthew were so often in a crowd of boys, who all had to shout to make themselves heard, they both spoke, when more than six or seven people were present, in very loud voices.

'We were joined to Antarctica once, but since then we've drifted north. We've gone one thousand one hundred and fifty kilometres already.'

'You haven't told them about Gondwanaland,' shouted Matthew.

'Gondwanaland was the supercontinent we broke off from. Us and Africa and South America and part of Asia.'

'When was this, Dom?' enquired Steven in a low courteous voice.

'One hundred and fifty million years ago.'

'Then we won't worry about it now,' said Rosamond. She put a hand to her forehead. 'I am feeling rather distracted, darlings, so off you go. Don't keep Em and Jazz waiting.'

'I forgot to tell you,' shouted Dominic as they went, 'that we're still drifting.'

'It hardly seems worth cooking this lunch,' said Rosamond. 'Min, shall I put Imogen down for her sleep?'

Imogen, her eyes blurred and unfocused, was almost asleep in Hermione's arms. 'No, I will,' said Hermione.

Stewart stood beside Sylvia's chair. 'Nice little kid,' he said abruptly, as Hermione carried Imogen away.

Sylvia was looking through the big window. Everything she saw, she was also seeing for Harry: observing, collecting, to please and interest him when they were together again. 'What a dazzle,' she said, 'out there on the water. The harbour's sun struck.'

'I wish you could see it on a better day,' said Rosamond.

'But the day is perfect.'

'I mean without all those weekend yachts. They make it so spotty. Tell us what you think of Sydney, Sylvia, after all these years?'

Sylvia touched her pearls, at which everyone had looked, and on which nobody had commented. 'The spaciousness is wonderful,' she said. 'You can't imagine it ever being the slightest bit fusty or musty.'

'We are supposed to have smog,' said Steven modestly.

'So you may have, but there always seems to be a breeze to keep it moving.'

Stewart said, 'You should say, "So *we* may have", Syl.'

'I should, too,' said Sylvia.

'Because if you're not Australian,' said Stewart, 'you're nothing.'

'Sylvia is an international,' said Rosamond.

'She's never even been to the States,' protested Stewart.

'Then she is a European,' said Rosamond.

'Stewart's right,' said Sylvia, smiling, 'I'm nothing.'

'We'll take you in hand,' said Steven. 'We'll have you saying "we" in no time.'

Across the doorway to the hall passed, without a glance, a bare-footed man in shorts. 'That's that beast Merrymen,' remarked Rosamond. 'The treasurer. I wonder what he's doing out of the cabinet room. Oh, here's Min. Min darling, your drink.'

Hermione took her drink from Steven's hand, and without looking at anyone else, sat down as if she were tired. Merrymen passed across the doorway again, carrying a bundle of files. 'Oh,' said Rosamond, 'running a message for the prime minister.' She made wide brushing movements across her skirt, and spoke in a higher voice. 'Do tell us you're tempted to stay for good, Sylvia.'

'Well, you see,' said Sylvia, as if in perplexity, 'I've made plans to live in Rome.'

'If you wanted,' said Stewart, ' you could teach Italian here.'

'Mmm?'

'I've been around a fair bit,' said Stewart, looking from face to face, but omitting Hermione's, 'and I've admired what I've seen over the other side, and in the States too, but I would like to know where else in the English-speaking world you can live so damned comfortably as here in Sydney.'

'Yes,' said Sylvia promptly, 'there can't be many other places where for seven months of the year you can get up in the morning, shower, and put cotton clothes on your body, and sandals on your feet, and be dressed for the rest of the day. I do love that.'

'In Europe,' said Rosamond, 'I get so terribly tired of the formality. I buy clothes over there, and back here they make me feel over-dressed.'

'And this is a great winter climate, too, don't forget,' said Stewart.

'That's true,' said Hermione, in a provisional tone. 'The climate is quite good.'

Everyone looked at her, but she raised her glass to her lips and said nothing else. Steven said, 'Well, for two months of the year, it's hot enough to make you want to aestivate, but in compensation it never gets cold enough to make you want to hibernate. Sylvia, I don't know whether you know this, but there's a very good demand for teachers of Italian here. So many Australians want to go there.'

'But the catch is,' said Rosamond, 'so does Sylvia.'

'It's true,' said Hermione, 'that so many Australians want to go there. Having mucked up our own country, and made it hideous, we rush about looking at the remnants of beauty in other countries.'

Sylvia was startled to hear this calm dogmatic voice pronouncing what might have been a thought of her own. 'Do you really regard it as mucked up?' she asked.

'Of course it is,' said Hermione.

'How?' asked Stewart.

'Oh, Min will *tell* you,' said Steven wearily.

'Don't tell us, Min,' begged Rosamond.

But Hermione had to go on. 'The only thing wrong with this country is the people. The country itself is beautiful, it's the stuff the people have put on it. If we had a population with any spirit and depth and courage, we would have an architecture. As it is, we have none.'

'We were unlucky enough to inherit the British bungalow,' said Stewart. 'But don't worry, we'll get rid of that.'

'And put what in its place?' enquired Hermione.

Rosamond flung out both hands. 'This is Sylvia's homecoming.'

But now it was Steven who had to speak. 'Lack of intelligent town planning—that's the problem.'

'A second-rate population,' said Hermione. 'That's the problem.'

Steven said, 'Min doesn't take into account—'

'And *my party*,' said Rosamond plaintively.

'—that we may not be the kind of people who express our spirit and depth and courage, as she puts it, through architecture, or any of the arts. It may be our talent to express it in areas like agricultural research, or biochemistry, or aviation. We've done good work in all of those fields, perhaps great work. To give a few examples—'

While he gave his examples, Sylvia watched Hermione lower her dark rosy face over her red drink. But the moment Steven stopped speaking, she flung back her head.

'Yes, and so we force all these clever people to live in ugly blighted cities—'

Rosamond jumped to her feet. 'Everyone will have another drink except Minnie Fyfe.'

'I'll have another Campari,' said Hermione.

'Only if you promise to shut up.'

Hermione's sudden beautiful laugh instantly lightened the mood of the room. 'All right.' She held out her glass; Stewart hurried to take it from her and give it to Steven.

'We have lovely statues, anyway,' said Rosamond consolingly, as she poured the drinks and gave them to Steven. 'All those governors in breeches with pigeons on their heads, and navigators holding telescopes, and the explorers lying down and dying, and Henry Lawson with his mate and his dog. And the politicians, I like those best, I've always wanted a long metal overcoat myself. And then in the suburbs and country towns all those little Anzacs from the first world war. And I adore those, because you can see the people were too poor to put up a man-sized one, or maybe just mean, so they made them about the size of Jazz. And they hold their guns so neatly and nicely at their sides, and don't point them at anyone, which would have been more expensive. And of course, Sylvia, the Roman statues are perfectly marvellous, they seem to be having such a good time. I can't say I like the London ones much, too grand and military, so many men riding horses and pointing with swords into the distance. It was quite a relief to get over to Dublin, where they were all reading books or had rolls of paper in their hands, and one even had a pen, and was just about to write something. And speaking of architecture, Stewart, what do you think we would get for this house?'

Stewart stopped laughing and looked keenly up at the ceiling. Steven and Hermione both looked into their glasses. Stewart stroked a cheek. 'These Spanish-type houses have stood up pretty well, generally speaking.'

'Well, I should hope so. Have you ever been through it?'

'Not that I recall.'

'Min, be a love and take Stewart through the house. I must go and see to the food. Take your drinks with you. The only room you can't go into is the cabinet room, or board room or whatever, where those two are. Steven love, would you take the glasses and cutlery down to the table in the garden. And Sylvia can come and talk to me in the kitchen.'

While Rosamond finished and assembled the food, Sylvia made a salad dressing, and Steven set cutlery and glasses on a tray.

'Needless to say,' he said to Rosamond, 'Min and I had just been looking at houses.'

'It must be painful to hold out for excellence,' said Sylvia. 'And more painful, perhaps, here?'

'It's not painful so much as silly,' said Rosamond; but Steven said, 'It is painful, Sylvia. And hard on Min herself.'

'It attracts enmity everywhere,' said Sylvia. 'Yet someone must do it, or no one gets anywhere near it.'

When Steven took the tray into the garden, Rosamond said, 'Though it's true Min can't help it. Sylvia, I want to say how pleased I am about you and Harry. I don't believe everything Guy tells me, but that sounded like one of his likelier stories. Have you had a chance to talk to Poppa about giving mother the money to carry on?'

'Rosie, I don't think Greta would like me to.'

'Oh, darling, of course she would. As soon as this thing of Ted's is off my mind I must go up there myself, I really must. Guy tells me she's selling things from the house. Put some of that dressing into this little jug, Sylvia, and I'll take it in to those two crooks.'

Rosamond, thought Sylvia with admiration, was like an actress who keeps within the confines of a light part, and rejects all temptation to enlarge it. From her present knowledge, Sylvia saw that Greta had once chosen the same way, and had played her part with the same nerve and skill. It was only now, by her comparison of the two, that Sylvia was able to estimate the extent of Greta's faltering in her part.

'That must be the cabinet room,' said Stewart.

'Ted's study,' said Hermione.

As they came out of a bedroom, they had seen Rosamond close the door of the study, and were now watching her disappear down the stairs. Hermione was holding her glass in both hands. 'And in there,' she said, turning only her head, 'is Matthew's bedroom.'

'You and I are always looking through houses.'

'What else?' said Hermione with a shrug.

'You can't say this house is ugly.'

'I didn't say every single house in Sydney is ugly. It's strange how one can't open one's mouth without being misunderstood.'

'Not considering the things that come out of yours.'

'It's quite impossible that you and I should be quarrelling, or even arguing.'

'It might be impossible, but it happens every single time we meet.'

'Matthew's bedroom.' She turned and entered it. He followed. 'Bathroom en suite?' he enquired.

'That's what they call it.' Turning her back, she stepped over a discarded wet suit and went to the window.

'Well,' said Stewart, 'only a shower room, really. Okay, though. In tip-top order.'

But his glance into the bathroom was abstracted, and after taking a few strides round the room, drinking from his glass, and scanning Matthew's music equipment, he came and stood behind Hermione at the window. Down below in the garden, Sylvia, carrying plates and napkins, was walking down the sloping lawn to the round table on the level ground under the trees. Steven moved around the table adjusting wine glasses, while at the bottom of the garden Matthew held Jason in a headlock, and Emma, flapping strands of her hair upwards, stood talking to Dominic.

Hermione said thoughtfully, 'Sylvia is rather unapproachable.' Stewart, watching his sister join Steven at the round table, spoke in the same tone. 'She sort of draws a line round herself, and the trouble is, half the time, you don't know where it is. Or I don't, anyway. So I just ignore it, and barge on.'

'I didn't find her unapproachable before.'

'She's got this bug about money. She's imprisoned by her notions about money. There's only two important things about money—how to get it, and how to keep it, and all the rest's fancy intellectual stuff.'

'Rosie is quite at ease with her.'

'Oh, Rosie's a barger, like me.'

It was the first time they had ever spoken to each other without challenge or tension, and as if both realized it in the same instant, they stood together for a few moments in silence and reflection. Steven and Sylvia were walking back to the house. Jason hooked his ankle round one of Matthew's, and both fell together to the ground. Emma looked up, saw her mother, turned her back, and flapped faster at her hair. Hermione said heavily, 'Money.'

'*Money*,' retorted Stewart, not quite in triumph.

'I used to want the very best for everyone. Now I want it only for myself.'

'Your children?'

'Sometimes,' she said fiercely, 'only for myself.'

'That's practical, at least.'

'Is it?'

'You know it is.'

She said nothing. 'It isn't as if it would be a cold-blooded thing,' said Stewart.

'But wouldn't it?'

Steven came out of the house, carrying a casserole on a board. Behind him came Rosamond with a bottle of wine and a basket of rolls.

'Oh, doing it,' said Stewart, 'yes. But not between you and me. Right here, standing here right now, and me not even touching you, you know it's not.'

Steven put the casserole carefully in the centre of the table; Rosamond put down the wine and rolls. 'Is it?' insisted Stewart.

Rosamond had turned to give a long, unguarded, intensely searching look towards the window of her husband's study. Hermione leaned out of the window and waved both arms from her joined hands, like a swimmer doing breast-stroke.

'Rosie!'

It was like a warning; Rosamond looked blank at first, then smiled joyfully, and beckoned them with an arm.

When they went down, Stewart said confidentially to Rosamond, 'I'll ring and give you an estimate during the week.'

'Any time,' said Rosamond, frankly and loudly. 'No hurry. I hope you can stay to lunch.'

'Sure. As long as I don't get a call from the office.'

The native fig tree in the Cornocks' garden had so leeched the soil that no grass grew round its buttressed roots. In the ground beneath, only a slight hollow remained of the rut once made by the feet of children using the swing. The new rope dangled over its biggest branch, which was crossed by two scars where for so many years the old rope had been tied. The big branch, flattened on its upper side, suggested a giant arm outstretched. Guy, waiting for Siddy to come from the garage with the seat of the swing, first sat on this branch then lay prone along it, shifting his head this way and that, as if in experiment, until, turning it sideways, his face towards the house, he lay still. The bark, which looked from a distance as smooth as dark flesh, was hardly rough even to the touch. Guy's eyelids were opened very wide, his face expressionless.

Nearer the house, under the prunus tree, Jack Cornock sat in his chair. He wore his spectacles, and was reading, or pretending to read, the *Sydney Morning Herald*, holding it, folded in four, upright in his good hand. It was certain that he had been able to read it earlier that morning, for he had drawn an unwavering circle, with his red felt pen, round the story of Ted Kitching's difficulties. All morning he had been in a calm, swelling, satisfied mood, but since Siddy had taken the seat of the swing to the garage, he had become disturbed; every now and again he sent a glance over the top of his paper towards Guy, in the tree, then another towards the house, where Greta could be seen moving about in the kitchen. After he had sent her a number of these glances in quick succession, her figure stood still for a while, then she came out of the house and crossed the grass. She walked slowly and reluctantly. When she was near enough for an un-obstructed view of the fig tree, she saw Guy, and diverted her course from her husband to the tree.

'Guy, where has Siddy gone?'

Guy's staring eyes did not shift. 'I am the voice of the tree,' he intoned. It was a game he had played as a child.

'Guy, where is Siddy?'

'The sap rises. The tree says, "The holes in the seat were too small." '

Greta looked at the rope. Stiff and new, it made wide angles as it hung, and was curled at one end. 'Will it be long enough?'

'The tree says, "You are making conversation." Why?'

.She glanced at her husband, who had lowered his paper and was staring fixedly at them both. 'Oh, hush,' she said wearily.

'The tree cannot hush. But here is Siddy. The spirit of the tree returns to the sap.' He sat up suddenly, astride the branch. 'Jack,' he called out cheerfully, 'you have flowers in the brim of your hat.'

Jack raised his paper again. 'Guy got the wrong rope,' said Siddy in a comforting tone to Greta, 'but I fixed the holes to fit.'

Guy was swinging his legs. 'What time is Mr Burtenshaw coming, mummy?'

Greta looked at him in mute astonishment; Siddy muttered, behind his wagging cigarette, 'I would give him mummy.'

'Any time he pleases,' said Greta at last. 'Siddy, you will check the knots, won't you?'

As she returned to the house, Siddy passed the rope through the holes in the seat. Guy, astride the branch, wound it over the old scars and, while fastening it, set his teeth together and groaned as if from strain. Siddy rose from his knees, put a hand in the fork of the tree and looked doubtfully up at the branch.

'I'll get the ladder,' he said.

'The knots are okay.'

'I said I would check them, and I will check them. I'll get the ladder.'

Guy shinned to the ground in a moment. 'Look, it's easy. I'll give you a leg-up.'

Siddy shook his head. 'I know you, with your games. I'll get the ladder.'

Guy sat on the swing. 'You've made it too high from the ground.'

'It's got to drop yet. It's not made for your weight.'

'If it can't take my weight, it's dangerous.'

But Siddy had already turned his back and was trotting across the grass. The garage and toolshed were at the front of the house, opening onto Orlando Road. Over the edge of his paper, Jack Cornock watched him go. He looked towards the kitchen, but Greta was no longer visible. In the house, the phone was ringing. Jack Cornock looked at Guy, and lowered his paper about an inch. Guy, holding a rope in each hand, drew the seat of the swing back as far as possible. Standing at the far end of the old hollow, his legs and feet neatly together, he loudly announced, 'The intrepid test pilot!' He looked at the ground to his left and his right, then sat suddenly, raised his feet and legs, and swung forward. He was forced to keep his legs quite straight, and at a right angle with his body, so that they would not scrape the ground and halt the swing. The muscles of his arms and trunk worked hard to make the swing rise. He looked only to the right and the left, smiling like a child at his own prowess, and rapidly increasing the arc made by the swing so that his feet, on each forward oscillation, drew nearer to the man in the chair. Jack Cornock sat still and looked only at the smiling face of the man on the swing, but Guy smiled only to his right and his left. The arc increased; at the peak of each forward movement the pages of the newspaper stirred. Jack Cornock could ring his bell, or he could put down his newspaper and wheel his chair out of reach; but he continued in his role of man reading newspaper, except for his glaring and misdirected eyes, while Guy continued in his role of blissful child on swing until, on an ultimate oscillation, he shifted one buttock from the seat, stretched forward one leg, pointed one toe, and, gasping with laughter, kicked off Jack Cornock's hat. As his toe touched the brim, their eyes met for the first time. Jack's were triumphant, Guy's terrified. The movement unseated Guy. He twisted in the air as he jumped from the swing, and caught the reeling seat to prevent it from striking his head. This movement temporarily diverted the attention of Siddy, approaching round the corner of the house with the ladder, from the unusual sight of Jack Cornock out of doors without a hat. At that distance, there was nothing else about Jack to attract Siddy's attention, though a closer view would have shown him that Jack was swelling once more with his triumph and satisfaction.

'You've not broken that swing?' said Siddy to Guy.

'Of course not,' said Guy. He was close to tears.

'Well, what do you know! He's thrown down his hat.'

Siddy set the ladder against the tree, went to Jack Cornock's chair, picked up his hat, brushed the clinging blossoms from the brim, and put it on Jack's head. 'You look pretty pleased with yourself today,' he said with affection. 'But, hey, steady on with that paper.'

In spite of Jack's look of contentment, the newspaper he had just raised was quaking. When Greta came out of the kitchen, carrying a glass of apple juice, Guy was standing with one foot on the swing, looking up at the branch, and Siddy was bending over Jack Cornock.

'Your paper's got the jumps,' said Siddy.

Over the edge of his quaking paper, Jack Cornock watched his wife's tired approach with exultant eyes. When she saw the paper, she stopped short of his chair. 'I think you had better put that down,' she said.

Siddy took it gently from his hand, but now the hand itself, set on the tray, went into a spasm of light tapping. Siddy, whose devotion did not include tact, laughed. 'A pill, Siddy,' said Greta. 'And Guy—' She had to raise her voice '—would you answer the door. It will be the Burtenshaws.'

Siddy put the pill in Jack's mouth. Guy sprinted across the grass. Greta held the apple juice to Jack's lips, then put the glass on his tray. While waiting for the pill to take effect, she walked over and sat on the swing, pigeon-toed, holding both ropes, her forehead resting on one hand, her eyes shut. When Siddy called out that Jack wanted her, she opened her eyes, and rose laboriously from the swing. At the same time Keith and Marjorie Burtenshaw, with a woman resembling Marjorie, came out of the porch door. Keith Burtenshaw was carrying a brief case.

'Where is Guy?' asked Greta vaguely, as she went to meet them.

'He opened the door to us,' said Keith Burtenshaw, 'and said he was just going. He seemed in a great hurry. Jack looks excited.'

Jack was looking from one to the other and beckoning them all nearer with a clawed hand. After some hesitation and exchanges of glances, they clustered round him: Greta, dull; Keith Burtenshaw, attentive; Siddy, grinning; the two women, indulgent. Exultant, his hand shaking, Jack took his red felt pen, pointed to the swing, then, on his alphabet card, pointed out the word GOD. Though dubious, they nodded encouragingly. He pointed again. SUCK. But on looking round at the faces, the headshakes of denial, his exultance fade. When he tried again—LOCK—Siddy wandered off and mounted the ladder set against the fig tree, Keith Burtenshaw glanced at his watch, and Marjorie Burtenshaw, in a whisper, introduced her friend to Greta. Jack Cornock looked angrily from face to face, and then, as if on sudden inspiration, and with a garbled sound, seized his hat from his head and hurled it to the grass.

Keith Burtenshaw, as he bent to pick it up, tutted reprovingly. 'My word, Jack,' said Marjorie Burtenshaw loudly—for she, like Sylvia, instinctively felt that he was deaf—'my word, you've got as good a head of hair as any man half your age.'

He looked at her with contempt. She laughed uncomfortably. He snatched the hat from Keith Burtenshaw's hand, put it on his head, and slanted the brim rakishly sideways between a forefinger and thumb. Then, looking into the lawyer's eyes, his own eyes questioning, he made a movement with his good hand as if writing.

Keith Burtenshaw nodded and began to open his brief case. 'You won't mind if I leave you,' said Greta, turning to the house. 'And what do you think of this weather?' said Marjorie Burtenshaw at the top of her voice to Jack, 'Is this weather good enough for you?'

After Dominic, Matthew, Emma, and Jason had quickly eaten their lunch and left to visit Dominic's friend Derek, the adults settled to the relaxed occasion, eating and drinking and being easy with each other in the matter of wit and sense, so that bursts of laughter rose often from the table. After one of these outbursts, Stewart commanded them all to look at Sylvia's pearls, and to say whether she shouldn't wear them with something a bit better than that dress. Instantly, seriously, silently, gaiety struck from their heads, they all looked at Sylvia's pearls. She touched them and said quickly, leaning forward, 'Oh, but you see, because I wear them with clothes like this, nobody will know they're real, so they won't have them off me in Rome.' And in the dispute on this, that curious moment of concentration, stillness, was merged into the general benevolence. Later in the afternoon, little absences occurred when Rosamond, or Steven, sent glances towards the window (which retained the twisted black bars removed long ago from the others) where Ted was shut up with Merrymen; but these flashes of absence were brief, hardly noticeable, and retrieved in the next moment by remarks addressed again to the table.

Stewart and Sylvia left about five o'clock. Stewart was buoyant, moving with a sort of ironic preening, and Sylvia, slightly drunk, following him with Rosamond to his car, realized with surprise that he was the kind of man she had once imagined her father speaking to on the telephone—'the kind of man my father rings up'. They both kissed Rosamond and drove away, and Rosamond returned to the living room where Hermione and Steven, with Imogen, were waiting for the two elder children to return. Down in the garden Rosamond's household help, paid double time for Saturdays, was clearing the table. Round her neck hung a transistor radio; the only sign of Ted's presence had been when he called through the window and told her to turn it off.

Steven, while they waited, abruptly shook his head at Rosamond's offer of more coffee, or another drink. Nor did he take part in the conversation, nor watch Imogen dragging herself to her feet and standing alone for three seconds, but only kept looking at his watch as if waiting demanded every scrap of his attention. When Rosamond remarked that he made her feel as if she had fallen into a well, he said 'Sorry', but at the same time looked again at his watch. When Emma and Jason returned, he leapt to his feet and told them they must all leave immediately. To Rosamond, who bent to the car window at the last moment and smiled at him in puzzled conciliation, he said goodbye pleasantly, but the car was hardly out of her hearing when his indignation burst out.

'He might at least have showed!'

'Who might?' asked Jason.

'Really, Steven,' said Hermione, in a suffering voice, 'does it matter?'

'Who might?' cried Emma.

'Uncle Ted,' Jason told her; while Steven said to Hermione, 'It was so *bloody rude*.'

'You always say you have no respect for him,' said Hermione. 'So why care so much?'

'It isn't a matter of caring. It's a matter of mere politeness.'

'Oh, how I hate those obfuscating remarks you make. They're so cowardly.'

'*What*!' shouted Steven.

'You feel snubbed by Ted. You care. Right. Then say so.'

'Snubbed? It was the *rudeness*—'

But Hermione turned her head away, and spoke out of the window of the car. 'There is a lot to be said for people who simply say what they mean.'

Emma leaned forward against her constraining belt. 'Dad does. He does so!'

'Thank you, Em,' said Steven.

Jason, sitting behind his mother, also looked out of the window, while Imogen, belted into her high seat, suddenly flapped her arms up and down, like a little penguin, and crowed with laughter.

'We will be at least an hour late,' said Marjorie Burtenshaw.

'Yes,' said Keith Burtenshaw. They were driving through Bulahdelah.

'We can't blame Sue if she doesn't keep dinner waiting. In a case like that, I thought they could just make their mark.'

Since leaving Sydney she had talked of many things but, always, she had returned to Jack and Greta Cornock.

'Like people used to do when they couldn't read or write,' she said. 'Wouldn't his mark have done?'

'It wouldn't have done him. I would only have had to go back another day.'

'It wasn't much better than a mark.'

'Neither are a lot of other signatures.'

'It absolutely exhausted me.'

'It exhausted him.'

'And when Vera and I went back into the house, there was Greta, sitting there sewing and talking to herself, as calm as you please.'

'Talking to herself?'

'Well, whispering.'

'What about?'

'We only heard something about the same cloth. But when she saw us, she said out of the blue that she and her aunt used to do embroidery, and each work a different corner of the same cloth.'

Keith Burtenshaw said nothing; his wife looked at him sideways. 'She will have the house.'

'Yes.'

'She can sell and move to a nice unit. She didn't even mention the trouble Rosamond's husband is in. If that were happening to Sue, I would be out of my mind. Has Guy inherited his father's weakness, do you think?'

'If he has, it takes a very different form.'

'When he opened the door he looked absolutely crazy, as if he had been blubbering.'

'From what I've heard about Hugh Polglaze, he would be in his element these days. He would be a guru, or some such thing, and they would be throwing flowers at him. Guy's just a common or garden bludger.'

'Well, he won't be able to get much from Greta now.'

Her husband did not reply; she looked at him sideways again. 'She has her health. Plenty of women her age take jobs these days. They prefer it. If I had my health, I would prefer it. Of course there is all this unemployment. Is she qualified for anything? What was she doing before she married Jack? Working in a shop, wasn't she? Or demonstrating cosmetics from door to door?'

'I've forgotten. At one time or another she did both.'

'Then she has two strings to her bow. She will probably start a new life, surprise everybody.'

'She looked very sick today.'

'Yes, but as calm as you please, sitting there sewing and talking to herself, and there I was shaking like a leaf, and every bone in my body screaming.'

She did not return to the subject until they were driving through Forster, when she said, 'Jack Cornock is not one of your clients I have ever actually liked.'

'He's a terrible man,' said her husband.

'Is he?' she said, surprised.

'Terrible.'

'It's getting dark,' she said. 'Sue won't keep the children up. We won't see the children before they go to bed.'

'It's funny,' said Rosamond, from her chair before the big window. 'It's really very funny. I was handing Sylvia that little glass jug, and I said, "Put some of that dressing in here, and I'll take it in to those two crooks." And all of a sudden, as I said it, I knew I wasn't joking, and that I never have been joking, and that I had known for ages that you were.'

Ted did not pause in his pacing. He had been pacing the room ever since coming out to give Rosamond the news that on Monday

133

reporters would be knocking at the door, and that the boys had better stay home from school. Showered and shaved and dressed in a dark suit, he had contracted his pacing to a line between Rosamond in her chair, and the window full of purple-blue sky, shining dark water, and clusters of lights. 'You can't have known for ages,' he said. 'It's only been going on since the property wipeout in '73.'

'Four years.' Rosamond, who was crying again, dipped two fingers into her brassière, pulled out a paper tissue, and wiped her eyes. 'So we will still be rich,' she said. 'So who will be poor? Private shareholders? Small companies?'

Ted halted at last. 'I'm sick and tired of hearing about private shareholders and small companies. As if they were bloody sacred! When all they do is bellyache! Take small risks and expect big profits! Let the directors do the sweating, yes, and then whine and bellyache if they lose a few dollars. Ah, now, look, love—' He came and earnestly leaned over her, his hands on the arms of her chair '—get out of that old thing, put some stuff on your face, and put on that black dress, and let's go out and play the wheel for a bit.'

'That place we go to is owned by a criminal. I used to get a kick out of that. But now I've got my own criminal at home.'

Ted gave a smile, quirked an eyebrow. 'That one has convictions.'

'I'm sure you will soon have a nice conviction yourself.'

'All but impossible.'

She turned her head away. 'I simply don't understand that.'

'I can only grasp it myself by its tail feathers.'

'But . . . borrowing from your own subsidiary companies, and keeping the money for your own purposes . . . if I have got that right?'

'Very roughly,' said Ted with kindness.

'Well, that's stealing.'

'Not technically, love. Technically, what we've done can't even be done.'

'But it *has* been done.'

'Yes.'

'So they'll charge you with it.'

Ted hoisted himself upright and resumed his pacing. 'Who will? The Fraud Squad? I'll take any odds against it. A bunch of coppers. What do they know about stockbroking? merchant banking? company structure? the securities business? Oh, something, sure, they've done a little course. But as much as Merrymen and I do? Don't be silly. But okay, say they get help from this new attorney-general and his men, and they frame a charge, and it stands up, and they get me past the committal proceedings, and I stand trial? All I need to do is plead "not guilty", and sit back, and let the judge and jury wrestle with the evidence. Remember the Ollin trial? An acquittal after ten months. And the Greville matter? Into its second year, that one. So, see, what jury wouldn't get discouraged? Juries—' Ted made a wiping movement with one hand '—Fffttt! They're bushed in ten minutes. Forget juries. And while you're about it, forget judges, including Derek's bloody father. No, what the bench needs, and the Fraud Squad needs, and the attorney-general needs, is men who know as much as Merrymen and me.'

'They may have them,' cried Rosamond weakly from her chair.

'No chance! They can't match the money.' He came again to stand at her chair, but this time remained upright. 'Oh, come on, Rosie. I can't stay in tonight. You must see that. I've got to go out. I've got to let go. These last weeks have been rough on me, and today's strung me up tight, tight—oh, come on, love. Get out of that chair.'

But Rosamond said, 'The boys will have to leave their school.'

'I've told you fifty times they won't.'

'They will want to.' After a pause she amended it. 'Matthew will want to.'

'Matthew is a minor, and will do as he's told.'

'I'm not a minor.'

'What?'

She shrank before his stare, but said it again. 'I'm not a minor. I am an adult. I won't live with a crook.'

He said incredulously, 'Would you desert me?'

Also incredulous, she said, 'Desert?'

'Yes. Desert me at a time like this.'

She shook her head. 'Oh, I don't know. I don't know.'

'You don't know!' His astonishment was growing. 'There is one thing you don't seem to have taken into account.'

'What?'

'It's *me* who is going through this.'

'But—'

'And who *has* been going through it. Do you think I wanted to go through it?'

'But,' said Rosamond.

'We tried to trade our way out of it, you know that. But we got boxed into this corner, and we had to box our way out. But it's me, me, me, that's had all the sweat and worry.'

'But,' cried Rosamond, '*you did it.*'

'That's what I'm saying. It was me, not you. Yet all you can do is sit there and bellyache. Now are you coming with me or not?'

Rosamond pulled the tissue out again, and again wiped her eyes. 'Not,' she said. 'And if you go on with this fraud, I can't stay with you. I *can't.*'

Stewart drove Sylvia back to the Macleay Street flat, where she immediately lay on the bed and went to sleep. She woke in the dark, and looked with a gathering frown at the lighted windows of the tower block. Her uneasiness she soon defined as guilt for failing to keep one of those appointments implicit in love: Harry would have taken for granted that she would return directly to him. And indeed, when she rang him, he was curt, and not mollified either by her explanation of drunkenness. This made her determine to take her time. Again she improvised a shower cap from a plastic bag, and while standing before the mirror, taking off her pearls, she paused to consider their rosy lustre, and came to an agreement with Hermione that they ought to be worn with cloth of a refined texture. And in that moment she was overtaken by one of her old longings for luxury, the pressure of so many wishes, for so many things, giving the moment a craziness that left each thing undefined, yet in its flashing dragnet caught them all.

Her revulsion was not only fast, but complete. For the first time in her life, her decision that she did not want those things could be held up to the light, examined, and sustained. She felt free, buoyant; it was like that moment of smiles when the plane leaves the runway. She showered quickly, eager now to reach Harry, to tell him that this old mania, which she had secretly suspected of stubborn life, had truly withered and been sloughed off. Walking impatiently round the room as she dressed, she saw the used envelope on which she had scribbled one morning her calculations on money, and had ringed, with a flourish, the remainder on which she would begin life in Rome. Casually, while drawing her dress over her head, she mentally subtracted from that remainder the money she would need for her extra month in Sydney. It made her remember her years of sums, her years of calculations, and she thought, yes, that's the trick so many people perfect without knowing it. The practical mind goes tick-a-tock with its arithmetic, but is the mechanical servant of an ideal.

She walked through the Cross to the bus. Darlinghurst Road was so crowded that the traffic had slowed almost to the pace of the pedestrians through which she absently weaved and side-stepped. The blatant music and flashing lights, the spruikers' hoarse babytalk of little titties, big titties, and botties, the ageing motor cycle boys reeling among their black machines, clutching their blonded girls, she noticed as little more than irritants, interruptions of her thoughts. From the Quay she caught a ferry, and again moved about, standing at one part or another of the rail, or watching the water comb away from the prow. She found Harry at his desk, his lamp, the only light in the room, illuminating his hands on blue paper. She felt at once a tension that told her he was still angry. As she leaned over his chair, and set a cheek against his, she guessed that this mood had often greeted Margaret. Cautiously, she rubbed her cheek against his.

'I have such a lot of gossip for you.'

'You are so sweet,' he said, without turning his head, 'when you must be.'

She would not recoil. 'I could talk to you very seriously. Or we could make love? But gossip is more insidious.'

She was pleased when he laughed. His humour had always been his talisman, keeping him from priggishness, letting him concede a little to the other side. Her string of pearls, she thought later, when they sat talking in the dark by his window and her fingertips moved instinctively over them, would perhaps do the same service for her.

Six

Ted Kitching woke in a room with shabby pink walls and faded curtains drawn across sunless windows. At the dressing table, with her back to him, sat the Vietnamese girl with whom he had spent the night.

Her arms were raised, and she was winding and pinning up her long hair. She had been sitting naked on the dressing stool for nearly an hour, waiting for him to wake, but she was now careful to avoid his eyes in the mirror, and to act as if unobserved.

Her real name had been hard for the Americans to pronounce, so they had called her Jackie. Later, in an adaptation of her name to a French meaning she liked, she had added the name of Ton, but finding this sometimes pronounced Tun, she had added another N, and was now Jackie Tonn.

She was twenty-five, but in most Australian or American eyes would have no trouble in passing for eighteen. When she had pinned up her hair, she leaned forward until her eyes were only inches from her reflected eyes. With the utmost attention and respect she flicked, as if to remove a speck, the corner of one eye with a little finger. Then she turned sideways on the stool, her back very straight, and slipped her feet into high-heeled scuffs as she rose. Without sauntering, she crossed the room to the chair on which she had laid, over the top of her expensive and glittering evening dress, the briefs and dress she meant to wear today.

Ted looked around the room. 'Damned if I remember getting here.

Jackie made no acknowledgment of this reflective remark. While putting on her briefs she bent from the waist so that he would see that even in that posture the skin of her waist was not crinkled nor her breasts pendulous.

'Jackie,' said Ted suddenly.

'Yes.'

The sound she made, almost 'yuss', was not only an attempt to correct her American accent, which betrayed her age, but to sound as curt and contemptuous as possible. She had been brought to Sydney because she was giggly and cuddly, but had lately been told, by a Malaysian Chinese girl who now drove her own car and looked very remote and steely-eyed while doing so, that to be giggly and cuddly would get her nowhere fast. The place to get, in the opinion of this Chinese girl, could be recognized by its resemblance to the ads in certain glossy magazines.

'What's your other name, Jackie?' asked Ted.

Jackie picked up her dress. 'I tell you last night,' she said with neutrality.

'I've forgotten.'

Jackie dropped the dress over her head. 'Tonn,' she said with force. With a single undulation of her body, she settled the clinging dress, which was of a cold dark blue, very skilfully cut. Ted watched her fasten the belt, then looked about the room. Frowning, he looked again at the evening dress, and at the silver shoes on their sides underneath the chair.

'What the hell are you doing in this crummy place? And more to the point, what am I doing here?'

'I wait for lease of good flat,' said Jackie. 'Decent flat hard to find.'

But Ted, as if he had not heard her, looked again around the room, then at the evening dress, then, with amusement, into her face.

'Undercapitalized, eh, Jackie?'

His smile made her clap a hand over her mouth to suppress her response, but in a moment, Ted was roaring with laughter, and had pulled her down on the bed, and she could not help giggling again.

When Douglas Merrymen rang Rosamond at noon, he told her that Ted had rung him, and that they had decided that Ted should spend today and tomorrow, at least, where he couldn't be reached, even by her. Undeterred by her silence, he went on to say that he would himself give an interview to the press tomorrow, because he was better at that kind of thing than Ted, and that the story, though it would not be in the midday editions, would almost certainly appear later.

'I don't know about television. It depends on what else they have. But it's a moral for the evening papers. For sure, they'll want pictures of the house. Ted says not to let them catch the boys. Keep the boys home from school. And he suggests you don't answer the phone unless it's someone you've given a pre-arranged signal to. If he rings you, he'll give three rings, then another three rings. And after that you answer.'

'I don't like to hang up on anyone,' said Rosamond, 'even you.'

'It's no good regarding me as Ted's bad angel, darling. My wife thinks he's mine.'

Rosamond rang off. She was alone in the house. The boys had

gone off very early, taking wet suits and surfboards. After curling her legs up into her chair, and watching the Sunday yachts, and biting the side of her thumb, she rang her mother.

'Mother, I had better tell you this now, because tomorrow it will be in the evening papers.'

'We don't take the evening papers, dear. I was just about to ring you. Poppa is very ill.'

'You mean, worse?'

Greta's voice was mechanical, bright, and thin. 'He is in a coma.'

'Lord, Lord, Lord,' said Rosamond softly.

'He was acting very strangely yesterday. He took off his hat and hurled it down on the grass. Then he got a little better, but then, when we brought him into the house, this happened.'

'You have had the doctor?'

'Of course. Though it's no use.'

'How are you, yourself, mother?'

'Well, you see, I am waiting.'

'Is Poppa, will he stay at home?'

'That was his wish. You know how he felt about hospitals. Perhaps you will tell Hermione for me.'

'Yes,' said Rosamond, 'and I won't tell you what I was going to, because it's too long.'

'If it's about Ted, don't worry, Rosie. A man who has made one fortune can make another, and Ted's a young man still. I expect you will have to sell the house.'

'Mother,' said Rosamond, 'I don't want to add to your worries—'

'There's the doctor now. I really must go.'

Rosamond clutched the receiver in both hands. 'Mother, just a moment. I won't be answering the phone tomorrow, so if you need me ring three times twice first.'

'Ring three times twice first,' said Greta, in empty obedience. 'All right, dear. Goodbye, and don't worry.'

Rosamond rang off and burst into tears, making the harbour flash with silver stars. She had not watched the harbour through tears since the quarrels of early marriage, when she and Ted had lived in a flat at Elizabeth Bay. She dried her eyes and rang Hermione, and while waiting for an answer nervously moved her upper lip over her teeth, again and again. When there was no answer, she rang Harry. He greeted her news almost with formality.

'I'm very sorry to hear it, Rosie.'

'You don't sound surprised.'

'Well—'

'I am alone in the house,' she quickly interjected, to spare him. 'Ted is in hiding, like in the movies. Come to see me.'

'Sylvia and I are just about to go to mother's.'

'But will mother want—'

'I didn't like the sound of her on the phone. And Sylvia has the right—He is dying, you know.'

'I know.'

'Sylvia won't believe it. But don't be alone, Rosie. Where's Min?'

'Out, when I rang.'

'Ring one of your friends.'

'And say, "My husband is a corporate crook," and see what happens? One would stand it, perhaps two, but they're the very ones whose husbands wouldn't. Instinct. That's the way they keep the balance, and guard the house. Or perhaps only have two bob each way. Harry, I feel better for talking to you. Don't bother about me. I'll ring Min again, then wait for the boys to come home. I'll have to tell them. And Harry, if you want me, ring three times twice first.'

When she rang Hermione again, Jason answered. 'They've all gone to look at a house, Aunt Rosie.'

'On a Sunday?'

'It's a private sale. Excuse me, Aunt Rosie, I must go.'

'Why?'

'We're playing Mastermind. Me and Nicholas Smith.'

'Jason, ask your mother to ring me when she gets home. Tell her it's important.'

'All right.'

'Tell her to ring three times twice first. Now, Jazz! Write that down!'

'All right. Goodbye, Aunt Rosie.'

Rosamond sat on the floor and watched a nature programme on television. A bearded man stood with a frog on his forearm. 'This one's a little lady frog,' he said. She went to the kitchen, sat with her elbows on the table, and read the Sunday paper with mechanical thoroughness, at the same time listening to the voices of Mr and Mrs Curry talking in the back garden next door, and the convivial noises of a party further away. Then she got up and wandered through the rooms, looking about her with curiosity. Later in the afternoon she returned to her chair with a dish of biscuits and a glass of gin and tonic. A storm came up over the harbour; the sky flowed with slate and purple, and the water turned green and blew up scuddy tops of a brilliant white. Soon the boys came running in, noisy, wet and excited.

'Go and dry yourselves,' said Rosamond, pointing at them with a biscuit, 'then come down here. I want to talk to you.'

'We only came home to change,' said Dominic. 'We're going to Derek's.'

'You wanted to hear about your father's bankruptcy. I'll tell you when you've changed.'

They were instantly subdued. 'Tell us now,' said Dominic.

'There's no need to add to your troubles by getting pneumonia. Go and change.'

In the few minutes they took to change, the rain stopped, and the wind blew the purple clouds apart to reveal a fresh and radiant sky. 'Right,' said Rosamond, taking a mouthful of her drink, 'some of your father's companies have failed, but he is no poorer than before, and won't have to sell this house.'

'That doesn't figure,' said Dominic.

'Not unless he's a crook,' said Matthew with enquiry.

'You can ask him about it yourselves, when he comes home.'

'And when will that be?' asked Matthew.

'Yes, and where is he, anyway?' asked Dominic.

'He won't be home today or tomorrow. And I don't know where he is. And he wants you to stay home from school tomorrow, in case the press catches you, or perhaps the television.'

'What would they want to catch us for?' asked Dominic. 'What could we tell them?'

'I've given you the message,' said Rosamond.

'I'm not staying home,' said Matthew. 'The media can't make you talk if you don't want to.'

'They kind of can,' said Dominic uneasily.

'Well, I've told you,' said Rosamond. 'And there is one more thing. I'm leaving your father. You have never heard me say that before, have you?'

Neither of them responded. She took another biscuit. 'Have you?'

They shook their heads.

'Then you know I mean it. So now you may go, and think about it, and leave me alone with my drinking.'

Harry and Sylvia entered the Cornocks' garden by the gate in the back fence. Greta was sitting facing the house on one of the garden seats, so that they approached her from behind. When

Sylvia heard her whisper, she drew Harry to a halt, and looked at him with enquiry.

'. . . and that one stretched right round the corner of Pitt and King Streets. The jeweller's shop where . . .'

A sudden ringing of currawongs broke into the rest. Harry went forward.

'Mother?'

She turned her head and looked at them blankly for a second or two. When she smiled and got up, she looked so little disconcerted that Sylvia doubted if she even knew she had been talking to herself. But nor was Harry disconcerted.

'How is Jack, mother?'

'There's no change.'

'Is Siddy with him?'

'Yes.' She raised her piece of sewing. 'I am stitching new lace on the hem of this petticoat. Have you come to sit with your father, Sylvia? Well, go in. Only, let Siddy stay. Don't let him leave the room, in case he's needed.'

Sylvia went to her father's room. His figure, with the arms neatly disposed beneath the bedclothes alongside the trunk, looked almost oblong, as did the big head on the pillow. When she saw his greyish skin there flashed from her memory an old German woodcarving, deeply split, seen in some museum, the effigy of a big man. Siddy's eyes, as he nodded in greeting, were sad and conspiratorial. He was rolling a cigarette.

'Do you mind if I smoke, miss?'

She was sickened by his stale odour. She smiled and said she would rather he had it outside. 'I'll call you if you're needed, Siddy.'

Conciliatory as always, he quickly rose. 'I'll be out the front.' And with his tobacco still in his palm, and the cigarette paper stuck for safekeeping to his lower lip, he creaked in his stiff boots on tip-toe out of the room.

Harry, beside his mother on the garden seat, put his forearms on his knees, clasped his hands, and leaned forward to look into her face.

'Mother, what were you whispering?'

'Was I whispering?' She examined the lace she had already attached by spreading it over the palm of a hand. 'Before we threw out a garment, Aunt Edith and I would unpick any lace or braid, take off all the buttons, press studs, hooks and eyes, then cut out the least worn bits and use them for dusters.'

'We *know* about Aunt Edith. That's not what you were whispering.'

'We went into this once before.'

'I wouldn't persist—' He was raising and lowering his heels on the grass '—if it weren't obvious that you *want* to talk to someone. Or else why do you whisper?'

'If you have something you want to speak of, do you invariably come to me?'

'No.'

'Nor I to you.'

'Least of all to me, or to any of us.'

'Oh, you are all always rushing here, and rushing there. You all have so little time.'

'We would make time. I would make time. But it's as if you want to keep us—me—yes, all of us—inviolable.'

'Oh, it's too late,' she burst out with impatience, 'it's too late to alter old patterns. I shouldn't be asked to make that effort now.'

'Well, then, I'm sorry.' He unclasped his hands and leaned back in the seat. 'You know about Ted's troubles?'

'Oh, Ted and his troubles!'

'Rosie would like it if you gave her a ring today or tomorrow, mother.'

'Yes, yes,' she said with regret. 'Poor Rosie. I will.'

'First ring her three times twice. Before I go, I'll write that down on the telephone pad.'

'You speak as if I am senile.'

He never teased her, or condescended to her, but now he spoke as he might have done to a flagging colleague. 'You have a lot on your mind. It helps to make memos. When did the new swing go up?'

'Yesterday. Siddy and Guy put it up just before Jack's trouble started, and Keith and Marjorie Burtenshaw came with some woman who acted as a witness.' Again she spread the lace and examined it, tilting her head and retracting her chin. 'It seems possible that Sylvia will have a good deal of money. Is she quite set on returning to Rome?'

'Quite,' he said curtly.

She smiled at the lace. 'It isn't always a bad thing, you see—the barrier between us. Well, never mind, dear, she is too old to start having children. And in any case, she isn't the type.'

He laughed. 'True, I suppose. You sound much better than you did on the phone.'

'It's stronger at some times than others. Is that why you came?

Because of how I sounded on the phone?'

'Partly, mother.'

'Well, thank you, Harry. But as you see, I am all right now. Don't think me ungrateful, but I need to be quiet and undisturbed.'

'That's difficult, because Sylvia has the right—'

'Of course,' she said, in the prompt way in which she used to concede Molly's claim on Sylvia. 'But you are not Siamese twins, even though it may temporarily feel like it. Sylvia may come alone.'

'*She* doesn't intrude?'

'I can depend on her for that,' said Greta drily. 'There is a good train service. Let her come whenever she likes. Only, there is nothing she can do. Nothing. Today is a beautiful day. Now that she has done her duty, why not take her out somewhere?'

Harry got to his feet and put a hand on his mother's shoulder. When he bent and kissed her cheek, she dropped her sewing, and in a moment of disarray, gripped his hand with hers. 'I'm sorry, dear,' she said.

'Okay,' he said with resignation. 'I'll go and see what Sylvia wants to do.'

In the hall, he tore off a page of Greta's geometric scribbles and wrote down his reminder of Rosamond's signal. The door of Jack Cornock's bedroom stood half open; he tapped as he entered.

When he saw Sylvia kneeling on the floor, one arm outstretched to reach beneath a clothes cupboard, he hurried towards her, glancing sideways at the bed. Jack Cornock lay in disturbed sheets, one hand hanging over the side of the bed. When Sylvia heard Harry's footsteps, she turned upward a flushed face wet with tears, then scrambled to her feet with a single pearl in her hand. The others she drew from one of her pockets; they hung from a broken string. She stood holding them in the cup of her two hands, her shoulders hunched forward, while she looked indecisively into his face.

'Have you got them all?' he asked slowly.

'I think so.'

'Where is Siddy?'

'In the front garden. I told him he could go.' She smiled faintly. 'It was the smell.'

Harry went to the bed, straightened the sheets, put Jack Cornock's hand outside the covers, and stood feeling the pulse in one of his wrists. 'Was he conscious?' he asked in a low voice.

She hesitated. 'He can't have been.' Then she said stupidly, 'He opened his eyes, he opened his eyes . . .'

'We had better get Siddy to come back.'

She nodded. As they crossed to the door she said, 'When he opened his eyes, he thought I was Greta.'

'Why do you think so?'

'I once saw him look at her exactly like that.'

Outside the door, he halted them both, and put his hands beneath her cupped hands. 'I've been afraid of something like this.'

'Afraid for your mother?'

'Yes.'

'Is she?'

'Not of this. I don't think it's of this. She's cautious, that's all. Very cautious.'

'I've seen his enmity.'

'His threat,' said Harry. 'I've seen his threat. But I didn't want to make anything big of it.'

'Well. that's it. One doesn't. Greta will have to get him into a hospital.'

'Yes. But before we go out there, how about putting those pearls away, and doing something to your face.'

'I left my bag in there.'

Harry went back and picked up her bag. Jack had not moved. Again Harry felt his pulse, and as he put the hand back on the bedcover, he lightly, consolingly, patted it. He called Siddy from the garden, then took Sylvia's bag to the bathroom. She was at the handbasin, drying her face.

'When did it all begin? she asked. 'I don't mean the real beginning. I know about that. But when did it become so active?'

'I first noticed it between the two strokes,' said Harry. 'Just after the first one, mother found a lump in one of her breasts. And he was so pleased. It was pathetic. A childish joy. He couldn't suppress it. But then the lump turned out to be benign, and the next time I saw them, the cloud had come down. But I wasn't seeing them continuously, so I didn't put two and two together at the time. It's only these past few weeks that I've been really apprehensive. Not of his doing her great physical harm. He's not strong enough for that. But of violent episodes, perhaps.'

'Hostility, of course,' she said, 'is a common symptom.'

'Quite. But I doubt if it often takes the extreme form of what just happened to you. She doesn't want it brought out into the open, that's the difficulty. It's such a private thing between them, maybe even an intimate thing. I've hesitated. But I'll do it now. I'll bring it out now.'

'Guy knows. That's what he whispered that night at the car.'

'Then is that why *he* has been coming so often?' But Harry looked disbelieving even as he asked the question, and he rejected it to say, 'I hope to God she'll agree to getting him into a hospital without a lot of fuss.'

But when, after they had sat with Greta for ten minutes of carefully desultory talk, the suggestion was made by Harry that Jack be moved to a hospital, Greta cut off a new length of thread and murmured that it wouldn't be necessary. 'I have engaged a professional nurse,' she said.

As she raised her head to thread her needle, they both saw, on the side of her neck, the bruise formerly hidden by her collar.

'Now what good will a nurse be?' Harry asked angrily.

But the front doorbell rang at that moment, and Harry presently opened it to a thickset young man with curly red hair and a curly red beard, whom even a man still half immersed in a dream or a nightmare could not mistake for a woman. In a light sweet voice, he said his name was Benjamin Thomas, but that everyone called him Ben.

Harry and Sylvia drove to the Kuring-gai Chase and began to walk to the sea by crossing the sandstone tops on one of the narrow walking tracks. Sylvia remembered that she had once come here with school friends, and that while crossing the flat, stony expanse, among the insignificant low scrub, they had felt tall, bright, important; had capered, shouted, and sung. Today she was despondent and angry, yet unable to find a direction for her anger. At first she and Harry spoke in snatches of speculation about Greta and her father, but then Harry drew ahead of her and picked up a stick, which he occasionally beat against the track.

But when twice they passed other walkers, Harry was able to suspend his mood, and to smile, and to nod with a sideways twist of the head that acknowledged an appreciation shared. Sylvia also smiled. The low scrub was not as insignificant as she had once thought. Among the spidery or attenuated foliage were many flowers, some so small that she had to crouch to examine them. Only their profusion gave a brush of colour to the bushes. Harry fell back so that they were walking side by side. 'What mother was whispering about when we arrived,' he said, 'about one of them stretching round the corner of Pitt and King Streets. That would be one of the queues she stood in to get a job.'

'At her age, most people are only too willing to talk about early hardship.'

'She never mentions her humiliations.'

'That's your theory?'

'Yes.'

When the track began to descend, they stopped talking and went forward to the sound of their own footsteps. Sylvia would stop to look at flowers, or to pick up and examine one of the small pebbles, subtly shaded with tan or lavender, from the whitish ground of the track. In a gully, bushes rising high on either side reminded her of how she had walked through banks of flowers in the Gardens, and made her compare the rich opulence of those with the hard, tenacious growth of these, and that insistent perfume with this light occasional scent. Whenever she stopped, Harry would stop and wait with her, but with an air of abstraction. She understood that he was still immersed in thoughts of his mother, for whenever they had spoken of Greta, his mood had always continued quiet and abstracted. They had begun to speculate on Jack and Greta, very tentatively, while driving in Harry's first car, with Sylvia's hand, along the back of the seat, touching his shoulder. They had continued, less tentatively, walking round the city, or lying on beaches or in parks. But only four years ago, in London, in a long conversation which included Margaret, had Sylvia confessed to her early enmity of Greta, and then only in its lighter aspects. It had been her response to Harry's disclosure of an enmity towards Jack, but Harry added that he and Rosamond were so entrenched in their roles of helping Greta with the younger two, that in his care to maintain towards Jack an example of affability, he had found the worst of his enmity dissolved. Besides, he had no Molly to exacerbate his pity, and to egg him on.

The long conversation in London began when Harry told Sylvia and Margaret how the newspaper story of Jack and Molly Cornock's divorce, by its tone, its combination of crude humour, salacity, and indignant gentility, had teased his imagination, and had led him later, while waiting for books from the stacks, or after finishing a period of study, to make a practice of browsing in the newspaper room. In the columns of the twenties, among photographs of prize rams, sportsmen, young women about to be presented at court, and politicians laying wreaths on monuments to the Anzacs, he would see an occasional photograph of one of the Anzacs themselves, and would be haunted by his mother's father. He looked at goods for sale, noted prices, read stock market reports, looking for nothing in particular, yet hoping to gain from all this general information a distillation, an authentic whiff of the past. He saw the débutantes, the prize beasts, the sportsmen, and the politicians go forward into the thirties, while in the classified advertisements the jobs dwindled and died, and sales of houses 'by order of the mortgagees' swelled, as did offers to buy furniture, jewellery, or bank accounts at less than twenty shillings in the pound. Harry looked through these newspapers in the light of Greta's own disclosures on the times, the bright even stream of her everyday conversation. She produced on Harry's request photographs of her mother and father, kept for her by Aunt Edith, and a very faded one of Aunt Maud, to whom she had gone first, and whom she hardly remembered. For Greta's children, the actuality of their mother's life began when Edith had taken her from Maud. Harry and Rosamond, especially Harry, had their own clear memories of Aunt Edith, and the vague memories of the other two were reinforced by hearing her words quoted, and her habits cited.

When she took Greta, Edith was a spinster employed as a clerk in a shipping office. Harry gathered from Aunt Edith a suggestion of rescue in her taking Greta from Maud. In any case, Greta must have been happy with her Aunt Edith, for she mentioned her of her own accord; indeed, almost too much, so that for a while Aunt Edith was threatened with the fate of Jack Cornock's sack, and Rosamond and Sylvia, as they threw away laddered stockings, remarked that Aunt Edith would have sat up all night darning them. Aunt Edith and Greta shared the housework, and in the evenings would listen to a radio programme while they mended, sewed, or embroidered; or they would read a library book together, sitting side by side at the dining room table, Aunt Edith waiting for Greta to finish the page before she turned it, an order that was reversed as Greta grew older.

Aunt Edith lost her job in 1930, and about this period Greta was less talkative, only remarking how lucky it was that she was old enough to leave school and get a job herself. At thirteen, though inexperienced, she was cheap to hire, so perhaps she did not have to stand in too many of the queues. Her first job was in a big store, unpacking china, glass, and silver; she was always happy to talk about silver markings, and the patterns and quality of china.

Aunt Edith confided to Harry that by concealing the fact that there was an employed person in the house, she continued to collect her coupons to take to the shops, where they were exchanged for food. She was also careful who she let into the back

yard of her tiny rented cottage in Petersham, for Aunt Edith
believed that if the social service people got to hear about her
vegetables they would stop her coupons or, later, when money
was substituted for coupons, her dole. In this she was wrong, but
Harry found that belief itself instructive. Aunt Edith said that
Greta was also sworn to secrecy about the vegetables, but Greta,
laughing, said she didn't remember a thing about it.

It was Aunt Edith who earnestly told Harry never to believe
that his father had always been "like that". But here Harry's own
memory joined the track of Aunt Edith's stories; for he himself
remembered his father dressed in a dark suit, just about to go by
tram to his work in the city. Hugh Polglaze worked in the same
shipping office as Aunt Edith had done. She told Harry that
spiritualism, and such practices as table-turning, had quite a
vogue in those days, and that nobody thought it odd when he
began to read and quote books by Indian mystics. Nobody could
have foretold the beard and the handwoven blouses that got him
the sack at last, in spite of so many kindly warnings. When Aunt
Edith heard that he intended to take his family, with the people he
called his "followers", to live on a farm beyond Parramatta, she
begged Greta to come back with the two children to live at Petersham. Greta refused.

Aunt Edith took in a boarder, a pale, quiet, asthmatic young
man named Vincent. Occasionally Vincent drove Aunt Edith in
his car to see Greta, but Aunt Edith was always so disturbed by
what she saw that she went less and less often. Greta, against her
husband's edict, refused to feed her children on only the meagre
products of the land rented with money supplied by the followers.
She served in a grocer's shop in the nearest township, taking
Harry in the bus with her, and dropping him at the nearest
primary school. After school he used to walk to the grocer's shop
and sit in the back among the packing cases until Greta stopped
work and took him home. He remembered getting off the bus in
the dark, then holding the torch with which they lit their way
home across the paddocks. Greta was so extremely taciturn about
this period of her life that Harry could only infer, by talking with
Rosamond, that the other two children were looked after by
Hugh Polglaze and the followers. When Hugh Polglaze went to
prison they all continued to live as before in the farmhouse and
outbuildings, but at this point there was a small eruption of their
lives into public, for the case of Hugh Polglaze's objection to war
service, his appearance with his followers in court, their loose
clothes, long hair, and peculiar diet, made a story for the press

which Harry read later, with great attention, in the newspaper files. One of the Sunday papers had used as a lead Hugh Polglaze's aversion to cameras. SNAPS SATANIC SAYS SELF-STYLED SEER. When Hugh Polglaze came out of jail, his followers took his changed appearance and extreme emaciation for marks of holiness; but after leukaemia was diagnosed, they fell away, one by one, until all were disbanded. Aunt Edith may have been right when she told Harry that they were so superstitious and hysterical that they thought they would get it too. Greta took Harry and Rosamond to see their father before he died. Hugh Polglaze put his hand on Harry's head and said something about the earth that Harry immediately forgot. Then he told Greta that she was looking worried again, and that by her worry she was hampering God's will. Rosamond hid under his bed, where Greta let her stay, so to her he said nothing. He died the next day.

The persistence of Greta, a good-looking, practical, ambitious young woman, in such a marriage could be explained only by Aunt Edith's sighing verdict of love, hope and pity. Margaret and Sylvia and Harry, in London, had agreed on this, concluding that Greta had loved him deeply, hoped for many years that he would revert to his former ways and, in the last years of his life, had pitied him as deeply as she had once loved him.

After his death, Aunt Edith came and offered again to take the family into her cottage. Of all Harry's childhood memories, this was the most vivid. Aunt Edith said, 'It would be like old times, Grete,' and Greta replied, 'No, it wouldn't, aunty.' Harry was eating one of the cakes Aunt Edith had brought, and as soon as he understood that his mother was refusing the offer, he burst into tears and sprayed Aunt Edith and his mother with cake crumbs. After Aunt Edith went off in Vincent's car, he hung around Greta, whimpering, and asking why they couldn't go to Aunt Edith's, until suddenly she rounded on him and told him to shut up. And with that one action she stepped, for her young son, into the resolute, authoritarian, and secretive character she had maintained, with minor variations, ever since. Long after, he understood that they would have displaced Vincent, with whom Aunt Edith continued to live in contentment until she died when Harry was eleven.

Greta, pregnant with Guy, came back to Sydney with the three children. They travelled in a truck driven by a friend of the grocer for whom Greta had worked. Greta sat beside the driver with Hermione in her lap, and Harry and Rosamond sat in the tray of the truck, wildly happy, holding onto the fibre suitcases and the pram, and singing songs. In Sydney began the period recalled so vividly by Harry and Rosamond. Harry believed that at this stage Greta asked Hugh Polglaze's family for help, and was refused. He knew he had relatives in Sydney, but Greta, when asked about them, said she did not know them, nor want to.

After Guy was born, Greta worked in a dress shop where the commission on sales, added to her wages, gave her just enough to keep her family. But the war, which was barely over, had caused a great shortage of accommodation of all kinds. Large sums of money were illegally paid for the "keys" to flats and houses (and at least one Sydney fortune founded). With a year's wages, Greta could have bought one of these "keys". Harry, in the newspaper room of the public library, joined the track of public knowledge to his own when he saw columns of pleas for accommodation, often desperately worded, and, as in the early thirties with jobs, a complete absence of advertisements for houses and flats to let. Aunt Edith was still safe in her rented cottage in Petersham, but she was now working as a tea lady, so when she took a child to mind at the weekends it would be Harry, whom she could take out in her back garden to help to weed or dig or plant, who was sensible enough to talk to, and who seemed to know instinctively when Vincent was not well.

Some of their landladies were kind, and Harry thought it possible that all of them tried to be. Even the woman he butted with the carpet sweeper may have had good intentions at first. But somehow or other, the noise and chaos of four children, the wet beds, the tantrums, the colds and the strain and anxiety of their over-worked mother always wore them down, and either made them give up or turned them into martinets or bullies. When Harry, talking to Margaret and Sylvia in London, had tried to assess the influence on his mother's life of public events, it was never to the big or dramatic ones that he had given first place. It was not the first world war, the influenza epidemic, the Depression, or the second war; it was always that hum-drum event— hardly an event at all: a condition—the housing shortage after the war, when, he said, she must have felt like a stray cat with a yowling litter. Sylvia and Margaret argued that he gave it that importance only because he personally remembered it; but on this point Harry was adamant, and he had always admired his mother for getting them out of it and into a decent flat—and in charge of the Spanish girl he and Rosamond remembered with affection—without any help from anyone. But Sylvia would be silent when he said that, for Greta's job of demonstrating cosmetics from door to door seemed too profitable to be credible, and she privately agreed with Molly's loud and often repeated assertion that Jack Cornock had known Greta for longer than he had pretended, and had been giving her money from the start.

The track was still descending, and now a deep gully on their left disclosed at its end a triangle of sea.

'Can't we get down to it?' asked Sylvia.

'Not that way. At the end of the track we can climb down the cliff.'

She loitered, unwilling to leave the sight of those two slopes of hard, resistant, spiky land holding in a ragged V the dense seductive sea. When she caught up with Harry she said, 'Shall we have time to get down to it and back to the car before dark?'

'If we hurry.'

But when the track became steeper, and from the deeper soil of the gullies big trees with smooth trunks and branches rose towards and almost obscured the sky, she felt on her arms a few drops of rain. They stopped and looked up at patches of sky of an unchanged blue. But as they climbed down to the flattened floor of a gully still damp from past rain, the storm Rosamond had watched, as it drove over the harbour, reached the Chase and broke with great force. Harry and Sylvia found shelter under a projecting ledge in a massive assemblage of iron-grey stone beside the track. They crouched uncomfortably, their shoulders bowed, watching the water beat the scrub and scour the earth from beneath the sandstone ridges crossing the track. Presently two boys and two girls appeared on the track. All were about sixteen, and had been caught in light clothes. Their wet hair flat on their heads, and their sodden garments beaten against their bodies, they strolled as indifferently as through sunshine, breaking their casual gait only by the long springing strides needed to cross the sandstone ridges. Sylvia thought their nonchalance stylish; they made her critical of her own and Harry's concern for comfort and dryness; but when she suggested that they should crawl out of their ignominious niche and go back to the car, he absolutely opposed her, so that when the sun came out, and (since it was now too late to go on) they began the journey back, it was she who was silent. But when they reached the flat tops, and she felt the strong wind blowing, she was glad to be dry. The wind sounded eerie and relentless as it passed over the high flat land, opposed only by scrub. It resisted the passage of their bodies, and they put their arms round each other, and bent their heads, and trudged into it.

Seven

On Monday morning, Rosamond rang Hermione.

'Min, did Jazz give you my message?'

'What message?'

'Then he didn't.'

'Don't sound so accusing. Jason's only thirteen. And he's usually very good at things like that.'

'It was about Ted. I wanted to tell you about Ted . . .'

After Rosamond had told Hermione the story, she said, 'And now I want to say this, so that nobody else can get in first. Ted is a corporate crook. He is a boardroom swindler.'

Hermione was in the kitchen. She looked at the upright iron on the ironing board, then reached over and clicked off the switch.'Is that what they were doing shut up in the room on Saturday?'

'As it turns out, yes.'

'How awful.'

'That sounds almost polite.'

'What else can I be?'

Rosamond, curled into her chair, was once again alone in the house. Matthew, as she had predicted, had refused to stay home from school, and by the impetus of his pride and defiance had carried Dominic with him. Rosamond said, 'Try to be something else, Min.'

'Who will bear the losses?'

'I just told you.'

'I don't get it. Small businesses? Private shareholders? And you won't be poor?'

'Ted won't be.'

'But he'll be charged with, with, whatever it is. Fraud, isn't it? He'll go to prison.'

'He says not.'

'Why not?'

'He says that if he's charged,' said Rosamond laboriously, putting a hand across her forehead, 'all he has to do is plead not guilty, and they won't have the skill to convict him.'

'But he can't get away with that,' said Hermione excitedly. 'That's stealing.'

'Minnie, I said it first.'

'Or am I being simplistic?' asked Hermione bitterly. 'Because they *do* get away with it. There have been those other cases. And those men are at large, living on the fat of the land.'

'Oh, Min, don't mention fat. I've got such a hangover.'

But Hermione said with force, 'And even if they do go to prison, they come out to their money and houses and boats.'

'What was the house like?' asked Rosamond. 'The one Jason said you saw yesterday.'

'I don't even want to talk about it. Mother doesn't know about Ted. I rang her just now, and she didn't mention it.'

'She has probably forgotten all about it,' said Rosamond sadly. 'Only a few weeks ago, she would have been on this phone, trying to boss me about. But of course, she can only think of Poppa at present.'

'She has a professional nurse there, and Poppa's condition may go on for weeks. And it's no use saying you mustn't think of expense at a time like this, because you can't help it. And Keith Burtenshaw was there again on Saturday. Mother and her ridiculous pride! Playing the game by the rules. That's what you get for keeping the rules. Ted's got the right idea.'

'I don't want to go on with this conversation, Min. You're horrible to talk to when I'm in trouble.'

'Rosie,' said Hermione, with the vibrato of love. 'Darling! I'm sorry.'

Rosamond burst into tears. 'I've been awake all night.'

'Rosie darling, it's not your fault. You didn't know it was happening. It's no use lying awake thinking about it.'

'I wasn't thinking, I was drinking. And I suppose if I had made a real effort, I could have found out what was happening.'

'Hindsight. Don't be hard on yourself.'

'I'm going to leave Ted.'

'Are you?' Hermione's voice rose with each word. 'Oh, but are you *really*?'

'I can't live with a cold-blooded criminal. A hot-blooded one, yes. Oh, my head.'

'What about the boys?'

'I hope they won't choose to live with a cold-blooded criminal either.'

'But who will keep them?'

Rosamond shut her eyes, leaned her head against the back of the chair, and moaned.

'You see?' said Hermione. 'You'll have to accept money from Ted for their keep, which means you'll be accepting money got by fraud. So if his fraud is your reason for leaving, what's the point?'

'I love the way you put things, Min.'

155

'You do want me to be frank?'

Rosamond opened her eyes and raised her head. 'Well, I want someone to be. Yes, in fact, I'm glad of it. There's that Chinese ship going out, the one I watched coming in ages ago, when I thought everything was all right. When I hoped everything was all right, only knew it wasn't.'

'I saw a Chinese ship,' said Hermione slowly, 'one day when I went over to look at a house Stewart had for sale. You would miss that house, Rosie. You have great comfort, and some beauty, and some luxury. Oh, and I do think beauty and luxury are wonderful.'

One of their silences fell. Rosamond watched the Chinese ship, black and ochre, passing behind Shark Island. Hermione's voice, when it came at last, had its dogmatic intonation.

'It's useless taking a stand unless you have a body of opinion behind you. It's easy enough in the beginning, because it's exciting, but then when you settle down to it, you start coming on like a bit of a freak. Like Sylvia, with a sort of circle drawn round you. Or me, with my insistence on quality. You might as well stay with the strength, Rosie, and be done with it.'

'You really think the strength will be with Ted?'

'Much more than it will be with you, a poor woman of thirty-seven.'

'All the same, I think I must leave.'

'Well, perhaps Harry will pay the boys' school fees.'

'School fees!' moaned Rosamond, putting a hand again to her forehead. 'I did want them to have that continuity. I was absolutely determined. Oh, I don't know. I can't think. I'm too sick.'

'No one will be surprised if Harry marries Sylvia, and it looks as if *she* will have plenty of money. She came back at absolutely the right time. There's no doubt about it, Rosie, if you want to get money, or you want to keep it, you *can't have* scruples. You *can't be* nice. If I were you, *I* wouldn't leave Ted.'

'Min,' said Rosamond, 'I had better go and get some sleep. Merrymen says the papers and the telly may come here to get the story.'

'So what are you supposed to do?'

'Keep them from the boys. Because of the publicity. And because,' she added, 'Matthew would be silly, and hit them.'

'And you'll stop him?'

'Yes.'

'How?'

'I can't think of anything until I've had a sleep. They don't get out of school till three. And it may not even happen. No press people have rung yet. Nobody's rung but Harry. Min, I told Jazz to tell you this – if you want to reach me, ring three times twice first.'

'Jason must have forgotten,' said Hermione with control.

As soon as Rosamond replaced the receiver, the telephone rang. It kept on ringing, one call immediately followed by another. Rosamond put her hands over her ears and went upstairs. As she drew the blind of her bedroom window, she saw a car stop in front of the house. A television van followed it. She set her alarm for two o'clock, then lay on the bed and put a pillow over her head. She lay on her back, stiffly, trying to ignore the ringing of the telephone, and of the bell on the door in the wall protecting the house.

Hermione still stood in her kitchen, her arms folded along the top of the refrigerator, and her forehead resting upon them. Hermione and Steven, after the quarrel that had erupted on the way home from Rosamond's lunch, had passed Sunday in silence until the truce needed to look together at the house for sale. But after seeing the house, a new quarrel had broken out. Or perhaps the former one was resumed; to distinguish was impossible.

A train passed. Imogen crawled out of the living room and pulled herself upright against a bench. Hermione swore, and reached out to take the upright iron from the board and put it on its stand. Then she rang Stewart Cornock's office. A woman told her that Stewart was not in. Would she like to leave her name? Hermione replied curtly that she would ring another time. She rang off and said, 'Imogen, leave that *alone*!'

Imogen was taking the earth out of the pot of geraniums on the balcony. Hermione swept up the earth and put it back, then washed Imogen's hands. 'All the same,' said Hermione, out of her meditation, as she did this, 'you're the one I will take.'

Rosamond pushed the pillow off her head with both hands and jumped to her feet. Her face was red and her eyes were puffed with weeping and sleep. She stood for a while as if she did not know where she was, then said, 'Oh, my *God*!' and rushed to the window.

The cars and the van were gone; the telephone was not ringing. She looked at the bedroom clock. 'Oh, my *God*!' she said again, and rushed out of the room and down the stairs.

The clock in the hall confirmed that it was ten to three. In the living room, the telephone gave three rings, then was silent, gave three more, and was again silent. When the ringing resumed, she picked up the receiver.

'Oh, it's you, mother.'

'Who did you expect?'

'I suppose—yes, Ted.'

'Well, I saw this note by my telephone, dear, in Harry's writing, and remembered about Ted's trouble, so I'm just ringing you to tell you not to worry. If it's money you want, a man who has made one fortune can make another, and Ted's a young man still.'

Rosamond's face filled with awe as she heard her mother prattling off the same speech as yesterday. She said childishly, 'I've been asleep. I lay down for a few minutes and went fast asleep for hours and hours.'

'It will do you good,' Greta assured her.

'But I must pull myself together. The boys . . .' Rosamond put a hand to her forehead. 'But how is Poppa?'

'A little worse.'

'Oh dear, oh dear,' said Rosamond. 'All the same, I must go. This instant.'

'Of course, Rosie. Everything here is very calm. Ben is a blessing.'

Rosamond rang off and rushed up the stairs to the window. The car had come back, and the television van arrived as she watched. She ran into her bedroom, picked up the telephone directory, and swiftly turned the pages, muttering, until she found the number she wanted. When it answered, her voice was calm and assured.

'Alison?'

'Yes. Who is it?'

'Rosamond Kitching.'

'I thought it was,' said Alison Pyne flatly. The Pynes lived at the top of the street; Matthew and Dominic usually came home with their son Andrew.

'Would you do something for me, Alison?'

'What?'

'If the boys come home with Andrew, take them in there for a while. I don't know if you've heard—'

'I've heard.'

'Well, there's a telly van outside. If the boys could just stay there until—'

'No,' said Alison.

'Alison, the boys have done nothing.'

'The whole thing is absolutely indecent, absolutely rotten. A few crooks like your husband get all the rest of us a bad name. If you think everything can just go on as before, you're totally mistaken. If the law can't do anything, decent people can.'

'You won't go to heaven when you die,' shouted Rosamond.

'And now to make jokes about it!'

'I don't like to hang up on anyone—'

'You needn't,' said Alison Pyne, as she hung up.

Rosamond took off her dress and put on pants with a bursting zipper, a shirt, and canvas shoes. The phone was ringing again. She ran down into the garden at the back of the house, picked up a garden chair, and carried it to the side fence. At the third attempt she managed to hoist herself to the top, and for a moment hung with her head on one side and her legs on the other, and the top of the fence pressing into the soft flesh of her belly. Then, gasping with fright, she awkwardly drew up one leg. As she flung it over the fence, the zipper parted and the crotch of her pants tore. She flung the other leg over, fell into the Currys' bed of marigolds, sprang up, and raced across their lawn, ducking at one point to avoid the clothes drying on the hoist. She did not look towards the Currys' house. Rosamond was slightly knock-kneed, and as she ran she flipped her legs from side to side. The Currys also had garden chairs; she grasped one as she passed. The fence was the same as the first, but the chair was higher, so she managed to get over without much difficulty, though she broke one of Amy Gow's boronia plants as she dropped to the ground, and the branch of a rose bush, borne down with her, scratched her cheek as it sprang back into place. Amy Gow's ninety-year-old mother, sitting in the sun, wearing an Indian blanket and a straw hat with its brim compressed by a scarf and tied under the chin like a Regency bonnet, watched without surprise as Rosamond ran panting across the grass, snatching up a white cast-iron chair on the way. This chair was rather low, and she had to make a number of preliminary little jumps, or bobs, before she could get up the impetus to rise to the top of the brick fence, on which she lay sprawled for a while before falling bodily, striking a cheekbone on the way, onto the Pearsons' lettuce bed. Mr Pearson, a retired barrister, had just come home from bowls. Having put away his car, he came out of the garage in time to see Rosamond, whom he knew only by sight, running laggingly across the lawn. She was panting laboriously, her clothes were dirty and torn, her belly and breasts shaking, and her blue eyes staring out of a red, sweating, scratched, bruised face. He flung back his head and shoulders and watched in gentlemanly affront as she picked up the step ladder he has been using that morning, staggered with it to the fence, mounted it, and disappeared over the other side.

The drop from the Pearsons' wall took Rosamond into the Pynes' back garden. She stopped and wiped her face on the sleeve of her shirt. Drawing hoarse painful breaths, but no longer running, she crossed the garden diagonally and reached the driveway at the side of the house. Alison Pyne's head appeared at a window.

'Rosamond!'

Rosamond, with no wind left for anything but breathing, shook her head and continued to trudge up the driveway towards the street.

'Rosamond, I've been trying to ring you to say how sorry–'

But Rosamond did not turn her head. She had reached the front fence before Alison Pyne had time to run through the house and accost her.

'Rosamond, of course they can come in.'

Rosamond was getting her breath back. 'They can—go—and wait—in the public—library.'

Alison grasped Rosamond's arm. 'No. I would never forgive myself. Oh, if you *knew how you looked!*'

'Let me go.'

'Your pants.'

The boys—Matthew, Dominic, and Andrew Pyne—carrying their straw hats and their cases, turned the corner. Seeing the two women, one dirty and dishevelled in the extreme, and one at the other extreme of neatness, struggling with each other, they came to an uncertain halt.

'What's up, mother?' asked Andrew Pyne.

'Andrew, you are to bring Matthew and Dominic into the house.'

'No,' said Rosamond, pulling her arm free. 'Matthew. Dominic. Go to the library.'

'Your pants,' said Alison, into her ear.

'Tell us why first,' said Matthew. He did not look at his mother, who now stood with a hand covering her crotch.

'A television van at the house,' said Alison Pyne briskly. 'So come along.'

'Two,' amended Dominic. 'Look, you can see them from here.'

With determination, Matthew put on his hat and walked on. 'Hey!' called Dominic after him.

'Matthew!' called Rosamond weakly.

Matthew did not turn round. 'Oh, my *God!*' said Rosamond.

Dominic quickly smoothed down his hair, put on his hat, and went after Matthew, taking long strides. Alison Pyne took Rosamond's arm again.

'Well, *you* can't go, not looking like that. So come along in.'

But Rosamond, faintly crying, 'Matthew! Dom!' pulled her arm out of Alison's grasp, and with one hand still on her crotch, and her legs flipping from side to side, ran after the boys.

'Well, come on, Andrew,' said Alison Pyne. 'Don't stand there staring like a cretin. Come along in.'

Mrs Gow and Mrs Curry, though they did not make a practice of talking across the fence, were looking with bewilderment at their broken plants and saying that it must have been a very big dog. Mrs Gow's mother, who had already forgotten what she had seen, but who wished to be included in the conversation, said in her tiny voice that it was that big white dog of the Woodhouses, but this earned only a patient smile from her daughter, for the Woodhouses, and their dog, had been dead for a decade.

Sylvia, after driving Harry to work in the Western Suburbs, made the long drive up to Wahroonga. She was shocked to see Greta's face, the glaring blue and reddened whites of her eyes, the vertical lines so conspicuous on her cheeks, the long mouth slack. On her seat in the garden, she unwillingly raised her eyes from her sewing to greet Sylvia. Sylvia went and sat with Ben the nurse by her father's bed. Ben had brought his own little colour television and had set it up near the bed, but when Sylvia came in he turned it off. Her father's lips, formerly distinguishable from his face by only the faintest flesh tones, were now blueish. She thought of the slackening of the blood with the simultaneous sense of one of the great silent cosmic movements—a sun setting, a moon waning, a cloud breaking—and was awed by the gulf between him and herself, who was still so firmly among the tangible minutiæ of life. She got up and went to the window, but her wish for distance, the long view, was defeated by shrubbery. Her gaze fell instead on the slanted bricks of the outside sill, recently re-pointed with cement, and it seemed a madness, an utter tenacious absurdity, that anyone should have bothered to erect this house, brick by brick, and to have laid those particular bricks, at that particular careful angle, and to point and then re-point them. This kind of stunned moment, this sensation almost like a loss of sensation, had been a common occurrence in her childhood and adolescence, and though it had been forgotten or absorbed in the delights and interest of her life, these had provided no answer to it, so that it could still recur in all its first, bewildering strength. She returned to her father's bedside and looked intently, composedly, and with hopeless curiosity into his immobile face, and into her memory drifted the image of Greta's exhausted face. She said quietly to Ben, 'Mrs Cornock looks as if she needs to sleep for one whole day and one whole night.'

'Oh well, she's in that state, you know, where she can't.'

'Who watches at night?'

'Siddy and I, in four hour shifts. Approx.'

'Does she try to sleep?'

'No. She won't.'

'Then what does she do? Sew?'

'Oh, she cooks for us, you know. She goes to too much trouble. I tell her that. She's a great cook, though.'

When Sylvia left Wahroonga she drove down the Pacific Highway, through the city, and into the Western Suburbs. There was heat in the air; she rolled down the other front window. It was too early to pick up Harry at the foundry. She drove to her mother's house, but Molly was not at home. Standing on the coir mat at the front door, she heard the ring of the bell die away in a house that seemed abnormally, permanently, silent. Her relief as she drove away made her wonder at the attraction that had taken her there: the attraction which was also a weight. Feeling that the car under her was becoming a wandering aimless creature, she began to drive with conscious care. School was out, and boys and girls were sauntering on the grey bitumen streets, past the long straggle of shops. The scant tunics of the girls displayed limbs usually of great beauty, making imaginable the complementary beauty beneath the baggy grey clothes of the boys. Between boys and girls there was touching, jostling, leaning, lingering. Occasionally a couple in a poetic or mesmerized pose made her wonder if the best experience this city could offer was the sensual, the relation of a warm young body not only to others of its kind, but to the flow of air, the touch of sun, the pressure and caress of water. These boys and girls would have, she thought, two summers of physical excellence.

West again, towards the foundry, she drove in heavy traffic. As if stacked against each other were the frail narrow shops, among them big junky discount stores like aircraft hangers, and dusty little bungalows, some awaiting demolition. At forced stops she mused on newspaper billboards. TV STAR CANCER SCARE, she thought, combined beautifully two of the preoccupations of the evening newspapers. The other billboard—COMPANY CRASH FRAUD ALLEGED—she did not connect with Ted Kitching until Harry threw his case and papers into the back seat and got in beside her.

'I've just been talking to Rosie. Two television crews have been there. Let's hope they don't run it. Or if they do, mother doesn't see it. How was she?'

Eight

Ben the nurse, sitting beside Jack Cornock's bed, was watching the television news.

Matthew's head and shoulders filled the screen. His dark eyes looked straight ahead. 'But it isn't like that at all,' he said with assurance. 'In a few days my father will have it all fixed up.'

Matthew's head receded slightly, so that Dominic, and the stuccoed wall of the house, could be seen in the picture. The same reporter was asking, 'Then nobody will lose their money in the wipeout?'

Matthew continued to look, not at either of the men with microphones, but straight out of the screen: at Ben by Jack Cornock's bed, at Steven and Hermione sitting apart in their living room, at himself and Dominic in a pile of beanbags in their games room, at Rosamond standing in the doorway, at Harry and Sylvia turned from their cooking, and, straight out of the screen, with dark eyes more expressive than he knew, at his father.

'My father is wiped out,' he said, in the same decided way. 'But nobody else is.'

The other reporter said to Dominic, 'What do you think?'

Dominic, until then diminished in size, stepped forward and grew as big as his brother. 'Ar—' he said. A swing of the shoulders suggested that he was changing his case from hand to hand. 'Ar, I think so, too.'

'You think what?' asked the rather hectoring voice of the first reporter.

Dominic glanced at Matthew, distracted or confused by his brother's unwavering forward gaze. But before he could reply, both cameras suddenly left him to take in Rosamond, running onto the screen in all her dishevelment, one hand on her crotch.

'Matthew! Dom!'

Ben's and the Kitchings' colour sets gave full value to Rosamond's scratches and bruises, but on the Fyfes' and Harry's sets, both black and white, she looked rather as if she had a dirty face. With her free hand, she jerkily beckoned her sons as she ran to the gate in the wall. One camera concentrated for its ending on a back view of Rosamond and Dominic as with huddled shoulders they unlocked the gate, but the other dwelt on Matthew's eyes, which he kept focused forward as long as was possible while he followed his mother and brother. The Kitchings and the Fyfes

164

were watching the first of these programmes, but Ben, and Harry and Sylvia, were watching the second. When Siddy opened the door of Jack Cornock's room, and entered on tip-toe, in his creaking boots, Ben got up.

'Do you want it on, Sid?'

Siddy shook his head, while reproachfully putting a finger to his lips.

'Right,' said Ben, turning it off.

Siddy went to Jack Cornock's bed. The big head of the dying man lay pressing the pillow like a stone. His telephone, his alphabet card, his red felt pen, his spectacles, his mirror and combs and brushes, all his instruments of struggle and revenge, were still on the wheeled tray beside his bed. As soon as Ben left the room, Siddy spoke confidentially to his unconscious face.

'I'll see you right, boss.'

He took out his tobacco and papers, stuck a paper to his lower lip, put a dollop of tobacco in the palm of his left hand, and began gently to pestle it with the ball of his right. Ben had reached the kitchen, where Greta stood at the window and stared intensely, unblinkingly, at her kitchen equipment suspended in the trees of the moonlit, reflected garden.

'Ah,' said Ben with satisfaction, 'thanks for decanting it.'

He sniffed at the red wine in the carafe (he had brought his own supply of wine), then opened the door of the food warmer. 'Ah,' he said again, as he took his dinner out.

He sat down at the table. 'I just saw a woman on the telly who looked a bit like you,' he said.

'Was she selling something?' asked Greta distantly.

'I don't quite know what she was doing, to be honest. I missed the first bit. There was a boy, too. No, they weren't selling anything. Sit down and have a glass of this, why don't you? It's the same as last night, that you said you liked. You were up to the bit where you came back to Sydney with the kids in a truck. Where you made up your mind.'

'Jack made up his mind when he was only sixteen,' said Greta, coming to the table. 'The night he reached Sydney, he was arrested for vagrancy, and put in the lock-up. And in there he said to himself, "I'm going to make money if I have to go to hell for it." '

She raised the wine Ben had poured to her lips. 'He believes in hell,' she remarked, in her distant voice.

'What about that truck?'

When she began to speak, Ben cut a slice of bread, and a slice of cheese, laid both on a side plate, and pushed it across the table, and soon, as she was speaking, she began automatically to eat.

Matthew got up and turned off the television set, then rejoined Dominic in the hill of beanbags, where he sank low, his knees sticking up in two inverted V's. Rosamond took her hands from over her eyes, came out of the doorway, and sat sideways in a hard chair.

'Was the last part awful? I couldn't look.'

Dominic sat even lower than Matthew, the angle of his knees sharper. 'Opening the gate,' he said, 'you and I looked furtive.'

'You looked all right,' said Matthew. 'It was all right. It could have been worse.'

'Everyone will think dad beat you up,' said Dominic.

'As bad as that?' cried Rosamond.

'No,' said Matthew calmly.

'You shouldn't have come after us,' said Dominic to his mother.

'Why not?' asked Matthew.

But Dominic was still looking with hostility at his mother. 'What made you do it?'

'Momentum,' said Rosamond, in a stunned way. 'Sheer momentum.'

'You looked all right,' said Matthew.

The phone rang. Rosamond jumped up. 'Don't answer it!' But Matthew, his face joyful, had already struggled out of the beanbags. There was no extension in the games room; he raced past Rosamond, down the stairs into the hall, and lifted the receiver.

'Hullo.'

'I got the message, Matthew,' said Ted Kitching.

'Dad!' shouted Matthew.

'Yes,' said Ted, 'I got it, you dirty little bugger. You dirty black-mailing little bugger. So you decided to appeal to my sense of guilt, did you? Is that what you call fair play? Is that what I've paid all those fucking school fees to have you taught, you dirty black-mailing little shit?'

Rosamond had picked up the bedroom extension. 'Ted Kitching,' she said, in an intensely furious voice, 'shut up.'

'Oh, it's you, is it, darling? So you couldn't even keep them at home. You couldn't even do that much to help me. Who's been beating you up, darling? Your black-mailing shit of a son? Just stay put and I'll be along to finish the job.'

'Come on, then!' bawled Matthew in the hall.

But now Merrymen took the phone from Ted. 'It's all right, Rosie. I won't let him come.'

'So he's in your charge?'

'No, Rosie, he's not in my charge. But he's very drunk, as you can hear for yourself. Just wait till tomorrow afternoon, and he'll be home, and himself again, and as good as gold.'

'Tell him I won't be here,' yelled Matthew.

Dominic, who had only faintly heard Matthew's voice, and Rosamond's not at all, had extricated himself from the beanbags and was staring into a mirror with great curiosity. Ted Kitching and Merrymen, who, in a hotel suite, with Jackie Tonn and an Australian girl, had watched the programme that finished with Matthew's eyes, stood as if in a static embrace. Then Merrymen began to shove with his chest, still with his arms around Ted, and succeeded in making him walk backward until the edge of the sofa touched the calves of his legs, and forced him to drop back into it. Absently, Ted reached for his drink. Jackie Tonn picked it up, put it in his hand, and closed his fingers round it. Matthew lugged himself up the stairs and returned to the games room at the same time as Rosamond from her bedroom. Dominic turned to them from the mirror.

'I don't get it. Matthew and I are so alike. So what makes him photogenic, and me not?'

'I'm packing,' said Matthew. 'I'm going.'

Rosamond stretched out both arms. 'Now just a minute.'

'I can see what your father must have been like,' said Sylvia. She had been very much moved by the dignified boy. 'But there's nothing of the fanatic about Matthew.'

'He had three other grandparents,' said Harry, 'to dilute it. I wonder if Ted saw him.'

'Can Ted get away with what he has done?'

'The trouble with crooks like Ted,' said Harry, 'is that they don't keep their eyes and ears open to what the other side is doing. They get too isolated. They talk only to people who think as they do, and have no idea of what's going on in the minds of the honest people.'

'Australian tourists,' said Sylvia, 'used to be well known in London for thievery. And still are, for all I know. I've lost touch with them these days. But it does seem to me that here you have an enormous tolerance of laws that make thievery easy.'

'Not so much as we did. There's a new government in this State. Ted has a very good chance of finding himself in prison.'

'I wonder if *you* talk only to people who think as you do.'

'I'm talking to you.'

'Oh, I have no opinions. It's very hard on Rosie and her two sons.'

'If he can do that, they're better off without him.'

'He must have been extremely desperate.'

'So are the honest people.'

Steven and Hermione still sat before the blank screen. Each held a glass of vermouth; each was waiting for the other to speak. The presence of the children on Steven's arrival home, and the close quarters of their flat, by forcing them into a pretence of amity, had made real amity possible, but only the drama they had just witnessed made it inevitable so soon. Neither Stephen nor Hermione had anyone else to discuss it with; it was simply a matter of who would speak first. The children had been fed, Imogen was asleep in the room she shared with Emma, and Emma and Jason, having had their allowance of television, were doing their homework in Jason's room. Hermione got up, went into the kitchen, and looked into the oven. As she returned she said coolly, 'Are you still off starch?'

'I'll have a little rice. Locked in that room on Saturday, they must have been destroying evidence. I foresaw this some time back, you know.'

'It's all quite true, I'm afraid. Rosie told me about it this morning. Poor Rosie. I guess I should ring her.'

'I foresaw it at least a couple of weeks back.'

'Mother is unlikely to ring her, with Poppa as he is.'

'Let us hope Greta was too busy to watch television. The day I met him jogging in the gardens, I foresaw it then.'

'The criminality, did you? The bust, everyone did. I'll ring Rosie now. I keep wondering about her face. It looked so dirty.'

Using the given signal, she rang from the kitchen while the rice was cooking. Steven stood with his drink in the doorway, but Hermione only said, at intervals, 'Oh, dear' or 'Heavens' or 'So what will you do?' When the rice began to boil over, he moved behind her and took it from the stove; he was frowning irritably.

'Well, remember I'm here if you need me,' said Hermione. She rang off and took the pan of rice from Steven's hands. 'I forgot to cook a green vegetable. We must remember to have fruit afterwards.'

'How is she?'

'Her face was like that from the garden. Or gardens, I think she said. I didn't quite get that bit.'

'Where is Ted?'

'She hasn't seen him since Saturday night. She and the boys are discussing whether to go or stay. They'll stay, of course.'

'It would be extremely hard to go,' said Steven. 'Even given the circumstances, there would be feelings of disloyalty. But to stay would involve them in a situation of criminality.'

Hermione, serving the dinner, was smiling slightly. 'But Ted's criminality has been going on for years. How can they extricate themselves from it now? You have only to think of the packing. Will she take the ear-rings he bought her for Christmas? The clothes she brought back last time from Europe?'

'No,' said Steven.

'Right. But she can't reverse the trip itself. Or the boys' school fees. Or their food. The money he stole has gone into flesh and blood and bone.'

'That's the kind of argument used by dictators and fanatics.'

'Well,' said Hermione amiably, giving him his plate, 'my father was a fanatic.'

'You know I didn't mean that, Min. But I hate and mistrust that kind of extreme argument. Rosie would have to draw a sensible line, and take what she needs for the boys and herself to start afresh.'

Hermione was serving her own dinner. 'But just think,' she said with amusement, 'even we—virtuous us!—can't extricate ourselves from Ted's fraud.'

'Are we eating in here?'

'We might as well. Just think—shall we indignantly return the lawnmower Ted gave us when they got their new one?'

'That lawnmower cost me fifty dollars to repair.'

'Or that toaster?' said Hermione, laughing.

'We could part with the pressure cooker,' said Steven, joining the game.

'Sure. We never use it.'

They sat down, laughing, at the small formica table. 'And what about Imogen's carry cot?' said Hermione. 'Or that black shower curtain Jason stood on and tore?'

'I'll get them all out tomorrow.'

'And take them to the dump.'

'Absolutely!' Steven reached across the table, grasped Hermione by her upper arms, and looked into her face with glowing eyes. 'Min, tonight, let's put on the pot.'

'Yes, yes, yes.'

They brought their lips together and kissed. Marijuana, which happened to have the same effect on them both, they used occasionally as an aphrodisiac, hiding it in places which the increasing knowingness of the two elder children had made them change seven times, from its first innocent accommodation in Hermione's stocking bag, to its present cache in a broken vacuum cleaner.

'Only,' said Hermione, as they drew apart, 'this time we must make absolutely sure they're asleep.'

'And in the meantime,' said Steven, getting up, 'I'll open a bottle of wine.'

'Should we, if we're—'

'Only one.'

'Right, one bottle, one joint. Open one of the ones Ted gave us.'

'And tip it down the sink.'

'Naturally!'

But the wine, though encouraging Hermione's smiling mood, made her draw her smiles into herself, as if they were a private matter. It was rather a silent meal. Cossetting the glass, as she seemed to be cossetting those smiles, she neglected her food, and drank slowly, rolling the wine in her mouth. But at last she set the glass gently on the table.

'You see, it is impossible to be honest in a corrupt society.'

Steven had not finished eating. 'Has Stewart Cornock been quoting at you again?'

'No. I thought of that myself.'

'Herodotus thought of it first.'

'Is that where I pulled it up from? Amazing, what lurks down there. But how true it is! So why do we spoil our lives, trying to do the impossible? Give in—take what you need—enjoy your life. It's the only way.'

'What you need? Where do you take it from?'

'Wherever you can get it. However you can get it.'

'You can't be serious.'

'Darling, drink your wine. Drink your marvellous wine.'

But Steven frowned as he drank. 'It's such a rotten materialistic attitude.'

'It can't be rotten, when it makes me feel so wonderful. It's like this wine. It puts me back in touch with luxury. I remember my first feeling of luxuriousness. I was three—four—and I woke up one morning underneath fresh sheets and fluffy blankets trimmed with satin, and I saw a window with white curtains, and a tree outside, and everything was so quiet. And there it was—luxuriousness.'

'Those are things you take for granted these days.'

'Yes, but *then*—Rosie says it must have been just after we moved to our own flat, and had that Spanish girl to look after us. But I don't remember that. Just waking up, and the warmth, and the tree, and the peace, and the thrill of luxury, that's all I remember. It was supposed to be after mother got her wonderful job, but I think—though Rosie and Harry won't agree—that she had just met Poppa. Which raises the question, doesn't it, darling—' Hermione picked up her glass again '—of how Poppa got his money, the money that helped to make my blood and flesh and bones. So it's quite simple. I am only returning to my very own socio-biological situation. Or should I say socio-nutritional?'

'What's the difference, in such a totally fallacious content?'

'Tell that to Herodotus.'

Jason came into the kitchen to ask for help with his homework. 'Are you two still having that row?'

They laughed together. Hermione put down her glass 'We are both human beings, Jason.'

'I know,' said Jason patiently.

'And because we don't agree on everything,' said Steven, 'it doesn't necessarily mean we're having a row.'

But Hermione suddenly put a hand round the back of Jason's neck, turned his head towards hers, and looked broodingly into his eyes. 'Don't,' said Jason, shying away in alarm.

'It isn't impossible at all,' said Matthew to Dominic. 'Plenty of people live like that, so how can it be impossible? All we need to do is walk out of here, get jobs, rent a flat or a house, and live in it.'

Matthew was again sunk in the pile of beanbags, his feet on the floor, his chin on his chest, and his legs making two peaks. Dominic, in much the same attitude, occupied another part of that malleable accommodation, while Rosamond, looking exhausted, sat in the hard chair, eating salmon from the tin with a fork.

'I don't see what all the argument is about,' said Matthew, in the same matter-of-fact tone. 'You just do it.'

'Have you ever seen a cheap room or flat?' asked Rosamond.

'Plenty of people live in them, so they can't be impossible.'

'What about all the unemployment?' said Dominic.

'What about all the employment?' replied Matthew. 'People get jobs every day.'

171

'All I said,' said Rosamond, 'is that I don't want you to make up your mind when you're in an emotional state.'

'My emotional state isn't going to get any better,' said Matthew.

'All I said, is to wait till tomorrow to make up your mind.'

'How can I, when I've made it up already. You two can wait till tomorrow. But I won't. I'm going.'

'Go on then,' said Dominic.

'Don't be mad,' said Matthew. 'I'm not going tonight. It's too late. I'm going in the morning.'

'What's the time now?' asked Dominic.

Matthew looked at his watch. 'Quarter to eleven.'

'Are you taking your watch?'

'Of course I am.'

'Who bought it?' asked Dominic in triumph.

'I don't care if he did buy it. I'll need a watch. I'll need a few more things too. I'll make a list of what I need.'

While Matthew wandered around the room finding pencil and paper, Rosamond finished her salmon, and sat watching him, the empty tin in her hand. Dominic also watched him in silence. When he came back to the beanbags and perched at the edge, his pad on his knees, Rosamond said quietly, 'But you do want to be a marine biologist?'

'Sure I want to be a marine biologist, but I'll be something else instead. Plenty of people can't be what they want to be. And anyway, who says I can't. I might find a way.'

Dominic leaned over, and read aloud from Matthew's pad. 'Wet suit. Diving gear. Surfboard.'

'I've just crossed all those out,' said Matthew.

'Only after I read them.'

'Well, tonight,' said Rosamond, getting up, 'we must all go to bed.'

'Sure,' said Matthew, 'I'll go to bed as soon as I've made out this list. I don't mind doing that. I'm not unreasonable. But don't think I'm not going. Somebody would have to physically restrain me, and nobody's going to do that.'

Rosamond, gingerly holding the salmon tin, sidled across the room, stood by the beanbags, and looked across one shoulder at Matthew's list as he wrote it.

Jack Cornock opened his eyes. 'Dad,' he said.

Siddy removed his cigarette from his lower lip. 'Yes, son.'

Jack Cornock said clearly, 'I'm done for, dad.'

'You'll be right, son.'

Jack Cornock shut his eyes. Siddy waited for about five minutes, holding the cigarette delicately between a thumb and forefinger. Then he went to the other side of the bed, took the mirror from the tray, and held it to Jack Cornock's lips. As he returned it to the tray, he said with tenderness, 'I'll see you right, old cobber.'

He tip-toed to the kitchen, where Ben was drinking wine and reading science fiction. 'Where is she, Ben?'

'Sleeping.'

'She reckoned she couldn't.'

'Well, she has. She dropped off on the sofa. I just went and checked.'

'Well, he's gone.'

Ben put down his book. 'You sure, Sid?'

'Sure, Ben.'

Ben reflected for a while. 'No point in waking her,' he said then. 'She needs that sleep.' He drained his glass and got up. 'Well, work to do!'

'I'm going home,' said Siddy. 'I'll just get the last train. If she asks, tell her he just opened his eyes, and looked at me, and looked real happy and peaceful.'

'Right-oh, Sid, I'll tell her. Though whether she'll believe me or not, I don't know.'

Nine

When Ken, who was driving out of the garage to work, saw Molly crossing the lawn, one hand raised, her stumping gait fast and flustered, he stopped the car, idled the motor, and looked at her with forbearance. She signalled to him to wind down the window on the passenger side, which, after looking significantly at his watch, he did.

She thrust her head in. She was panting. 'Stewart just rung.'

Ken's look of forbearance changed to one of sympathy. 'Gone, is he?'

She burst into tears. 'Ken, Ken, I'm a widow.'

He looked at her blankly for a moment; then he said, 'You're a what?'

'A widow,' she bawled.

'Excuse me,' said Ken, briskly winding up the window. As he continued down the driveway, she could see him mouthing something to himself, but she continued to stand beside the concrete tracks, and to weep almost with the copiousness which had so infuriated Jack Cornock thirty years before.

Sylvia answered the telephone less than a minute after Harry had left for work. 'Oh,' she said flatly, when Greta told her. She sat abruptly, sagged, on the edge of the bed. 'When?'

It was the only question she could think of, and when Greta replied, she could only vacuously repeat—screening her own uncomfortable sense of postponement, of dodging—'Eleven.' But then she sat up straight and said quickly, 'Greta, if you want Harry, I could run down and get him before he leaves the car park.'

But Greta did not want Harry. 'Rosamond is coming, at her own insistence. Perhaps Harry could come after work, and bring you. Unless you want to come now?'

'Well . . .' murmured Sylvia. Her head and shoulders sagged again. She wore Harry's bathrobe, and her hair, still loose, hung like a curtain secreting her face and the hand holding the receiver. She felt as inept as on the days immediately after her arrival. 'Unless you need me . . .' she said.

'Well, if you don't want to see your father before they take him,' said Greta, almost answering the question as she asked it.

'Well, it's not the kind of thing—' But Sylvia rejected what she had been about to say ('not the kind of thing I go in for') because it could be interpreted as sardonic. She fell back on juvenile politeness. 'No, thank you, I don't want to.'

'As you wish. I rang Stewart. And when Hermione rang me, I asked her to try to get onto Guy. He can hardly be left out. I shall ring Harry when he gets to work.'

Greta's manner, calm, competent, slightly mechanical, suggested that she, unlike Sylvia, had no trouble in finding rules to follow. Sylvia remembered Greta's raised face as she held the eye of the needle to the light, the bruise on her neck; and she asked, with warmth and feeling suddenly released into her voice, 'And how are *you*, Greta?'

'I have had a good sleep, and feel much better.'

'Is Siddy there?'

'No, he went home. But Ben is here.'

Both had lowered their voices, and were speaking quickly, almost confidentially.

'How long will Ben stay?'

'Until Fernly and Gows come.'

'Fernly and Gows are—'

'Yes, the funeral people. Ben hasn't had breakfast yet. I must go and get it.'

'I'll come this afternoon, then, with Harry.'

'Yes, this afternoon.'

When Greta rang off, Sylvia lay back across the unmade bed and stared at the ceiling. Grief, she thought, would simplify everything; but she felt no grief. She hoisted herself into a sitting position and rang Stewart at his flat. When there was no reply, she tried his office. It was not yet eight-thirty; he answered the phone himself.

'Stewart, someone should tell mum.'

'First thing I did.'

Behind the frizzed hood of her hair, Sylvia's face was passive, her mouth mute.

'Mum was really upset,' said Stewart.

'Stewart—'

'What?'

'What's the procedure?'

'Well, it's a bit on the early side to ask Greta if there's a copy of the will about.'

She raised her head, holding her hair back with her free hand. 'I meant,' she said in a clearer voice, 'the funeral.'

'We'll be notified, Syl. About the will—Greta told me of her own accord that dad's lawyer's away, so that sort of cut me off. His partner might disclose the details. We'll just have to wait and see.'

'Stewart, I'm confused about the funeral. What do they do?'

'Just the usual. Take him away, keep him for a few days, then bury or cremate him, according to instructions, either from the will, or from Greta.'

'Then I don't have to do anything?'

'What did you expect to do?'

'I don't know.'

After a pause, he said, 'There will be some kind of service at the funeral.'

'Service? A religious service?'

'There always is.'

'Why?'

'Or maybe sometimes there isn't, but at every funeral I've been to, there has been.'

'I've never been to one. None of my friends has died, and this is the first relation—'

'The first for me, too, though plenty of them must have dropped off. Dad's father would have gone ages back, and the two brothers have most likely gone, too, and their wives, if they had wives. Their children, well, I don't know, there was a Kevin Cornock got killed in the war about the same time as old Brucie. But families like ours, we don't even get to hear about the lives, let alone the deaths, so it's the first relation whose funeral I've been to, too. But not my first funeral, not by a long shot. I've seen a few mates off, and of course I go in the line of business, so to speak. And at every one I've been to, there's been a religious service of some sort. The funeral companies have clergymen, parsons, people like that, on call, and now that there's this uniting church, no one—not Protestants, anyway—has to be picky about denominations.'

'I'll have to cancel the hire of that car,' said Sylvia.

'Yes, well, that's something you can do, isn't it?'

Sylvia cancelled the car, then took off Harry's bathrobe and picked up her Indian dress. As the cloth enveloped her head, and she smelled the pungent dye, she was attacked again by a dizzying onslaught of desires, out of which a voice—her own—silently told her that now she would be able to go to India, China, anywhere.

Ted Kitching, though steamed and frozen and beaten with birch

twigs, and dosed and barbered and dressed and scented, hinted at
his precarious state of repair in his cautious carriage and wild
reddened eyes. Rosamond's eyes were no longer red, and a strip
of plaster covered the scratch on her cheek. They stood face to
face in the hall, shouting at each other.

'. . . the sort of mother you are, to let him do it.'

'He was gone before I woke up.'

'So that's where the kooky grandfather comes out. In my own
son.'

'That is the final indecency.'

Ted had come in as Rosamond was leaving with two large
suitcases, between which she now stood, facing him. She cried
with fury, 'The final indecency, that you should bring that up.'

'You don't even know where he is.'

'I will never forgive you for that. Never! Matthew will write to
me care of mother.'

'Care of mother!' Ted, kicking one of the suitcases, betrayed his
condition by teetering sideways when deprived of the balance of
both feet. 'If you're only going to help your mother, why are you
taking those two fucking big suitcases?'

'I told you—I may stay there.'

'Only may, eh?'

'That's what I said when you first came in, and I was nervous.
Now I'm saying I *will* stay.'

'Stay then. Go out of that door, and you go for good.'

'Get out of my way then.'

He stood aside. 'Bloody ingratitude. Poor old Knocker's well
out of it.'

Rosamond picked up one of the suitcases. She spoke in a
normally pitched but aggrieved voice. 'My taxi will be here any
minute.'

Ted also spoke at a normal pitch. 'Has your car packed up?'

She was going through the door. 'I don't want my car.'

Dominic appeared at the head of the stairs, looking uncertain
whether to come down or not. A taxi, drawing up outside, beeped
twice. Ted watched, stupefied, as Rosamond staggered, bent
sideways by the weight of the suitcase, over the narrow area of
paving to the gate in the wall. But as she went through it, he came
suddenly to life.

'I hope you heard me,' he roared. 'Don't come back!'

Dominic disappeared from the head of the stairs. A hollow-
chested young taxi driver got out and lifted the lid of the boot,
which he held open while Rosamond lifted the heavy suitcase and

put it into the empty space. As he got in behind the wheel, and Rosamond got into the back, and was just about to speak, Ted appeared at the gate, carrying the other suitcase.

'Stay there,' he shouted.

'Will I?' the driver asked Rosamond.

She looked at Ted's face. 'Better not.'

But Ted made a lunge, and put a hand on the bonnet. The driver said, with a hard edge to his ease, 'What's up, man?'

'If she goes,' shouted Ted, 'she bloody well takes this too.'

'You want that one, too?' the driver asked Rosamond.

'Yes, please. I was just going to ask you to get it.'

The driver got out and opened the boot, but when he saw Ted lift the case high, he said, 'No, you don't, man. You don't chuck it in like that. You give it to me.'

Ted chucked the case into the boot, and made a lunge for the driver. The driver ducked while slamming the boot shut, and Ted fell to his knees, then rolled over onto his bottom. A passing car slowed down to watch; Dominic ran out of the gate; and the taxidriver ran round the taxi and got in behind the wheel. As he drew away from the kerb, Rosamond looked through the rear window and saw Dominic helping his father to his feet. The driver was watching her in the mirror. When she faced forward he said, 'Well, you got your suitcase, anyway. Where to in Wahroonga?'

'Frankly,' said Hermione to Rosamond, 'I don't know why we came.'

'I know why I came,' said Rosamond.

'I just felt the need to react *physically*—' Hermione made chopping movements with the side of a hand '—in some way, and the first thing I thought of was to drive up here.'

'I came because it was a way of easing myself out of the house by degrees,' said Rosamond, 'and not burning my bridges behind me. And then I went and burned them anyway.'

'You didn't, Rosie.'

'If only Ted and I could have talked.'

'You said you did.'

'We shouted cliches at each other. There must have been some other *real* things we could have said.'

'Your talks would have gone on forever.'

'Yes,' said Rosamond, 'now that they don't sort of automatically end up in bed any more.'

'It's certainly the only place where basic differences are thoroughly reconciled.'

'Unless you have young children, Min. They're reconciled in young children.'

'Ye-es,' said Hermione doubtfully.

Both sisters looked despondent. Greta had seated them in the living room, on the sofa, like guests, had asked them to do her the favour of listening for the phone and the doorbell, and had then excused herself and returned to the garden and Ben. Normally Hermione and Rosamond would not have hesitated to break her implicit embargo, but an uneasy awe for her bereaved condition, and for the presence in the house of the dead man, kept them where she had put them. Presently Hermione said, 'What do you think Mother is talking about to that nurse, out there?'

'They are planning to elope,' said Rosamond. She put her face in her hands as if she were about to weep, and laughed. Death and drama had aroused in her not only gloom, but a weak hilarity.

'And sewing,' said Hermione. 'Sewing away at that basket of clothes.'

'She feels virtuous when she sews,' said Rosamond, becoming serious. 'She told me that once.'

'I guess she's invoking the ghost of Aunt Edith. Rosie, what would you say if I left Steven for another man?'

'I would say you were a bad mother.'

'Look who's talking!'

'Oh, Min, I can't be bothered being tactful today. I don't say I'm a good one, but Matthew and Dom are older than Em and Jazz, to say nothing of Imogen.'

'How much do kids really care?'

But Rosamond had receded into self-absorption. 'In a way I'm glad Dom chose Ted, for Ted's sake. But in another way, it weakens my reason for leaving. And how am I to make sure that I continue to see him?'

'I often think children don't really give a damn.'

'You know they do, Min.'

'And that we are just biological instruments, used by nature and discarded.'

'Men, too?'

'Husbands, yes. Husbands and wives, biology's holy pair.'

Rosamond gave her sister a long look of curiosity. 'Of course, it's absurd to think I know all about you.'

'Yes,' said Hermione, with a downward look.

'But I know what you long for, so this other man, if he's not just an hypothesis, must be rich.'

'He says so. But you mustn't think that's his only attraction. I really *do* feel—Amazingly enough, I *do* feel—'

'It isn't Ted?' cried Rosamond.

Hermione threw her head back and began to laugh, then, recalling the presence in the house of the dead, she put her hand to her mouth and looked at the open door as if expecting reprisal. But having paid that recognition, she turned again to Rosamond, smiling.

'Rosie, you're a monomaniac.'

Rosamond flung herself back on the sofa. 'Well, so I am! Min, it's all very well for Matthew to ring and tell me he's all right. But I want details. *How* is he all right? Where will he sleep tonight, for example?'

'That's the kind of thing he wants to find out. But Rosie, even to *think* of Ted and me—'

'Not so funny. I remember once, at that party we had—'

'Rosie, Ted was drunk. He doesn't even like me.'

'I know, but I wasn't thinking of liking.'

'Doesn't Ted like me?' asked Hermione sharply.

'Min, you just said yourself—'

'Why doesn't he like me? What have I ever done to him? Well, that's news to me, that Ted doesn't like me. Well, I don't like him, either. You're doing absolutely the right thing, leaving him. What is he but a thief, after all?'

'Min, *I* can say that.'

'Well, you did, didn't you? When you rang yesterday. Which seems to prove it. But it's ridiculous to think he won't go to prison. I bet you anything you like he will.'

'Ted?' asked Guy, coming into the room. 'I'll take fives against. No, threes.'

'Oh, shut up,' said Hermione.

Guy was carrying a mug of coffee and a thick, loosely constructed sandwich on a plate. He sat down carefully and drew towards him, with a foot, a small table. 'Wait till you see the gear in Jack's clothes cupboards,' he said. 'There's enough to outfit the whole cast of Arturo Ui.'

Hermione sat up straight in indignation, but Rosamond appeared concerned as she said, 'You went in there, and looked through his cupboards?'

'I was looking for a copy of the will,' said Guy. 'I thought he might have got Siddy to hide it somewhere.'

Hermione, who often proclaimed that she would not encourage Guy's exhibitionism, pulled a note pad from her bag and began to check her shopping list; but Rosamond, who had so often protected and cared for him in his infancy and who had borne for him, in his beautiful childhood, an almost maternal pride, drew her brows together as if there must be an answer to the questions in her mind. Guy, careful of his clothes, cupped a hand beneath his chin as he manœuvered a corner of the thick sandwich into his mouth. After he had finished chewing, watched by Rosamond, he said, 'I'm dying to know how he left his money, aren't you?'

Hermione looked up. 'Mother will be provided for,' she said, with curt finality.

'It's impossible to doubt it,' said Rosamond.

'Is it?' Guy took another big mouthful and ate it before he spoke again. 'Keith Burtensahw brought the latest will here on Saturday. But do either of you two know whether he signed it or not?'

The sisters exchanged cautious glances.

'You don't,' said Guy. 'Neither do I. I was here just before Keith Burtenshaw came, and I thought if I gave Jack—'

He took another mouthful, chewed again; the sisters waited.

'—thought if I gave Jack a bad fright, he might die before Keith Burtenshaw arrived, or get to the stage of not being able to make his name. It wasn't planned, or anything, just an impulse. But he loved me trying to do it. He loved showing he could beat me, and survive. Yet he didn't, for long, did he? And I still don't know whether he signed it.'

Hermione and Rosamond again exchanged glances: Hermione exasperated, Rosamond worried. 'We know you're horrible, Guy,' said Hermione. 'You don't have to prove it.'

'I'm not trying to prove anything,' said Guy. 'I kicked his hat off, onto the grass.' He took the last bite of his sandwich.

Hermione went back to her shopping list. Rosamond said, almost with pity, 'He took his own hat off, Guy, and threw it on the grass. Mother told us.'

Guy's mouth was too full to reply, but he fully dilated his eylids and rolled his eyes. Rosamond said to Hermione, 'Do you know if Keith Burthenshaw does all kinds of legal work, Min? I'll need somebody.'

'If you won't take anything from Ted, how are you going to pay Keith Burtenshaw, or anyone else? You'll have to apply for legal aid. I don't see you going on with it, myself.' Hermione got up. 'I'm going to ask mother and that nurse if they would like some coffee.'

Guy finished eating. 'I asked them, and they said they would. So I made it and took it out with mine. But before I could sit down, mother said, "Thank you. And now if you will excuse us, Guy." So I had to slink off.'

'What were they talking about?' asked Hermione.

'She was describing the kind of place she went into to demonstrate cosmetics.'

Rosamond and Hermione turned on each other the looks of exaggerated amazement they had so often employed in the jokes of their youth.

'Never look back!' said Rosamond faintly.

'It's unhealthy,' said Hermione in the same tone.

'What door do they come to, Rosie?' asked Guy.

'The funeral people? The front door, Guy. We're listening for the bell.'

'That's our little task,' said Hermione.

'Why isn't Sylvia at this send-off?' asked Guy.

'Harry is bringing her,' said Rosamond, 'after work.'

'I wonder if she'll be rich.'

'I guess she'll get something,' said Hermione.

'Are you really leaving Ted, Rosie?'

Rosamond turned up both hands in her lap. 'You see me here, Guy. I have left him.'

'You'll go back.'

'You almost make me realize I won't.'

'When are you going to leave Steven, Min?' asked Guy.

Hermione did not bother to reply.

'Who's looking after the kids today?'

'Mind your own business. Penny Newman,' said Hermione.

'With your looks, you must often think you could do better. And what's wrong with that? If you worked in an office, and someone offered you a better job, and you took it, everyone would think you had advanced yourself. And so they would if you did that, after a while, because advancing yourself is what the whole thing's about.'

Hermione got up and went to the door. 'I'm going to make coffee, Rosie,' she said, in her tired voice of reproach. 'Do you want any?'

'Yes, please, Min.'

'She's like me,' said Guy, when Hermione went. 'She's dying to know who'll get the money.' He took a toothpick from his pocket. 'I guess she thinks if mother does, she can bite her for a bit towards the house she wants. If mother doesn't, I'm going to lose my backstop. Nobody else will stand me for long. And the older I get the less they will. The quality of the shelter,' he said, taking the toothpick from his mouth and looking directly at Rosamond, 'must decline.'

'For me, too,' said Rosamond.

'Stains, cigarette burns on the carpet,' said Guy, meditatively picking again. 'Dirt on the banisters. Green garbage bags, bottles, cartons—all day long at the end of the hall.'

Rosamond put a hand in front of her face. 'Don't!'

'And the smells, the smells. You would think mother would ring David Sole.'

'Who's David Sole?'

'Keith Burtenshaw's partner. But even now Jack's dead, she won't let him provoke her into caring about the money. If he can provoke her, he wins. She and he were terribly alike. They both had to win.'

'You're wrong,' said Rosamond. 'He had to win, and she couldn't afford to let him. And his last illness was his last chance, and she still couldn't afford to let him. But because he was so ill, she was kind and patient.'

But Guy said, picking his teeth, 'Talking her head off out there, as if he could still get at her. It's amazing, how superstitious people are.'

When the telephone rang, he leapt to his feet. 'I bet that's David Sole,' he said, as he went to the door, while Rosamond, as she followed, said nervously, 'Perhaps Ted . . .'

'That was Guy,' said Greta to Ben, when Guy had put down the coffee, and been dismissed.

'He was how old then?' asked Ben.

'Only twelve months when I started. About eighteen months when I turned it to real profit by casing the joints. That sounds very tough and gangsterish, but it's what my contacts actually called it. I started because I was desperate, but once I started, I can't tell you how much satisfaction it gave me.'

'It did?' said Ben, with interest but without surprise.

'After all those years of penury, and the despair I had to hide, it lifted me up as nothing else could have done. It wasn't only the things I could buy—the key to a flat, the labour of a kind reliable girl, good beds and food and clothes for the children. No, it was doing it. I would have gone with them to break into the places if they had let me. I felt ashamed only once, with the woman I was telling you about when Guy came out. She told me her troubles. Well, they often did. Only, hers were bad. But I wasn't ashamed for long. Good enough for her, I thought, if she takes what they hand out.'

'You were punishing yourself,' said Ben, 'for taking it when it was handed out to you.'

'Those psychological explanations are often so blurry round the edges.'

'I've found that too,' said Ben. 'And bits spin off the blurry edges, and roll around out there, and form little spheres of their own.'

The birds drew their twittering membrane from tree to tree, and the currawongs carolled into the upper air. A layer of brownish flowers lay at the foot of the garden seat, disturbed by their feet and Greta's big basket of sewing. Ben looked up through the bronze-green leaves at the sky. He was wearing a blue muslin blouse and a long silver necklace. 'What made you give it up?'

'I was nearly charged with being an accessary to breaking and entering. I happened to go to a good lawyer. He got me out of it, and got my name suppressed as well. It cost money. He doesn't like to be reminded of it now. I'm so glad you came, Ben. I didn't imagine anyone like you. So of course, I had to give it up. I was no longer justified in taking the risk, however much I enjoyed it. A mother in jail wouldn't have been any good to the children, to say nothing of the bad example. I wanted them to be insiders. I wanted them to be safe inside. And besides, I had got what I wanted. To go on would have been sheer self-indulgence. So I went back to working in a shop. But I had got my health back, and my looks, and it was a good shop, and I had quite a nice home background, too. So I remarried. It was the lawyer who got me out of it who introduced me to Jack. I could have married another man, a good respectable man, clever in his speciality. But he seemed like a child. Jack Cornock is the only kind of man I could have considered.'

'It's a wonder,' said Ben, 'that when he got to the stage of trying anything, he didn't threaten to spill the beans to the kids.'

Greta shook her head over her sewing. 'He wouldn't have done that. That would have been to break the base, the foundation of our compact.'

'Even in these last stages?'

'Even then.'

'I don't understand that.'

'No?' said Greta. 'Well, never mind. You've been wonderful.

And perhaps the only man who understood that is dead.'

'You haven't drunk your coffee,' said Ben.

She went on sewing. 'It would make me sick.'

Surreptitiously, Ben looked at his watch; Fernly and Gows were late. He said, 'Guy wanted to have his coffee out here with you.'

'Let him annoy those two women instead.'

'Is Guy like your first husband?'

'On Sunday, you can't have been listening.'

'I may have missed—'

'It seemed as if he were going to be the most like him of all, but suddenly he changed, and grew in quite another way. His father, when I first met him, was unusual only because of his handsomeness. Have I given you another impression?'

'No. From what you told me of yourself as a girl, I don't see you marrying anyone odd.'

'I wouldn't have. *I* was an insider. But the clothes men wore in those days—so thick and proper—and the way they were trained to be so alike—disguised them. We come from one of the military nations, and they are so good at disguises. I thought I was lucky that the man I loved so much should have a secure job as a shipping clerk. I hoped he would rise to be head of the branch and buy us a brick bungalow. There was a tea trolly in Beard and Watson's I coveted . . . I ought to have looked at his eyes. Blocked out all the rest, and isolated his eyes. They had a sort of skittering distant unprotected look.'

'I know it!' cried Ben.

'The thick clothes, and the quiet deferential manners, and the shaved face, and the cropped hair—they anchored him to earth. But all the time, the eyes were pulling him away.'

'Do any of your children have his eyes?'

'None. Nor the grandchildren. I've looked for it in dread, and been thankful not to find it.'

'Most times I would agree with you,' said Ben. 'It's very combustible, spirituality. You can see why churches want to catch it, and discipline it.'

'Imogen is still so young. Can it come later, that look?'

'I think they're born with it. Here is one of your daughters now.'

Rosamond was crossing the grass. Greta, with a look of patience, took off her spectacles and held them by the nosepiece. Rosamond stopped in front of them and, because Ben was looking with such intense curiosity into her eyes, spoke nervously.

'Mother, two things have happened. Keith Burtenshaw has

Jessica Anderson

come back a day early, and is on his way over. And Fernly and Gows are at the front door.'

Keith Burtenshaw got out of his car as Fernly and Gows' van drove away. Since he was of an age to remember the ceremonies, he took off his hat and held it for a moment against his breast. Greta stood in the open door with Ben at her side; they silently stepped aside to let him pass. Rosamond, Hermione and Guy were in the hall, Rosamond and Hermione in each other's arms. All were crying, but as if from startlement rather than grief. Keith Burtenshaw touched Greta's arm, and indicated the door of the living room with his hat.

'Shall we—?'

But Greta shook her head. 'Say it at once, Keith, to everyone. Then it won't need to be said many times.'

'I'll go and pack,' said Ben.

Greta turned and grasped both his hands. 'Thank you. Thank you.'

'Nothing to it,' said Ben.

'And who may that be?' asked Keith Burtenshaw as Ben left.

'The nurse,' chorused Rosamond, Hermione and Guy, expectant through their tears.

'What are we coming to,' said Keith Burtenshaw with disgust. He put his hat on the hall table. 'Well, Greta, as we have always known, the house is yours. The capital, which is considerable, goes—well, apart from a small bequest, two thousand dollars, to Siddy—the capital goes to Sylvia after her mother dies, but her mother is to have the interest on it in her lifetime.'

Greta looked interested, the three others stupefied. Only Hermione spoke. She breathed out, hardly audibly, *'Her* mother!'

'It is not a thing,' said Keith Burtenshaw, looking from face to face of the younger three, 'that would be easy to upset, even if your mother were prepared to risk the money and the nervous energy an appeal would cost, which, according to my understanding, she is not.' He looked at Greta. 'You are not?'

'Most certainly I am not,' she said with vigour.

'Now may we talk alone?'

But in the living room, he seemed to have nothing of importance to say, unless it was that if she should have need of his services when selling the house, he would be glad to act for her as a friend. Greta nodded as if she were not listening. Then she smiled and said, 'That was a good one. He wants me to contest it.'

Keith Burtenshaw leaned out of his chair, so that his face was

186

closer to hers. 'Greta, he may *have* wanted you to.'

'Oh, yes,' she said absently, 'I must remember.'

He leaned back, sighing. 'Is his daughter very much attached to her mother?'

'Attached? I don't know. I don't think they like each other, but attachment is quite another thing.'

'A damned shame she came back when she did.'

'I shall never believe she persuaded him.'

'She did something.'

'Acted as a reminder, perhaps. But it's the kind of thing he was quite capable of shaping out for himself. I only wonder he didn't do it before. It's as perfect as it could be. To contest it would kill me.'

He was looking at her probingly, with worry and gloom, as if thwarted by her placid exterior. 'It's too early to ask if you have plans,' he said.

'Much too early. I will know when I am quite free. I will feel it.'

'At these times,' he said cautiously, 'tranquillizers are a great help.'

'I will get some,' she said dismissively.

'I must see the daughter, of course.'

'They came in a moment ago. I heard Harry's voice. I wish they would all go away. Well, I'll send Sylvia in to you, Keith. I must go and give Ben his money.'

When Sylvia and Harry arrived, Rosamond, Guy and Hermione were still in the hall, standing close together and talking in low voices. Sylvia knew she would never forget her shock as the three faces turned towards her. It was an onslaught of naked and unfriendly speculation, an intensification of that moment in Rosamond's garden when all eyes had turned on her pearls. She flushed, and put a hand to her throat, forgetting that she had left the pearls with a jeweller for restringing. When Harry took his hand from her arm, she turned to him in confusion and supplication. But he would look only at Rosamond.

'Where is mother, Rosie?'

Rosamond recovered with grace, coming forward to kiss first Harry, then Sylvia.

'Mother is with Keith Burtenshaw. I expect he will want to see you, Sylvia.'

Sylvia was frowning in attempted recollection. 'Who is Keith Burtenshaw?'

It would have been a chorus again had they not all called Jack Cornock something different.

'Jack's lawyer.'

'Poppa's lawyer.'

'Your father's lawyer.'

'His lawyer.'

Sylvia remembered the man she had spoken to on the telephone; she blushed again, deeper than before. 'I see.'

Greta came out of the living room. 'Sylvia, please go in to Mr Burtenshaw. Harry, dear.' She kissed Harry, and then Sylvia. 'I wonder where Ben has got to.'

'I'm going,' said Guy, loudly and angrily.

'Ben has gone to pack,' said Rosamond.

'As he *told* you, mother,' said Hermione sternly.

Guy ran out and banged the heavy door behind him. 'One of these days, he will break one of those glass panels,' said Greta mechanically, as she turned away.

Rosamond went with Hermione to her car. 'I'll never forget the way we all looked at Sylvia,' she said. 'Even Harry. It was so absolutely uncouth. I could feel it while I was doing it, but it was too late then, it was done. It had flowed out of my face. Min, the savage creatures we have inside us!'

'It wasn't that at all,' said Hermione, belting herself into her seat. 'Not with me, anyway. It was only that the door was open, and I didn't hear them on the path, and they took me by surprise. I suppose Sylvia thought she was getting it straight away. She's in for a bit of a shock.'

Ben came running out of the house, carrying his possessions. 'Can you give me a lift to Crow's Nest?'

'Don't you have a car?' asked Hermione.

Ben was already putting his television set in the back. 'Nope.'

He got in beside Hermione, and Hermione pulled a face at Rosamond, and drove away.

Keith Burtenshaw sat on the low sofa with his long forelegs sideways, his thin wrists crossed, and the sour taste in his mouth very much in evidence.

'The investments will be made by Sole and Burtenshaw, Mrs Foley, in accordance with your father's instructions, and you may be assured that they will be as safe as possible in times like these—'

'But my present position is unchanged?' asked Sylvia.

'—in times like these,' continued Keith Burtenshaw, reproving her interruption by briefly lowering his eyelids, 'when inflation is rampant, computerization is overtaking us, a world fuel crisis is inevitable, and almost certainly our whole monetary system will change. Yes, your present position is unaltered unless you avail yourself of the services of those people who lend money on wills. I shouldn't advise it—though it is not for me to advise you – unless you are in desperate circumstances.'

'I'm not,' said Sylvia absently. Looking beyond him, she was tracing with difficulty her own emotions. He was not a man she would normally have confided in, but since he was sitting opposite her, it was on him that she presently turned her look of pleasure, of surprise.

'I'm rather relieved.'

'Then you did consider the possibility, Mrs Foley?'

The pleasure left her face. 'After I came back, yes. When it was mentioned to me. But I put it out of my mind.'

He nodded. 'Always a wise precaution.'

'But before I came back—never.'

'You find it necessary to make that disclaimer?'

'Your face makes it necessary,' she said angrily.

'In that case,' he said, without appeasement, 'I'm very sorry, Mrs Foley.'

'And your attitude towards me, ever since I came into this room. How ridiculous that you should make me mistrust my own motives. You make me wonder if, after all, something in me—' She pointed to her chest, speaking incredulously '—something I don't acknowledge, made me act for my own profit.'

'Or against Mrs Cornock?'

'Against Greta? No,' said Sylvia, shaking her head. 'No. I won't have that.'

'Or will you?' he asked, closely watching her face.

She took the bag from the floor beside her chair, and set it in her lap. 'No,' she said. 'Absolutely not. I won't be forced into a position of guilt that I've done nothing—consciously at least—to deserve. I think you are making me the butt of your own bad temper.'

He looked at her thoughtfully, his mouth a little less sour. 'I have known Mrs Cornock for a very long time.'

She softened at once. 'I see.' She leaned forward. 'But the house is still hers.'

'Oh, yes.'

'Well?'

'Yes, well, let it rest there. It may be years before you get the capital. And it's quite possible that you are relieved. Many people are afraid of the responsibility of money. And this will give you time to get used to it.'

'Is that what made him do it?'

'What? Because he wanted—'

'Yes, to give me time.' But then she shook her head. 'No, it's more likely to have been something I said about my mother.'

'Since you've mentioned it, may I ask what it was?'

'No. I'm sorry. It was something private.' And she added, 'Something pathetic.'

'And you believe—' Now he was incredulous '—that he made that change, out of pity for your mother?'

'Why not? He did treat her very badly.'

'There's no doubt about that,' mused Keith Burtenshaw.

'So, to make amends—'

'Strange amends,' he said.

'Strange?' She reflected for a moment, then her eyes widened in comprehension. 'You know my mother?'

'I haven't seen her for many, many years. But I remember her well.'

'Have you told her?'

'I rang her before I came here. She became extremely excited. I can't believe your father meant to make amends. He was a man who knew a great deal about the effects of money.'

'Then why did he do it?'

'Well, certainly to deprive his present wife. As far as that's concerned, this last change is quite consistent with all the others, merely a culmination. And perhaps we have already hit on another motive, and passed it over without justification. He may have wanted to give you time to get used to it.'

'At my mother's expense.'

'*She* will never think of it like that.'

'All the same,' said Sylvia heavily.

'And nor did he, I'll be bound. He probably thought of her only as a device.'

'A device,' said Sylvia. She got to her feet. 'A device. And I suppose,' she said, 'I shall have to ring her, and say how pleased I am, or some such thing.'

He had risen at the same time, and now went with her to the door, but in the doorway she stopped, detaining him.

'My father may have known a great deal about what money can do, but I wonder if he knew what it can't do.'

'Of course he did,' said Keith Burtenshaw tartly. 'He knew it couldn't get him accepted by certain people, cure certain illnesses, or stop death. But in the fields of persuasion, he knew it could do a very great deal, and so it can.'

'But not everything.'

'Almost everything,' said Keith Burtenshaw impatiently. 'Would you mind telling Mrs Cornock that I had to go?'

After he went, Sylvia stood in the hall listening to the voices in the kitchen. She heard Rosamond, Harry, and Greta, but not Hermione or Guy. She felt diffident to the point of shyness about exposing herself again to the shaft of their concerted and irrepressible emotions. In the dining room she hesitated as, when she was a child or a girl, she would hesitate before the door of the school principal to whose office she had been called to explain her truancy or other delinquency. But she had not then been shy on behalf of the principal as well, as she was now shy on behalf of Harry.

Harry came out of the kitchen and himself hesitated in the same way. But then they came together with a cry of regret, their arms round each other, each solemnly holding the other as tightly as possible.

Rosamond and Greta were still talking in the kitchen. Harry released her and said quietly, 'Mother wants us both to stay to dinner. But we mustn't. It's asking too much of her in every way.'

'Rosie will be here?'

'Oh, yes. Indefinitely, she says.'

On this pronouncement of Rosamond's they were able to exchange a sceptical and smiling glance.

'I'll ring my mother from your place, then,' said Sylvia. 'It will give me more time to think of something to say.'

When the doorbell rang, Molly moved down the hall at a pace so much faster than was usually possible that it made her limp.

She opened the door, said, 'Ah, love—' and leaned forward with a shriek of laughter into Stewart's arms. Then she pulled away and said, 'Only Ken's spoiling the whole thing.'

'You can see his point of view.'

She set her head back and gave him a squint-eyed look. 'Rung you, did he?'

'Yes.'

'The cheek.'

'Did Syl ring you, mum? She told me she had.'

'She rung,' said Molly, with grim brevity.

She turned and led the way, with her limp of excitement, back down the hall. In the dining room, Ken sat in front of the television, his head erect, and his arms folded high and tight on his chest. The sound was turned up very loud.

'Here's Stewart,' shouted Molly. 'Turn it down.'

'When I've seen what I want,' shouted Ken, without turning his head.

Molly winked at Stewart and nodded towards the door of the kitchen. 'He's being independent,' she said, as they went through. He's wild, though. Ooo, he's wild. He can't open his mouth without he rouses on me. Here, love, you open this.'

She took a bottle of champagne from the refrigerator. 'I wouldn't have got it in specially, on account of it being a bereavement too, but it so happens I got it in for Syl, never dreaming— Ah, what a day!'

'What did Syl have to say?'

'Oh, just congrats and so on,' said Molly with evasion. She flopped into a chair and fanned herself with a hand. 'I still don't know whether I'm Arthur or Martha. Have you worked out how much per week yet?'

'Only Keith Burtenshaw can tell you that, mum.'

Molly said nervously, 'I don't like to trouble him.'

'Now none of that, old dear. You're quite entitled to trouble him.'

'Well, just say what you worked out, Stewart.'

'At least three hundred.'

'That's the same as Fergy.'

'Only don't take it for gospel. Who's Fergy?'

'Ferguson down the shops has the footwear. Where Emmericks used to be.'

Stewart, removing the wire from the cork, slightly pursed his lips.

'After I rung you, I never knew who to tell,' said Molly. 'Nobody home either side, nor at the Talbots neither. So I went down the shops, walked, never had the gumption to get a taxi. It hadn't struck home yet that I can get all the taxis I want. There's some down there remember him still. It was his guilty conscience, they all said. And it was, too, love, like I told you on the phone. It's sad to think of it gnawing away at him, all those years. Though in my heart I always knew. Anyway, when it died down at the shops, I make my mind up all of a sudden to go out to the job and tell Ken, and I go in a taxi, being a wake up by now. But just in case you think he was pleased, you can think again.'

'Pop,' said Stewart quietly, as the cork hissed out.

'He just pushed me back into the taxi and told the driver to take me home. And talk about humiliation! I never had enough money in the house to pay. Lucky the Talbots was home by that time. Well, all that's changed, at any rate.'

'I thought Barry and Gavin and the kids would all be here,' said Stewart.

'Ken says he's not going to carry on like a madman, even if I am, and it's time enough to tell them when we see them. But if you ask me, he's narked because I didn't think to tell them first. Talk about a let-down! Although there is the bereavement, too, of course.'

Stewart took three glasses from a shelf and put them on the table with the champagne. He went to the door. 'Going to join us, Ken?'

Ken turned down the sound, but kept his hand on the knob. 'Pardon?' he said, blinking rapidly at Stewart over his shoulder.

'How about joining mum and me in a drink, Ken?'

Ken got up and came slowly into the kitchen. 'All right, I'll have a drink with you. I'll do that.' He went to the refrigerator and took out a can of beer. 'But this'll do me, thanks all the same.'

Stewart poured two glasses, then raised his own. 'Well, folks, here's to your good fortune.'

'Pretty cheerful for a man whose father just died,' remarked Ken.

'I'm not pretending to be knocked about, Ken.'

'Fair enough.' Ken raised his beer can. 'Here's to my penniless retirement.'

'Ogh!' Molly put down her glass and turned from the table. 'I've had enough of you, you scotty thing.'

'Now,' said Ken to Stewart, 'it was you who asked me in here. I didn't ask to come. You asked me. And now, if nobody minds, you'll listen to what I have to say.'

'Sure,' said Stewart. He sat down and pointed to the chair nearest Ken.

'No,' said Ken. 'I'll stand, if nobody minds.'

Molly, sitting sideways to the table, said 'Ogh!' again with a force that made her head tremble. 'Okay, Ken,' said Stewart. 'Fire away.'

'What I said would happen when I rung you to come and control her,' said Ken, 'has happened. Not twenty minutes after that, Ralph comes up and says, "Well, Ken, what d'you think? You've had a fair crack of the whip, and there's fellers waiting on a job." '

'You can see his point of view,' said Stewart.

'Too right!' said Molly.

'I'm not saying you can't, Stewart. I'm not an unreasonable man. I can see his point of view. Never mind what I did for his father in the years when labour could hardly be got. I'm not wanting to trade on that. What I would have done, only for her busting in on the job like she did, was, in my own good time, after I saw how this thing worked out, I would most likely have gone and resigned. "Well, Ralph, I'm tossing it in, so you can give one of those unemployed young fellers a chance," See what I mean?'

'You never would have,' said Molly, 'you stingy thing.'

'But you do see the difference,' said Ken, bending from the waist towards Stewart, 'don't you, Stewart?'

'Yes,' said Stewart. 'I thoroughly appreciate that difference, Ken.'

'But she had to come busting on like a mad woman. Lipstick all over her face. "Ken, Ken, I'm rich." It was disgusting.'

'Well, mum's impulsive, aren't you, mum? Here, old dear, let me top that up.'

'Wait on,' said Ken. 'I haven't finished what I have to say. So here I am out of a job, which had to happen sooner or later, Stewart, as you told me on the phone, and with which I quite agreed with you. And when that happened, I would have got the pension for us both, a hundred a week, and with the interest on what I've put by, and what I can grow in that backyard, and the odd job on the side for a neighbour, we would have got by, no worries, and run the car too.'

'But now you'll do better than that,' said Stewart. 'There's no means test over seventy, which you both are. So you'll get the full pension, plus mum's money. You'll have four hundred a week.'

'Yippee!' cried Molly, while at the same time Ken pointed at Stewart and said, 'Taxable!'

'Sure. Well, say tax takes eighty. You'll have three twenty. What's wrong with that?'

'Who,' asked Ken, bending from the waist again, 'will have three twenty?'

'See his attitude?' cried Molly. 'It's because it's me what's got it, and not him.'

'Now hang on,' said Ken, patting the air. 'Hang on. We're being reasonable about this. Stewart, when your mother went down the shops to tell all and sundry her private business, she also happened to order a washing machine. Did you know that? And also a mixmaster. Because she happens to have a friend in the electrical goods, she bought those two things.'

'They're fairly useful,' said Stewart.

'Untried and untested.'

'Guaranteed,' said Molly.

'Stewart,' said Ken, 'I wouldn't begrudge your mother a washing machine or a mixmaster. But you remember what I said when you wanted to buy her those things? You can't teach an old dog new tricks, and what chance has she got of learning to use them at her age?'

'I don't mind the old copper,' said Molly, with sudden doubt.

'Those things are dead easy to use, Ken,' said Stewart, 'or they wouldn't sell like they do.'

'I quite like to get out there and boil up that copper,' mused Molly.

'Well, Stewart, leaving that aside, in the meantime, she also arranges to go to the races with the woman in the fruit, and when I come home, sacked, I find her all ready to go to a restaurant to celebrate, which I discover she thinks she can easy do once a week. Now before you say anything, Stewart, which I see you are just going to, do a little sum. Washing machines, plus mixmasters—or substitute any other such appliances as will catch her fancy in the years to come—plus the races, plus eating out, and what do you think would be left out of three hundred and twenty a week? Oh, I forgot about the new carpet for the lounge she happened to mention. Fancy me forgetting that. Cheers.'

'Cheers. I think three twenty a week will run to that, Ken, provided mum doesn't go mad with the horses.'

'I'm not that keen on going to the races at all,' said Molly. 'It was just half a joke. You want a man to go to the races with. It's not the same with a girl friend.'

'And no account taken of inflation in these plans of hers,' said Ken. 'Or a drop in interest rates. Or provision for lengthy illnesses. Or old age. Or insurance. Or repairs. That guttering's going. You haven't got where you are, Stewart, without knowing I'm talking good sense. What I'm talking is just plain common dog-fuck, and anyone but your mother could see it.' He put his empty beer can on the table. 'Aren't we eating tonight?' he asked Molly.

'What do you want?' returned Molly.

'Anything that's going. I'm not hard to cook for.'

'I'll cook yours first, then I'm eating out.'

'Got the first instalment already, have you?'

'Listen,' said Stewart. 'Ken, whatsay I take mum out to dinner? It's time I took her out to dinner, anyway.'

'She's your mother,' said Ken, turning towards the door.

'You come too, Ken.'

'No thanks, Stewart. You don't know what you're getting.'

Molly got up and reached for her apron. 'I'll grill you those chops.'

'Stewart, I would like a word.'

'Won't be a minute, mum.'

Ken and Stewart went out to the back verandah. 'Stewart,' said Ken, standing close to Stewart, folding his arms, and looking up into his face, 'that sister of yours. Is she a women's liberationist?'

'I wouldn't know,' said Stewart.

'Because your mother's been getting ideas lately.'

'That's no crime, Ken.'

'You think I'm hard on your mum, don't you, Stewart?'

'I'm not a married man myself, Ken.'

'You might think I've been on the mean side, but that's not the case at all. The truth is, your mother's a wrecker of currency. Give her currency, and she wrecks it. If I hadn't kept a rein on the currency, I don't know where we would be now. I know you've been working a bit her way these last twelve-thirteen years, maybe with the implication that she doesn't get enough from me, but you're her son, and I haven't taken offence. Okay, but what do you think she's got to show for that money? How much do you think she has of that money today?'

'It wouldn't have amounted to fifteen a week,' said Stewart.

Ken's little eyes rounded with surprise, but he said steadily, 'That doesn't answer my question, Stewart. Which was, has she got any of it today? And the answer is no, she's wrecked the lot.'

'But what you call wrecking, Ken, some people just call spending.'

'Do they, Stewart? Well, maybe those are people with no responsibilities. But I shouldered the responsibility of your mother, and I've been good to your mother. There's nothing owing at the shops today, which wasn't the case when I married her, I might point out. And she's always had plenty of good tucker, and no worries about illness, present or future, and I've never so much as looked at another woman.'

'Mum's done her part, too, don't forget.'

'She has. I appreciate that. I've never wanted for a cooked breakfast or a clean, well-ironed shirt. But I know this about women, Stewart, you can't give them an inch. Give them an inch, and you've had it.'

Stewart rubbed his jaw, pushing it to one side.

'Smile if you like,' said Ken, 'but you not being a married man, as you said just now, you have a different attitude. But you were married once, I seem to recall, and there was some trouble with your wife's sister in the first week of that marriage.'

'There was,' said Stewart. 'I've always regretted what I did to those two poor kids. I was a crude and greedy type in those days. These days I hope I'm a bit more refined.'

'I hope so, too, Stewart. We learn by experience, which is what I've been trying to tell you. There's nothing like the lessons of experience. I suppose you're wondering what made your father leave his money like that. I think I can tell you. He was out to get me. Dog in the manger. He never knew me, but never mind, I know that type, he's had it in for me all this time.'

'You reckon?' asked Stewart, with his lively, flattering interest.

'I do. Well, that's that. We've had our talk. No hard feelings.'

'God, no,' said Stewart.

They shook hands.

'Stop here and have tea with us, why don't you?' asked Ken, as if on a sudden inspiration. 'And I'll take a run down to the pub for a bottle of wine. How's that?'

'Well, that would be great, Ken. But I've promised mum now. Another time.'

The restaurant of Molly's choice was in one of the neighbouring suburbs. Called *El Paso*, it featured arched doorways and silhouettes of red bulls and black matadors on the walls. Stewart impassively scanned a menu of what he would usually have rejected as 'pay-night food', and advised his mother against her intention of starting with garlic prawns; but Molly replied, half haughty and half belligerent, that just for once in a way she was going to have what she wanted; so he ordered the same thing, and a bottle of the champagne she liked, and they toasted her good fortune while they waited for the prawns.

'And here's to him that's gone, too,' she said. 'Forgive and forget. I'm having a new frock made for the funeral.'

'The funeral?' said Stewart.

'I'm coming. It's natural.'

'You don't think it will upset you too much?'

'I do not. I am entitled after all this time to see her face to face. It's me he chose to leave his money to, don't forget. And I expect you to be good enough to ring and tell me when it's on.'

'I'll do better than that,' said Stewart, cheerful in his resignation, 'I'll take you.'

197

Now she was inclined to apologize. 'You see, son, I would never forgive myself if I didn't pay my last respects.'

'Right. And if you change your mind in the meantime, that's okay, too.'

'I won't,' said Molly, belligerent again.

There was a silence, rather bridling on Molly's part, after which she looked around the restaurant and remarked that it was novel, but too dark.

'I'll get the waiter to light the candles. What did Syl say, mum, when she rang?'

'Nothing much,' said Molly. 'I've forgot.'

He took her hand across the table. 'There was no need to refuse to talk to her, mum.'

'Why is everyone pimping on me to you, as if I was a kid done something wrong?'

'Yeah,' said Stewart. He released her hand. 'Yes. It's a bit rough.'

'Look, love, I don't want her round, reminding me.'

'Now look, old dear—'

'I don't care what you say, son. I don't want it. You asked me, and I'm telling you. She needn't think she'll get it in a hurry, either. She's seen fit to stay away twenty years, and now she thinks she only has to bide her time to get the lot. Well, she's got another thing coming. That time's going to be a lot longer than what she counts on. I've even heard of cases where it's the daughter goes first. Not,' said Molly in fright, looking round for wood to touch, and grasping the pepper grinder, 'Not that I wish that on her. I swear before God I don't.'

Stewart also touched the pepper grinder; he looked serious. 'Oh, come on,' said Molly, 'cheer up. I didn't mean nothing.'

But she herself was unable to cheer up. 'They're taking their time with them prawns. You know what, Stewart?'

'No.'

'You know what I keep thinking?'

'No.'

'I keep thinking I could leave Ken now, if I wanted.'

'Sure. But you don't.'

'I don't know so much about that. There's life in me yet. I could rent a nice flat, do a few of the things I've always wanted.'

'You would be lonely as hell, mum.'

'Who says! I would let him stay on in the house, I would do that.'

'Mum, never make champagne decisions. You're fond of Ken's family, and they're fond of you, and you know it.'

'Do I but? It's really only a case of us all been thrown together, and made the best of it. Gavin and Barry are real nice chaps, but they're that busy, like everyone else these days, they got no time for anything but the odd joke and the pat on the back. And Joy and Susan are nice—wonderful wives and mothers, we all know that—you'd think it was a perfession, the way they go on—but they haven't got much conversation, nor a sense of fun. It's only the young kids I get on with really, that I can take down to the shops and have a talk and a joke with. But it's no use of saying one thing and meaning another—as soon as they get to nine or ten they'll sort of slip me off like the others did, like the cicada cases you see on trees. And the two babies, Stewart, now I'm going to be frank with you, they're too much for me. Sometimes the smell of talc mixed with baby poos, poor little mites, makes me sick to the stomach.'

'Would you like me to have another word with Ken about it?'

'The last one done no good.'

'Because you didn't stand by me, mum.'

'I don't like to refuse, love.'

'They wouldn't mind a bit.'

'That's what they say to your face, but not what they go away thinking. No, it would be easier to leave, and be shot of the lot of them. With what happened to Brucie, and you and Syl never staying married and having children, I got no close family round me like Ken has. I'm just a sort of appendage. And anyway, if you're that keen on families, get married and have one yourself, why don't you?'

'I think our prawns are on the way.'

'So you're thinking of it!' cried Molly, with one of her flashes of intuition.

'Not of having a family, mum.'

'Getting married, though.'

'Only thinking.'

'Well, I'm that glad,' said Molly with chagrin. 'Who is she? What's she like? How old?'

'Hey, hey, steady on. She hasn't said she'll have me. Not in so many words.'

'She's mad!' declared Molly.

'Or I am,' he said soberly.

'Well, you might be. You want to be careful, son.'

The dark young waiter brought the prawns, and as he set them down, and lit the candles, was complimented by Molly with a pomp curiously charged with coyness. But she had not eaten half the dish before she put down her fork and said she felt sick, and that all she wanted was a plain bread roll, and to get out in the fresh air. Stewart, who was hungry, quickly finished his prawns, paid the bill, wrapped two rolls in a paper napkin, and hurried to join Molly, who was waiting for him under the lamp of amber glass and cast iron suspended from a bracket above the arched doorway.

Solicitous, he caressed her elbow. 'Would you like us to find an all-night chemist, mum?'

'I'll be alright once I get that roll into me.'

'Eat it now.'

'I will not. I will not eat in the street.'

He placed her wrist in the crook of his arm, and they walked slowly past the shops, which were all shut and brightly lit. At the window of the menswear shop, a young man and woman, with a small boy in pyjamas and a manly little dressing gown, stood talking in lethargic tones about the clothes. Two men sat on the steps of the A.N.Z. bank, drinking from a wrapped bottle they passed from hand to hand. A collarless fox terrier, so newly discarded that he was still plump and hopeful, trotted along looking alertly to right and left. Many shadowed faces, profiles or swivelled ovals, were carried past in cars and trucks. Stewart walked with a slight sideways inclination, adapting his height to his mother's. As they stood at the crossing, waiting for the lights to change, he attempted a joke.

'Now that you're a rich girl, beware of rich food.'

'I hope that's all that's wrong.'

'What else would it be?'

'I'm not saying that word. It's unlucky.'

As they crossed she looked nervously at the headlights of the arrested vehicles, muttering that half the time they didn't wait. Yet on the other side, she suddenly said that she had half a mind to go on an overseas tour.

'Why should Syl be the only one to go to Rome?' she demanded with spirit.

A narrow lane beside the town hall led to the bitumen car park, nearly empty, where Stewart had left his car. Sitting in the front seat, they ate the rolls. The area was in process of expansion, and on one side, the partly collapsed paling fences of demolished houses marked the boundaries of former back gardens, in one of which still grew a peach tree in fresh leaf, and in another a rampant choko vine. In the centre of the car park stood a new brick toilet block. The bitumen was littered with waxed paper cups, blue drinking straws, wrappings of various food, and the dispersed sheets of an evening newspaper. As Molly finished her roll, she sent a sidelong glance at Stewart's face.

'You got one of your depressed moods, love?'

'You can always tell,' he said, to please her.

'I can always tell,' she proudly repeated.

'You're feeling better, aren't you, mum?'

'The roll settled me, and I've got Dexsal at home.'

'That's the place to go, then.'

In front of the house, when he had helped her out of the car, and kissed her, he said, 'You know, mum, it's not every day a man gets the sack.'

'I know that. But if Ken hadn't puffed himself up so big, there wouldn't be so much to get let down.'

In the house, she put her bag on the bed, then went to the kitchen, glancing with sly appraisal at Ken as she passed through the dining room. He sat in front of the television, his hands clasped at the back of his head, his legs casually crossed, and one foot violently kicking. In the kitchen she took a dose of Dexsal, washed up his dinner things, then loudly said, 'Well—' and came to stand behind his chair.

'What happened tonight in "The Restless Years?" '

'Stop home,' he replied, in prompt triumph, 'and you'd know.'

'I can ask Mrs Talbot tomorrow.'

'Do that.'

'We had a lovely dinner.'

'Good.'

'Well, I'm off to bed. I got to be up early tomorrow, and go for a fitting for my new frock for the funeral.'

He abruptly unclasped his hands and stopped his kicking foot, but then, just as abruptly, reclasped his hands, and resumed his kicking. She waited behind his chair for a while, then stumped out of the room, muttering that he was a scotty old thing.

Stewart, very hungry, drove towards the city, parked in a lane, and walked quickly in the direction of an Italian restaurant owned by a man who had once attempted a career in the real estate business.

Passing alongside a terrace of small, low, darkened, semi-detached cottages, he came to one with the front windows curtainless and brightly lit, and saw in the room beyond a young man and a girl sitting on the tops of two step ladders, talking across to each other. He did not slacken his pace; the five steps that took him past gave him time enough to take in the information that they had already painted the ceiling white, and were now resting while painting the walls a pale yellow, and that from the ceiling was suspended, clear against the yellow, a round white paper lampshade like a moon of hope.

GRILLED STEK was chalked on the blackboard at the end of the Italian menu, for although Silvano Marinori had learned how to spell the word after making that mistake for the first time, he persisted in it because his Australian customers found it cute, and his compatriots didn't care one way or the other. After bringing Stewart his grilled steak, he sat down at his table.

'How's business, Stewart?'

'Fair. How is it with you?'

Silvano shook his head and said, with the dramatic solemnity that always amused Stewart, 'Terrible. Terrible.' But when Stewart failed to smile, he became serious.

'Something wrong, Stewart?'

'Not really.' But then Stewart said, 'My father died last night.'

'Your father? That's bad. A man's greatest friend, or a man's greatest enemy. Or both.'

Stewart said tersely, 'He wasn't my greatest anything.'

'No? But that's why you feel bad.'

'Forget it,' said Stewart. 'Nice bit of beef, Silvano. How's the Mafia these days, Silvano?'

At last Sylvia found herself able to write freely to Richard and Janet Holyoak.

My father died on Monday night. I can't say how I feel. I can't quite get at what I feel. There's something there, waiting. It's heavy, and it's waiting. It's not sorrow, though I do feel sorrow. I suspect it's responsibility. He left me his money, though I am not to have it until after the death of my mother, who is to have the interest on it in her lifetime. It isn't a great fortune. My brother Stewart calls it a useful amount. But why don't I want to say how much it is? Why this instinct for secrecy? I was never secretive about my lack of money. I won't be secretive. It's between three and four hundred thousand dollars.

In spite of my father's stroke, he sized me up pretty well, as I sat there and chattered in a kind of tamped-down panic about nothing. The more I think of it, the more I am convinced that he delayed my possession of the money for my own good. I was so set in my habits, so determined on my providence, so thoroughly resigned to keeping it up for life, so

triumphant over all my silly old temptations, and so much in control, I
hoped, of the rest. Suddenly to get all that money would have been too
drastic, a shock that could have made me do all kinds of absurd quixotic
things, or perhaps reversed my triumph over all those trivial old
temptations. Now it is my mother who takes the impact of the shock, and
who cushions it by giving me time.

If my father had not been my father, I would have disliked him. Since
I was twelve I have been able to stand off far enough to know that. But
he was my father, so there was —is—the love engrained in childhood,
unreasonable and indestructible, and liable to show itself in ways
surprising to myself, such as weeping into my breakfast coffee. And
while I weep, I think that my mother has freed me for this, too—freed me
even for grief—and that makes me weep more. Harry, with whom I am
still living, or staying—we don't know which yet—looks at me over his
coffee, and doesn't touch me, or say anything, but sends out waves that
do. I have a dry-eyed sorrow, too, but that is a generalized sorrow for all
people who are taken up and knotted and warped as my father was. I
don't like it. I think it is rather an insulting kind of sorrow. I shouldn't
like anyone to feel it for me. No, the personal, particular kind, weeping
into the coffee, is the kind I would rather have.

The funeral is to be on Friday. I am nearly forty, and have never
been to a funeral. Fractured families like mine, cracked across and
across, don't collect for occasions. My mother means to attend, but
my brother means to head her off, because she wants some kind of
confrontation with Greta. Stewart is very wily, and I'm sure he will be
able to do it. I hope so. The prospect makes me tremble in my shoes.

I have three pupils—the first one a friend of Harry's, and then two
friends of that friend—and I am to give nine lessons a week, beginning
on Monday. I could have two more, but they are serious, and would
need a whole year, and I don't know where I shall be in a year. My plans
are as fractured as my family. Between Harry and me from the very
start there has been the unspoken question of my staying here, to which I
said no by reaffirming my intention to settle in Rome. But it has slowly
made its way up from underground and become a full-blown, spoken
question, and now we are speaking of setting up a household—not
marriage. No children, so no point—and as he works here, and is
committed to the place in other ways, too, and is in any case a thoroughly
untransplantable Sydneyan, it would mean my living here. So if you get
a letter asking you to send my tea chest here, don't be surprised. It says
something about my state that although I still rent the flat in Macleay
Street, and the wisdom of experience tells me that I ought sometimes to
spend a night here, I never do. Nearly all of my things have somehow
crept over to Harry's, and I come here only to see if there is any mail,

and if there is, to sit down and answer it, as I am doing now. On the other hand, to give up Rome, my haunted city. And to give up London, which I have taken so much for granted. When I think of London now I think of a big rich dark cake . . .

Ten

'I don't even know where that is,' said Marjorie Burtenshaw. 'Where is it?'

'Out George's River way,' said her husband.

'I've never heard of it,' she said. 'Everyone we know goes to the Northern Suburbs Crematorium. It will take hours to get right out there.'

'You don't have to worry. You're not going.'

'I'm not well enough to go.'

No preliminary meeting was arranged; there was to be no attempt at a cortege; every car was to make its way out separately. Sylvia was to be picked up by Greta and Rosamond, in Greta's car, because Harry, the only one for whom Jack Cornock's choice was not extremely inconvenient, would go directly from work.

'I should have thought Stewart would bring Sylvia,' said Rosamond to Greta, as they left the house behind them.

'So did I,' said Greta, taking the corner too sharply. After she drove out of the next street she frowned, and leaned forward to wipe the windscreen with a hand, although it was faultlessly clear, having been cleaned by Siddy just before they left. Siddy sat in the back, smelling only of the mothballs in which his blue serge suit had lain for so long. When they arrived at Neutral Bay, Rosamond ran in to fetch Sylvia. Sylvia, looking rather frightened, opened the door while still pinning up her knot of hair, which she went on doing in front of the mirror in the hall.

'How is Greta, Rosie?'

'A model of calmness. But the car is very nervous. The way it's leaping about, there'll be four more funerals soon.'

'Four? Is Guy with you?'

'No. Mother shunted him on to Min and Steven. Min was furious. You'll be next to Siddy, but he has had a bath.'

Sylvia shut the door and they hurried together down the stairs.

'Sylvia, I wonder if Ted will be there.'

'Will you mind if he is?'

'It's ridiculous, but I will be shy. I won't know where to look.'

'Are you thinking of returning?'

'No. But in the evenings, I get anxious, and feel there's something I must do, but can't remember what. And that's because whenever I've been away, I've rung Ted every evening.

So I know now that we're stitched together, and will have to be unpicked.'

'Yes, it's very painful.'

They were near the car; Rosamond lowered her voice. 'You offer to drive, Sylvia. I offered, but mother may let you.'

But Greta said, 'Certainly not, my dear. You look rather tired. Just relax in the back.'

About forty minutes later, Sylvia said uneasily, 'It *is* a long way out.'

'Would you like me to take a turn at the wheel yet, mother?' asked Rosamond.

'It's not so far now,' said Greta soothingly.

Yet the car skittered along, and was hooted at by other drivers, and Greta leaned forward now and again and wiped the windscreen with a hand or a tissue. Rosamond leaned round the back of the front passenger seat and peeped at Sylvia, consulting her with her eyes, but Sylvia shrugged, and looked out of the window. Guessing that the traffic from the Western Suburbs must have joined the road by now, she tensely watched for Stewart's car, though Stewart himself had been confident that he could dissuade Molly from coming, or that she would lose her nerve at the last minute. She was conscious of Siddy's knobbled hands, lightly clenched and motionless on each blue serge knee. He had said not a word since their departure, but had occasionally cleared his throat.

'Min and Steve just passed,' said Rosamond suddenly.

'I don't see Guy in the back,' said Greta.

'Min probably put him in the boot.'

'That was mother's car,' said Hermione to Steven.

'I was watching the road,' said Steven.

Hermione, looking back through the traffic, muttered that Greta was driving in the most erratic way. 'And she is usually such a wonderful driver,' she said, as she faced forward again.

'I'm curious to see if Ted will show,' said Steven.

Guy was slumped low in the back seat. 'And if he will bring Jackie Tonn.'

Hermione was not speaking to Guy, so although her head jerked sideways, she recovered at once, and said nothing. 'Whoever Jackie Tonn may be,' said Steven casually.

'She's Chinese. Or Vietnamese. Or a bit of both. He takes her everywhere. He tells everyone he's in love with her.'

'I don't believe it,' said Hermione to Steven.

'Ted stood up in a restaurant and made a speech about it. He picked her up at a baccarat table last week. She's a whore.'

'He must have gone off his rocker,' said Steven blithely.

'Although I suppose she's a concubine now.'

'It's not true,' said Hermione with contempt. She opened the road guide in her lap. They were passing over the bridge spanning the George's River. 'It looks a bit like rain,' she remarked. 'Is that old umbrella still in the boot?'

'As far as I know,' said Steven. 'Is Ted drinking, Guy?'

'He wasn't drunk when he made that speech in the restaurant.'

'You mean to say,' said Steven, 'that stone cold sober—'

'I suppose Guy heard him,' said Hermione.

'I did,' said Guy.

'—that stone cold sober—'

'Not stone cold, but not drunk.'

'Ted's just trying to get at Rosie through Guy. It can't be much further, Steve.'

'You're the pilot,' said Steven. 'What's she like, Guy?'

'Those Asian girls make the local product look so beefy and coarse. They'll take the cream of the trade, nothing surer.'

'And of course,' said Hermione, 'it's well known that they can do terribly sexy things, like tying themselves into knots. Isn't it wonderful having someone in the car who knows so much about life, and who can give us poor, fat, coarse, single-jointed suburban women so much thrilling information?'

'Look,' said Guy, sitting up straight. 'There's a hearse, up there ahead. I bet that's it.'

'Oh, of course,' said Hermione. 'It's so easy to tell.'

'Look,' said Rosamond, in Greta's car. 'Even the climate is different out here. It's another country. It's cloudier, and I'm sure it's warmer.'

Sylvia was reminded of those Londoners, residents of such places as Kensington or Chelsea, who would murmur, 'Goodness, wherever can we be?' while driving through Watford. The car was passing over a bridge. Motor launches lay on the river below, and on its banks stood large, neat houses. Siddy cleared his throat.

'This is where he used to say he would live when his ship came in.'

'I recall some talk of the kind,' said Greta absently.

Sylvia was pleased by this evidence against Stewart's claim that Jack Cornock's choice had been made with the intention of giving the most possible trouble to everyone concerned. She turned and looked through the rear window, but there was still no sign of Stewart's car.

Steven turned the car through the gates, down a driveway lined with spring annuals in flower, and into a parking lot also surrounded by beds of flowers.

'Stewart has arrived,' said Hermione, leaning forward to look across Steven. 'There's his car.'

Guy got out of the car, slammed the door, stuck his hands in his pockets, and went off towards a small sign—OFFICE—which protruded from the wall under a heavy archway dividing the long brick building which hid all else from their view. His feet crunched loudly on gravel.

'Min,' said Steven, 'why, when we are with Guy, do you descend to infantile brawling?'

Hermione was so used to the question that she no longer acknowledged it. She took from the boot a broken black umbrella like a dead bird. 'Ted's car isn't here.'

'So I shan't have the trouble of ignoring him.'

'You wouldn't. Here, you carry the umbrella.'

'Why? It's not heavy.'

'I can't, with this dress.'

Hermione was magnificent in her claret dress. Steven took the umbrella. 'It could easily be true about Jackie whatever her name is,' he said.

Hermione banged the lid of the boot. 'That he's *in love* with her?'

'One can imagine that in the general crash, in the atmosphere of letting things rip—'

'Pooh, pooh, pooh,' said Hermione, crunching away across the gravel.

Five minutes later, Greta's car trundled uncertainly through the gates. In the parking lot, Sylvia looked at once for Stewart's car. When she found it, she wondered again if she should warn Greta that Molly may be present; but, still trusting in Stewart's persuasion, and Molly's bouts of timidity, she instead said nervously, 'Harry isn't here yet.'

'Min and Steven are,' said Rosamond.

It seemed to take them all a long time to get out of the car. Greta, out at last, stood looking helplessly about her, at a level which precluded the word OFFICE, until Siddy pointed it out. Then, with sudden confidence, she hurried at his side towards it. Sylvia waited for Rosamond, who was dabbing at her hair, fishing for a brassière strap.

'How neat and pretty it all is,' said Sylvia.

'It's the least they can do.'

They stepped onto the path, crunching gravel. 'Though this gravel is rather insensitive,' said Rosamond.

But their few steps along the gravel now gave Rosamond a view of a car formerly hidden by others. She halted, momentarily shutting her eyes. 'Ted's car,' she said faintly.

'Be brave,' said Sylvia lightly.

'I can't. Tell mother I've decided to wait here.'

'Oh, come along,' said Sylvia, walking on. But a few more paces gave her a side view of Ted's car, of which she had formerly seen only the rump. She turned back to where Rosamond stood, slightly swaying. 'There's someone in Ted's car.'

Rosamond moved forward and saw the Oriental face turned cautiously towards them from the seat beside the absent driver's, the connubial seat. Jackie, perhaps puzzled by the irresolute steps on the gravel over which other feet had strode so boldly, had leaned forward to look. Meeting Rosamond's stare, she put the back of one hand under one heavy strand of her loose hair, lifted it slowly upward, let it fall, then as slowly leaned back to disappear behind the peak of the seat.

Sylvia touched Rosamond's arm with an authority that brought Rosamond, dazed and obedient, to move forward at her side. Greta and Siddy were waiting under the arch, below the sign saying OFFICE.

'Mother, there's a Chinese girl in Ted's car.'

'Is there, dear? Well, I'm glad Ted came. It's only decent.'

Greta was looking around her, again at a uselessly high level. The brick archway, though grave and heavy, was domestic or civic, like the flower beds, avoiding gloom.

Siddy waved an arm. 'We go down there.'

Emerging from the archway, they halted on a wide terrace overlooking a steeply graded lawn, its slope broken by flower beds in narrow terraces, and by low brick walls. On the flat lawn at the foot of the slope stood a number of L-shaped buildings, towards one of which Siddy, their shepherd, again waved an excited arm. About thirty men, all in dark clothes, and two women, stood on the paved and roofed strip around the inside of the L. Sylvia saw Stewart moving about the clusters of darkly dressed men, and by the regular inclinations of his back, guessed him to be bending from his height to shake their hands. Neither of the two women was her mother. On a long breath of relief, she said to Rosamond, 'Perhaps Harry couldn't get away.'

'There's Guy,' said Rosamond. 'And there's Hermione and Steve, all by themselves, saying how awful everyone else is.

And—is it?—yes, it's Ted, talking to some of those Mafia-looking men.'

Behind Greta and Siddy, they descended broad steps. Sylvia saw that the low brick walls on either side contained metal drawers, or boxes, and wondered if the idea had derived from the safety-deposit rooms in banks. 'Oh well,' she said to Rosamond, 'they have to do something with us. And we can't all be buried in Père Lachaise or the Protestant Cemetery in Rome. And at least it wouldn't encourage ghosts.'

'Not ghosts who wanted a full life,' said Rosamond.

They reached the foot of the stairs; Rosamond grasped Sylvia's arm. 'Ted is coming to speak to mother,' she said, with great curiosity, 'and he hasn't once looked at me.'

Ted took Greta's hand. Greta reached awkwardly backwards with her free arm. 'You remember Sylvia, Ted.'

'Sure,' said Ted.

While Ted took Sylvia's hand. Rosamond stood slightly in the rear, with an air of patient waiting. When Sylvia went on with Greta and Siddy, she said in a light informative voice, 'Ted, there's a Chinese girl in your car.'

He was looking very well, standing with the palms of his hands together, as if just about to rub them. 'Hello, Rosie. She's Vietnamese, actually. Where she goes, I go. I'm in love with that girl.'

'You can't be,' said Rosamond. 'You're in love with me.'

'Not any more, Rosie. My whole world blew up, and when I came down, I found that beautiful child in my arms.'

Rosamond repeated with a silent mouth, 'beautiful child,' while her eyes looked into his face with incredulity. She said, in a lagging voice, as if partly anaesthetized, 'How is Dom?'

'Adapting very well. Why not ring him?'

'I have. But how is he, really?'

'Great. Great. Have you heard again from Matthew?'

'Not yet.'

'Let me know when you do. Well, we can't just stand here, Rosie. We've got to join the throng.'

Passive, but still amazed, Rosamond went to stand with her mother and Siddy. They were joined by Hermione and Steven, and, from another direction, Guy. Groups of the old men were taking turns to cluster round Greta, each man respectfully shaking her hand and speaking words of condolence, or making sounds which could be understood as such. The two women, wives, also took her hand. Again Greta made those awkward backward movements with an arm.

'You remember Siddy ... And these are my daughters ... And Steven Fyfe ... Guy, my younger son ... Jack's daughter, Sylvia ... Sylvia, friends of your father's ...'

Sylvia scarcely needed the introduction. In old age, shrunken, their heads sunk into their stiffly tailored garments, they were still recognizable as 'the kind of man my father rings up'. Smiling, she moved aside and began to make her way towards Stewart, who now stood alone at the far end of the L.

Wreaths, some crossed by a broad ribbon, lay close to the wall or were propped against it, making a pale floral background for the polished black shoes and the dark trouser cuffs of the men. Most of the men held umbrellas, and some now accompanied their confabulations by sharp taps on the stone flagging. Sylvia scrutinized the flowers as she passed, weaving through the groups of men. One group surrounded Ted, who, rubbing his hands together, was explaining something that held them spellbound. A few laughed. The wreaths bore cards.

AUSTRAL MANAGEMENT SECURITIES ... A A A FINANCE ...
STAR ACCEPTANCE...LANCETT MOTEL SUPPLIES...

When Sylvia reached Stewart, she said, 'They are all from companies.'

'Not actually, Syl. Most of these blokes still have an interest or two. And like that, they're a tax deduction.'

As he spoke, he bent his courteous height towards her, and she remembered that he too was the kind of man her father had rung up. Not wishing to be overwhelmed by the tears that kept rising to her eyes, she told herself they were tears of nerves, not of grief. 'So mum changed her mind,' she said.

'Let's hope so. But that's why I'm hanging on here. She spotted my reluctance, and told me not to call for her. Said a black hire car was the proper thing anyway. Isn't Harry coming?'

'Yes. He's late.'

A door in a wall opened a little, and a young man wearing a clerical collar appeared in the long aperture, scanning the groups of people with eager, nervous eyes.

'Perhaps it's his first time, too,' said Sylvia.

Stewart looked at his watch. 'Nine minutes to go.'

The laughter among the clusters of men was louder. One man indeed laughed so much that he had to take off his hat, reel away from the others, and wipe his forehead with a white handkerchief. Siddy now stood apart from everyone; he held his hat against his leg and looked far away as if in contemplation. Keith

Burtenshaw came rapidly down the broad steps, with an occasional twirl of his rolled umbrella. He shook Stewart's hand, nodded to Sylvia, then walked quickly round the L to join Greta and her family. Hermione, coming towards Sylvia and Stewart, coolly acknowledged him as they passed.

'Stewart, mother says will you and Sylvia join us.'

'We'll hang on here for a bit, Hermione.'

'I think she meant, will you stand with us inside.'

'It doesn't matter much, does it?'

'I don't think so, either. But, well, you know—Well, forget it. I'll see you on Tuesday.'

'You're sure about wanting to see that house?'

'I've made up my mind.'

Sylvia noticed how his eyes clung to her face, and hers to his, with an hypnotic tension not in accord with their commonplace words, but before she could vault the old assumptions that obstructed her understanding of what was happening between them, her attention was drawn to a figure at the edge of her field of vision, and she turned and saw her mother approaching the head of the broad stairs. As she touched Stewart's arms, her gaze still on Molly, she was aware of Hermione's tall figure moving away.

When Stewart saw his mother he made a sound of startled concern and hurried across the grass towards her. Molly was dressed quietly enough in grey, but her festoons of jewellery, and her big black cartwheel hat trimmed with a long floating gauzy scarf exposed her sense of the occasion, and of her own importance in it. As she came down the steps with her lurch and wobble of fright, the wind lifted the hatbrim, making her clap one hand, then the other, on the crown, so that her handbag slid up her arm to the shoulder. But now Stewart reached her. In the lee of the stairs the brim subsided; she took her son's arm, pressed back her shoulders, and looked for the first time in the direction of the mourners.

Among the men, all laughter had stopped, and the voices had become murmurous and enquiring. Greta, after her first glance at Molly, raised a cuff to look at her watch. Keith Burtenshaw spoke a few words to her, and they turned away together and examined the cards attached to wreaths, he pointing with his umbrella. Siddy smiled, and raised his umbrella uncertainly, as if to wave. Rosamond mouthed at Hermione, 'Old Molly,' but her face was nearly as dismayed as Hermione's. Hermione, indeed, with Steven at her side, stood as if in a trance of dismay.

'Well, we always *did* know . . .' murmured Rosamond.

'We didn't know how bad,' said Hermione. 'How *grotesque*—'

'It makes our jokes mean.'

'It does, it does,' said Steven.

'It makes them weak,' said Hermione.

Sylvia was walking stiffly across the lawn to join her mother and Stewart. They were still out of earshot of the groups round the building. As she drew near she heard her mother say, 'I never dreamt the car couldn't come right up.'

'Hello, Mum.'

'Syl.' But Molly drew back her head from Sylvia's profferred kiss. 'I got something to tell you, Syl, and it might as well be right here and now, to your face.'

'Mum,' said Stewart, 'this isn't the time—'

'It's this,' said Molly. 'You aren't going to get your hands on it in a hurry, so don't think you will.'

'Mum,' said Stewart again. But Molly, though as red as her blushing daughter, was pressed irresistibly past the barrier of her own nerves.

'You seen fit to stop away twenty years, so as far as I'm concerned, you can stop away another twenty. You'll be sixty then, won't you? And don't forget inflation. And don't bother to ring me, and think we can be chums, and all lovey-dovey, neither. Come on, Stewart.'

But Stewart released her arm and turned back to Sylvia. 'She's not herself, Syl.'

'You're mistaken,' said Sylvia, turning away her tearful eyes. 'Go with her, Stewart. You may be able to mitigate—'

Greta, with an intention so sudden that she pivoted on a heel, left the paved strip and quickly crossed the grass, her knees slightly bending with each step, towards Molly. Her face was serious; one hand was extended. Molly again pressed back her shoulders and raised her head, while her face struggled to express something deadlier than mere malice, and her voice for words that would exceed the capability of words. But her face crumpled, and her only sound, as she sagged forward with a cheek against Greta's cheek, was a moan. Her jewellery tinkled and clashed, the brim of her hat was pressed backwards, and she and Greta put their arms round each other, and Molly wept.

Now on a few of the old faces a grin broke out, while others murmured, 'Well, I'll be buggered,' and others remarked that this was a turn-up for the books. Guy did not grin; his amusement took on another and inward look. Keith Burtenshaw (followed by

Siddy, who looked nothing but delighted) hurried across to Greta and Molly, so that when they disengaged, and Molly was wiping her eyes, he was there to fill the awkward gap, or to spoil the sequel, with his sour stylish smile, the twirls of his umbrella, and his brisk words.

'This isn't the first time we've met, Mrs Fiddies. And, of course, it won't be the last.'

'I'm sure,' said Molly, with a shy but ingratiating movement of her shoulders.

Siddy came forward, broadly smiling. 'Remember me?'

Molly was aghast with amazement. 'Siddy Dickerson! Well, I never!' She threw up her arms, shrieked, then lowered them again, for her eyes had fallen on one particular old man. She went forward, with Stewart and Siddy at her side, pointing a forefinger.

'Ronnie—don't tell me—Ronnie Carmody!'

And now there was much loud laughter, and cries of 'Molly!' 'Moll!' 'My oath, Moll!' while in return she shrieked, 'Geoff! Jim! Pete! Olaf! Betty!'

Stewart stood aside, smiling, his annoyance forgotten. Ted eased his way out of the congested group of men, and stood at Stewart's side, and they spoke together, nodding and consulting, Ted rubbing his hands. From the end of the downstroke of the L, Hermione and Rosamond silently watched. Greta, with Siddy and Keith Burtenshaw, now rejoined her children and Steven. Peaceful and business-like, she looked again at her watch. Guy was laughing.

'She's rather an old sport.'

Sylvia, lingering alone on the grass, saw the double doors open. For a moment nobody else noticed them. Then one nudged another, who spoke to yet another, and they began to shuffle and press indoors, taking off their hats. Sylvia sent a last look at the stairs for Harry, and was surprised (so little had gone right) to see him running down, with Matthew Kitching at his side. She ran towards them and, meeting Harry almost with a collision, they kissed, while Matthew ran to Rosamond, who left her mother's group and greeted him with extended arms.

'Darling,' said Rosamond, 'did Harry bring you?'

'I came by public transport,' said Matthew impressively.

'Darling,' said Sylvia to Harry, 'join your mother and the others. It seems to matter where people stand. Family in the front.'

'So come to the front.'

'Please, my love. I'll get chopped up in there. I want to stand by myself.'

So Sylvia stood at the back, with the old men. In the front row, on the right hand side of the aisle, Molly stood with Stewart. Ted also slipped into this row, and beside him stood Keith Burtenshaw. On the left hand side stood Greta, Harry, Rosamond, Hermione, Matthew, and Steven. As there was no room for Guy, he asked Keith Burtenshaw to move up, and was presently joined at the end of that row by Siddy.

On the dais, the coffin, with a wreath of flowers on its lid, stood on what looked to Sylvia like a trestle. Behind were bronze curtains, and with these as his background, the young clergyman stood beside the coffin, watching the mourners reach their places. Presently, though the young clergyman remained silent, Molly, Keith Burtenshaw, Ted, and all the old men bowed their heads. Sylvia, bowing hers, realized that she was acting not only in imitation, but also to obliterate the coffin from her view, and its contents from her thoughts. So she raised her head and looked at the coffin and the young clergyman, and then saw that Greta and her family, Stewart, Steven, Siddy, and Matthew, had not bowed their heads but were looking with expectation at the clergyman, as if wondering at his long silence. He put one foot forward, and grasped with the opposite hand the lapel of his jacket.

'None of you know me,' he said. 'And I know none of you.'

A few of the old heads jerked up in surprise, but were quickly lowered again. The young man's hand moved in agitation on his lapel, but he went on in a resolute though strained voice.

'Nor did I know the deceased, and nor did he know me. That's the way it is today. A stranger called in by strangers, called in for christenings and weddings and funerals, and ignored all the rest of the time. Some people don't call us at all any more, and those are the honest ones, but most do, and some of those are the godly ones, and some are the superstitious ones, and some just tag along. You will all know in your hearts which you are.'

The bowed heads were still. The raised faces were expressionless except for Steven's, which was interested, and Greta's and Rosamond's, which were politely expectant, as if saying, 'Oh, yes? Do go on.' Sylvia felt the shell of her courtesy drawn over the body of her live, warm hostility; she slightly tilted her head. Oh, yes? Do go on.

'As I did not know the deceased in life, I had to make enquiries about him. He was born in the north-west of this State, but from the age of sixteen was engaged in business of various sorts here in Sydney. He leaves a widow—'

Molly half-raised her head, but quickly dropped it again.

'—and two adult children. He prospered, so he must have been industrious. He gave money to charities, and in that, whatever his motives, was an element of good. We are therefore here today to mourn the passing of a man who was industrious and charitable—'

'And to pray for his soul,' cried Siddy in a loud voice.

Matthew leaned out of his place to look across the aisle at Siddy. The young clergyman coloured, and tightened his grasp on his lapel. 'And to pray for his soul,' he said, addressing Siddy only, and speaking in a slower, deeper voice. Then to the others he said, 'My friends, let us say the Lord's Prayer. Our Father, which art in heaven—'

'Our Father, which art in heaven,' everyone said, or appeared to say, for some only mumbled, or moved their lips.

'—hallowed be thy name—'

'Hallowed be thy name—'

Steven's experienced voice rang pleasantly out, as did Siddy's confident cry. The young clergyman allowed a pause after the Amen, then turned to the coffin, and as if addressing it directly, in words of his own choosing, commended the soul of Jack Cornock to the care of God. Some of the old men raised their heads at this, but lowered them again when they saw that the coffin had begun to slide towards the curtains. Slow music flowed from an unseen source. The coffin advanced on the curtains, which parted to receive them. An old man near Sylvia whispered to his neighbour, 'Untouched by human hands.' The music swelled, the coffin disappeared, and the curtains slowly closed.

Sylvia moved among the men towards the doors, hearing their low comments.

'How'd you like to cop his reverend when you go, Ralph?'

'He's green. He'll learn.'

'Get's paid, doesn't he? That's his game, isn't it?'

'Something in what he said.'

But as they drew near the double doors, their laughter took them again.

'He'll burn well.'

'No, he won't. He never got enough of the turps into him.'

'Jack was abstemious.'

'Jack was only a boy. Look at Charlie Trout. Ninety.'

One man softly sang, *'Goodbye Jack, goodbye, Joe . . .'*

The opening of the big doors disclosed light rain.

'Lucky I was made bring a brolly.'

'. . . *goodbye, Mick and Mary* . . .'

'Geoff's got no umbrella. Here, Geoff, come up with me.'

'. . . *for I'm off on a long long trip. I'm off to Tipperary.*'

'Remember how particular old Jack was about not getting his shoes wet?'

'I know what I could do with, and it's not what you think it is, either.'

'Quicker the better, in this.'

The rain was heavier. Now concerned only with getting to their cars, the men flung forward their umbrellas, pressed the catches on the handles and with the speed of wizardry inflated the cloth into black domes. Alone, or huddled with another man, and two with women, they hurried out of the shelter of the low roof, to be seen by Sylvia as a dark swarm against the fostered green of the grass and the bright flower beds. Behind her she heard Molly, and stepped aside to avoid her. Ted came through the door, and ran at his lumbering gait across the grass, winding between the men, and started up the steps. Molly, coming out in the van of the 'family' parties, clapped her hand to her hat.

'The brolly's in that hire car.'

Keith Burtenshaw was directly behind her. 'If you care to wait while I have a word with Mrs Cornock, Mrs Fiddies, I'll see you to your car.'

'I will,' said Guy. He deftly filched the umbrella from Keith Burtenshaw's hand. 'Back in a tick.' And before Keith Burtenshaw could turn round, he had opened it, and was ushering a gasping Molly, beneath its shelter, out into the rain.

Greta emerged looking detached and thoughtful. She took a collapsible umbrella from her handbag and slowly opened it. Sylvia, after a moment's hesitation, obeyed the invitation of her eyes, and her beckoning finger, and crossed the open doorway to join her. Harry came out, serious, impatient; he kissed Greta and Sylvia, waved to the others, and ran off through the rain. As Hermione and Steven stepped out together beneath their broken umbrella, Keith Burtenshaw was joined outside the doors by Stewart. Somebody inside shut the doors behind them, and they stood, these two tall thin men, and spoke together without interest as they watched the others move off. Siddy, in a courtly manner, offered shelter to Rosamond; Sylvia shared Greta's umbrella; and Matthew ran ahead uncovered.

'I think I'll chance it,' said Stewart.

'Oh, don't get wet,' said Keith Burtenshaw. 'Wait, and share mine. Guy won't be long. He took your mother up.'

Matthew joined Steven and Hermione under the brick archway, near the sign that said OFFICE. Presently Siddy and Rosamond appeared.

'Rosie,' said Hermione, 'mother ought to complain about that clergyman.'

'I thought he was sweet,' said Rosamond distractedly.

'Making the most of a captive audience,' said Steven with a smile.

'If someone could drop me in the city,' said Matthew.

'Come home for just one night,' pleaded Rosamond.

'Home?'

'To my house, Matthew,' said Greta, arriving with Sylvia.

'Please,' said Rosamond.

'Okay. Just for tonight.'

'Mother, that clergyman—'

'What about him, Hermione?'

'Giving us a bloody lecture.'

'Poor young man. He obviously found it hard to do.'

'Since it was my first funeral—' said Sylvia, turning away from them all with a shrug.

Rosamond spoke softly to Hermione. 'Matthew dreaded facing Ted, but Ted just said "Hi" to him, as he pushed past to race back to his beautiful child.'

Before Hermione could reply, a cloudburst began to send rain down in vertical strokes, and Steven urged them all to hurry to their cars. As they reached the parking lot, a big black car drove out of the gates. Steven and Hermione were belting themselves into their seats when Stewart came leaping over the ground. He leaned down, his head and shoulders wet, to look through the window on Steven's side.

'Have you seen my mother?'

'Yes,' said Hermione, busy with her belt. 'We saw your mother.'

He looked across at her briefly; she did not return his look. He spoke to Steven. 'I mean, just now. Did you see a black car drive out?'

'We did, in fact.'

'Then where the hell is Guy? He took Keith Burtenshaw's umbrella.'

'We didn't pass him on the way up,' said Steven, 'but there could be another way . . .'

'Steven,' said Hermione. 'Penny Newman will be furious.'

Stewart rose to his height and leapt towards Greta's car, but she was turning into the driveway, and before he could reach her, she drove slowly away.

Steven was backing out of the parking lot. 'Should we wait for Guy, then? I'm confused.'

'Don't be. Guy didn't take that umbrella back.'

Steven, turning the car in the driveway, laughed. 'Surely he wouldn't—'

'Oh, wouldn't he! He has carried off the prize.'

'Then we could take our umbrella down to Keith Burtenshaw.'

'Oh, there'll be someone down there with an umbrella. And Penny–'

'All right. Right.' He drove towards the gates. 'I managed to avoid Ted.'

'Yes, darling. But did he notice?'

Stewart, behind the wheel in his own car, took off his wet coat and draped it over the next seat. He took a towel from the glove box and vigorously rubbed his hair. As he combed it, looking up at himself in the driving mirror, making deeper the three lines across his forehead, he muttered flatly but with force, 'Bugger it all, bugger it all, bugger it all . . .'

Keith Burtenshaw stood alone among the wreaths. An attendant of some sort had gone away saying he would see what he could do about an umbrella, but had not returned. The rain continued without abatement, and presently, when two men appeared and began to gather up the flowers, Keith Burtenshaw thoughtfully scrutinized again the wreath nearest his feet, which was very big, and encased in plastic.

At Greta's dinner table that night were Harry, Sylvia, Rosamond, and Matthew.

Greta, by remarking that Guy had not turned up, disclosed that she had expected him, and by twice saying that Imogen was cutting a tooth, she seemed to pronounce an excuse (for herself as well) for the absence of Steven and Hermione. Sylvia was interested by this evidence that Greta wanted all her family gathered around her for the occasion. She remembered Greta's plan for a Sunday lunch in the garden, and wondered if Greta would revive it; but Greta presently answered this surmise by saying, 'We will leave our lunch party until Christmas time.'

'Sylvia won't be here,' said Rosamond.

As this pointed to the question still unresolved between Sylvia and Harry, both were silent, and gave their attention to their plates. Rosamond, who was sitting with her elbows on the table, suddenly put a hand on each temple, pressed back her hair, pulling the skin taut round her eyes, and said loudly, with entire seriousness, 'Now I will have to start thinking what to do. There is no more excuse for delay.'

'Perhaps we are all in the same boat,' said Greta drily.

'I'm not,' said Matthew. 'I only have to think of what to do first.'

When dinner was over, and the things were washed and put away, Matthew went out to the workshop where Siddy was sorting Jack Cornock's gardening and household tools. It had been part of Jack Cornock's providence that if he wanted, say, a soldering iron, he would buy two, so that if one were broken, stolen, or lost, it would not need to be replaced at an inflated price. Greta had told Siddy to take home all the duplicates he could use, and Siddy, under the searching fluorescent lights Jack Cornock had had installed, was assembling at one end of the workbench an array of tools. Many were still in their original wrappings, and Siddy, as he discarded the dusty paper or plastic, offered them for Matthew's inspection.

'They don't make them like that any more. Everything's shoddy these days.'

'Diving gear isn't,' said Matthew.

Matthew hung around as if he expected something of Siddy. He plugged in electrical tools to watch them working; he sat on an upturned packing case and watched Siddy sort the dusty un-opened boxes of nails and screws and hooks; he jumped up and vigorously planed a piece of wood. Siddy looked old under the strong fluorescent light, which revealed what even the sunlight did not: that the healthy-seeming pinkness of his skin was com-posed of innumerable tiny broken capillaries. He was cheerful, delighted with his legacy. He told Matthew he would have his verandah enclosed with glass, and buy a colour television.

'It gives you something to do at night. The daytimes are all right. You can keep busy. It's the nights.'

Matthew, planing the wood, drew his dark brows together in puzzlement.

There had been no rain at Wahroonga. The light of a half moon shaped the trees, and the grass was damp only with its own and the earth's juices. Harry and Sylvia sat on a garden seat facing the house. Harry sat facing forward, and Sylvia sideways, turned towards him. She had put an arm along the back of the seat, a hand on his shoulder, and was trying to demonstrate with caresses the reluctance of her decision.

'It was only today, in the car on the way home, that I knew for certain. Something always does come between us, Harry. And now it's this country.'

'You've scarcely seen this country.'

'That's an evasion. I'm an urban person, and so are you, and it's here in Sydney we would live if I stayed.'

'Then why did you speak of this country.'

'A Londoner may speak of England, and mean the whole country, the people, their general ways. And here, one is always aware of the country, out there, at one's back.'

'One is more aware of it when one has seen it. But I'm not trying to talk you out of going.' He suddenly turned his face to hers. 'I'm amazed, that's all.'

His features were indistinct, but in the angle of the head turned to hers she divined his sharpness, his aggression. She said, 'I want to explain. I don't want you to think I don't love you.'

He faced forward again, and spoke in his former tone, cool, rather idle, with a hint of asperity. 'I know you do. But not enough.'

'Enough to accept living here. Well, no, it's evident that I don't.'

Feeling the shrug of his shoulder, she withdrew her hand and gripped the back of the seat.

'This place has no wholeness,' she said. 'I've repressed what I felt about it, even with you—especially with you, because I've felt it would be like walking into someone's house and belittling it. But now, if I am to make you understand, I must say these things. It has an effect on me of mess, muddle, discontinuity. It's all bits and pieces. I feel this with my body, as well as my mind and eyes. And I find it painful. I've been about enough now, seen enough—and what is there? Of course there's the harbour, but I hardly want to mention it. It hurts too much to think that they should have had that great opportunity, and have bungled it so badly. I've even wondered if it's the source of the trouble—as if, having that, they rested on their unearned laurels, and took pot luck in everything else. Because what else is there? Don't remind me about the National Parks. They're wonderful. They're marvellous. But they're places of pilgrimage. You can't live in a park. No, first, there's that heavy Teutonic concrete city, and you can see they know it's wrong, because someone has been dabbling about here and there, trying to prettify it. And once out of the city, there are only the suburbs, miles and miles of them. That day I drove to the mountains, every time I thought I was getting out of the suburbs, along came another batch of houses, then a space littered with rubbish and corpses of cars, then another batch—Oh, Lord! But please don't think I'm comparing those far western suburbs with ones like this. I'm not. One doesn't need to. They're all fundamentally the same. The rubbish and corpses of cars aren't fundamental. They could be cleaned up. What is fundamental, and what they all have in common, rich or poor, green or grey, north, south, east, or west, is a lack of any focal point, any centre, any heart. Unless of course you're content with a supermarket and a row of shops, and perhaps a public library . . . Oh, I had better stop this, hadn't I?'

'Not unless you've finished.'

Even though his voice was so quiet, and his words so reasonable, she felt his stubbornness and anger. 'That's the trouble,' she said, 'I never would finish.'

'Well, there must be some truth in what you've said, or it wouldn't be said so often. Yet to me it always sounds excessive. It seems to me that people like you work the argument up, and pursue it for its own sake, and forget the physical facts. I've seen parts of England, France, Italy as discontinuous, as broken and muddled, as anything we have here.'

'I know. I agree.' Recognizing some justice in his accusation, she was eager, almost pleading. 'But there, you do have the consolation of the old. And so much of the old is good. There's enough left of excellence, quality—so the old parts still provide hearts for the rest, not matter how bad.'

'Well, I'm not content with a supermarket and a row of shops, but nor would I be content to live off other people's hearts.'

'One has to live as best one can, and if I can't find a heart here, what else can I do?'

'You're like Hermione. Not so covetous, but interested chiefly in how things look.'

'It must be important, how things look—'

'In fact, infatuated with how things look.'

'But it must be important,' she insisted, 'or else why do so many Australians go to Europe just to admire how things look? They know there's something wrong here, they know it, or else why do they go in such droves, so restlessly, again and again? And why do so many of the young ones never come back? No, wait,' she said, as he was about to speak. She put her hand on his shoulder again, enclosing the curve of it with her palm, and inclined towards him, speaking earnestly, pleading. 'I want to tell you what I thought, or thought I *knew*, today after the funeral. I thought, these are people who have repudiated tragedy, and have flattened out their lives into a comfortable utilitarianism. And of course, I asked the question you are going to ask. What is the alternative? Elaborate rituals of some religion they don't believe in? No, they reject that. I believe they are honest—'

'They *are* honest,' he broke in to say. 'They express what they believe in.'

She took her hand away and leaned back in the seat. 'A jocular stoicism.'

'It's not always jocular. It's not always stoicism, either. But supposing it were, can you define anything better? Can you say what you want?'

'I want something else. And so do they. That's another thing they go to Europe for. Other people's rituals.'

The kitchen was suddenly full of light. Rosamond appeared. She picked up an apple and went out, taking the first big bite, leaving the light on. Sylvia said quietly, 'Now you're thoroughly sick of me, and thoroughly impatient with me.'

'Not thoroughly,' he said.

In the increased light, each took a hostile yet anxious glance at the other, then both looked forward again.

'Not yet,' said Sylvia with challenge. 'But think of what it would be like if I stayed, if we lived together.'

'There's an alternative. You could avoid that kind of criticism.'

'Oh, I would,' she said promptly, 'if I stayed. I would be afraid to do anything else. It's not so bad for Hermione. She's so big and beautiful that they're forced to accept her. But they wouldn't accept me. They would say, 'Of course, she is so *sensitive*,' in that certain tone. But about Hermione, I imagine they say, "Oh, she gets so *angry*," which is better.'

'Hermione gets angry because she hasn't enough money.'

'Hermione is angry because she is caught here, and the best she can do is to make her few square metres of it as good as possible, and for that she needs money.' Sylvia hesitated. 'Well, *I* will have money . . .'

She drifted for a moment into speculation, but shook it off and returned to her theme. 'Hermione is caught here by love. You don't rant about a place, and keep it up, as she does, unless you're bound to it by ties of love. I didn't start to get hot about it until I began to love you, really to love you. At first I was irritated, and knew I wouldn't be like that if it weren't my native place. But I was cool, too. I was a sojourner. I would soon be gone. So I was polite, and smiled, and mentioned only the pleasant things, and repressed the others.'

'Nobody would ask you to keep that up.'

'I would have to repress them, Harry, for your sake, or I would risk undermining your love of the place. The person you live with can rob you. Every day, they can take a little bit away from you. I don't want to do that. I know what it's like to love a city. So I would be tactful, and watch my P's and Q's. Or I would meet Hermione now and then, or someone like her, and have a hate session to let off some steam. But neither of those courses is attractive.'

'I can see they're not,' he said. 'If you stayed, and didn't come to some real reconciliation, or real acceptance, we would certainly fight.'

'The prospect is quite unbearable,' she said, in a light prim voice.

'Okay. If you can't find a way of bearing it, don't face it.'

Matthew wandered round the corner of the house, but when he saw them together, he diverted his course towards the swing.

'I think Matthew wants to see you,' said Sylvia, in the same light voice.

'In a minute. You rushed me past something I wanted to say, and now I'm going to say it. Generally speaking, I think it's a very bad thing when so many people leave a country in its formative years, and congregate in a place where a culture is already consolidated, and never come home to use what they've learned. Exceptions must be made, but generally speaking, I believe it's objectionable to deprive one part of the world to over-enrich another. I believe that's as true of culture as it is of food. Among the people I know, it's an opinion that gets a very poor reception. They agree about the food, but not about the culture. But I hold it, all the same.'

'I would not have believed it of you,' said Sylvia. 'It's so incredibly parochial.'

'You have hit on the usual word. Just as you would be called sensitive, and Hermione is called angry, I am called parochial. I envy your brother Stewart, who simply accepts it all, the bad and the good, and thinks it's the best place in the world. My difficulty is, I don't think it is, but I feel it is. You say you feel your dislike with your body as well as your eyes and mind, but I feel my affection in exactly the same way.'

She got to her feet, pulling down the rolled cuffs of her shirt. 'If we were eighteen, we would be shouting at each other, and I would be crying.'

'I wish we were eighteen.'

'Matthew is getting impatient. I'll go. In the car on the way home, he said he wanted to ask you about fruit picking.'

'That's not a private matter. Stay.'

'I want to be by myself for a while.'

But when she reached the kitchen, she did not want to be alone after all. Matthew was sitting beside Harry on the seat. She went to look for Greta and Rosamond, but outside the door of the living room, she heard the engrossed tone of their conversation, and turned away again. She felt uneasy, on edge, as if waiting for some event of which she was not certain, some guest already late. She returned to the kitchen, and took an apple from the big dish on the table. Matthew was still sitting on the garden seat, but Harry was now on his feet, facing him, moving about restlessly, talking while the boy listened. Sylvia plunged her teeth into the apple and creaked off a huge bite. In the car on the way home, Matthew had sat in the back between Rosamond and herself. Rosamond had taken his nearer hand, turned it palm upward, and under pretence of reading his fortune, told him that wherever he went, he would always feel compelled to send a brief report to base. 'That is ordained in your hand,' Rosamond had said. While Sylvia, seething with her thoughts about the mourners, about the poverty of their rituals, their repudiation of tragedy, and the wistful interest of such people in the old rituals of Europe, had wished, then too, to be alone, so that she could follow these thoughts, which seemed to her so urgent. And now she was alone, and she did follow them, or rather, was drawn after them as they raced ahead, informing her in one second that in her observation of the mourners, she had selected those attitudes that were true of herself. It was she who had repudiated tragedy, and she who needed other people's rituals.

She was eating the apple in big bites, examining the remainder as she chewed each mouthful with the strong teeth whose care she had included in her area of providence. She nibbled the core close, threw it into the bin, and went out into the garden. Matthew was facing the house, and by the altered direction of his gaze he indicated her approach to Harry. Harry turned as she came to a stop, and without hesitation put out an arm and drew her into his side, while he continued to talk.

'The asparagus didn't cut out till about Christmas, but check that. Then you could fill in on tomatoes — tomatoes are a great summer fill-in—till the grapes come on. When I was doing it, there weren't so many vineyards as today, and at first I went for the prunes. I don't know how they harvest prunes now, but then it was what the Americans call stoop labour, and for the first few days you thought your back was broken. I'm not likely to forget it, all the same, going out in the early mornings in that truck. Not bad.'

A look of curiosity had entered Matthew's eyes, for Harry and Sylvia, as Harry went on speaking, had begun gently, and as if unconsciously, to rock. Clasped together, in a perfect, slow rhythm, they swayed this way and then that, first his outer heel slightly leaving the ground, then hers.

'There were two kinds of prunes in those days, Robes and D'Argents, but the D'Argent was gradually taking over. In the fourth year, I went to the Hunter Valley for the grapes.'

Eleven

On the Monday after the funeral, Keith Burtenshaw drove again to Greta's house. Rosamond opened the door.

'Mother has gone to the shops. Mr Burtenshaw, think of some kind of job I could get.'

'Has she gone in the car?'

'Of course.'

Keith Burtenshaw sat on one of the chairs in the hall. 'This is very embarrassing. I hoped she would understand without my having to explain. A house doesn't mean a house and car. The car's not hers.'

'Oh,' said Rosamond, resuming her seat at the phone. The table and floor were littered with pages from the phone pad; Rosamond had been ringing up for two hours. 'She will be furious,' she said, 'or would have been, only she has suddenly turned into a saint.'

'These contentious wills always cause bitterness. Always. Sooner or later it comes out. I'll wait for her. It must be done.'

'While you're waiting, think of some job I could do.'

'You're serious in this separation, Mrs Kitching?'

'Absolutely.'

'I shouldn't have thought it of you.'

'I shouldn't have thought it of myself. I try to imagine myself living in a room, rushing home with my arms full of parcels, and spilling oranges on the stairs. There will be a lettuce on the bed and a bath towel drying over a chair. And when I want a widdle I will peek out of the door to see if the dunny's free.'

'I suppose it's too late to start a career as an actress.'

'I treasure my amateur status.'

'Could you be a saleswoman?'

'No.'

'Why not? Inexperienced people start such jobs every day.'

'You sound like my son Matthew.'

'A fine looking lad. Where is he?'

'Left this morning for the country,' said Rosamond, with tears in her eyes. She bent to pick up the pages from the floor. 'Nobody seems to want to give me a job at all.'

'Keep trying. Don't take this as a professional opinion, but I think it very likely that your husband will go to prison.'

'*He* doesn't. He is quite demented. I rang him half an hour ago.

I wanted to hear a human voice after talking to all those job people. And I wanted to hear more about his beautiful child. He didn't at all mind telling me. I think he tells everyone.'

'It hasn't reached me.'

Rosamond told Keith Burtenshaw about Jackie Tonn, and while she repeated Ted's words about the girl, imitating the slow harsh cavernous yearning voice in which he had spoken of her, Rosamond became serious. 'So you see, even if I wanted to, I couldn't return.'

'Many wives sit these things out.'

'Not when they've depended so much on the understanding that they are *in love*.'

'A great mistake,' said Keith Burtenshaw, looking aside. The metal door of the garage had just rolled up.

Greta came in looking tired, mild, and vague. 'Oh, Keith . . .' But when he told her about the car, she looked at him first with incomprehension, and then with a growing tension of the body, and an icy-blue blaze of the eyes, such as Rosamond had not seen for a long time. She took the car keys from her bag, and it looked for a moment as if she would throw them at him; but she did the next best thing by placing them, too carefully, on the table near his hat.

'You do remember, Greta,' he said, 'that I tried to dissuade you, when Jack stopped driving, from selling the second car, which was in your own name?'

'Oh, no doubt,' she cried. 'No doubt at all that you knew what was in his mind.'

'I was in his confidence—in an awkward position.'

'Oh, you always are.'

'Mother, let me make you a cup of tea.'

'I shall make my own tea, Rosamond.'

'What have *I* done?'

Greta was marching off, but under the arch of the dining room she turned again to face Keith Burtenshaw.

'What about the furniture?'

Keith Burtenshaw put the car keys in his pocket; he picked up his hat. 'It belongs to the estate.'

'I am left with an empty house?'

'My instructions are that the effects are to be sold. There are taxes, expenses—funeral expenses for one—and certain debts.'

'Such as the debt for your services?'

'That isn't a debt to me, Greta. That's a debt to Sole and

Burtenshaw. I have already offered my legal advice to you, free, as a friend.'

'I don't need a lawyer.'

'Mother, when you sell the house—'

'Be quiet, Rosamond. And after all the things are sold, Keith, and all these taxes and debts and expenses paid, what about the remainder?'

'It becomes part of the capital.'

'And suppose there were no effects to sell. How would all these expenses be paid then?'

Keith Burtenshaw drew down his upper lip, and scratched the side of his nose with a fingernail. 'From the capital?'

'You seem strangely uncertain, but I take it that that is an answer and not a question. Well, you have the car keys. You may sell the car, since there is no question about its ownership. But I would like to see you or anyone else prove that the contents of this house belonged to Jack, and not to me. Rosamond, Mr Burtenshaw will see himself out.'

But Rosamond went with Keith Burtenshaw to his car.

'Mr Burtenshaw, I'm so sorry.'

'Your mother is on a dangerous course.'

Yet both of them seemed pleased, and were trying not to smile. Keith Burtenshaw said, 'If I hear of anything for you, Mrs Kitching, I will certainly let you know.'

'Mother tells me not to worry, and that however bad times are, one can always think of something to do.'

'Oh, does she?'

The next day, Sylvia and Hermione were to come to help Rosamond clear out Jack Cornock's wardrobes and drawers. Hermione arrived first, carrying Imogen, and complaining about Penny Newman, who had refused to mind the baby out of her turn. Greta was out. Anger had released in Greta a great energy. She had set out at nine o'clock, walking up Orlando Road on her strong muscular legs, her step fast, indignant, and springing. No neighbour who saw her pass, on this street where she had lived for thirty years, did more than reservedly nod, and if they speculated on why this woman, who was always in a car, was now on foot, they gave no sign of it. Molly's neighbours, if Molly had driven a car, and suddenly stopped, would have come to their gates and called, 'Where's your car, dear? What's up with your car? Is it on the blink?'

Hermione was dull and cross. 'Where has mother gone? Imogen, *put that down*.'

Rosamond took the shaving brush from Imogen, and told Hermione what had happened yesterday. 'So she has gone to see the man who bought the rugs, to get him to come and give her a price on the furniture.'

'She could have rung him.'

'She felt like seeing him. And I don't think she felt like seeing us, especially Sylvia.'

'I knew it was too good to last. Where are Poppa's clothes to go? To the Smith Family?'

'Only the worn things. Everything else,' said Rosamond, speaking in Greta's voice, and waving an arm, 'everything, everything, is to be sold.'

'Oh,' said Hermione. 'Just as well she is out, then.'

They put Imogen down for a sleep, and settled to sorting the clothes.

'They are all perfectly clean,' said Hermione, 'yet they smell of him.'

'He was a man with a pleasant smell.'

'Yes, but you feel it should have evaporated. It's like a ghost. Oh, Rosie, I am so depressed.'

'How is your lover, Min?'

'He wasn't my lover. He was a man who made me a financial and sexual proposition. The financial proposition was good, and the sexual one would have been, too. So good, that to give it up will mean staying apart in space. It was always only a matter of staying apart in space, but that was easier to do before the financial proposition was put.'

'Still, it's the right way, Min. There are Steven and the children.'

'I was going to take Imogen, and leave Emma and Jason.'

'You had actually worked out—'

'Yes. I am relieved, too, of course.'

'As close as that? Do I know him?'

'You have never set eyes on him,' said Hermione promptly.

'And now you have told him—'

'He understands without being told. I suppose mother will get in a separate man for the clothes.'

'Yes. Guy once suggested a theatrical costumier. He may have something there. Oh, look, Min, look at all these boxes of handkerchiefs. All unopened.'

They both looked into the low drawer Rosamond had bent to pull out. 'And the socks,' said Rosamond. 'All brand new.'

'And the camphor mother put in with them, and always

renewed. What good care she took of him.'

'She had the habit of it,' said Rosamond.

'It was like a career.'

'You can't help but be sorry, in a way, that all that kind of thing is over.'

'It's unreasonable,' said Hermione. 'But you can't.'

Rosamond sat back on her heels. 'What she's doing now, selling everything, must be illegal.'

'Right. So don't mention it to Sylvia. What it amounts to is this—that she's selling Sylvia's things.'

'Right. We are doing Sylvia a favour. She will never know how mean he could be.'

They burst into laughter, traces of which were still on their faces when Sylvia arrived, wearing her Indian dress and her pearls, her bag over her shoulder. Their smiles dilated the joy in Sylvia's face, but when she saw the sorted clothes on the floor, and the open cupboards darkened by their solid contents, her joy died away, and she stood staring.

Hermione and Rosamond cried out to her not to help, if she didn't want to, if she felt like that. But she shook her head, and slowly let the bag slip from her shoulder.

'No. I want to.'

Rosamond jumped to her feet. 'We will all have lunch first.'

Greta arrived while the three women were in the kitchen at lunch. She looked well satisfied. She kissed them all, then sat down and poured herself a cup of coffee.

'Sylvia, I am selling the furniture.'

'Mmm.' Sylvia's mouth was full. She took it for granted that the furniture was Greta's to sell, and vaguely wondered at the challenge in the remark.

'I have two men coming this afternoon, and two more tomorrow.'

'So soon,' murmured Syliva.

'Why not?'

'Well,' said Sylvia, disconcerted by Greta's sharpness, 'Rosie and you will need tables to eat from, beds to sleep in . . .'

'One table, two beds, and perhaps four chairs. Those pearls you are wearing, Sylvia, as they were a recent gift, I believe they are part of the estate.'

'Oh.' Sylvia dropped her sandwich and raised her arms to unclasp the pearls. 'Then shall I—'

'No, no, no,' said Greta, with a broad gesture across the table.

'Keep them, my dear, keep them, and we shall say nothing about them.' She sent a consulting glance at her daughters. 'Don't you agree?'

'Yes, yes,' chorused Hermione and Rosamond.

'What I suggest,' said Greta, in her old warm, confidential way, 'is that if there is anything any of you want—any small thing—you should feel free to take it.'

'I suppose I had better take something sensible,' said Rosamond, 'like brooms and mops.'

'I would like that blue lustre vase,' said Hermione.

'That is only physically small, Hermione. But you may have it, all the same.'

'Harry and I need another bed,' said Sylvia, 'now that the summer's coming on. But that's not small, so I would like to buy it.'

'Sylvia,' said Rosamond, 'aren't you going to Rome?'

'I'm staying with Harry.'

'You mean for good?' asked Hermione.

'And when we find another flat,' said Sylvia, 'we'll move, because I'll need a room for teaching.'

'Sylvia,' said Rosamond, 'I'm so pleased. Mother, isn't that wonderful?'

'Very nice,' said Greta. 'There's no question of marriage?'

'Not legal marriage, no.'

'Much more sensible,' said Greta. 'You can both move on without fuss. These modern temporary arrangements are a great improvement on the old rigid ones. Choose whichever bed you like, my dear.'

'But I must buy it.'

'If you insist.'

Sylvia was surprised at the price Greta asked for the bed. She had not imagined that beds were so expensive. But it was a good bed. She bounced up and down on it, testing its springs.

'I have never owned a bed before.'

Rosamond and Hermione laughed. Greta's continued force and energy had put them all in that state in which problems can be happily postponed. Siddy arrived, and Greta asked him to move furniture from against the walls, so that inspection could be faster.

'There is no borer in any of *my* furniture.'

Siddy, as he shifted the furniture, refused to take off his hat. After he went, carrying his small fibre suitcase and an army duffle bag, Rosamond said to Greta, 'Have you thought about who is to do the garden?'

'I will do it myself, until I sell.'

'All of it?'

'As long as you're here, you can help me.'

Rosamond looked with commiseration at her soft pale hands.

'Siddy says he can get plenty of work closer to home,' said Greta. 'And although he doesn't like to say so, he would feel uncomfortable in a house not commanded by a man.'

At three o'clock, Hermione had to leave. She drove out of Orlando Road, up the hill, and onto the Pacific Highway. When pausing for lights, she turned round to check on Imogen strapped into her seat in the back. Stewart, passing in the other direction, saw her in that posture, her face turned, on a strained neck, to cozen and smile at the baby, and her wide sleeves falling away from her arms. She did not see him. He turned abruptly into a side street, and pulled up outside a brick fence over which flowering shrubs protruded like risen bread from a tin. Sitting in deep reflection, he absently watched a man, behind the wheel of a parked car facing in the opposite direction, turning the pages of an order book. After about five minutes, Stewart departed as abruptly as he had come. He joined again the northbound traffic on the Pacific Highway, and drove to Wahroonga.

Rosamond opened the door. 'You know about Sylvia staying in Sydney?'

'Sure. She rang me. Time she came to her senses.'

One of Greta's buyers had arrived, and was in her charge, and the other came while Rosamond was still ushering Stewart into the hall. Greta had remarked that it wouldn't hurt them to know that there was competition, and that she intended to sell the furniture piece by piece, fighting all the way. Rosamond, as she showed the second buyer to a chair in the hall, told Stewart where he could find Sylvia; so Stewart, who had not come especially to see Sylvia, found himself facing her across the room in which Jack Cornock had died.

'There's really nothing left to do in here. Hermione and Rosie and I did it together. But this room was inspected first, so I came in here to be out of the way. Harry's coming after work.'

'Greta's a bit quick off the mark, isn't she?'

'It's a good thing that she's so much occupied.'

'As long as Keith Burtenshaw knows.'

'Oh, I'm sure he does.'

'Oh, well—I really came up on a bit of business of my own.'

'You're out of your territory.'

Both were restless, moving about as they spoke. 'A man came to

see me,' said Stewart, 'wanting to sell in the east and buy
something up here. I thought Greta might be interested. I would
have rung, only I wanted to check on a few details of the layout. I
would have been here earlier, but at Roseville I had a bit of
trouble with the car. I passed Hermione, in fact, Hermione. On
her way home.'

'We were all very energetic.'

'You must have been.' Stewart paused to peer glumly into a
carton, then, coming alongside Sylvia, he laid an arm across her
shoulders, and briefly hugged her. 'Don't let anyone talk you out
of what you're doing, Syl.'

She thought that he had made this long journey (so laboriously
explained) especially to tell her this, so instead of saying, 'Nobody
is trying,' she said meekly, 'I won't.'

'Don't talk yourself out of it, is what I really mean. Settle for it.
Don't argue the toss.'

'I'll try not to. Does mum still feel disinclined to see me?'

'More than ever, now that you've decided to stay.' He had
picked up his father's watch. Holding it in his palm, he moved his
hand up and down as if testing its weight. 'Best to humour her.'

'I've no alternative.'

'It won't last.'

'Given her reason, it will.'

He wound the watch, and held it to his ear, looking at her
sideways. 'There's a flat coming vacant towards the end of
October near Redleaf Pool. Two bedrooms, needs painting.
Would you and Harry be interested?'

She laughed. 'You're a real man of business. Does it face that
dreadful road?'

'The other way.'

'The harbour. Oh!'

'Harbour glimpses.'

'Oh. Well, I am certainly interested. I don't know if Harry's
wedded to the north side. I'll ask him.'

He put down the watch. 'Mum's as nervous as hell about going
to see Keith Burtenshaw. I tell her it's not an exam. She wanted
me to go with her. I suggested she take Ken.'

'Is Ken capable—'

'He doesn't have to be capable. She's in good hands with Keith
Burtenshaw. But Ken needs something to do. He can read the
documents,' said Stewart, with a faint smile. 'Save her putting on
her specs.'

'So Ken doesn't know either?'

'Keep calm.'

'These men!'

'Before you blow up, Syl, remember mum's had plenty of practice hiding it.'

But Sylvia walked away from him, hugging herself as if to contain her indignation.

'Well, if you want to blow right up, Syl, you might as well know mum's arranged to go to the races with Guy.'

She span around. 'With *Guy?*'

'Cool it. She reckons she and Guy have interests in common, by which she means horse racing.'

'So she'll pay him—'

'Oh, he'll get his corner, or he wouldn't be doing it. She'll supply the bank, she reckons, and he'll supply the expertise.'

'And read the form guide,' said Sylvia in despair.

'And read the form guide,' Stewart calmly repeated. 'She also said she needs the companionship. Now think that one out.'

Sylvia sat down, an elbow on the arm of the chair, her forehead in her hand. 'I made an effort,' she said

'I know. I mean, I know it *was* an effort. But sometimes it's gone too far. It was like me and Dad. We got on all right these last few years, but it was a rickety old bridge we slung over that gap, it wouldn't have stood another ounce. And anyway, say you and mum got along fine, it still wouldn't be enough. I get on fine with mum, and I'm not enough, either. Nor Ken, with all his family. No, what she wants is to go out in public, with a man at her side. And a man—you've got to say it—she can be a bit flirty with.'

'Oh, Lord,' said Sylvia wearily.

'It's in her nature,' said Stewart. 'But it can't last long. There's not enough in it for Guy. He won't stick it. In fact, what I'm scared of is he won't even show up for the first flutter. I would like her to have a flutter or two before he pulls out. And don't worry, I'll keep an eye on her. If Guy does stick it, and she looks like losing too much, I'll get her out of it, even if it means getting Guy in a quiet corner, me and someone else.'

'Metaphorically speaking!' cried Sylvia.

'Metaphorically speaking. I guess I'll go and cast a fresh eye on that back garden, Syl.'

Stewart strolled round the back garden. He sat in the centre of each garden seat in turn, stretching his arms along the back and looking up into the trees; he stood under the fig tree, gently kicking the seat of the swing to cause the ropes to wind and unwind. It was here that Greta joined him, when it was nearly dusk.

'Well, Stewart?'

'I have this man and his wife in Bellevue Hill. Wife brought up in these parts. Pining to get back, but will wait for suitable house. Must have garden, garden very important, missing those autumn leaves, etcetera. I wouldn't handle your sale myself, but I would put you onto a good man up here, and the advantage for me is that I would handle theirs.'

'I'll let you know. If I agree, I'll do my own selling.'

He looked doubtful for only a moment. 'Fair enough. And if you want any advice, you know where to come. As long as there's no commission, I'm free to help.'

'Thank you.' Greta peered at her watch. 'I expected Guy by now. Harry will come, of course, since Sylvia is here. Can you stay to dinner?'

'No, thanks, Greta. Thanks all the same.'

She put a hand on his wrist. 'There wasn't time to talk at the funeral. How are you, Stewart?'

'Bloody unhappy.'

'He was your father,' she said with sympathy.

'I don't want you to get the wrong idea, Greta. It's a bit of everything.'

'I understand.' But she turned away as she spoke; Guy had opened the kitchen door and was crossing the grass.

'Old age looming, for one thing,' said Stewart, 'and so on and so forth.'

'Its looming is worse than its arrival.'

Guy kissed his mother. 'Harry risked leprosy, and picked me up on my way from the station.'

'Guy, where did you get to after the funeral?'

'I don't remember.' Guy looked at Stewart. 'Out of your territory, aren't you, Stewart?'

'I guess I am,' said Stewart pleasantly. 'I guess everyone should keep in his own territory, Guy.'

Rosamond went with Stewart to the front door.

'It was good of you to think of that, Stewart, and to take the trouble to come up and see mother yourself.'

'I don't want you to get the wrong idea. I had another bit of business up this way, that didn't come off.'

'I feel this one will. One out of two, that's not bad.'

'Weren't you once a typist, Rosie?'

'Was I *not*!' she said, rolling her eyes.

'Why don't you brush it up?'

'God help me, I suppose I'll have to. Though nowadays there are all these computers around.'

'Computers have their limitations.'

She stayed at the open door and waved to him as he drove off. Then she shut the door and hurried back to the living room, where Sylvia and Harry sat on the sofa, with drinks on the low table in front of them. Harry at once picked up again the roll of notes he had been offering to Rosamond when Stewart had put his head round the door to say goodbye.

'Here, Rosie. To go on with.'

'I don't like to,' she said, with a wriggle.

Harry and Sylvia laughed, but when Rosamond still did not take the notes, Harry became serious.

'If you can't take this –' He jolted his forearm, admonishing her with the notes ' – if you, of all people, can't take this from me, of all people –'

'Oh, all right.'

But Rosamond, as she took the notes, looked dubiously at Sylvia, who, though she was peacefully smiling, had said nothing.

Sylvia was pleased to see Rosamond take the money, but it had not occurred to her to add her voice to Harry's persuasion. She had not thought of it as her business; she was unpractised in connubial ways.

Molly and Ken sat in Keith Burtenshaw's office. Molly was wearing her funeral dress, with a smaller hat, but Ken, to demonstrate that he was not impressed by the occasion, was wearing his shorts, short-sleeved shirt, and sandals. Molly had said that by dressing so differently from her he made her look ridiculous, and Ken had replied that she did the same for him. The journey in the train had been absolutely silent, but they did present some kind of unity as they sat in two similar chairs, in similar, square-set postures, and faced Keith Burtenshaw across his desk.

'Actually,' said Keith Burtenshaw, 'it's more than that. These last few months the interest has been allowed to accrue . . . Excuse me.'

While he answered his phone, Molly leaned sideways and whispered to Ken to ask when the money would start to come in. But Ken's meditative expression did not alter; he made no reply, and before Molly could repeat her plea, Keith Burtenshaw put down the phone.

Ken extended a hand over the desk. 'Just let me run an eye over that document again, will you?'

'Certainly.' Keith Burtenshaw passed the will across the desk. I've had a copy made for you to take home,' he said.

As Ken scanned the page, Molly took her spectacles from her handbag, put them on, and leaning sideways in her chair, also appeared to read it.

'What about the furniture?' asked Ken at last.

'I was coming to that.'

'It says "house" here, not "house and contents". What happens to the contents?'

Molly took off her spectacles and gave an impatient sigh. Keith Burtenshaw said, 'Mrs Cornock claims very strongly that the furniture belongs to her.'

'She can't do that,' said Ken. 'What about what it says here?'

Keith Burtenshaw plucked the paper from his hands and laid it before Molly. 'You're quite right. I would like Mrs Fiddies to read it very thoroughly, and then, if she has any questions, I'll be pleased to answer them.'

Molly put her spectacles on again, took the will in one gloved hand, pursed her lips, lowered her gaze to the paper, and moved her eyes from side to side. Ken folded his arms and crossed his legs. 'She doesn't understand the legal terminology,' he quietly confided to Keith Burtenshaw. Keith Burtenshaw picked up a piece of paper at random, and blinked at it. Molly laid the paper down and took off her spectacles.

'Let the poor soul keep the furniture.'

'Poor soul!' Ken uncrossed his legs and leaned forward from the waist. 'She's got a house worth a fortune.'

'Quite a good house,' murmured Keith Burtenshaw chidingly. 'Mrs Fiddies,' he said to Molly, 'please tell me if there is any part of this—' He put a forefinger on the will '—you would like me to explain.'

Molly pushed it towards him. 'You explained it already.'

'Not about the furniture,' said Ken.

'I was coming to that,' said Keith Burtenshaw again; while at the same time Molly said crossly to Ken, 'Well, he's explained it now, hasn't he?'

'Yes, he says it's ours, yours.'

'I'm not getting any younger, Ken,' said Molly. 'And if she feels goaded, she could easy turn round and contest the will.'

'I feel bound to say,' said Keith Burtenshaw, 'that she was quite decided about not contesting it.'

'See!' said Ken.

'I don't care,' said Molly. 'I've got an intuition.'

'You're mad,' said Ken.

'Start arguing about these things, Ken, and there's holdups all the way. I've heard of cases held up years. We aren't getting any younger, Ken.'

Keith Burtenshaw allowed his chair slightly to swivel. 'Mrs Cornock relinquished all claim to the car. Not very willingly, I feel bound to add.'

'See, Ken!'

'I see one thing,' said Ken, with covert significance.

But he did not enlarge on this theme until they were out in the street, and walking towards Wynyard station.

'I see one thing, and that's that half these lawyers are crook.'

'Oh, go on!' said Molly. The weight of money, which had at first so excited her, now made her placid; it seemed that nothing could unnerve her. They reached Martin Place. 'Let's have a sit-down, Ken.'

'I don't need to sit-down.'

'I do.'

'It's those shoes.'

They sat on a semi-circular plastic seat in the flickering shade of the poplars. 'You never asked when it would start coming in, Ken.'

'You heard him say he would ring you.'

'You got to egg them on.'

Ken folded his arms tightly high on his chest. 'The whole thing's a disaster. He's done for me, all right, that old Jack Cornock has.'

'Would you like to go to Pauls, and look at some electric things for your workshop?'

'What electric things?' asked Ken with scorn.

'How would I know what electric things? You're the one knows that.'

'I don't need any electric things, as you call them.'

'All right. You would only be loaning them half the time, anyway, to Barry and Gavin and Jim and Les, you're that generous with your things.'

'What is life for,' asked Ken, 'if you can't help others?'

But she could not inveigle him into going to Pauls. They continued towards Wynyard. When Ken stopped to look at a news stand, she stopped with him; when she stopped to look in a shop window, Ken walked on. Thus he reached the barrier before her, but he had both the tickets, so here he had to stop and wait for her, his hands on his hips, and his angry face turned to watch her stumping calmly down the ramp. On Platform 3, they sat waiting for a train.

'You only want it to start coming in,' said Ken, 'so you can start going to the races with your pick-up.'

'You can't call him that, with the families so closely connected, Ken. And why shouldn't I have some pleasure in life? You got your pub Saturdays, and I'll have my races. And I won't keep you short, Ken. I told you you can control the lot. Bar this hundred a week I'm keeping for myself.'

'A hundred,' moaned Ken. 'A whole bloody hundred.'

'It's not much these days.'

'If you must be a fool, and give your money to the bookies, why not go with that woman down the fruit?'

'It's not the same with a woman.'

'Why isn't it? Why isn't it?'

'It's just not, that's all. It doesn't feel as natural.'

'A young feller that age. And a bludger, too, from your own past account.'

'All I know is, we got on, him and me. From the moment he come up, with that umbrella, courtesy itself.'

'You bloody fool. Would he want your company if you didn't have this money? Ask yourself that.'

'Well, money comes into everything, doesn't it? Would you have married me, come to that, if I hadn't owned a house, and put it in both our names the minute we was married.'

'And which straight away I had to turn round and start repairing,' swiftly countered Ken.

'Oh, I know you done your part. Look at that girl, Ken. Those dainty florals are all the rage again, after all the years of jeans, jeans, nothing but jeans.'

'The truth is, you've picked up with a fancy man.'

'Don't be mad,' said Molly. But her laugh, after its initial shriek, settled to such an intimate and satisfied chuckle that Ken got indignantly to his feet, and went to stand at the very edge of the platform, with his back towards her, until the train came in. They sat together in the train, but though Molly tried to make conversation, saying, 'More flats going up,' and 'The sky's stormified again,' he would not reply.

Twelve

Rosamond made astrological forecasts in which she used the word ordained. 'It lets you out,' she said. 'If it's ordained that you're to be a typist, what's the use of fighting it?'

She practised on the hired electric typewriter for six hours every day, and Greta made the mistake of showing her annoyance only in her efforts to suppress it. In the big, slowly emptying house, the footsteps of the two women, audible on the bare floors, were as far apart, and as circumspect, as each could make them.

Rosamond used in her forecasts the language of popular astrology, but admitted that her sources were different.

'Uranus is traversing my watery sign,' she said to Harry and Sylvia. 'There will be outstanding career opportunities for Pisces in the three weeks before the festive season. The last three months of 1977 favour buying and selling, and moving and resettling, for Pisces, Acquarius, Leo, and Sagittarius. Those people of Stewart's have been to look at the house. Did mother tell you? And Min and Steven have seen something at Turramurra not too utterly disgusting. And you two have your flat. That leaves me. But it will happen to me. It is ordained. Besides, when mother moves . . .'

On the night Harry and Sylvia moved to their new flat, they turned their backs on the unpacked crates and boxes and went to eat at a Vietnamese restaurant in Oxford Street. The place had been converted from a milk bar, and on the walls traces of the former proprietor were retained in prints of gum trees, blue hills, cattle, and of intensely floral English gardens. Manet's soldier boy was also present. Here Harry and Sylvia were served delicate food by a graceful woman and a swarthy, smiling girl. It was the last dinner they were to eat at leisure for some weeks. An election was called by the government long before its term of office would normally have ended, Malcolm Fraser choosing his time, according to his own party, with his usual astuteness, and, according to the Labor Party, with the cynical opportunism everyone had come to expect of him.

Sylvia was impressed by the doggedness and good humour with which Harry set himself to work in a campaign Labor could only lose. She half expected him to ask her to help, and when he did not, suspected that he remembered too well the remarks she had made to him and Margaret about her own involvement, with

Geoffrey Foley, in politics in London. For she had said that the chief impression remaining with her was of the *bad aesthetics* of politics, of how she had wasted so many evenings in bleak halls, under leeching lights, facing two men, or a man and a woman, at a table. And nor, at that level (she had said) were right-wing politics any different, adding to the scene only a bunch of flowers, often plastic, and a coloured print of the queen. But if Harry remembered this, he did not say so, and Sylvia not only found the time inappropriate for repeating it, but doubted if she could repeat it with her former aplomb.

Sylvia now had nine pupils. She formed them into classes of three each, taking two classes during the day, and one at night, so that it often happened that Harry cooked himself an early dinner while Sylvia was teaching in the sitting room, and that when he came home, he would find her finishing a late dinner in the kitchen, her book propped against a bowl of fruit. It suited them both, this freedom that contained at its centre the intimacy of shared quarters. Yet in Sylvia's commitment to Harry there was much of conscious resolve, of management, of setting herself to a task as she had once set herself to divide her year. In his commitment to her she sensed none of this; he seemed to accept her as naturally as he accepted his place in his own country; she admired and envied him for it, but could not change her own way. In a long letter to the Holyoaks she wrote:

> . . . *so please send my tea chest to this address. It will take such a long time by sea that by the time it arrives we will have bought something to empty all that paper into. At the moment we have only the strictest necessities. We haven't had time to get anything else. No, that's not quite true. I'm so used to living in a provisional way that I want to postpone the days of buying. But they will come. Harry says, 'When this election is over, let's ask the so-and-so's to dinner.' So we are a couple, and will entertain our friends, and will need table mats, and china, and candlesticks. And if one owns such things, they might as well be beautiful, so they must be bought with care. So here I am.*

Sylvia had never voted in her life, but was now forced to enrol, and on the tenth of December, to take her ignorance to the polls. Walking out into the westerly wind of that day, she wondered how many others, in this land of compulsory voting, were as ignorant as she. As she filled in the squares on the ballot papers in obedience to the Labor leaflet Harry had given her, she remembered Molly's frequent and virtuous proclamations that she always voted the way her husband told her to. Angry at being forced into a similar act of docility, she was tempted simply to fold the papers and put them unfinished into the ballot box, but refrained because such an act would seem to show contempt rather than the rebellion she intended.

Sylvia, though partly relieved by Molly's edict that her daughter must leave her alone, could not accept it calmly, and complained about it to Stewart. Her relief was less than the soreness it gave her. She would have preferred her mother and herself to continue to limp along, in all their bungling and awkwardness, rather than lose the hope of reviving, even if it were for only a moment, an old ease, so obscured that it seemed like a goal in a dream. The hundreds of letters she had written to Molly she no longer saw as the lifeless relics of a lost unity, but as a stubborn assertion that unity still existed. Her mind would not leave Molly alone, but returned again and again to ponder on her life with Ken Fiddies, or to perplex itself with her new association with Guy. She questioned Stewart, who was curt with her. Yet she persisted, as if by these thoughts and questions alone, she could change Molly, could nag her into reform.

Harry had taken for granted the defeat of Labor, but the resignation of Gough Whitlam from the leadership of that embattled party—the actual, emotional event—plunged him into silence and bitterness. Sylvia dropped the remark that in Australia today, there must be many children for whom the name of Gough Whitlam would carry an emotional charge similar to the name of Parnell in the Ireland of James Joyce's childhood. But Harry was not comforted by the literary allusion, and rather made her feel, by his continued silence, that she had been tactless and glib in making it. She supposed that there was no end to the possible obstacles between them.

Harry's bitterness passed in a day, or was absorbed into a firmer resolve, but Sylvia saw that for many other supporters of Labor, bitterness was the mood hardest of all to subdue. Suddenly offered more pupils than she could accept, she realized with amazement that these people intended to emigrate.

'But do you imagine that politics are any more reasonable in Italy?' she asked.

The reply of one woman sufficed for most.

'I know they're not, but I shan't care about them there. They won't be my business. I can't stay here and stop caring, and to stay here, and keep caring, hurts too much.'

But even as she looked incredulous, Sylvia began to see, in these perverse patriots, a reflection of herself. Her frequent sharp offendedness with the people of Sydney was the product of attachment, how ever much overlaid. It established her as a sort of patriot, just as her grief for her mother's dull and trivial fate established her as a sort of daughter. For when had she been so offended by, for example, fat and mendacious Romans, or grieved for the fate, when less than tragic, of anyone else's mother? She had exposed her wish, long hidden and denied, that the people of her country should excel, and that her mother should be wise and ripe.

Molly would have told Sylvia what to do with her grief. The law moved slowly, and when she had proposed to borrow on her expectations from the A.A.A. Finance Company, Ken had stepped in and offered to advance her five hundred dollars at the same rate of interest he got from the building society in which his savings were lodged. Keith Burtenshaw drew up the document on which both clamorously insisted; and so Molly got her betting bank, and Ken's ferocity took on a slightly forced air.

On the Saturday of the elections, Molly left for the races after Ken had gone to the pub. She went to the polls on the way. After scribbling all over the ballot papers (as she had done in every election of her life), she folded them neatly, and with a reverential air, dropped them into the stout, locked, supervised ballot box.

In the taxi, she sat beside the driver, fiddling with her scarf, her hat, her new necklace, and telling him about her luck.

'How many meetings has it been like that?' asked the driver.

'Three so far.'

'You might be worth following.'

'So others think. Last Saturday two blokes come up and touched me for luck. It isn't beginner's luck, neither, though I don't say my long spell away from the horses hasn't played a part. Do you know what I reckon it is? Only, don't laugh.'

'I won't,' said the driver.

'I was recently widowed,' said Molly, 'and I can't help thinking the luck what my husband had, which was famous in its day, he passed on to me.'

'How would he have done that?' asked the driver.

'There's a lot in this world we don't know.'

'Sure enough.'

'My husband reckons it's mad, but I've always been a bit on the fey side.'

'I thought you said you were a widow.'

'I married again.'

The driver glanced at her sideways. 'Well, and why wouldn't

you? A good-looking sort like you.'

Guy was waiting near the gate. Molly gave him a quick scrutiny before he saw her. Last week he had appeared without a coat and tie, but with their winnings Molly had fitted him out with a lightweight suit, a pink muslin shirt, and a Dior tie. In the spaces of their day, Molly would place questions about Greta—Had she sold the house? What was it worth? What was she buying? Why didn't she dye her hair? Guy rationed his answers.

From the way he kissed her in greeting, smackingly, on both cheeks, any spectator would have seen that he appreciated the comedy of his own situation. Molly, after her shriek and chuckle, touched her new necklace, and preened.

'How do I look?'

He had learned the words she liked. 'Very smart. Very chic. Today we've got to change our strategy. We don't want people following us around, shortening the odds.'

'Just as you say.'

Again they made a profit on the day's betting, but it was not so large a profit as on those first three glorious days, and in Molly's anxiety, as they left the race course, may have been found justification, after all, for Sylvia's grief.

'It's not the amount that matters. That's just what you've got to learn, Guy. It's staying on top. Staying with that winning streak.'

'Sure. Till it runs out.'

'It needn't run out. They don't always. I knew one never did. We're still on top, with plenty to spare. We'll meet Friday as usual, and go over the form. Eh? Meet Friday? Guy?'

On Molly's home journey, there were three other passengers in the taxi, and the driver was one of the glum sort. As they turned into her street, Molly took off her new necklace and put it in her handbag. But she did not encounter Ken on her way into the house, and was able to get into her bedroom unobserved, and to put on the house dress and slippers which she knew would soothe him. Ken was regaining his ascendency. By her winnings, she had seemed to tear herself away from his first efforts to pin her down by advancing her the money; but he need not have worried; habit was on his side. The tiny daily accretions of habit, built up in Molly during her fifty years of married life, and by her childhood observations of her parents' marriage, stood solid for Ken. Even if she continued to win at the races, Ken would regain his ascendency. A reversal in her luck would only speed a victory already, as Rosamond might have said, ordained.

In his retirement, Ken shopped. He did not buy; he became a

scrutinizer and valuer. Round the shopping streets of his and the adjacent suburbs, he steadily walked on every fine day. When attracted by a window display, he would halt abruptly, but instead of turning to face it, would fold his hands behind and scrutinize it, with keen suspicion, along one shoulder. If he decided to go in, and challenge the salesman, and tell him what shops were offering goods for less, or on better terms, he did so with great deliberation, always shaking the man's hand first. In the pub he was given a new name.

'Here comes the estimator. Get ready for the relevant information.'

Ken produces papers from his pocket as he approaches. He slaps them down on the bar.

'Brian! That lawnmower you're thinking of buying. Here's the relevant information. Go to every shop in Sydney, and you won't do better than this. Schooner please, Jean.'

'Honest to God, Ken, you should take a percentage.'

And Ken replies, with that faint sarcastic hint of self-knowledge, 'It's a poor world where you can't help your mates.'

At first, Ken's sons and their families came less often to the house. Molly's brave resolve to 'tell them everything to their faces' had been reduced to an insistence that Ken should tell them that she needed a bit of a break. But Guy and the races did not occupy all of her week, and she soon found herself, for all her money, stuck in front of the television, just as before, and without even Ken for company, for now that his family did not come to him, he went to them. So, bit by bit, and pretending to be grudging about it, Molly let the sons and wives and families back.

'And she's minding those babies again?' said Sylvia to Stewart. 'And cooking all those great meals?'

'It's better than it was,' said Stewart. 'The older kids are made to get off their arses now, and give a hand. She gets more respect. It's the money.'

Stewart had come to Harry's and Sylvia's flat to give them a moving-in gift, a rug which he carried over his shoulder like a bent column. When he had spread it on the floor, and the three of them stood at different points of its permimeter, and it had been admired, and he had been thanked, Harry suddenly addressed him across its coloured field.

'Why do you look so disconsolate these days?'

Harry and Stewart, who seldom met, and had hardly an idea or a belief in common, were always at ease with each other, like friends or brothers from a buried life, of which only this amity had survived.

'I don't know about disconsolate,' said Stewart. 'That means hard to console. Well, yes, you're right, I'm disconsolate.' Surprise made him laugh. 'Eh? Disconsolate. Who would have thought I would ever be that?'

'Is it dad?' asked Sylvia.

'Well, he was always the one I had to beat. As long as he was alive and kicking, I didn't need the goal, I had the spur. Then, bang, I lose the spur, and at the same time it so happens I lose what could have been a goal—a woman. So if I'm disconsolate, it's for my old enjoyment in making money. That's what it boils down to. I don't have that any more.'

One night in early November, Stewart had another prospective buyer in his flat, a thin small man of about fifty, with long flapping feet and a wide crescent grin. One of the naked women on the wallpaper in Stewart's bedroom reminded him of the greatest lay he had ever had in his life, and after telling Stewart about this lay, his grin fixed all the while, he went on to describe a more recent pleasure.

'Five of us kicked in, and we got these five girls, and they stood against the wall on their heads and hands, with their legs apart about that much—' He put his elbows together and parted his forearms in a V through which appeared his grin '—and they all have an oyster in their fannies. Now I'm a guy who's eaten oysters in all kinds of places, from all kinds of dishes. But I see I'm boring you. You've heard this before.'

'Not lately,' said Stewart.

'What's up with it?' asked the man, his smile in place. 'It's only nature.'

'I'm kinky. I like to know my women personally. Do you want to buy the place?'

'It's not the standard of residence I'm looking for.'

After he had shown the man out, Stewart went to the telephone and rang Rosamond.

'Girl in my office is leaving. Typing's necessary, but not as important as the phone, putting people off nicely, and turning them on nicely, and having a look at the people who come in, then telling me what they're like, etcetera.'

'Well,' said Rosamond thoughtfully.

'Well, what?'

'Well, it would be so embarrassing if you had to sack me.'

'There's a risk in everything. What I have in mind is that maybe later, when you know a bit about the business, you could show people houses, do the preliminaries, then I could move in to sell. Then you could do your real estate exams, set yourself up.'

'You astound me.'

'Why?'

'Such faith.'

'Will you?'

'Let us both think it over. I'll ring you tomorrow morning. But in any case, Stewart, thank you.'

'Wait.'

'What?'

'How's that son of yours?'

'Matthew or Dom?'

'The one at the funeral.'

'Matthew is harvesting asparagus at Mudgee.'

'What about after the school holidays?'

'Harry says if we can't get him to go back next year, we'll try again the year after. He has always wanted to be a marine biologist.'

'What about the other one?'

'I worry about Dom.'

'I expect you do,' said Stewart with satisfaction. 'We'll talk again tomorrow, then.'

Rosamond went out to the back garden, where Greta was walking behind the motor mower. Rosamond fell into step beside her. 'Stewart has offered me a job in his office,' she shouted.

Greta turned off the motor, and they both halted, facing each other beneath the leafless boughs of the jacaranda, on which the flowers had just begun to appear. 'What is he offering?' asked Greta.

'Lord, I forgot to ask.'

'Never mind. There will be an award. And in any case, Stewart would not be paltry. Take it.'

'I will. It means I can move, mother.'

'No hurry, dear. There's nothing signed yet. My sale may come to nothing.'

'But it's such a long journey each day,' said Rosamond, shrugging and looking aside, 'if I don't move.'

'Well,' said Greta, 'it hasn't been too bad, your being here, has it? Considering.'

'Not bad at all,' said Rosamond, laughing. 'Considering.'

They embraced, laughing, kissing each other's cheeks. 'In some ways,' said Greta quietly, as she turned again to her mower, 'it's been a very good thing to have you here.'

And indeed, as soon as Rosamond moved away, Greta entered a seclusion of a kind that none of her children could break. Rosamond and Hermione made a point of ringing her frequently, and Harry and Guy began to hover again; but although Greta usually replied to questions, she instigated no conversation, and without evident intention on her part, would often absent herself, would drift away, and then would not reply to questions at all.

When she was alone, there were no more whispered soliloquys. At these times she wore the true face of her solitude, her eyes staring with an animal sadness, and her mouth clamped down in a long crooked line resembling that of Jack Cornock in his last months. Her sewing lay half-finished in various places. Only the garden attracted her. Working without gloves, sweating into her hair and her clothes as the days grew hotter, pulling violently, stubbornly, at the weeds which now grew tall among the annuals and spread like discs on the grass, she presented unlikely ground for the regeneration that would become apparent in a few months time, and would take such an unexpected form. Yet regeneration had begun. In the late afternoons, when the shadow of evening scuttled across the grass, fast as a revelation, and entered the pockets of foliage, she would sometimes raise her head, suddenly, and look intently aside. Her face would become peaceful, and she would settle, with the knuckle of a soiled thumb, the nosepiece of her spectacles before bending once more to her work.

But to her family, who witnessed only her sadness and suppressed violence, her defeat seemed complete and irreversible. Rosamond and Hermione conferred by telephone.

'Steven says, and I do agree, that she made one great mistake. She expected an end product.'

Rosamond was standing at the pay phone in the hall of the block she lived in. Bulging green plastic garbage bags were piled against the wall at her feet. 'You mean, she expected us to make it all worthwhile.'

'Or one of us. She expected one of us to be *good enough*. Then when we all turned out to be imperfect, one of the grandchildren.'

'You may be right. I don't know.'

'Did I tell you we're having another baby?'

Hermione always dropped important news in this off-hand way, but did not expect an equally off-hand response.

'*No!*' said Rosamond. 'Oh, Min, how lovely.'

'We thought we might as well,' said Hermione languidly. 'We do seem to be quite good at it, and it will be company for Imogen. And whether it's a boy or a girl, we can still get by with only three bedrooms. Steven said he could enclose the verandah of the new house with glass, but I *will not* have it closed in.'

'No,' said Rosamond, 'don't you.'

'It would make the house look *boxy*.'

'It would, too. Will you have moved by Christmas?'

'No, we won't, after all. We think early in January.'

'Has mother mentioned Christmas Day to you?'

'No. And when I mentioned it to her, she didn't answer.'

'When I mentioned it, she said there was no need to think about it so soon.'

'So *soon*? A fortnight away.'

'We have always had it in her garden,' said Rosamond. 'I can't imagine Christmas without jacaranda trees in bloom.'

'It's hard to know where else we can have it.'

'Not in my so-called flat, certainly. And Matthew will be down.'

'What about Dom?'

'He will share his day between Ted and me. He longs to see Matthew.'

'How horrid it must be. I'm sure mother hasn't any real objection, Rosie. It's only a matter of getting through to her.'

'Have you told her about the new baby?'

'No, and I don't want to, either, not while she's like that. I'll tell you what—I have to take Imogen for her first injection on Tuesday. I'll drive up and ask mother if she would like to come. She still smiles at Imogen. How is your job, Rosie?'

'Quite lively, really. Stewart is teaching me things about it. We stay after work and eat takeaway food and drink beer.'

'You don't!'

'No. We drink wine. But beer sounded better with the takeaway food.'

'And I suppose you put your feet up on the desk.'

'He does. I don't. My legs are too fat.'

One of their silences fell. Rosamond put a hand on a hip, and a foot on a garbage bag. Hermione said, 'Rosie, why do you always feel compelled to *please*?'

'You used to ask me that in 1963. I still don't know.'

'Excuse me, Rosie, I must go. *Imogen*!'

A few days later, Greta and Hermione, with Imogen sitting propped on Hermione's right arm, stood talking in the clinic while they waited for the nurse to give Imogen her injection.

'Rosie and I were wondering about Christmas Day, mother.'

Greta was looking through the glass wall into the parking lot. She said, as if trying to remember, 'You always come to me.'

Lately, when speaking to her mother, a hectoring note was audible in Hermione's voice. 'Well, you will still be in the house.'

'Yes. I move on January the eleventh.'

'None of us has even seen your new flat.'

'There's nothing to see. It's clean and convenient.'

'But what a waste of money to rent, when you could buy.'

'All that trouble. I couldn't be bothered.'

'Oh well, you can always buy later. And in the meantime you will be quite near Sylvia and Harry, and that will be nice. Now about Christmas Day? We'll come to Wahroonga as usual?'

'Of course,' said Greta, looking through the glass at the parking lot. Most of the cars were small. On their clustered roofs, of red and yellow and acid green, the sun shone down so straight that on each lay a colourless scintillating disc.

'Then we will bring food and drink. You mustn't worry about anything. Rosie and Sylvia and I will arrange it all. It will be a picnic Christmas. Here she comes. And about time, too.'

Imogen was scarcely awake. She swayed on her mother's arm, and needed the spread of her mother's hand at her back. When the needle was inserted, Hermione was speaking across Imogen's head to the nurse, so that it was only Greta who saw the baby's face. Imogen's dark eyes, swimming with sleep, did not alter as the needle was inserted, but her mouth opened wide. Then pain sharpened her eyes, and the expansion of her chest, the retention of her yell, was like that moment when the plane pauses at the end of its run to gather its forces for the rise. While force gathered, Imogen raised her other arm and slowly beat it in the direction from which came the unbelievable assault. Then, after that hard start, out came her cry, immediately at its fullest pitch, and her cheeks were flooded with tears while her arm continued, feebly but faster, to beat the enemy away.

Hermione kissed her cheek, murmuring in comfort, but Greta turned abruptly away, and walked to the glass wall, and stood looking steadily at the blazing cars.

The couple to whom Greta sold the house turned out to be as separate from Orlando Road as she and Jack Cornock had been; but with this difference: that everyone would have been glad to know them. Not only had he been a distinguished diplomat, but

she had written children's books on which many of the women
nearby claimed to have been brought up. Even some of those close
to her own age said they had been brought up on her books,
though she was thirty before she had begun to write them. In any
case, she and her dignified and very acceptable husband chose not
to make friends with their neighbours, so that once again those
neighbours said, as they had done about Jack and Greta Cornock
(though with a different intonation), 'I don't actually know them,
but they seem very nice.'